PHILIP MARTIN'S
GANGSTERS

Deathtouch

Published by Candy Jar Books 2021

Candy Jar Books
136 Newport Road
Cardiff Road
CF24 1DJ

www.candyjarbooks.co.uk

Editor: Will Rees
Editorial: Shaun Russell

Printed and bound in the UK by
4edge, 22 Eldon Way, Hockley, Essex, SS5 4AD

ISBN: 978-1-913637-58-3

Philip Martin wrote professionally for over forty years.
His television credits included *Z Cars*, *Doctor Who* and *Star Cops*, but his most famous work is the postmodern BBC series *Gangsters*.

Productions of Philip's stage plays have been performed at the National Theatre; the Royal Court Theatre; the Traverse Theatre; the Liverpool Playhouse; and his local theatre, The Duke's Playhouse, Lancaster.

He also wrote numerous plays and adaptations for Radios 3 and 4, including *Dead Soldiers*, voted radio play of the year.

Philip's long-anticipated returned to the *Doctor Who* universe, *Sil and the Devil Seeds of Arodor*, won multiple prizes and earned an official selection from the Philip K. Dick Science Fiction and Supernatural Festival 2020.

In memory of the dear departed

BOOK ONE
THE DICTATES OF SHEN T'ANG

1

From the outside it appears to be a Birmingham engineering workshop that has seen better days.

A dozen Chinese workers, all carrying lunch boxes, approach the large, closed, heavy wooden door, eager to enter the premises.

Harry Sen jostles amongst them, a part of the throng.

The crowd passes a solitary glass kiosk that sells burgers and hot dogs. Inside sits a watchful Chinese who surveys the side streets that lead to the grime-tainted workshop. His left hand hovers over a red alarm button.

Harry Sen is familiar to the gatekeeper, a burly ex-boxer, Roy 'Slasher' Sturt, sometimes known as 'Shtum' on account of his vocal cords, slashed by an assailant's machete. Holding a voice amplifier tube to his scarred neck, he intones, with a metallic boom, 'Hello-Harry-got-something-for me?'

Harry greases the palm of the doorman with a fiver and is allowed inside through a creaking lower door.

The workshop smells of machine oil, stale cigarette smoke, human sweat. The ceiling is high. Morning sunshine leaks in through grimy windows, casting a dim light on the crowds of gamblers hunched over their games of chance. There is a low hum of activity, the click-click-click of mah-jong tiles, the shuffling of banknotes, the passing of wads of money back and forth, occasional stifled squeals of delight over a winning play.

Harry places himself next to a giant Butler Planing machine upon whose broad table the main gambling action is taking place.

Watching the lines of play is the plump figure of Mr Yan. Harry's gaze shifts towards a bench that holds a drill and a small hand press. On this a more sedate game of dominoes is being played for insanely high stakes. Leaning against the bench, not taking part in the game, is a Chinese man with a hollow face. Harry nods across to the thin man, indicates a move towards the back of the workshop. Alert, Mr Yan watches Harry's progress intently. A jerk of his head sends two henchmen after the stocky figure.

Harry and Chen meet up, a swift exchange of a sealed package is made before both are seized from behind. There is a fracas, a struggle, Harry knees the guy who seeks to grapple with him, darts away as his attacker squeals in anguish. Chen is punched in the gut. He sinks to the greasy floor, groaning and puking.

At the same time, outside, the watcher from the hotdog stand sees a uniformed official striding purposefully towards the building. The lookout jams down on the red alarm button, hard.

Inside the workshop a hooter blares out a warning. Instantly, games are halted, boards hidden, money stashed away. Gamblers become factory workers as machines are activated. An extractor fan starts up with a whirr of throbbing sound. The table of the Butler machine begins its long stately progress, forward and back, forward and back…

Roy Sturt presses his voice activator to his throat, booms out instructions.

'Masks!'

Four young Chinese 'workers' step forward. They raise metal welding masks to their faces.

'Weapons!'

Four flaming welding torches point towards the door that shakes under a pounding from outside. Sturt turns towards the entrance, Harry joins him, points, asking to be let out. Sturt eases the door part way open, lets Harry through before glaring at the uniformed official who attempts to enter.

'What-do-you-want?' the voice box intones.

'I've come to read the gas meter.'

'We-don't-have-gas-piss-off!'

Sturt slams the door in the official's face.

2

Anne Darracott follows John Kline out of the council offices, watches him crumple the application document then hurl the ball of paper back at the Victorian building.

Hurrying along Colmore Row, dodging through the morning traffic, she tries to keep up with the tall, muscular guy in the grey suit.

'It's not over, we can appeal. John, it's early days, the business doesn't even have a name yet.'

Kline's voice is bitter, his hands bunched, knuckles white.

'The authorities have it in for me, first at the Maverick, now at the restaurant. Without a booze license, we're nothing but a hash joint.'

'Did they give a reason?'

'Police objections. No detail.'

She trots along beside him.

'What about, Khan? You've done that bloke favours, ask for one in return.'

'Mr Khan has taken a powder, disappeared out of the country. Maybe we should do the same.'

3

Birmingham seems a world away as Zahir Khan waits for the train to stop outside his home village of Jallundar, Pakistan. The land lies flat, open, a vast sky above. A few white cumulous clouds, precursors of the monsoon season, dot the sky. On the heavy air the faint aroma of spiced cooking mixes with the acrid smoke from the engine of the train.

Stepping down at the small country station, Khan sees his father waiting to greet him. Smart in a white linen suit, a club tie, a panama hat, the old man seems a little more stooped than before but still proud of bearing.

Father and son embrace, awkwardly but warmly. The elder Khan gazes up enquiringly.

'How is Queen Elizabeth?'

'Well.'

'And England?'

'As ever.'

'What brings you here?'

'I'm investigating Asian highway drug traffickers. The trail starts here in Pakistan, goes through Hong Kong, Amsterdam, into England and perhaps on to America.'

'Opium?'

'Heroin. There is an influx into the UK. A new source of supply.'

'Crime never sleeps.'

It is a phrase the ex-inspector of police had often used. It gives Zahir Khan a comforting sense that he really is home.

They begin to stroll towards the village. Behind them the four carriage train chugs away, sending a smudge of grey smoke up into the sky. Struck by a sudden worrying thought, the old man halts, grasps his son's arm.

'It's topping to see you, of course, but you mustn't waste time visiting me if duty calls you elsewhere.'

'There's little I can do at present. We suspect the new influx of Class A drugs is being channelled through Chinese gangsters. Their Triad societies are difficult to penetrate but we have seconded a pair of undercover agents from Hong Kong. I hope to receive their findings when I return to the UK.'

'Good, good…'

Khan senior pauses as he sees, running towards him, an eight-year-old boy.

'Here's your nephew, come to greet you…'

Zahir Khan smiles, opens his arms to greet the excited youngster. A little way behind, racing along the dusty track, he can see other village children shouting cries of welcome. Soon they are surrounded by the crowd of youngsters, all bubbling with questions.

'Are you really a policeman?'

'Have you caught many crooks?'

'What's Britain really like?'

'Tell us!'

'Tell us!'

Khan's father holds up his arms before his son can speak. The kids quieten.

'England is exactly as I say it is.' The old man says.

The children cheer. Zaheer Khan says nothing; he has no wish to contradict his father.

4

Holding a half-smoked cigarette, Anne Darracott leaves a public toilet cubicle. The cistern flushes behind her. About to douse the ciggy in a bucket of sand, she sees used hypo needles lying amongst the fag ends. Her expression darkens. She hears, from behind a closed door, a cry of pleasure as a hit strikes home.

The door of the cubicle is covered in obscene graffiti saying who did what to whom and in just what way. Anne hears giggles on the other side of the barrier, wonders who is shooting up inside. Veteran junkies? School kids? Anne feels an invisible hand move her towards the cubicle. She puts her arms out, presses her hands against the door, makes herself breathe, forces herself to turn about. She leaves the junkie haven, heads out to re-join John Kline.

5

The Church of Saint Stephen lies in the heart of Birmingham. It is empty of worshippers except for a visiting organist who plays a few bars of 'All Things Bright and Beautiful' before sashaying into a thunderous version of Bach's *Toccata and Fugue in D Minor*. The sonorous notes fill the church with glorious sound.

The music filters down into the crypt below, a musty space that belies the name of the group that has rented it, the Hong Kong Charity Foundation.

Chen, the thin man last seen puking on the factory floor, lies spread-eagled on the dank flagstone floor of the basement. He groans under the weight of two gravestones pressing down on his puny chest.

Shen T'ang, middle-aged, conservatively dressed, in appearance more a member of the Chamber of Commerce than the leader of the murderous mob 'Hong Ming' or 'the Red Disciples', watches impassively as their prisoner groans with pain. Standing next to the Triad leader is his second in command, Mr Yan.

A little to the side, gazing down at the suffering Chen, is Shen T'ang's daughter, Lily Li T'ang. Tall, not yet twenty years of age, she is beautiful in a cold, contained way. Impatient for action, she gestures to Jian and Chang, two would-be members of the Triad society. They lope over to a pile of abandoned gravestones stacked around a pillar of the gloomy crypt. With an effort, they lift a stone that faintly reads 'Robert Sinclair, Man of God, 1847-1899'. The Chinese youths stagger out of the shadows, holding the gravestone. They wait for further instructions. Mr Yan bends down, stares into the bloodshot eyes of the infiltrator.

'Chen, what did you give to your colleague, Sen, before he ran away?'

Struggling to fill his lungs against the weight of the stones, Chen spits his defiance.

'Something that will destroy you all. You will never find Harry Sen.'

Yan steps aside, Shen T'ang takes his place. With a polite smile he addresses his victim in slow measured tones.

'We know your Hong Kong police colleague works undercover as a cook, we will search him out. His betrayal, like yours, will be avenged.'

The Triad leader gestures to the initiates. Carefully and slowly they lower the gravestone of the long dead parson onto the others placed on Chen's chest. The added weight soon takes effect. Chen's eyes bulge, blood surges up into his throat, fills his mouth, chokes him. Unable to breathe, he kicks out in a final spasm of agony. Lily smiles, turns to speak to her minions, issues her orders in a cut-glass English accent.

'Thus perish all traitors. There are stone coffins back there. Hide the remains of this creature inside one of them.'

6

Khan's father leads his only son into a graveyard containing rows of sun-bleached headstones. Around the perimeter lie unruly grasses that may contain cobras. In the oppressive heat, shrubs and trees wilt, bowing down towards the parched earth. The elder Khan removes his hat, holds it to his chest, bows his head in a gesture of respect. His wistful gaze travels along the lines of gravestones.

'I often visit this sanctuary. It is how I imagine an English graveyard to be. Here they sleep, the British dead. Some of them are the chaps I instructed in the ways of the sub-continent. They would have become able administrators had not the blunder of '47 put an end to the order of things.'

The old man begins to wander among the graves, pausing from time to time at a name he recognises.

'Ah, yes, Captain George Fowler, died of a fever, poor fellow. Well, let's not become morbid. We are alive, you have a fine job, working to uphold the law in that most green and pleasant land across the sea.'

'Father, why not visit England, compare it to the land of your imagination?'

'No, no, that is not necessary. With the help of Rudyard Kipling, I have created England here…'

He smiles, taps his temple.

'Yes, yes, the downs, the valleys, the hills, the towns whose children have slept secure for a thousand years.'

Zahir glances down at his father. This is not the time to disillusion him. The old man misreads his hesitation.

'Am I to assume you will shortly be recalled to your duties?'

'Yes, I must soon return to England's green and pleasant land.'

7

The confines of St Stephen's church crypt have become a place of initiation. Between stone pillars stands an altar surrounded by a pantheon of Chinese gods and demons. Their contorted features are illuminated by candles and flaming torches. Joss sticks fill the dank air with the scent of sandalwood.

Before the altar stands Shen T'ang. He is dressed in red satin robes and the snakes' head crown of Triad high office. Lily Li T'ang, on his right-hand side, wears white and crimson vestments. Around her plaited hair is coiled a brown-tasselled headpiece. She holds a ritual brass bowl that is filled with blood.

Behind them, the Master of Incense, Mr Yan, dressed in a white ritual robe, sports a ruby red headband. He holds a thin, curved knife in a sheaf. He makes a beckoning sign towards the pool of darkness beyond the altar.

From the shadows, two Chinese youths crawl across the stone floor towards the waiting triad leaders. Both initiates are naked except for scarlet loin cloths.

On reaching the feet of Shen T'ang they are summoned to rise by Mr Yan. They stand, each extends an arm, joining their separate thumbs together. Lily steps forward to hold the sacrificial bowl beneath their linked hands. Mr Yan unsheathes his knife, slices across the underside of both the offered thumbs. As the blood of each novice flows down into the receptacle, Shen T'ang intones the ritual response.

'Know that I am Shen T'ang, president of our most honoured society, Hong Ming.'

Lily offers the bowl to initiate Chang. He drinks. His companion, Jian, waits his turn. When both men have tasted blood, the Triad leader continues to intone his blessing.

'Know that your blood is now one with the true disciples. Pray that one day their blood will honour yours, pray that their courage will become yours. You may now call yourself initiate but you must both be aware that the next step required to seal your entry will be one of hazard.'

Lily takes the bowl of blood away. The arms of the youths are lowered. With bowed heads, they prepare to receive the benediction of Shen T'ang.

'May you survive to wear the red robes of honourable membership.

May old age and wealth be yours in the service of this, our most ancient and revered society, Hong Ming.'

Mr Yan and the initiates slowly retreat from the altar. The shadows flicker and dance as if to celebrate their induction.

Lily takes up a soft-headed drumstick and gong. As Yan and the youths bow with respect and obedience to Shen T'ang, she strikes the gong. The resulting boom fills the underground space with an ominous resonance.

8

A shower of rain has swept the streets of Rawalpindi clean. Khan and his son, on their way to Islamabad airport, have decided to make a brief sightseeing visit to the busy town. They are unaware that they are creations in a writer's emerging script, as he dictates text instructions sitting inside a recess under a sign that reads 'English Typing Done'.

After the brief downpour, Saidor Road soon returns to its customary bustle. The Writer sits next to the typist, a middle-aged Asian with a neatly trimmed white beard. The typewriting machine is a vintage model that P.G. Wodehouse would have recognised. The Writer watches the crowds passing by, the swarm of auto taxis plying their trade. He plays with his sunglasses, thoughtfully. The typist waits, the Writer begins to dictate. The keys fly and commit his words to paper.

'Exterior. Rawalpindi. Day. Khan and his dad stroll past the camera on Saidor Road. Follow them as they skirt a large greasy puddle then…'

He pauses, where should the next scene take place? Ah, yes…

'Cut to- Interior. Chinese Ritual Basement, Birmingham. Day.'

9

Inside the basement of St Stephen's church, the two new recruits, Chang and Jian, now fully dressed, stand before Shen T'ang and his daughter Lily. Mr Yan waits behind. It is the final stage of the initiation. The torches splutter and spark, the candles burn and shine their light on the demonic gods of chaos and destruction. Shen T'ang shows the initiates a photograph of Harry Sen.

'This is the man whose life you must claim to prove your worth to our society.'

'Who—?' Chang starts to ask.

Yan slaps the taller recruit across the face.

'Do not question, obey!'

Jian and Chang bow to the Triad leader.

'Please, master, where is this man to be found?' Jian asks, humbly.

'Our information is he works at a restaurant,' Shen T'ang replies.

'Of what name?'

'It has no name.'

10

It is almost lunchtime when Anne and Kline return to the restaurant. Anne shares Kline's frustration over the setback. The sale of the Maverick club has provided enough funds for this new venture, but without a license to sell liquor how can they make a profit?

Not talking much, they walk past the lines of empty tables, push through swing doors reminiscent of a western saloon, enter the kitchen, there to be greeted by Harry, their Chinese cook.

'Bit've lunch, boss?'

'Great.'

'Drink?'

'Best thing I've heard today.'

'Miss Anne?'

'Soda water, on the rocks.'

Kline sits at the kitchen table, sprawls his long legs. He undoes his necktie as if releasing a hangman's noose. Anne watches him, decides to keep her mouth shut. Their drinks arrive. She fumbles for her methadone tablets, takes one down with a swallow of soda water. Her companion notices but makes no comment. Behind them, inside the rear cooking area, Harry is busy preparing their lunch. Anne decides to break the silence.

'Is it the license thing that's pissing you off or is it something else?'

'Like what?'

'Me?'

'Just not used to having to do things by the book.'

'It's what we decided.'

'I know, I...'

He stops. Two Chinese youths are peering over the swing doors. Kline waves a dismissive hand, calls, 'We're not open yet!'

He frowns as the two Chinese guys shoulder their way in, just as his cook brings bowls of noodles, prawns and vegetables to the table. Jian, the smaller of the two visitors, addresses Kline as Harry returns to the kitchen.

'We desire to see the owner of the restaurant.'

'You're looking at him.'

'Yes, what is name?'

'Kline.'

Anne grins.

'He means the name of the place.' She spells it out. 'It hasn't got one.'

'Yet,' Kline adds. He helps himself to a mouthful of food as he regards his visitors.

'You waiters?'

'We look like waiters? We want to talk.'

'No charge for that.'

Jian looks around the kitchen.

'I worked here once. Before it was closed for illegal gambling. You know Chinese bet hard?'

'I've heard.'

'Heard, have you? Now, since bigwig judge close dens, we need places. You have storerooms behind kitchen. Let us use them, you get cut from every game.'

Kline glances across at Anne. She gives him a stony look in return.

'No deal,' Kline says.

The taller Chinese rubs his fingers together under Kline's nose.

'You not like money?'

'Not when it's fishy, like your fingers.'

Chang helps himself to a prawn from Kline's plate, sucks on it.

'Not bad, you have good cook.'

He reaches for another helping. Kline grabs his hand.

'You've no manners, want me to teach you some?'

'Want your hair parted with a meat axe?'

From the corner of his eye Kline sees Anne wince at the growing aggro. The smaller thug pushes himself forward.

'Lots of restaurants in this town need protection.'

'Is that what this is about?'

'Rent out your space, we pay you; refuse, you must pay us.'

'For protection?'

'Hey, you catch on pretty good.'

Kline sighs, looks towards Anne.

'This is where I came in.'

He stands, fills his lungs, exhales. Grabs the intruders by the scruff of their necks, pushes them through the swing doors, hustles them across the restaurant. Pauses at the exit with a final instruction.

'Beat it!'

He propels them towards the street.

Jian stumbles and falls, Chang pulls out a knife, steps towards Kline threateningly. Anne emerges from the kitchen as Kline grabs a decanter from a side table, ready to crack the first skull that comes within reach.

Jian scrambles to his feet, pulls Chang away from the growing confrontation. They retreat into the street. The door bangs behind them. Kline relaxes, chuckles to himself. Anne is less than impressed.

'Enjoy yourself?'

Kline shrugs, his expression hardening.

'That pair of yellow perils used the word "protection". I did three years because of that word, you know.'

'Yes, I know, you keep telling me.'

11

Harry Sen can scent imminent danger. He suspects the visit of the Chinese duo was a scouting mission. Were they waiting for him outside? What had become of his partner, Chen? Murder? What of their secret mission? How could he protect their findings? The cook looks around the storeroom then down at the chicken he is holding. He takes out a wad of papers wrapped in polythene from his pocket, rolls them tightly, inserts the document deep into the innards of the bird.

Holding the carcass by the neck, Harry places the chicken next to other frozen poultry within the freezer. He moves to the back door of the kitchen, eases it open, checks the alley for danger. Seeing none, he steps outside.

Kline and Anne are perched on stools at the restaurant bar. Both are leafing through lists of names, consulting dictionaries. Kline looks up, a gleam of triumph in his eyes

'Got it.'

'Go on.'

'Kline's Cuisine.'

His fellow researcher thinks about it. Shakes her head, her blonde hair swirling. Kline gives up, slides down from his stool, heads behind the bar, selects a glass, pushes an optic, brings down a shot of scotch.

Anne ploughs on. She reaches the letter 'N' in her dictionary. *'N' for what? Narcotics? Oh, sure, thanks a lot. 'Nefertiti', the Egyptian queen? Mm, décor would be… what? Funeral masks? Hieroglyphics decorating the menu, waiters in loincloths?* Then she sees it. Reads the definition, knows the search was over.

Kline sips his scotch, looks quizzically as Anne gives him a seductive smile, speaks in a husky voice.

'Ready?'

'Hit me.'

A pregnant pause.

'Nirvana.'

'Nir… What?'

Anne smiles seductively, breathes the words in a low sexy voice.

'Nirvana. Where all desire is extinguished. The consummation of bliss.'

Kline pictures her naked on their bed. He smiles.

'I'm all for that.'

Kline raises his glass to her as the swing doors crash open. Harry, their chef, staggers into the bar. He attempts to speak, blood froths from his lips. He turns. They see the handle of the knife buried between his shoulder blades. Anne cries out in fear. Kline rushes to support Harry, catches him as he falls.

'Harry, who did this?'

The cook stares up at Kline, tries to mouth a message.

'Roo… Heart… of the rooster…'

'What?'

Kline feels the life ebb from the body he holds in his arms.

'Harry…'

There are no more words from Harry Sen, only a dark gush of blood from his mouth. Gently, Kline lowers him to the floor.

'He's gone.'

Anne begins to shake, trying to make sense of the horror.

'Why this, for Christ's sake?'

'It can't be to get back at me, not for a few quid's protection.'

'What was he trying to say?'

'Something about a rooster, heart of the rooster.'

'What?'

John Kline watches the blood of Harry Sen slowly form a pool on the floor. He feels an anger, a need for revenge, a growing desire to discover the truth behind the last words of a man who has become his friend.

Anne senses his rising rage, his excitement at the prospect of being drawn back into a dangerous world, one she had thought no longer part of their lives. A dark world of mystery, mayhem and, now, murder.

12

Islamabad airport is overcast by rolling grey-black clouds. On the runway, the green and cream livery of the PIA aircraft glistens in the drizzle of early monsoon rain.

Khan and his father stay together until it is time for Zahir to enter the departure lounge. As the last call for his flight back to the UK chimes out, he smiles down at his dad.

'I will try and holiday here soon.'

'That would give us a chance to compare notes on crime detection. Yours the somewhat devious, mine the more traditional.'

'Or perhaps you would let me show you modern Britain.'

'Yes, perhaps.'

He frowns.

'What is it?' Khan asks.

'There was a fellow turned up at the village last month. The things he said regarding England, vicious propaganda. I soon sent him packing.'

'What did he say?'

'Never mind. Now, look here, as an agent of the Crown it is your duty to protect her Majesty's realm from, what did you say? Ah, yes, Triad gangsters. Bring them to book, really bring their crimes home to them.'

'I will.'

It is time to go. Father and son embrace. Zahir Khan picks up his hand luggage, goes through the gate that leads to passport control. The old man watches until his son, after a last wave of his hand, disappears.

13

John Kline hates police stations, but his years in the army have taught him endless patience. So he sits impassively inside an interview room facing a police detective, who from his dishevelled state has either been heavily on the piss or hasn't slept for days.

DC Marks stifles a yawn as he writes notes on the interview. Kline sits back in his grey plastic chair, wonders if Anne is receiving the same treatment. The police's aim would be to compare their accounts, look for differences between which to drive a wedge. Basic stuff. He worries about Anne's fragile state of mind, hopes she will be able to cope with any enquiry. After all, they have nothing to hide – a novel situation for them both.

The cop's notes are now up to date. He rubs his eyes, squints at Kline.

'These mysterious Chinese visitors, did they mention what they were after?'

'They tried to hustle me into paying protection.'

'And?'

'I said I didn't need it.'

'You didn't get into a fight about it, the cook got involved, ended up dead?'

'Nope.'

'What did they look like, give me a description.'

'One was taller than the other. They both had sallow skin, black hair.'

'That fits two billion Chinese.'

'That's my point. I've been through what happened. First the Chinese guys, then my chef pitching up with a knife in his back. Think the two might be connected?'

'If they exist.'

'Why would I stick a knife into my chef?'

'What if he wasn't just a chef?'

'You've lost me.'

Marks yawns. 'Let's go through it again.'

'Let's not. If you suspect me of involvement, charge me. Otherwise, me and my partner walk.'

'The fuck you talking to, Kline?'

'I know how you bastards work.'

The detective stands, clenches his right fist, steps menacingly forward. Kline, SAS trained, is unimpressed. The DC glowers down at him.

'You belong inside.'

'Try and put me there.'

'Give us time.'

'Time's what you've just run out of.'

14

The restaurant soon to be known as Nirvana is in darkness, except for light streaming into the hallway from the kitchen. Kline, on entering, looks down reprovingly at his companion.

'Annie, lights.'

She casts her mind back, realises.

'I switched them off, I know I did.'

They hurry towards the kitchen, push through the swing doors.

'Oh, Jesus!'

Chairs are overturned, cooking utensils thrown around. They enter the storeroom. The upright freezer gapes open, frozen foodstuffs lie scattered on the floor. Anne walks up and down, desperate for an explanation, trying to make sense of the destruction.

'Is it kids, just hungry kids breaking in?'

'Maybe…'

Kline bends down, picks up a frozen chicken.

'They couldn't eat this, it's still frozen.'

They start to collect the poultry, begin to pack them back into the freezer. Anne lifts a bird by its neck, grimaces.

'Ugh, this one's still got its head on.'

Kline glances across, notices the red coxcomb.

'Rooster.'

He reaches for another frozen carcass, pauses, realises the import of the word. He takes the fowl from her. It has a softer feel than all the rest.

'This is only half frozen.'

'So?'

'Rooster, "heart of the rooster", they were Harry's last words…'

Kline turns the bird upside down, catches a glimpse of polythene inside. He slowly extracts a packet containing a wad of papers.

'This is what Harry tried to tell us about. This…'

He opens the papers, scans the first page, sees lines of unintelligible characters.

'All Chinese to me. Look…'

Anne backs away.

'Don't ask me, I want nothing to do with it.'

'Why? Don't you wonder why a bloke uses his last breath to try and tell me about this?'

'That was his problem, please don't make it ours.'

'Maybe this is what the law were hinting at.'

'So give it to them.'

'Huh, I should do them favours?'

Kline toys with the papers. Anne watches him, wary. He notices the worry in her hazel eyes, but it doesn't stop him.

'Do you know what I think we should do?'

'Nothing.'

'That isn't an option, Annie.' He toys with the wad of paper, smiles to himself.

'What is it with you?' Anne asks.

'Fancy some fish and chips?'

15

The Empire Fish Restaurant has a Chinese proprietor. Leaving Anne outside, Kline joins a small queue of hungry customers.

Anne feels the gnawing of a different kind of hunger. The mixed smells of stale frying fat and the fumes from the passing traffic almost overwhelm her. She reaches into the pocket of her voluminous green coat, feels the cold comfort of the small bottle containing pills of methadone. It is there, waiting to dull the pain when her fears become too sharp to bear. She hugs her coat around her, shivers, although this is a warm autumn day.

Inside the fish and chip shop, the last customer to be served is John

Kline. He orders a packet of chips to take out. While his order is being shovelled into a paper cone, Kline eases the mystery writings from his pocket. Once the bag of chips is paid for, he produces the bundle of Chinese writings.

'Do us a favour, tell me what this says.'

He watches the expression of the man as he scans the first few lines. There is a flicker of fear. He thrusts the papers back across the counter.

'I do not understand, this language is different from mine.'

'But I thought your written language was the same for anyone Chinese?'

'I do not understand. Please, go away. I have no time, go away!'

He backs toward the safety of his back room. Kline follows him along the counter. Shoves the papers at him once again.

'Just the first page. Look, even the opening line will do.'

'Please go away!'

The frightened owner retreats. The door to the rear of the restaurant slams shut after him. A puzzled John Kline helps himself to salt and a dash of vinegar then joins Anne outside. She looks up at him hoping that the Chinese letters are merely someone's shopping list. Kline offers her a chip.

'The Chop Suey deepens, my dear.'

16

Aslam Rafiq, settled in his seat in the members' enclosure of the Edgbaston cricket ground, is watching a match between Warwickshire and Surrey.

The game is petering out into a tame draw. Rafiq doesn't care. He is mulling over the state of his various business enterprises, some legitimate, others less so.

Rafiq becomes vaguely aware of an upper class woman's voice wittering away behind him. *Women and cricket, oh dear.* Rafiq gives a slight shudder. He remembers trying to explain the rules of the game to the woman he was once married to in Lucknow. A pointless exercise, as was the marriage. He sighs. Love is an unsolved mystery, sex a temporary need to be appeased from time to time. Once more the woman's voice intrudes into his thoughts.

'Daddy, why do those men in white keep trotting between those sticks of wood?'

This is too much to bear. Rafiq turns in his seat, opens his mouth to insist on silence. The words die on his lips. What he sees is an elegant young Chinese woman wearing a peach-coloured floral blouse and a pleated skirt of the same material, Seated next to her is a dapper gentleman who must be her father. Out of a clear sky, Cupid's arrow finds its mark. Rafiq musters an engaging smile.

'Might I offer my services to instruct you in the nuances of the great game?'

Lily Li T'ang glances towards her father.

'What *is* he talking about?'

'Cricket.'

'Oh, that.' She looks across the field of play, gives the flannelled fools no more than a cursory glance.

Rafiq stands, bows, breathes in the musk of her perfume, produces his business card.

'Sir, I would be delighted to have an opportunity to further our acquaintance.'

'I too would welcome such an occurrence,' Shen T'ang replies in his slow, considered tones.

'And your daughter?'

Lily fixes her almond eyes on Rafiq. She takes in the cut of his expensive suit, the smooth brown skin, his sleek, well cut hair. She smiles her most scintillating smile, revealing teeth as white as the sightscreen below. Rafiq takes her hand, lays a devout but respectful kiss on its silky skin. Around them members tut at this show. Damn foreigners indulging in manners unbecoming.

At that moment, on the pitch, a fast yorker crashes into the stumps. Amidst the applause, gazing at the loveliness of Lily Li T'ang, Rafiq realises that he, too, has just been bowled over.

17

Standing beside a hedgerow, on a country road near Henley-in-Arden, Zahir Khan looks up at the grey monsoon-like sky and wonders if it has travelled back with him from Pakistan.

He is here to meet with an undercover agent. Why the meeting should take place at this isolated spot he cannot fathom. He strokes his moustache, gazes across the lush green fields, fails to notice on the horizon of the sullen sky an aircraft drifting by.

The whining sound of an approaching car focuses his attention. A cream Ford motor slows, halts. A passenger alights, a man of mature years who carries a fawn briefcase. The car drives away. Khan looks at the stranger. The stranger looks at him. No sign of recognition. They both look away. Another car sweeps up. Another Ford. A door opens, the unknown man gets inside. The black saloon car roars away.

A further five minutes go by before Khan becomes conscious of a faint whirring sound in the distance. The sound is ominous, mysterious, and it grows ever louder. He realises the low-flying object is aiming straight at him. It swoops; he hears the *whap-whap-whap* of a helicopter's blades, feels the rush of air swirl around him, sees the red markings on the hull coming ever closer. He starts to run. There is no cover, no cornfield to take refuge in. The 'copter soars above his head, banks, climbs, turns and clatters back towards him. Khan makes himself stand still. The helicopter descends, flattens the vegetation all around, settles, lands in the middle of the country road.

A side door slides open. A black woman, late twenties, wearing an olive green combat jacket, tucked in trousers, boots, a forage cap, shuttered sunglasses, ducks away from the down draft of the still whirling blades, approaches Khan. She snaps out a jaunty salute and speaks with a Californian accent.

'Hi, glad you could make it. I'm Sarah Gant.'

Aboard the helicopter, strapped in next to Sarah Gant, Khan looks down at the expanse of the English countryside unfolding below, trying to come to terms with the disturbing news the DEA agent has just passed onto him.

'You're certain of this?'

'Harry Sen got it in an alleyway yesterday. Stabbed.'

'And the other agent, Chen?'

'Missing. He has family in Hong Kong, but they say there's been no recent contact.'

'Amongst Harry's belongings was there any sign of a report?'

'No. We searched his room. I found some papers written in Chinese, but they turned out to be letters from his wife in Hong Kong.'

'Not a coded report of Triad activity?'

'Nope.'

'Do you still have those letters?' Khan asks.

'Sure, why?'

'They may be useful. Without Sen's report, we're on the back foot. There were supposed to be names, addresses, details, the drug routes the Triads intend to use into Britain.'

'If the report exists, we'll find it. He worked for John Kline.'

'Kline? He still around?'

'Yes. We have some history. He knew my sister, Dinah. I suggested Harry apply to work for him.'

'Kline had no idea Sen was an undercover agent?'

'No. Police interviewed Kline, had to let him go. No evidence.'

'Or he didn't want to offer any. I'll talk to him. He's a useful tool to have on one's side.'

'Tools are always welcome in my line of work. The bigger the better.'

Khan turns his head to Sarah Gant. She grins back at him.

'I knew the United States Drug Enforcement Agency were sending over an agent. There was no mention that it would be you, Mrs Gant.'

'I've been here before. But I was given no choice. One of my hookers ratted me out. The DEA closed my restaurant, all my houses, busted my dealers. They offered me a choice: fifteen to twenty behind bars or a mission overseas. Stop the Triads or it's jail time for Mrs G. So here I am, back in beautiful Birmingham.'

'This is a tough assignment, Mrs Gant.'

'My whole life's a tough assignment, baby. We need to work together. I've access to DEA files in Europe but for the local stuff I'll need your help. What about it, ready to jump into bed with me?'

Through the window of the chopper Khan can see the tower blocks of Birmingham come into view. Any help would be welcome, but can he trust this brazen woman who has been foisted on him? Sarah rips open a packet of salted peanuts, pops several into her mouth.

'Mrs Gant, you are here only in an advisory capacity.'

'I'm here to save my ass. Let me give you the mantra I give my whores: "Fake it, shake it, but be sure you make it". We need to send those Triad gooks down the tube any which way we can.'

'Let's agree we have a mutual understanding of what's at stake.'

Sarah Gant looks sideways at him, flutters her false eyelashes.

'You just wanna hold hands? OK, that's a start. Peanut?'

18

John Kline sits at the kitchen table puzzling over a liquor license appeals procedure booklet. With a muttered 'bollacks', he tosses the booklet aside. Sitting across from him, Anne purses her lips like a disapproving schoolmarm.

'Study time over, is it?'

'Council bullshit.'

'Want me to look at it?'

'I just need to get my head around it, that's all. We'll have to take the appeal to a magistrate's court. Legal fees, all that crap.'

Anne watches him. He is moody, at odds with everything. Is it her insistence that they stay within the confines of the law? Or something else? Is he becoming bored with her? Kline drums his fingers on the tabletop. It reminds Anne of a death rattle. She decides on a change of tack.

'Nirvana.'

'What about it?'

'If that's the name, we need to hire a sign writer.'

'OK, price them up.'

'Also, the menu will need to be part eastern. Thai, maybe, to go with the name.'

'That means an Asian cook?'

'It does.'

A bitter half smile flickers across the lips of John Kline.

'Better not tell him how the last one left our employ.'

Anne shivers. She sees Harry, his shocked, staring eyes, the handle of the knife buried in his back, the stain of blood on his jacket. She tries to wipe away the memory.

'I'll contact the catering agency. You do the interviewing, OK?'

Her tone is icy, her manner hostile.

'Annie, what is it?'

'You. Doesn't it matter to you that Harry was murdered right here?'

'It matters a lot. I intend to find out why. With or without your help.'

Anne stares at him as if he has suddenly become a stranger. Without a word she turns, leaves the kitchen, runs up the stairs.

Once inside their bedroom, Anne sits on the side of the bed. She feels tears begin, fights them back. She has never cried over a man. She wipes her eyes with the back of her hand, falls back on her pillows. She wonders if the 25mg of methadone per day is enough. She can feel the craving for something else emanating from rogue receptors in her brain. Nibbling. Rats gnawing away at her resolve. She gazes at the bottle of pills on her bedside cabinet. Where's the harm in taking a further half? That would make, what, 37mg today, might even give her a dull high. Why stop at a half tablet? Why not take a double dose? Never mind the dangers, coma, heart attack, it would give her peace. Jesus, what she wouldn't give for a hit, a boost to cope with everything this shitty life could throw at her. Anne reaches for the bottle, stops herself. Stands, forces herself to walk away, go down the stairs, head towards the kitchen.

Inside, John Kline sits at the pine table. She notes the bottle of Johnny Walker beside him. She's not the only one seeking aid from a false friend.

'I need to visit the clinic, don't know how long I'll be.'

'Anything I can do?'

'No, this is down to me.'

Kline watches her waif-like figure push through the swing doors. He wonders if the woman he fell in love with will ever return.

19

The red Vauxhall of Mr Yan is parked on the broad driveway of the detached residence of Aslam Rafiq. The house is an imposing one. Grey weathered stone, its bay window frames painted black and white. Above the mansion a rising moon appears. Its light throws shadows across the wide, tailored lawns.

Inside the dining room a meal has been cleared from the white damask tablecloth. Rafiq watches a servant serve wine to his visitors. To the left of him sits Lily Li T'ang, ravishing in a pale rose shantung silk dress. A hanging Lalique lampshade casts a soft light down onto the table.

On an ornate wooden sideboard sits a statue of the goddess Kali, black as night with the red of her lolling tongue just visible in the spill of light from the table. Shen T'ang, wearing evening dress, sits opposite to his host. Mr Yan, in a grey business suit, completes the foursome. Rafiq turns his attention from Lily to her father. He smiles engagingly.

'I was most impressed by your daughter when we encountered each other at Edgbaston earlier today.'

'And she with you.'

'Really?'

Rafiq turns to Lily, who smiles encouragingly. His voice lowers in response.

'Forgive me, I find myself intrigued: the name Lily one associates more with France than the Orient.'

She leans towards him, he leans towards her, anxious to drink in every word.

'I owe the sobriquet to the girls at my prep school. My name is Li Li, which became Lily, hence Lily Li T'ang.'

'Ah, Lily Li T'ang, what a wonderful a name. Like cool water on a parched tongue.'

Shen T'ang takes a sip of wine, savours it, speaks in his slow, measured way.

'Li means a beautiful tree.'

Rafiq waves an appreciative hand towards the young woman beside him.

'A beautiful blossom on a beautiful tree. What an apt description, Lily. May I call you Lily?'

'You may.'

'Your accent?'

'I was educated in Sussex.'

'Ah, Roedean.'

'Hence the clarity of consonants and the god-awful tone.'

'Oh no, no, not at all.'

Aslam Rafiq notices the dull gold of the head piece that holds back her shoulder-length dark hair. Its colour matches the coiled snakes that decorate the head rail of the chair behind her lovely head. His eyes meet with hers, their look lingers, until the brisk tone of her father intrudes.

'Mister Rafiq…'

Rafiq tears himself away from the lovely Lily.

'Mister T'ang.'

'May we speak openly?'

'Of course.'

'My daughter is no lover of the game called cricket.'

'Oh, what a pity. The game has much to offer.'

'You must wonder why she should be attending a stadium where the game is being played?'

Rafiq wonders about many things but contains his impatience with an indulgent smile. He sees Shen T'ang nod towards Mr Yan. Yan speaks with a directness absent from the meeting so far.

'I knew of you, Mister Rafiq. I suggested you to Shen T'ang as having the correct credentials for what we require.'

'Credentials?' Rafiq aims the question towards Shen T'ang, who leans forward intently.

'A position of trust as a leader of your community. Multifarious business enterprises.'

'I find such interest very flattering, although I must confess I do not understand its purpose.'

'I'm a man of business who seeks an alliance to help in the distribution of our wares.'

'Well, I prefer to do business with a man of business, although what business is proposed can alter that preferment.'

In his peripheral vision, Rafiq sees Lily extract a cigarette and place it into an ivory holder. Rafiq smoothly takes a table lighter and lights her cigarette. Lily touches his hand as she bends to the flame. Her gesture, slight as it is, inflames his desire to possess this young woman, make her his own. He notices dragons intertwined above her breasts, a motif of delicate pink. Pink as the nipples beneath? Lily draws on her cigarette, exhales.

'My father is a dealer in pharmaceutical supply.'

The businessman in Rafiq recognises that the point of the evening has now been reached. He phrases his next words casually, delicately.

'Which are imported without government approval?'

Shen T'ang, too, acknowledges the moment of opportunity. He toys with his table napkin.

'If I said yes, would that terminate the possibility of our alliance?'

'Perhaps not immediately.'

'I see. Mr Yan, you may elucidate further.'

'Mr Rafiq, you have heard of the Chinese associations called Triads?'

'Triads, yes.'

'Do you know in what merchandise they deal?'

'Protection, terror and what else? Oh, yes, a drug that I believe is called heroin.'

Yan glances at his leader for guidance. Shen T'ang gets down to business.

'We have been hampered and restricted recently by the activities of two undercover Chinese detectives from Hong Kong. I am pleased to say that both impediments have now been removed.'

He glances towards Yan, who, Rafiq is pleased to note, proceeds at a livelier pace.

'There is the problem of distribution. Agents, dealers. This is not London or Liverpool; the Chinese community in the West Midlands is slight by comparison. But other immigrant communities, such as yours, possess the same advantages as our own. They are insular, loyal and true to their leaders.'

Rafiq nods. 'That is indeed true. My constituents speak a language the forces of the law cannot easily penetrate.'

With the word 'penetrate' his eyes stray towards Lily. Shen T'ang suddenly becomes agitated. Rafiq wonders if he has read his lascivious thoughts but it soon becomes apparent that there is another cause. The leader of the Hong Ming rises to his feet, raises his arms as if to welcome a new dawn.

'In the year 1841, Great Britain created Hong Kong to flood China with opium. I wish to return the compliment. Soon it will be raining heroin all over Britain. We will need many, many receptacles to catch the fall.'

Rafiq stands, mimes the catching of a cricket ball.

'To catch the fall!'

All stand and lift their glasses to toast the success of their enterprise. When settled around the table once more, Shen T'ang sheds his urbane image. The cold steel of the Triad leader shows through.

'I do not care what colour are the hands that bring us profit. Yellow, black, white or brown. All may be associated with our great cause.'

Enthused by the opportunity, Rafiq raises a clenched fist.

'All may share in the commonwealth of the dragon!'

Mr Yan strikes a sober note of warning.

'But only those who have the wisdom to follow the dictates of Shen T'ang.'

Lily turns to Rafiq, leans in a little. Drawn to her, he takes in her lustrous hair, her oval face, her deep, dark brown eyes, her fine nose, her lips delicately outlined with carmine, the same hue as the tongue of the goddess Kali.

Rafiq waits for Lily to speak, to hear once more the lilting clarity of her voice.

'In China…'

'Yes?'

'The dragon brings rain, causes rivers to flow. It can wing across an ocean and bring love to the hearts of men.'

'And women?'

Lily smiles, her voice rich with the promise of further intimacy.

'Of course.'

'Then only a fool would not welcome the arrival of such a celestial creature.'

They are very close, faces almost touching. Rafiq looks down, sees the dragons on her dress rise and fall each time she breathes. Across the table, Mr Yan and Shen T'ang exchange satisfied glances. Lily has done her work well. Soon Rafiq will belong to them.

20

Anne, in bed with Kline, cannot settle. The increase of methadone dosage, small as it was, makes her restless, tired but unable to slide into longed for sleep. She wants comfort, to be held by the man who lies naked beside her, but all he seems interested in is studying a booklet on how to gain a liquor license.

Her gaze is level with the bedside table. Beside an alarm clock rests the bottle of methadone pills newly issued to her. She recalls her journey to the drug clinic, the fevered trip past all the familiar staging posts, the pubs, the clubs, the street corners, the dark places that almost led her to self-destruction. Yes, she'd paused by one or two, exchanged words with dealers, but had somehow managed to side-step them all.

At the clinic, she convinced a doctor to increase her dosage, a 5mg daily boost. There was a pep talk from a woman psychologist who obviously had never ingested any drug stronger than aspirin. Anne was to think about 'maintenance' rather than 'treatment'. Anne sighs, punches her pillow. Nothing from her companion, who still pores over the appeals procedure requirements. Anne turns to him, moves up against his body, seeking warmth. She traces the hard muscles of Kline's belly. She lets her hand wander down into the wiry tangle of his pubic hair. Absentmindedly, Kline removes her hand before it can make any further progress. He turns a page of the appeals booklet. Anne flings herself back to her side of the bed, turns her back to him. Waits for a conciliatory word. Nothing. After another thirty seconds of silence, Anne hauls herself up, plucks at her white cotton nightdress.

She stares around the bedroom. She enjoyed decorating, choosing the décor, matching covers to the subtle design of the grey wallpaper, searching for the bamboo design headboard that she now rests against. Creating a haven, a nest for them both. All for what? She makes a derisory noise. Kline sighs, looks up from the page.

'What is it?'

'You. You pretending to want what I want, to turn away from the flash, the cheap thrills, the easy lays.'

Kline mutters in protest. She cuts him off.

'Shut up, give me one minute. Today, when trouble came to call, I realised that you were happy for the first time since you sold the Maverick.'

'I'm not happy, just curious to know what it is about a Chinese puzzle that is worth killing for.'

Anne's voice reflects her frustration, anger, fear.

'Why bother? Why not let it be? You might be the next one killed. Or is that the charge needed to boost your machismo?'

'Talk English.'

'What you need to get it up, get it off.'

Kline does not consider his reply; the words are out before he can stop them.

'And how much methadone do you need to get you through the day, baby?'

'Bastard.'

'Yeah, aren't we?'

Hurt and angry, she turns towards him.

'I've gone six months on methadone, that's something, some sign of how much you mean to me.'

She waits for his response. He looks away.

'That really embarrasses you, doesn't it?'

Still no response. Kline stares ahead.

'Talk! I want you to talk, use soft words, woman's words.'

'What words you want to hear, Annie?'

'Just something beyond "want", "have", "take". Something like "need", "trust".' Anne hesitates. '"Love"?'

Kline's tone is unyielding. 'Words like, "I do"? My name on a mortgage?'

All the events of the day bear down on Anne. She feels helpless, held in an ever-tightening vice. Her words gush out like she is trying to vomit them away.

She hurls herself, crying, onto her pillow. Kline comes across to her, wraps his arms around her.

'Annie, I never resist the run of things. I won't be held responsible for what may never happen. I want to know what the Chinese papers say. I want you with me, *you*, not the house frau you're trying to become, but the sexy, tough, gritty woman who did a heroin deal with that Chinese geezer...'

He stops, realises what their next move could be.

'What was his name?'

Anne hesitates. The house frau would lie that she can't remember. The tough woman with a brain full of heroin would give out the name and to hell with the consequences. She feels the arms of her tighten around her. Anne knows the next words she speaks might change her world forever, either send her away or keep her bound to this man. But words won't form. She feels Kline breathe into her ear as he has once before, when he extracted a name from her that that had brought deadly consequences to so many lives.

'Annie, what was his name?'

After a long pause. 'He's called Mr Yan.'

21

The defunct engineering factory is once more a gambling den. At his post behind the locked gate, Roy Sturt's befuddled brain realises someone is trying to gain entry.

The large wooden door shakes, the bolt on the smaller entrance door rattles. Sturt frowns, shambles over to squint through the spy hole placed low on the door. All he can see from that angle is the lower part of a woman's blue jeans, a fawn pair of high heeled shoes moving impatiently on the grimy pavement. Always hoping for a stray shag, Sturt opens the door. He finds himself looking not into the face of a willing woman but at the stern features of John Kline.

'Hello, Roy baby, got your voice back yet?'

Before the ex-pug can reply he is yanked out into the street. The two face each other like a pair of rutting stags. There is history between them, a violent history.

Sturt crouches into his fighting stance. Kline grins. He doesn't mind mixing it with boxers. They tend to attack above the waist, a habit that plays well with someone trained in a different discipline. Sturt opens with a left jab, Kline counters with a savage kick to where a protective cup should be. As his attacker doubles over in silent pain, Kline hooks him to the side of the head. Sturt pulls Kline into a clinch, the pair crash back against the wooden door.

No fan of fisticuffs, Anne ducks through the door and enters the workshop. Her searching look takes in the hectic games of Mah Jong, the swirl of cigarette smoke above groups of Chinese gamblers immersed in their games of chance. Anne spies Mr Yan, who has his back to her as he watches the action, keen to collect his commission on every game being played. She walks across the concrete floor, a seemingly confident figure in her heels, blue denim and close-fitting white sweater.

Anne comes up behind Mr Yan, taps the shoulder of his charcoal grey business suit. Yan turns, controls his surprise at the identity of his unexpected visitor.

'Miss Darracott, I thought you had melted clean away.'

'Not quite. Can we talk?'

'Of what? His eyes gleam. 'Business?'

'Maybe.'

Yan's eyes shift beyond Anne to where Kline is walking towards them, dabbing at his lower lip and tucking in his shirt. On reaching Yan he takes out a wad of papers from his jacket pocket.

'You read Chinese?'

'What do you think?'

The pair eyeball each other. Anne intervenes.

'Please, Mr Yan, we'd like you to help us.'

Kline hands him the papers. Yan glances down, reads the first page.

'Where did you obtain these, Miss Darracott?'

'A fortune cookie. What do they say?'

Yan scans through the pages, shrugs.

'They seem to be a man's diary. He writes of his life in Birmingham, his work as a cook, his longing for his wife and children in Hong Kong. There are several poems about this, not of great merit.'

'That's all?' Kline shows his disappointment. Yan shrugs.

'What did you expect, instructions to find a treasure trove?'

'I didn't know what to expect. You can pass them back now.'

The papers change hands. Kline senses a little reluctance. He gives a curt nod of thanks, turns to leave. A dazed figure with a bleeding nose staggers back into the workshop. He holds his voice activator to the side of his neck.

'Bastard-I'll-get-you!'

Unseen by Anne and Kline, Yan holds up a warning finger. He does not wish the couple harmed, not just yet. Kline approaches Roy Sturt, who lifts his fists. Kline smiles.

'Sorry for the roughhouse.' He grabs the ex-boxer's voice tube, places it against his own neck. 'It's-a-cut-throat-business!'

The device starts to buzz angrily. Kline can't switch it off. Anne takes it from him, quietens the sound, hands it back to the seething keeper of the gate.

'Thanks for letting us in, Roy, it's been a pleasure,' she says, sweetly.

Sturt forgets to activate his means of an audible reply, but the silent words 'fuck' and 'you' are very apparent.

On the street outside the factory, Anne and her companion mooch along thoughtfully.

'What do you think, was the Yan guy lying?' Kline asks.

'Why would he lie?'

'He didn't want to give the papers back. I'd like a second opinion from someone, somewhere. Any ideas?'

About to shake her head, a memory clicks into place.

'There's a guy I used to supply. He moved out into the country.'

'Give him a call.'

In a tatty office, at the rear of the factory, Shen T'ang sits at a desk counting the take from the morning's play. Standing behind him, elegant in a black Chanel two-piece suit, Lily Li T'ang checks her make-up in a hand mirror. The door is thrust open, Mr Yan bustles in. He halts, bows respectfully to his leader.

'What is it, Yan?'

'We have a problem with the man called Kline.'

22

Within the city morgue the air is chill. The décor is as anonymous as death itself. Khan stands on one side of the container holding the corpse of Harry Sen, on the other Roy Sturt stares down at the dead agent. Across the room, Sarah Gant lounges against the wall playing 'he loves me, he loves me not' with a posy of faded flowers.

'What did you know of Superintendent Sen?' Khan asks.

'I-didn't-know-he was-dead! He-paid-me-to-tell-him-who-went-into-the-gambling-club!'

'Tell me.'

There is a pause during which Sturt rubs his forefinger and thumb together, indicating his need for reimbursement. Khan glances across to Mrs Gant, who nods acceptance. Khan looks sternly at the swollen face of the ex-boxer.

'We will see. What do you have?'

'Kline-and-Anne-came-to-see-Yan-today!'

'Why?'

'Kline-had-a-bundle-of-Chinese papers!'

Khan takes out the letters Sarah has gathered from her raid on Harry Sen.

'Did they look like these?'

Sturt nods.

'Anyone else visited Mr Yan?'

'Money-first-money-money-quick-quick-quick-my-batteries-are-running-out!'

Banknotes change hands.

'More-more-give-me-more!'

'A name, Roy, a name. Who else visited?'

'Rafiq.'

Sarah Gant saunters over.

'You'll get more cash when you deliver more information. Double cross us, you'll end up like him.'

They all look down at the still features of Harry Sen.

23

Shen T'ang regards the dozen members of the Hong Ming Triad crowded into the factory office. He is about to delegate the task of capturing John Kline when a telephone jangles on the desk behind him. He motions for Lily to answer it. She languidly removes a pendant earring, holds the receiver so it doesn't quite touch her skin.

'Yes? How soon? Excellent, thank you so much for the information.'

She replaces the telephone, addresses the gang, her voice sharp with authority.

'You will not need to search for Kline and his floozy. My father and I will attend to the matter.'

Anne and John Kline have rarely visited the countryside together. Not wishing to risk his motor on the rough track that leads towards the stables, Kline parks alongside a farm gate. The couple amble down the tractor way that leads to the rear of the stable buildings. Around them lie wide green fields, a show jumping course set up with red and white poles, rustic planks. A slight breeze plays with Anne's hair. Kline, wearing a leather jacket, surveys the terrain for dangers, places for ambush, but sees only a scattering of trees, the swell of gentle hills against a cloud-filled sky.

When they reach the stable complex, a diminutive Chinese in his mid-thirties is waiting for them. While Anne and Joey Fu exchange greetings, Kline scents the aroma of horse dung. He watches a middle-aged huntsman, replete in red coat, white breeches, shiny black riding boots, come towards him. The huntsman leads a horse who must stand all of seventeen hands. The men nod to each other. Kline can't resist touching the muscled flank of the massive chestnut nag as it passes by. It leaves a faint trace of horse sweat on his hand.

'John, you interested in what Joey has to say?'

'Sure. What's the word, Joey?'

The Chinese groom indicates the papers he holds. When he speaks, it is with a Birmingham accent.

'Menus, Chinese menus. Scribblins for a Chinese cookbook.'

Kline looks down at the groom.

'You're certain?'

'I just said, didn't I?'

'Straight from the horse's mouth.'

'If you say so.'

Anne intervenes.

'OK, thanks, Joey, I'll let you get back to cleaning up after the gentry.'

'It's a living. Nice to see you again, Miss Annie.'

'You were one of my best customers.'

'Great times.'

'Seemed so. Thanks again.'

Joey Fu watches the couple stroll from the yard. When they are out of sight he hurries into the stable corridor that leads through to the front yard. He sees a father and daughter wearing riding habits and mounted ready for the hunt. He signals that their quarry has emerged into the open. Shen T'ang wears a red riding jacket, Lily wears black. She settles her riding helmet firmly on her head. They turn their mounts and with a clatter of hooves, leave the stable yard.

Kline and Anne wander across the showjumping course. Now that she feels her duty has been done, Anne feels chatty, made lightheaded by the sweet country air.

'Joey was an apprentice jockey, had a few rides in public, lots of rides in private with rich ladies. Then smack got his number until he couldn't raise a gallop in or outside the bedroom.'

'A big shagger, that little guy?'

'There's good stuff in little packets.' She laughs, nudges the tall man walking beside her then indicates herself. He grins down at her. 'So I've heard.'

She pretends indignation. 'Heard? Don't you know?

They reach the tractor path on their way back to the car. Kline reviews the state of play as they walk along.

'So, it's a bunch of menus, a book of poems, someone's diary.'

'Or something else.'

'Something scary. Something valuable?'

'I haven't got any other contacts. This is only a suggestion, Johnny, but how about turning the stuff over to the authorities?'

Her companion shakes his head. He isn't going to let go that easily. They stroll along in silence, each lost in their thoughts. Behind the couple, further down the pathway, two riders urge their horses forward.

'There's Khan,' Kline says, 'maybe he knows someone. I've still got his number. Or Rafiq, he's still around.'

'Why should Asian guys make sense out of Chinese writing...?'

She pauses. Something is wrong; she hears the thud of horse's hooves. Kline turns, sees a pair of horses galloping at speed towards them. He pushes Anne away from the path, yells, 'Run, Annie, run!'

Anne veers away, stumbles, regains her balance, hits her stride, speeds across the grass of the hillside, running for her life. Her pursuer sends his mount charging after her.

Kline takes another direction, belts away but finds the ground uneven. He zig-zags, tries to prevent the rider in his wake from gaining a clear run at him.

Shen T'ang enjoys the chase. In his youth, he had been a polo player. He spurs his mount after the woman who scampers along ahead of him, her coat flying behind her in the breeze. Shen T'ang gallops up alongside Anne, reaches down, scoops her up and throws her ahead of him across the saddle. Anne, winded, scared, sees the ground racing beneath her. Shen T'ang orders her to keep still unless she wishes to have her neck broken by a fall.

Kline is just beginning to believe he can outfox the horse and rider behind when his luck runs out. He loses his footing on a loose patch of ground, pitches forward, rolls onto his back. Half a furlong behind, Lily Li T'ang sees his fall. She kicks her horse in its belly, yells exultantly as she whips her mount towards her prey.

Struggling to regain his feet, Kline sees the oncoming galloping hooves almost upon him. He turns, tries to protect his head, but a flying steel-shod hoof smashes into the base of his skull. Kline crashes to the ground, out for the count.

Lily pulls up, turns in her saddle, looks back. Smiling with satisfaction at the sight of Kline's sprawled body, she turns the head of her mount, is just about to trample over her quarry once more when she sees a tweed-clad country person hurrying across to offer aid to the stricken Kline. No fan of *The Archers*, Lily has no wish to indulge in 'oo-aar' chit chat. She sees her father in the distance with his prisoner slung over his saddle. She smiles to herself as she canters away towards them. The sport is not over.

24

In a side room of Queen Elizabeth's hospital, Sarah Gant watches Zahir Khan empty a clear plastic bag that contains personal items belonging to John Kline. There is a red leather address book, a pack of untipped cigarettes, a gold lighter inscribed 'Love from Anne'. The final item he extracts is a wad of paper. He sees the Chinese writings they contain. He shows them to Sarah Gant.

'What do we have here, Mrs Gant?'

'Sen's report?'

'Perhaps.'

'I'll get it translated. This John Kline guy, how come he has the missing report?'

'I suggested Harry work in Kline's kitchen, undercover. Kline must have come across the report. He is very resourceful but also dangerously inquisitive. I've used him before.'

'Can we use him again?'

'Perhaps.' Khan pauses, a plan forming. 'Tell me, do you still have the private letters you found in Sen's lodgings?'

'Sure, you said they might be useful.'

'So I did. Shall we make an exchange?'

'What a great idea.'

Sarah produces the letters from a side pocket of her combat jacket. Khan takes them from her and in return hands across what he hopes is the missing crime report. He places the letters from Sen's wife into the polythene bag, together with the other personal items belonging to John Kline.

25

John Kline comes back to consciousness with a thudding headache. It feels as if he has been kicked in the head by a horse. Then he remembers, he has been kicked in the head by a horse, a bloody great galloping horse! He struggles to sit up in… what? A bed, a hospital bed? He looks about him, sees a small room and, sitting by his bedside, a figure from his past. An Asian wearing a stone-coloured suit, a dark moustache and a thoughtful air. Kline's headache worsens considerably at the sight of Zahir Khan.

'You.'

'Yes. Good afternoon, Mr Kline.'

'Where the hell am I?'

'Casualty. They noticed my police telephone number in your address book. So here I am.'

'The angel of bleedin' death.'

'You are not going to die, Mr Kline.'

'I nearly did.'

'What happened, a riding accident?'

'Something like that. Why are you here?'

Khan extracts the red address book from the plastic bag. He shows his contact number to Kline, who scowls, grabs the bag, looks inside, sees the Chinese writings are intact. Khan watches, impassively.

'Problems, Mister Kline?'

'No. Where's Annie?'

'Anne was…?'

'She was with me.'

'What's this all about, Mister Kline?'

'I don't know but I've got to get out of here.'

He swings out of bed, goes to the window, looks down into the hospital car park.

'They bring my car in?'

'I believe so. Can I help find your lady?'

Kline winces as he struggles into his leather jacket.

'I'll let you know after I get back to town.'

'Are you fit to drive? Perhaps I can—'

'No thanks, I know what lifts from you can lead to.'

He plucks his address book from Khan's grasp and heads for the door. Left alone, Khan allows himself a little smile. Quite like old times, using Kline as a stalking horse. The door opens, Sarah Gant looks in.

'He on the hook?'

'Yes, although he doesn't know it yet.'

26

After returning to the Nirvana restaurant, Kline sits beside the telephone, waiting for a call he feels sure will come. He swallows a couple of paracetamol tablets with a mouthful of Bell's scotch to ease the throbbing pain in his neck. The telephone rings out, he picks it up straight away.

'Kline…'

A woman's voice sounds in his ear, cold and clear.

'Ah, Mister Kline, we find you in residence at last. We thought you might have met with a riding accident. This is just to inform you that your lady is quite safe. I trust your cooperation will help her remain so.'

'Cooperation over what?'

'We hear you have been touting a collection of Chinese texts around the town and adjoining countryside…'

'Get to the point.'

'Bring us the papers and your floozie will be restored to you.'

'Alive, I take it.'

'If we receive your full cooperation.'

'Who am I speaking to?'

'Should we say a well-wisher?'

Kline grips the phone as if it were the caller's throat. He controls his anger, keeps his voice calm.

'You can have the damn papers providing Anne stays unharmed.'

He listens to the voice that he suspects belongs to the bitch who ran him down. He is to meet her emissary in the shopping centre of the Bull Ring. The cold arrogant voice warns him of the consequences should he be foolish enough to involve forces of the law. Kline gives his agreement; the call ends abruptly after her final instruction that he has just one hour to effect the exchange.

Seated at Shen T'ang's desk, Lily returns the receiver to its cradle. She looks towards her father, who nods his approval as to how she handled the call. Lily stares around the office, a room that once housed a factory foreman. She wrinkles her nose in distaste at the sight of the bilious green-painted walls.

'Daddy, I do wish you would smarten up the décor of this place. It is a most unbecoming setting for a man in your position.'

27

John Kline hurries from the Nirvana, his thoughts seething with apprehension. Given Anne's fragility of mind, he must rescue her as soon as possible, to hell with any information the mysterious papers stuffed in his inside pocket might contain.

As he guns his Avenger away from the restaurant, heading for the centre of Birmingham, he fails to notice a sand-coloured Ford nose out into the traffic behind him.

The Bull Ring is busy with afternoon shoppers, but Kline soon spots the Chinese youth he has been ordered to meet.

From a vantage point above the shopping centre, Khan watches Kline and the teenager meet and confer outside a burger bar. They move away together. Khan guesses they must be heading for a multi-storey car park on Queensway.

Khan hurries down the steps leading to the lower level. He keeps them in sight until they enter the confines of the car park. He sprints to where his car is parked in a side road, drives back to the NCP exit.

He does not have to wait long. Kline, with his Chinese escort beside him, emerges from the car park exit. Khan starts up his engine, follows the black Chrysler as closely as the traffic allows.

Kline has a survivor's instinct. The sand-coloured Ford has appeared in his wing mirror too many times. He pulls to the side of the road, abruptly. The Chinese guy protests, they are wasting time. Kline tells him to shut it. He sees the driver of the Ford as it sweeps by. He recognises Mr Khan. John Kline fires his motor, makes a three-point turn, roars away. His passenger complains that this is not the quickest route to their destination. A savage look from the driver kills any further comment.

Speeding down towards the Aston Expressway, Kline is ready to believe he has lost Khan until he sees the Ford in his rear-view mirror once more. Growling with annoyance, he accelerates, notices the open front of a fire station on his left-hand side. No time to think, he turns the wheel. He sees a board announcing, 'Foam Test Today', but is too late to turn back. The Avenger drives into a giant bubble of foam that engulfs the car in a complete whiteout.

On the other side of the yard, a manned fire engine starts up and charges towards the exit, answering an alarm call from the Jewellery Quarter.

Driving down the expressway Khan has lost sight of the black Avenger. A fire engine exits a station, turns and sweeps past him. Khan drives past the fire station, glances inside, sees nothing apart from a giant cloud of foam. With a grimace, Khan concedes defeat. He drives back in the direction of his office, annoyed at losing a chance to locate the hideout of the Hong Ming.

The mass of foam shows little sign of dispersing. Kline decides, as time is running short, to take the bull by the testicles. To the consternation of his Triad passenger, he puts his foot down on the accelerator and drives blindly forward. The speed of his progress clears the foam from the windscreen in time for him to avoid crashing into the foot of the training tower. He brakes, turns the Avenger back towards the entrance to the main road. Once there, he pauses, looks in every direction but sees no sign of Mr Khan. The Triad gangster thrusts an imitation Rolex watch in front of Kline's face.

'You're running out of time, mate!'

'I'll drive, you do the navigating.'

'You know Snow Hill?'

'Had a battle there once.'

'What you mean?'

'Nothing, ancient history.'

This last said absentmindedly as Kline realises the traffic is slowing to a halt in front of him. He casts a worried glance at his watch: ten minutes left. He turns to his surly passenger.

'You know a different route to this rendezvous?'

'Much longer way. You've no time, not if you want your girlfriend to keep the nose on her face.'

'We need less traffic. There must be a way, what is it?'

'How should I know, I'm no traffic controller.'

'Show me the other route.'

The Chinese shrugs indifferently. Kline slams an elbow into his ribs. The youth squeals.

'We turn up late, if anything's happened to Anne, I'll mash your mug into egg foo yung.'

'There, side road, there.'

'That's better.'

The mobster rubs his ribs. His mouth opens in surprise and fear as Kline blasts into overdrive. The Avenger corners into the side road with a screech of protest from its smoking tires.

28

Backed up against the altar, surrounded by leering demons, Anne faces the leaders and disciples of the Hong Ming Triad. Most members wear crimson robes, except for Yan and Lily, who are clothed in white. Lily's long satin smock is decorated with panels the colour of newly spilled blood. Her jewelled headdress catches the light from the red candles burning on the table of the altar.

Lily leaves her father's side. Anne sees her raise the curved knife she holds in her hand. Yan calls out a warning to her in a dialect Anne cannot follow. Whatever the words, they provoke a savage reply. When Lily has finished her harangue, Mr Yan, suitably chastened, bows his head in acquiescence. Lily turns back to Anne, regards her like a buyer in a slave market.

'You are somewhat attractive. I'd have thought your gentleman friend would have arrived post haste.'

Anne holds down her rush of panic, attempts a calm, logical approach.

'He'll be here. You can have your bunch of hieroglyphics. It's no problem, why didn't you, you know, just ask?'

'That would lead to bargaining, haggling over prices like common market traders. No, this is a more secure system of exchange.'

She raises the long knife, regards it lovingly before turning her attention back to her prisoner.

'I might as well warn you that I am not renowned for my patience. If this John Kline person does not turn up very soon your life will be forfeit.'

Lily lifts Anne's chin upwards with the point of her knife blade. Anne looks into the brown eyes inches from hers, into the soul of Lily Li T'ang. She sees a monster lusting for blood. Without shifting her gaze Lily calls back to her father.

'Daddy, it must be past time, surely.'

'I'm afraid it is.'

Anne sees the face of the young Chinese woman take on the look of an executioner. With a slight smile Lily whispers, woman to woman, her blade at Anne's throat. Her voice is casual, as if cancelling a lunch appointment.

'So sorry about this.'

Anne backs away, trapped against the altar. Lily Li T'ang, avid for pleasure, follows, raises her knife. Her father's voice calls out.

'Lily, stop, there is no need!'

Lily turns, sees the tall figure of John Kline standing beside her father. She trembles with the desire to stab her victim, longs to see blood spurt, life fade from those round hazel eyes. A disciple, at a signal from Shen T'ang, advances towards Lily and pulls Anne out of danger. Kline strides towards Anne, takes her into his arms.

'You hurt?'

'No.'

Kline presses Anne to him, regards the exotic creature that is Lily Li T'ang. He sees her fancy dress, looks around at the group of Chinese men in their ritual robes. He is not impressed. He has long-standing contempt for the get up of judges, lawyers, politicians, bishops with their silly frocks and pointed hats. He smiles at the leader of the Triad mob.

'End of paperchase.'

'Let us hope so.' Shen T'ang holds out his open palm. Kline reacts quizzically.

'Just like that?'

'I give you my word, should the papers prove genuine you will be released without harm. If you indulge in trickery, I will be merciless.'

Kline guides Anne away from the altar. They slowly advance towards Shen T'ang. Lily follows in their wake. When he is almost within reach of the Triad leader, Kline asks Anne to move towards the door. She attempts to do so but is forced back by shadowy figures guarding the entrance to the crypt. She recognises them as the thugs who muscled their way into the restaurant. The killers of Harry Sen.

Kline pulls the papers from his pocket, hands them to Shen T'ang with a mocking bow. The documents are passed to Mr Yan, who thumbs through the pages, frowns. Shen T'ang notices Yan's unease.

'Is this the report you witnessed?'

'No.'

'You are certain?'

'Yes, this is not the police report on our activities. These are letters of love from a lady in Hong Kong.'

He passes the papers back to Kline, who realises the danger he and Anne are now facing. He sees knives appear, hatchets, machetes. Lily is the first to lift her long knife and move. She is eager for the slaughter to begin...

To be continued...

BOOK TWO
THE RED EXECUTIONER

29

John Kline realises this gang of gooks mean business – deadly business. He sees Anne held by the two thugs last seen at his restaurant. His survival instincts go into overdrive. Playing for time he pastes what he hopes is an easy grin on his face as machetes and meat cleavers are raised against him. Then a solution surfaces, a way to avoid annihilation. He addresses the middle-aged man in the red frock.

'You didn't really expect me to bring the real papers, did you?'

Lily's knife pricks his belly.

Shen T'ang holds up his hand, Lily and the others pause. The dragon head of the Hong Ming scans Kline's face for signs of duplicity. He finds none.

'You knew these papers were not the police report we seek?'

Kline nods at the two mobsters who must have knifed Harry Sen. Now he knows what all the fuss is about he can embellish the truth a little.

'The guy who worked in my kitchen, your boys didn't kill him right away. He lasted long enough to tell me the value of that report.'

Shen T'ang shoots an angry look at Yan who glares in turn at the initiates. Anne huddles next to Kline as Yan gazes suspiciously at them both.

'If you knew what the papers referred to, why seek translation of the documents from me, Mr Kline?'

'To establish the asking price.'

Lily steps forward impatiently, points her knife at Anne.

'You mean a price beyond the life of your paramour?'

'With the information in that report, the police could wipe you out.'

'Asking price,' Shen T'ang intervenes, 'what might that be?'

'Ten grand, our release, in exchange for the right papers.'

Lily turns to her father, speaks angrily in Cantonese.

'These persons have nothing, are nothing, they deserve nothing!'

Shen T'ang is not so impetuous. He smiles at his guests, speaks with a semblance of politeness.

'My daughter is not convinced of your bargaining position.'

Mr Yan joins in, speaks vehemently in Cantonese. Shen T'ang translates the gist of his argument.

'Mr Yan is frugal in the extreme. He doesn't see why we should spend ten pence, let alone your inflated price. My daughter also fails to understand why we should spend anything at all.'

Lily reverts to English.

'End this bargaining! Let me go to work on the white face woman, you'll soon get your information!'

Lily tucks her knife away, takes a cigarette from a pocket in her robe, inserts it into an ivory holder. A disciple takes a candle from the altar and offers her its flame.

'Thank you, most kind.'

She lights her cigarette, draws in smoke, exhales, stares at Anne.

Shen T'ang, undecided, drifts towards the altar. Once there he bows his head, communes with the spirits. Kline counts the group: eight, most of them armed. There is no chance of escaping given such odds.

The Hong Ming leader turns and faces them. His decision has been made. He waves a limp hand towards his daughter. Lily draws on her cigarette, examines the glowing tip, saunters towards Anne.

'I'm told smoking can be bad for your throat.'

A disciple pulls back Anne's head, tugging at her hair, exposing her throat. Kline starts forward, is pulled back in turn. Mr Yan looks from Anne to Kline, speaks with quiet menace.

'Tell us, Mr Kline, where the report is to be found, or Miss Darracott will need a tube to speak love to you.'

John Kline makes himself wait. Anne can feel the heat from the tip of the cigarette as it almost touches the skin of her throat. She sees Lily's cruel smile, hears her mocking words.

'Hope you have plenty of roll-neck sweaters to hide the scars.'

She looks across at Kline. 'Well, where exactly is this tiresome report to be obtained?'

'Her Majesty's stationary office?'

With a squeal of anger, Lily goes to burn a hole into her victim's neck. Shen T'ang catches her arm, speaks to Kline.

'My daughter likes to play with fire.'

'Tell her to go to hell.'

Anne sees the burning tip dart towards her throat, she twists her head away, cries out.

'John!'

Kline admits defeat.

'OK, enough.'

Released from danger, Anne slumps. Lily gives a childish smirk of triumph as she looks around the group.

'Told you.' The smile fades, she addresses Kline. 'Yes, well?'

'Back at the flat above the restaurant, in a box by the writing desk.'

Mr Yan holds out his hand. 'Keys.' Kline hands them over. Shen T'ang reasserts his authority.

'Should the papers not be where you say, there will be consequences.'

'No doubt you'll know where to find us.'

'Yes, you will both be held prisoner here. Do not consider escape, my disciples will destroy you. Adieu, Mister Kline.'

The gang begin to disperse. Lily cannot resist a parting shot. She moves close to Kline, gives a small seductive smile, gazes into his steel blue eyes. Kline stares back at her. Lily nods.

'Should fate decree that we shall not meet again, Mr Kline, it really has been most enjoyable. Goodbye.'

Kline ignores the hand of Lily Li T'ang. She grins, cheeky as a naughty schoolgirl, before clapping her hands and saying, 'Let's go collect this damn report!'

Left alone inside the crypt they hear steel bolts slot home in the heavy wooden door. Anne begins to shake with rage. Kline goes to her, tries to explain why he had to prolong her ordeal.

'I'm sorry, I couldn't give in too soon.'

'My throat…'

'It's OK.'

'That yellow-faced bitch! A few moments alone with that cow, that's all I'd need to wipe that supercilious smile off her sodding face!'

'There's every chance we'll see her again.'

'Good!'

'Not good. The papers won't be where I said they'd be.'

'Why?'

'I don't know where they are. Switched by person or persons unknown. I was too busy chasing back across town to think things through.'

Hope drains from Anne.

'We've nothing to bargain with?'

'All we've bought is a little time.'

Kline notices a grille above the altar. He climbs up among the idols to test it, quickly realises it is firmly embedded in concrete. He tries it, anyway, but it is immovable. He jumps down, looks around the dismal chamber. Anne echoes his thoughts. Taking in the empty crypt, her voices rises in panic, 'There's no way out of here!'

Her cry echoes around the crypt.

On the altar behind them a red candle gutters out.

30

Waiting for Sarah Gant outside the department of Asian and Oriental studies, Zahir Khan surveys the grounds of Birmingham University. Lawns basking in gentle sunlight, just the scene his father would conjure up when dreaming of his imaginary England. Greenery, blue skies...

'Hey, have I got something for you.'

Sarah offers him the Chinese police report together with a translation of its contents. Khan scans the first page. Names, addresses...

'No wonder murder was done to protect this information,' Sarah says, reading his thoughts.

'Yes, indeed,' Khan says, turning a page.

Inside Kline's flat, the raiding party soon locate the box by the writing desk. Mr Yan opens it. The box, lined with green felt, contains nothing but air. Shen T'ang frowns, Mr Yan scowls. Lily, with a scream of rage, hurls the offending box across the room.

In the basement below the church of St Stephen's, a morose Anne Darracott sits, her back against the altar, and nervously waits for the return of their captors. Without medication, her skin crawls, her mind dwells on knives slashing at her throat. The time Kline bought by lying to the Hong Ming is running out, fast.

Kline, restless, prowls around in the semi-darkness, still seeking a way out, but the chamber is sealed, the heavy wooden door immovable as he shakes it one more time. Nothing for it, he must mount a frontal attack, allow Anne a chance to escape. A slim chance but better than nothing. How many attackers could he take out? Two, three? He hears angry shouts from outside. Here we go. He rushes back to Anne, pulls her to her feet, speaks urgently.

'If you get a chance to run, take it.'

The door is thrown open. The first of the Triad Disciples charges in, brandishing a meat cleaver. Kline recognises the youth as one of the assassins from the restaurant. Kline stands his ground, dodges the slashing blade, karate chops him to the throat. With a gurgling cry the disciple crumples to the stone floor. Kline grabs Anne by the hand and together they rush towards the open doorway, just as a figure steps inside, barring their escape. Kline raises his fists ready to wreak mayhem. He pauses, his fighting stance frozen in mid-air. He sees a familiar face, a smiling face.

'Is that any way to greet your rescuer, Mr Kline?'

Kline is lost for words. Anne looks at Khan, relief turning to trepidation.

'You again.'

'Yes, shall we step out into the sunshine?'

The church grounds are occupied by law officers escorting handcuffed Chinese mobsters towards waiting police cars. Kline and Anne emerge into the sunlight, together with their rescuer. They shade their eyes, eyes that have grown used to the gloom and shadow of the underground crypt.

A red Vauxhall Viva is parked on a side road. Inside, Yan, Lily and Shen T'ang watch the raid on what was their secret headquarters, together with the arrest of half their gang members. Lily is the first to break the shocked silence. Her tone is bitter and vengeful.

'This is John Kline's doing. He has betrayed us to the law!'

31

Seated at the bar of the Nirvana, Kline pours himself a whisky. He pushes a soda and lime towards Anne, who sits beside him. Her focus lies further down the bar, where Zahir Khan stands. If Anne's set gaze bothers Khan, he shows no sign of unease. Kline looks at him enquiringly.

'Drink?'

'Orange juice.'

'I should have remembered. It's been a while.'

'Yes, it has.'

Khan gives his easy smile. It provokes a question that has

preoccupied Anne ever since their return from the crypt of St Stephen's church.

'Why that particular basement?'

'A calculated guess.'

'Not information?'

'Does it matter? You are safe.'

Kline slides the orange juice down the bar, western style. It slows and stops in front of the agent of the law. He nods his thanks. Kline watches him sip the juice. He is trying to work out a probable sequence of events.

'Something on your mind, Mr Kline?'

'Whoever took that report put our lives on the line.'

'You chose that line when you refused my offer of help, when you evaded my attempts to follow your progress through town.'

'The only person who could have switched that report for the letters was you.'

'How?'

'When I was in the casualty ward, lost in dreamland.'

Kline pauses, begins to see, with some clarity, the progression of events. His manner hardens as he follows his train of thought.

'We know how long it takes to find somebody to translate Chinese, and you thought, "Why wait?" Why not manipulate the situation in the hope that I might lead you to the hideout of the Hong Ming?'

'We are conducting a war against the Triads, Mr Kline.'

Anne and Kline exchange looks. Anne turns to Khan.

'You don't deny that's what you did?'

Khan shrugs. Kline stands, walks along the bar holding his glass of scotch. He looks down at the lawman with loathing.

'The only difference between you and a bucket of crap is the bucket.'

'You have a way with words, Mr Kline.'

'Have a drink, you slimy double-crossing twat!' Kline tosses his drink into Khan's face.

Wiping the spirits from his face, Khan stands, tries to control a situation that is escalating far too fast for his liking.

'Mr Kline—'

'Shut your lying mouth. I'm nothing to you. My life, Anne's life, is nothing to you. We're just pawns to be sacrificed to your advantage or the law's.'

'You have benefited in times past.'

The two men are close to each other. Anne watches. She knows that John Kline is at his most dangerous when his tone quietens, when his words become clipped, as they are starting to become now.

'Benefits? Tot it up. Profit and loss. Most of the trouble I've ever been in is down to you. As for benefits, I can't even get a liquor license for this place.'

'I can easily—'

The smooth words trigger a burst of anger. Kline grips Khan by the lapels of his jacket. Stares at him, up very close.

'Arrange it? Take your favours, your job under the law, wrap them up in that license and shove it right up your shit chute!'

He hurls Khan away from him. The agent stumbles against a dining table. Khan regains his balance, his mask of sociability gone as he points a finger.

'You better reconsider your position, Mr Kline. You are now an enemy of the Hong Ming, you will need all the protection you can get.'

Kline laughs, turns to Anne.

'Everybody seems to think I need protection.'

'It's your little boy lost manner.'

'I wondered.'

With a great effort, Khan attempts to repair the trampled fences. He approaches the couple at the bar. Kline has his back to him. Anne watches Khan approach, sees the easy smile reappear, the teeth white in contrast to the dark moustache.

'Mr Kline...'

'Annie, tell him sharks are not welcome in these waters.'

Anne smiles, her manner icily polite.

'Mr Khan, the management reserve the right to refuse admission. So we'd be most grateful if you would not only urinate off out of it but maintain a polite distance in the future.'

With a shake of his head, Khan tut tuts. Anne tuts straight back. Kline, hunched over the bar, considers whether to eject the infiltrator from the premises by force. Instead he asks Anne a pointed question.

'Has he stopped smiling yet?'

'For the moment.'

Kline turns to regard the agent who has dogged his progress ever since he was first released from prison. He leans back against the bar.

'You heard what the lady said?'

'Yes.'

'Yet you're still here.'

'Only to wish you much luck and great good fortune. You will need both if you hope to survive the onslaught of the Triads.'

Anne frowns. 'Thought you were onto them. Arrests today.'

'Only low-grade members, all too frightened to name their leaders. Hong Ming is not the only triad operating in the Midlands, there is another called Wo Shing Wo. Very dangerous, as will be the Hong Ming once they reform their numbers. The Triad snake heads in Hong Kong will wish to make an example of you to deter others. Both your deaths will be a priority.'

'We'll manage.'

'Alone? No, Mister Kline, that is not possible. Not if you wish to survive long enough to open your restaurant.'

32

Aslam Rafiq, dapper in a white suit, shirt and tie, occupies an antique Bergere armchair in his luxurious sitting room. Feeling the fates are on his side, he blows pipe smoke up at the ceiling and plays a subtle game of denial with his visitors.

'John Kline… John Kline? Oh, yes, we've had some slight acquaintance, why do you ask?'

Shen T'ang, seated opposite, wears a well-tailored grey business suit, white shirt and yellow and blue-patterned tie. He looks towards his daughter, Lily, seated on the settee, her long legs encased in knee high boots and yellow satin knickerbocker trousers. She nods, encouraging him to recount the disastrous events of recent days. Shen T'ang begins to speak in his carefully enunciated English.

'John Kline has provided the means of temporary confusion. The agencies of law enforcement now know of Triad addresses, names of couriers and their network of distribution. It has caused us a painful setback, standstill, reorganisation at basic level.'

This news causes Rafiq to tear himself away from the contours of Lily Li T'ang's thighs. He reacts with alarm.

'Is our association also contained in this report?'

'It is extremely unlikely. Mister Rafiq, now is the time when we need the support of friends such as yourself.'

Lily fits a cigarette into her holder. Rafiq takes a table lighter across to her. Once the cigarette is lit, Lily allows smoke to drift lazily from her lips before speaking softly to him.

'Not simply support but active help with distribution.'

'Distribution under the guise of what exactly?'

The crux of the discussion is about to begin. Rafiq, urbane but watchful, listens as Lily's father begins to outline his proposal.

'My superiors consider the trade of antiques a suitable mask for smuggling heroin via your export and import facilities. That is, should you approve of the arrangement.'

'To what degree of profit?'

'Commensurate to the risk.'

Shen T'ang displays all the digits of his right hand.

'Of what gross?'

Shen T'ang uses his hands to describe a circle in the air that grows and grows.

Excited by the prospect, Rafiq sits next to Lily on the settee, places his arm along the back, feels her hair touch his hand. A tremor of desire flows through him. He tries to concentrate, to deal with business matters. Shen T'ang, his arms spread to symbolise unlimited wealth, waits for an answer. Rafiq tries to put all carnal thoughts aside. It is not easy to suppress his lustful desires. *Business, to business*, he exhorts himself. He speaks in what he hopes is an agreeable manner to the man whose daughter he intends to seduce.

'Well, Mister T'ang, perhaps we can do business, explore the ways that will lead us to ultimate pleasure, ah, I mean, profit.'

Lily's father regards his daughter and Rafiq sitting side by side on the sofa.

'Mr Rafiq.'

'Mr T'ang.'

'Are you the father of any children?'

'All in my community.'

'I meant of your blood.'

'Well, not to my certain knowledge.'

'Being a father to a daughter is not easy.'

'No?'

'She causes me much worry. Now that this man Kline has passed on such damaging information, the time could be ripe for takeover and exploitation.'

'Takeover and exploitation by whom, Mr T'ang?'

'By rival Triad gangs such as Wo Shing Wo. Also, I must attend an inquest to be held by my superiors in Hong Kong. It would be a comfort to me if Lily could remain in a safe house, away from danger, in case I should be held responsible for our recent failures.'

Pouncing like a greyhound catching a hare, Rafiq is quick to reply.

'Oh, she must remain here!'

'You care for Lily?'

'I would be delighted to take care of Lily.'

'I am filled with much gratitude.'

'Oh, I assure you the gratification will be all mine.'

Rafiq gives Lily a gentle squeeze on the nape of her neck, stands and skips to the table. He raises a tiny brass bell, makes it tinkle mightily to summon a servant, who appears almost immediately.

While Rafiq issues orders for the accommodation of his unexpected guest, Shen T'ang opens his arms to Lily. She comes to him. They embrace for a long moment before Lily steps away from the Triad leader.

'Bye, bye, Daddy, have a safe journey. I hope you will return soon.'

Shen T'ang's voice is tinged with sadness and foreboding.

'I hope I will be allowed to do so.'

He turns, holds out his hand. Rafiq clasps it with his, puts on his most sincere expression.

'Adieu, Mister T'ang, have no fears for Lily, she will be in good hands.'

Shen T'ang nods sadly, bows. When he has finally exited, Rafiq circles the table in the centre of the room. He whistles a little with happiness at his good fortune, wonders how best to begin, what honey words of seduction to use. He sits himself in the chair that the father of his prey has just vacated. He gazes across at his quarry seated demurely on the sofa opposite.

'Lily...'

'Yes?'

'I have a confession to make.'

'About what?'

'About you.'

'Oh, really?'

'After our most enjoyable meal together here, after you left, I felt so lonely. I wandered around, desolate at heart. Something guided my steps, I found myself standing before the statue of the goddess Kali. On an impulse I prayed to her, asked her to grant me my most heartfelt wish.'

'And what was that, pray?'

'I beseeched her for a boon, a blessing, I asked her to bring you into my life. Now here you are!'

Leaping from his chair, Rafiq bounces enthusiastically across the space between them, sits next to Lily, who gazes ahead, composed and unresponsive. Rafiq kisses her cheek, seeks her mouth, strokes her hair. Lily, shocked, moves away from his fervent embrace.

'Mr Rafiq!'

'Yes?'

'My father has not left the room above a moment ago. He has scarcely vacated the premises and already you are making declarations of a most intimate nature.'

This is delicious, the girl is indulging in irony. Wonderful. Rafiq rubs his hands, joyfully.

'Oh, Lily, please, such phrases, "declarations of an intimate nature", "vacating the premises", you are teasing me, surely?'

'No, but if I happen to amuse you, so be it.'

'Humour is vital in a relationship. I find myself bored with most women. Their petty ploys, their silly stratagems, their sly hints create in me nothing but ennui. Believe me, darling Lily, the prize must be rare indeed for me to summon up enough will to play the games required to achieve consummation. We are above such silly rituals, you and I.'

Lily feels his hand clutch at her left breast. She lets it linger no more than an instant before she rises to her feet, leaving her would be lover in a confused heap of thwarted desire. She lights a cigarette, looks around the room, peers through a parlour fern placed before a bay window.

'Is this a large house?'

Recovering some composure, Rafiq stands, adjusts his dress, joins her.

'Oh, extensive, wings and things. This house once belonged to a designer chap who created sets for the cinema. Many rooms are decorated in differing styles. This room, for instance, is in a traditional Art Nouveau style. But others are far more modern.'

'Really?'

'Yes, really. I often sleep in a different, newly discovered bedroom, just for a change of locale…'

He fixes a soulful gaze upon Lily, sighs for effect.

'One does that sort of thing when one lives alone.'

'I would enjoy a peek into these mysterious bedrooms.'

'Oh, but you must choose one for yourself. I should be delighted to give you a tour.'

He holds out his hand, ready to lead her from the room. She ignores it.

A little flustered, Rafiq hurries to open the door. Lily sails through into the hallway. She wears a smile of mischief that bodes ill for her would be lover.

33

The shopping mall that curves around the Bull Ring is busy with noonday shoppers. Amongst them Khan waits for Sarah Gant to join him from an outlet that sells the nuts she seems to thrive on. She joins him, offers him a cashew, he declines. They walk along. Sarah pops nuts into her mouth as Khan shares his worries.

'Kline is adamant, so is his woman. They believe I've used them as pawns.'

'Which you have.'

'Which *we* have, it was a joint strategy.'

'Are Anne and Kline still important?'

Khan halts, watches the traffic circling below.

'The Triads practice the policy of destroying all who disobey or thwart them. A deterrent that works; all the Chinese gang members arrested so far refuse to name their bosses.'

'Omerta, that's what the Mafia call it back home.'

'Yes.'

They resume their progress. Sarah sees a shoe shop plastered with 'sale' signs. She gravitates towards the window, surveys a display of boots and shoes. Khan tags along. Sarah takes in the rows of sales items, assessing prices and styles.

'Mrs Gant...'

'Don't worry, I can shop and think at the same time. So, the Triad guys can't help but believe Kline turned that report over to us.'

'They might decide to bring in an enforcer to exact revenge against both Anne and Kline.'

'That Captain Marvell character mentioned in Sen's report? Hey, would those mustard-coloured boots go with olive green?'

'No, they would clash alarmingly.'

'You're right. Let's go, there's nothing here but overpriced junk.'

They resume their progress. After munching a few more nuts, Sarah looks enquiringly at Khan.

'What did the report call this assassin guy, Scarlet Stump?'

'Red Stick, sometimes known simply as number 426. He could be brought in to destroy Kline. That might be an opportunity for us to arrest one of their most powerful enforcers. Of course, to achieve that, we would need someone placed in the vicinity of the restaurant.'

'Oh, who might that be?'

'I can't request your secondment from the DEA but our agencies do share the same aims.'

'Let's cut the formal stuff. If I'm to get the agency off my back, I need to take the heat. I've catering experience, think I'd be welcome in Kline's kitchen?'

'He has a vacancy in that department.'

'Then I'll apply.'

With a nod Khan helps himself to a cashew nut.

34

After much deliberation, Lily Li T'ang has chosen the all-white room to be her boudoir. A room of white furnishings, a ceiling draped with muslin and cotton, white lace screens, a dressing table painted to match the unsullied white of the carpet. At the centre of the ceiling hangs a chandelier, heavy with droplets of cut glass, that casts a soft light down upon Lily as she sits demurely on the bed with its virginal white covers.

Several trunks of her clothing have been delivered and carefully unpacked by the servants of Rafiq. She has informed the master of the house that he may enter her chamber at a certain hour after she has bathed in preparation for his visit. She is dressed in satin pyjamas, all white apart from an almond blossom motif that lingers at the side of her breasts then curves down towards her slim waist.

An eager tap-tap on the door announces the arrival of her would be lover. She calls an imperious 'Enter!' Rafiq, dressed in a white suit with matching shirt and tie, enters immediately. He carefully closes the door and advances to the centre of the bedroom. His rapt gaze takes in the vision in white before him. He clasps his hands together, joyfully.

'Oh, my dear, darling Lily.'

'May we talk?' Her tone is business like.

'Of course…'

Rafiq hurries to sit beside her. They are very close. Lily goes to speak, Rafiq places his forefinger against her lips.

'Later, we can talk afterwards.'

Lily shifts away.

'My daddy placed me under your protection, Mr Rafiq.'

'Aslam, call me Aslam.'

He takes her hand, raises it to his lips, speaks in a voice made husky by his mounting desire.

'I promise that I will do nothing you do not want, desire or approve.'

'My father—'

'Yes, I know, Shen T'ang, but he is not here…'

'I feel—'

'He is far away, but we are close, so very close…'

Lily shifts away, assumes a serious demeanour.

'I fear for the safety of my father. He has failed in his mission. He will be held accountable for all the police raids, arrests, loss of income and damage to our society here and in Hong Kong. I must say this…'

Rafiq is hardly listening. He is entranced by the light that shimmers on the darkness of her shoulder length hair.

'Aslam, please pay attention.'

'Yes, yes, I am, what is it you wish to say, my darling?'

'The girl you want knows much of the world, she has desire, ambition but is not yet a woman. I have not known a man, and when I do it will be a commitment that is total. That man must be my equal in love and loyalty. Do you understand?'

All Rafiq understands is that Lily Li T'ang is a virgin and that his ardour must be tempered just a little to take in the unexpected circumstance.

'Yes, I understand. But will you understand that my ultimate wish is to possess all of you?'

His declaration brings only a baffling reply.

'Yes, yes. Did I mention Hong Kong may employ the services of someone known in the Chinese community as Red Stick.'

'Red… what?'

'Well, if one breaks open another's head, the implement used does tend to stain red.'

'What an apt description of the fellow's function.'

Rafiq watches the play of emotion in Lily's eyes, her growing animation, her excitement, her clenched fist.

'Red Stick must be strong. A tiger trained to kill and bring destruction to all who oppose our will!'

'Lily, my love…'

There is no stopping her.

'He will arrive in Birmingham tomorrow. His mission is to arrange the demise of this Kline individual. An example must be set, revenge must be taken against all who bring confusion to our affairs.'

'Yes, yes, but such things are for tomorrow, what about tonight, what about our assignation?'

Lily ignores the question.

'My father may be replaced. I have intimated to those who matter that I consider myself worthy to become head dragon of the Hong Ming Triad, aka the Red Disciples. I will require the services of Red Stick to instil order. I will also need advice, help and support from others too.'

She takes Rafiq's hand, moves closer to him, places her thigh alongside his, speaks seductively.

'I've heard that colleagues who work together can become friends.'

'Even lovers sometimes…'

'I must give myself to someone sometime soon.'

'Yes, but that someone mustn't be just anyone. He must possess special qualities. The first purveyor of love is most important.'

'I so agree.'

'I will be most grateful to receive that honour.'

'Yes, I'm sure you will.'

She stifles a yawn. Rafiq is taken aback.

'You are not bored, you cannot be bored, surely?'

'How can I be when I am so very close to you? Forgive me, the emotion of the day has been quite exhausting. Tomorrow, I must rise early, I have important business to attend to outside the city. Please understand, Aslam, it's best our liaison waits for a more propitious time.'

Before Rafiq can reply Lily has left him, walked away from the bed and opened the door. There is nothing to do but to hide his disappointment and retreat from the field with dignity. He joins Lily in the doorway.

'Goodnight, my darling Lily.'

'Goodnight, Aslam. Thank you for your understanding.'

She places a chaste kiss on his cheek.

Left alone, Lily Li T'ang leans back against the door, surveys the white room. Her mind is alert, her weariness no longer apparent. She strides across to a white telephone, dials, waits. When the connection is made, she speaks with authority.

'Lily Li T'ang. I wish to know if 426 has left Hong Kong as I requested.'

35

In woodland outside the city, a wind keens through the trees of pine and birch, scattering a grey mist before it. In a clearing a Chinese man sits, naked to the waist, waiting for the sun to rise. Beside him is a pile of neatly folded clothing on top of which lies a red shirt.

Minutes later the sun appears. The man, known variously as 426 or Red Stick, ends his meditation, rises and begins his internal exercises. Around his waist is a scarlet sash that contrasts with his baggy black pants.

After several stretch exercises, he throws a series of feints and jabs, ending with a tiger claw step and punch against an imaginary opponent. After a final sequence of open-handed chops and double dragon fists, Red Stick swings his arms, twirls, projects a series of kung fu kicks into the early morning air. This done he breathes deeply, stills his body for a second, then explodes into action. Producing Ninja throwing stars from his sash, he hurls three to the left, three to the right. In a blur of motion, the six-pointed blades bury themselves into the trunks of pine trees on either side of the clearing.

The assassin pauses in his morning ritual to listen intently for sounds that might carry to him on the rising wind. Hearing only the chatter of a pair of crows, he begins to run, a low loping run that takes him to the edge of the wood where a trio of paths converge. He looks down each in turn, sees nothing. He returns into the wood, halts before a mature birch tree. Red Stick gathers his strength, focuses his inner power and with a 'HIYAAAA!' strikes at the bole of the tree with the edge of his hand. Chips of white birch wood leap into the air. Red Stick steps back to observe the tree. It totters, teeters then, with a final crack, crashes to the ground.

36

At the same time as the demise of the silver birch a yellow Spitfire 1500 noses along the widest of the pathways and draws to a halt. A tall, lithe woman steps out of the sports car. She wears a pink bandana that matches her tailored jacket and contrasts with the black material of her dress. She adjusts her sunglasses, looks about her, notices a pathway that leads into the wood.

Emerging into a glade she sees a small bundle of clothing on top of which lies a crimson shirt. She crouches down, runs a lingering hand across the garment. She hears a swishing sound, looks up into the sky. A whirling figure is somersaulting towards her. Red Stick lands faultlessly. He crouches down with her, face to face. Both rise in unison. Lily Li T'ang pulls the Triad enforcer towards her. Their embrace melts into a long and brutally passionate kiss.

37

John Kline and Anne Darracott are still abed. Anne asleep, her companion smokes his first cigarette of the day, watches the play of early morning sunlight filtering through the curtains, chasing shadows from the room.

Beside him, Anne is locked into a heroin dream where she is held prisoner. A faceless man holds a spoon and a needle. He draws up the opiate into the syringe, reaches for the main artery of her neck, inserts the needle, sends the heroin home. There is a rollercoaster surge, a freeing of fear as her body reacts to the hit.

Anne wakes, sweating, her back turned to Kline. Slowly she realises that the high didn't happen, it was her dream trying to satisfy the longing. Anne turns to her bedfellow. He stares at the window, pulling on his cigarette, ignoring her. She hauls herself up into a sitting position, clears her throat, asks, wearily, 'What is it?'

'Nothing. For the first time, I'm enjoying doing nothing.'

With some relief, Anne realises that his voice has no tension in it. He is in a surprisingly mellow mood. He turns to her, stretches out his naked body, rests his head on her lap, looks up at her.

'You know, you were right, what you said the other night…'

'What did I say the other night?'

'About me needing excitement. Watching it get light just now, seeing the sunshine show its face, I understand that peace might be found in an ordinary life.'

Anne wonders if she is still immersed in a dream. This man is talking to her in a way he never has before. She furrows her fingers into his hair, smooths a strand away from his forehead. Kline continues the run of his thoughts.

'It's tough, you know, for me to get used to not having a screw or a drill sergeant ready to kick my arse for lying in bed. It's also a novelty waking up alongside the same woman more than two times in a row…'

They gaze at each other, Anne puts her head to one side, speaks softly.

'Are you trying to tell me something?'

'No, for once I'm just saying what's in my head.'

She bends down to kiss him. Their kiss grows in intensity. Anne realises her lover means business. She pulls her nightdress up over her head and throws it aside.

In the street below the restaurant a yellow sports car pulls up. Lily applies the hand brake, surveys the exterior of the restaurant with its partly completed name of 'Nirv…' painted above the wide lower windows. She looks up to the curtained bedroom window. She turns to Red Stick.

'We will wait.'

Anne rides towards the top of the hill. Only recently has her capacity to orgasm returned. She straddles Kline, driving towards a climax.

Below her the thrusts increase and increase until she has a golden release, the next best sensation to the high she still craves. But this will do, this will do very nicely, thank you. She falls onto his chest, allows the aftershocks to have their way. Slowly she realises something, something she has noticed a few times before. She props herself up on an elbow and asks the question.

'Why do you never come?'

No reply. He looks away.

'John…?'

'I don't want to talk about it.'

'Say what's in your mind.'

'No.'

'Just for once, you said you would share what's in your mind. So let's have it, is it fear of making me pregnant or am I simply not exciting enough?'

'Annie, no, it's the reverse.'

He touches her cheek, she pulls away.

'What's that mean?'

No reply. Kline sighs, shakes his head. Anne stares down at him. Hard.

'I said, what exactly does that mean? Is it a medical problem?'

He shakes his head, unhappily. The warmth and closeness between them begins to fade. After a long silence, Kline begins to speak in a halting way, a way that Anne has never heard before.

'Don't take this the wrong way but it's because of someone else.'

'What are you saying?' She pushes him away.

'Wait… Wait… OK? It's like this… You really want to know? When I make love to you there comes a time when I want to prolong the pleasure, for me as well as you. Not come, shoot my wad, whatever you want to call it. That's when I think of other things…'

'What things?'

'Patrolling the streets of Belfast, that used to take the edge off things. But that no longer seems to work. Other images come into my mind, an image of a particular woman.'

Anne reacts as if he has spat into her face.

'You're thinking of her when you're fucking me?!'

'No, well, yes, but not in the way you think. Listen, you asked for an explanation, this is it, hear me out.'

He uses her chill silence as an invitation to continue.

'When your ex-boss was hunting me throughout the city, there was a woman, a young black woman, a stripper in one of Rawlinson's clubs. A club that once belonged to me. The Maverick. She helped me escape capture and later took me into her bed. She didn't have to, maybe she didn't realise the danger. I did. I took what she had. After nigh on three years of fucking my fist, I let my prick rule my head. She paid for that with her life. One of Rawlinson's mob, Malleson, gave her a heroin overdose as punishment for aiding and abetting me. Months later her sister turned up, Sarah Gant. She blamed me, tried to bump me off, but when we found her real killer, she changed her mind. She had no need to condemn me, I'd done that myself.'

'How long were you with her sister?'

'Dinah? Couple of nights, no more than that. Dinah Carmichael wanted to return to Jamaica. She got her wish. The last time I saw her she was dressed as a bride, dead in a coffin, waiting to be flown out for burial.'

'You loved this woman?'

'No, but that makes it worse. I used her the way people use me. Because of me, people die. I try not to think about that but that's what I see, each time, Dinah in her coffin, you in yours, both because of me. Every time we make love, that's what I see…'

Anne turns over the revelations she has just heard, sifting his bleak explanation. Her emotions surge. She hugs him to her.

'John, let it go, it's just guilt fucking with your mind. Christ almighty, don't hold back with me, if it lasts one minute or ten, I don't care. As for death, I know that fucker, he's no stranger, every time I shot up there was a chance that I wouldn't come out of the high alive. So, baby, I'll take my chances with you. Compared to the needle, you're a safe option.'

The thought makes her giggle, then laugh. After a moment of puzzlement, Kline joins in. They hold each other, laughing and laughing, until finally the release of tension subsides. Anne wipes her eyes with the back of her hand. Kline watches her, thoughtfully. Anne feels a sudden pang of alarm, wondering what's coming next. When Kline finally speaks, she is in for a surprise.

'I've been thinking…'

'Uh, oh…'

'Relax. Is there any reason you couldn't take out a license for this place? You've no record.'

'No... No, but it's your place.'

'It's your name that will be over the door.'

Here was commitment, here was the need to accept his trust. Part of her says, no, you don't deserve it, but the healing part says, go for it. She nods.

'If you like.'

'Good. Well, that being settled, maybe we should think about doing some work in our restaurant.'

'OK.'

She watches her lover swing out of bed and walk naked towards the window. She feels the first nibble of the grey rat inside, a parental voice that says, *you don't deserve any of this.*

She reaches for her bottle of pills.

Parked in the street below, Lily Li T'ang alerts as she sees the curtains in the room above the restaurant open. She sees a glimpse of a naked male torso and the sight of John Kline looking out into the distance. She turns to the assassin at her side.

'All right, they're in residence. We can now proceed with their destruction.'

38

Little remains of a hectic night of gambling other than a fug of stale cigarette smoke. The factory-cum-gambling den is now almost deserted apart from a couple of players hunched over a scatter of cards laid out on a table, perched on the bed of the giant planing machine.

Yan, holding his final playing card, stares at his opponent.

'It is up to you, Mr Sturt.'

Roy Sturt glowers down at his remaining card, his mind fuddled by lack of sleep and the effects of too many blows while following the noble art. He must decide, all in? *Bugger it*, he thinks, *my luck must change soon*. He activates his vocal tube, a reedy voice booms out.

'Raise-you-again!'

Mr Yan is a card counter. He assesses the upturned cards. Reasonably certain of the outcome, he responds.

'And again. And another twenty.'

'Raise-you-again-and-see-you!'

Roy Sturt adds the last of his cash to the pot. Mr Yan turns over his card.

'Mrs Banks, the scientist's wife.'

'Ah-bollacks!-I've-got-the-bleedin'-scientist's-daughter-again-haven't-I?'

He throws down the offending card. Mr Yan gathers his stack of banknotes, lost in the joy of being blessed by the gods of chance. Only the sudden echoing sound of the factory gate slamming shut alerts him to the presence of Lily Li T'ang. She is accompanied by a man who, even at a distance, radiates quiet menace. Yan, clutching his winnings, hurries to greet his superiors, his footsteps clattering on the factory floor. Roy Sturt, sunk in black depression, remains at the card table.

Yan mumbles an excuse, bowing as he does so. 'We were just finishing the last session of the night.'

Lily looks pointedly at the banknotes.

'Quite a profitable one, obviously.'

'This, oh, this is nothing. The guard at the door, every morning I pay him his fee, he challenges me to play Happy Family, I take fee back from him.'

He chortles, seeks to share his greedy delight. Lily does not oblige him.

'I wish to place the Kline contract in less expendable hands than those of my companion here. I have much more pressing tasks in mind for the hands of Red Stick.'

Lily looks across to the raised bed of the planing machine, where Sturt sits on his stool, slumped like the beaten fighter he is.

'What about that person there? Might he be a possibility?'

'Sturt? He has need of money, also he has little affection for the man John Kline.'

'Summon him.'

'Roy…'

Dimly, Roy Sturt realises he is being called. He scrambles down to the factory floor and shambles over to join the group. He raises his voice amplifier to his scarred throat.

'Hello-how-are-you?'

'We are very well, thank you.'

Yan's eyes shift to Lily. She indicates he may proceed.

'Like to make some money, Roy?'

'More-Happy-Families?'

'Not exactly.'

Lily takes charge.

'I believe you are no lover of the person known as John Kline?'

'He's-a-right-bastard!'

'I quite agree, when I last met with him he looked at me in a most unsavoury way.'

'You-want-him-done-over?'

'A little more than that.'

'Maimed?'

'Should we say eliminated on a permanent basis.'

'That-will-cost-you!'

'Mr Yan will attend to the terms of the contract, half in advance, half on completion.'

'For-the-right-price-I'll-make-sure-Kline-meets-his-bleedin'-maker!'

'That consummation will satisfy my dearest wish.'

'I-don't-understand-you!'

'We will be most pleased when you fulfil your contract.'

'Got-you. Consider-it-done!'

He looks at Mr Yan.

'Let's-talk-about-the-money!'

39

Ensconced in the office of his home, Rafiq is less than pleased with his world. Troubled by his failure to bed Lily Li T'ang, he now has a business problem in the shape of an Asian youth standing before him. Rafiq toys with a paper bag containing five hundred pounds. Not for the first time Rafiq misses the assistance of his erratic but loyal assistant Kuldip, who at present is serving a sentence within the confines of prison. He sighs, decides needs must and addresses the successor to Kuldip sternly.

'Repeat back to me what it is you must do.'

Suraj adjusts his hearing aid, nods, a spaniel eager to please.

'I will go to the Bar Two café on Broad Street. I will possess an up to date copy of the *Financial Times*. I must not read it, but place it folded on the table before me.'

'Yes, good. Then what?'

'I wait for a man to join me. When he appears, he will say, erm, he will say…'

'How is the rate of the rupee?'

'What?'

'That is the password the man from the embassy will use.'

'Yes, yes, "the rate of the rupee", that is what he will say.'

'And then?'

'I will say "fluc… Fluct…" '

'Fluctuating, as always.'

'Yes.'

Rafiq strides across to the whisky decanter, pours himself a drink, wonders why there are so many slow people in the world and why they all must be employed by him. He drinks, returns to his instruction.

'When you have responded accordingly, an exchange will then take place.'

'Of what, master?'

'Your paper bag for his.'

'Ah, yes, I see.'

'Once this is done you will bring the passports and visas back to me here. You will not pilfer any of the money beforehand if you wish to remain in the land of the living.'

'No, master.'

'One more thing, Suraj, should anything untoward happen, you have no knowledge of my existence. Your story will be that an unknown man approached you and asked, as a favour, for you to make the exchange.'

'Does the unknown man have a name?'

Rafiq gives a long sigh

'No, that is why he is unknown. My God, Kuldip was no inimitable Jeeves but compared to you he was a paragon of ignoble virtue.'

'I don't understand such words, master.'

'No, all right, be about your business. I've made the exchange as idiot proof as I can, now go and test my hypothesis.'

'What is that?'

'Out, out, please, please, just get out!'

Suraj starts to back out of the room. Rafiq lifts the brown paper bag containing wads of banknotes, holding it out before him. Sheepishly, the young man returns, takes it from him, stuffs it inside his shirt, hurries from the office.

Left alone, Rafiq has a vague foreboding that all may not go as planned, but he dismisses it as mere worry. There are other problems to be dealt with. Defections to rival illegal immigration networks, failure to prime incomers with enough knowledge to dupe immigration officers. He is just about to pick up the telephone and call Pakistan when he hears the click of the office door opening behind him. He turns, expecting to see the hapless Suraj, but instead finds a vision of womanhood posed in the doorway. A ray of sunlight catches her silver choker, causing it to gleam and sparkle. Rafiq is entranced.

'Ah, darling Lily. Did you have an enjoyable early morning drive?'

Lily gives a secret smile.

'Mmm. Most invigorating. It might just have put new life into me.'

40

Deep inside the council building, in the heart of bureaucratic darkness, Anne Darracott sits across from a middle-aged woman who wears her hair swept back, isolating a face that would sink a thousand ships. The official wears a baggy blue suit and a starched white blouse.

Anne watches Doreen Chambers reading through her application for a license to sell intoxicating spirits at the Nirvana restaurant. The omens do not augur well. Doreen tuts from time to time, refers to a file in a pale brown cardboard folder. Anne wonders about the alien world that lies outside her experience. Sometimes she feels like a time traveller who has pitched up on planet Ugly. Finally, Doreen looks across the neat shiny polished desk at her. When she speaks, her voice is surprisingly soft.

'This application has been made before.'

'It has.'

'It was rejected on police advice.'

'I don't have a police record.'

'But Mr Kline, your partner, does.'

'He wishes me to be responsible for the license.'

'I feel I must refer this matter to my police colleagues.'

She closes the file decisively, her mind almost made up. Anne sees the drawbridge being pulled up. There is only one way to halt being shut out. She plunges in, keeping her question as cool as she can.

'Might one of them be called Khan by any chance?'

Doreen refers to the file. Glances inside, looks up, a little too fast.

'I really can't say.'

'If Mr Khan is part of the equation, before you turn me down, would you please consult him and say I would be grateful for a character reference?'

Doreen begins to fuss with her papers.

'This is most unorthodox, Miss Darracott.'

'Give him a call, please.'

Doreen considers, an aunt deciding whether to allow her niece to visit a sweetshop.

'Khan, you say?'

'Yes.'

A decision is reached.

'Please wait outside.'

41

On the steel table of a universal milling machine three green bottles are being primed with petrol. Billy Dudley, aka 'Dodger', because of his ability to sidestep the repercussions of his nefarious activities, stands back to assess his work. Beside him, smacking his left fist into the palm of his right hand, is Roy Sturt. Dodger glances at him, speaks in his native Brummy accent, his lugubrious tones echoing in the deserted workshop.

'Do yow trust these Chinky Choos, Roy?'

Sturt nods. Activates his voice box.

'They've-given-us-a-contract-to-do-money-money-money!'

'I can't tell what they're thinking. Especially that silent bloke. He gives me the heebie-jeebies, a right spectator at the feast. He able to speak or what?'

'Don't-know-maybe-I-should-offer-him-my-voice-box!'

Dodger grins as he inserts the rolls of cotton into the neck of each bottle. He watches the petrol rise to soak each wick in turn.

'Who's going to serve Mr Kline these Molotov cocktails, like?'

Roy mimes an overhead throw, brings his hands together, opens them up in a dramatic gesture to illustrate an explosion of flame. Dodger considers all the angles, chooses the one that carries the least danger to himself.

'Yow do the chucking, I'll do the driving. That's a fifty-fifty split of labour, same as the fee.'

The ex-boxer nods his agreement. The Dodger looks about him furtively.

'Be OK if I stash some personal effects here? I don't like to have ID about me on a job. Same with cash; we find ourselves in the nick, the thievin' coppers will help their selves.'

Sturt shrugs indifferently. They both take a step away. Dodger empties his pockets, hides his wallet under a bundle of cotton waste. He indicates the trio of Molotov cocktails, solemnly makes the sign of the cross, intones a blessing over each bottle.

'God the father, the son and the holy ghost.'

He starts with alarm as he sees Roy stick a cigar into his mouth and pull out a lighter.

'What yow doin'! There's petrol in them bottles, no naked flames until yow light the wicks for real, right?'

His fellow arsonist loads a bottle into each pocket of his leather jacket. The other he jams into a trouser pocket. He chews on his unlit cigar, places his voice box to his throat.

'Let's-get-on-with-it-sooner-Kline-goes-up-in-smoke-the-sooner-we-get-paid!'

42

The café is full of office workers chomping on a hurried sandwich before returning to their desks. There is a background of chatter, gurgling coffee machines, jangling cutlery, all of which play havoc with Suraj's hearing device. Perspiring, he sits uncomfortably at a table. He looks up nervously as a city financier pauses beside him.

'Mind if I borrow your *FT*, just to check the closing prices?'

Suraj jiggles his hearing aid, not certain what he has heard.

'Sir, did you perhaps mention the closing rate of the rupee?'

'No. Your paper, can I borrow it for a moment?'

'You will find the rupee fluctuating more than somewhat.'

'I'm sure…'

Quickly, the financier checks the closing prices on oil futures, frowns at what he sees, replaces the *FT*, strides away. Suraj eases the soggy paper bag of money away from the sweaty skin of his stomach. When he looks up, an Asian man now occupies the seat opposite him. The man picks up the salmon pink newspaper.

'Does this belong to you?'

'Yes.'

There is a pause, both wait for the other to speak.

'I bought it to check the rate of the rupee.' Suraj eases his shirt away from the bag of banknotes.

'How is the rate of the rupee?'

'Fluc… Fluctuating, as always.' Another pause, each looks at the other. Suraj takes the initiative. 'Do you perhaps have something for me?'

'Like what?'

'Passports, visas…'

'No, but I can show you something else.'

Khan shows his police ID to Suraj, who makes a bolt for the door. Amongst indignant yells and the crashing of overturned tables, Khan gives chase, grabs Suraj's shirt. It rips, Khan wrestles the young Asian to the floor. The paper bag bursts open, banknotes flutter all around them like autumn leaves.

43

The kitchen of the Nirvana restaurant is enveloped in steam. Kline watches the new chef, Ali, scalding every surface with a steam cleaner. Ali seems fanatical about hygiene and cleanliness. Kline hopes that he has equal flair for the yet undecided menu. Dimly, through the clouds of vapour, he sees Anne emerge through the swing doors and enter the kitchen. She looks around at the activity dully. The chef and his assistants know where she has been. Seeing her doleful expression, they fear the outcome is less than hopeful. Kline is the first to act. He strides across to her, takes her by the arm and leads her out of the kitchen.

Seating Anne at the bar, he looks down at her.

'What happened?'

Anne shrugs.

'They turned you down?'

'No, we got what I went for.'

'We did?'

Kline thinks she is playing games, pulling a gag, she will soon grin and laugh with delight. It doesn't come. Kline, puzzled, lifts her face to him. He sees the pain in her expression.

'Annie, what is it? You got what you went for. Why the face?'

'I didn't make it on my own. I had to enlist someone's help.'

'Like who?'

'Mister smiley face.'

'Khan?'

'Don't look at me like that. We were about to fail, nothing to offer our customers 'cept water and soft drinks. I played the Khan card. I felt I had to.'

It takes a moment for the implications to manifest themselves fully. Kline sits down next to Anne. They stare across at the well-stocked bar, the spirits, the wines. Eventually Kline puts his arm about her.

'We'll handle him.'

'Can we?' Anne gives him a worried look.

'We have so far.'

'Khan will expect more than a free orange juice.'

'Maybe so, but right now we're in business. We can serve booze. Talking of which...'

Kline leaves her, goes behind the bar.

'What can I get you, Madam?'

'You allowed to serve liquor in this joint?'

'We are.'

'Well, seeing as it's a celebration, I'll have a fizzy water.'

44

Roy Sturt's Morris Minor has seen better days, years and years of them in fact. With a pair of unpainted replacement front wings, the car has a distinctive if decrepit look. Not one to bother with servicing, Sturt has always had a problem getting the starting motor to fire. Today is to be no exception. Dodger tries the choke in a vain attempt to get the show on the road.

Roy leaves the passenger seat, goes to the rear of the car, puts his shoulder to the immovable object and heaves with all his strength. The Morris Minor moves a little, jerks into motion, the engine fires, Roy Sturt falls flat on his face. He feels the bottle of petrol in his trouser pocket disintegrate. The sting of petrol floods down his leg, his trousers soaked with gasoline. Up on the count of three, the ex-pug empties the glass fragments from his pocket, hops back into the car. The Morris Minor takes off with a jerky motion that will take them to their date with destiny.

45

The foreboding Kline had about their new cook and his ability to produce English grub is proving all too justified. Sitting at the bar, Anne turns over the undercooked cod and its accompanying overdone chips.

'Not good.'

Kline pushes his hardly touched plate away.

'Should've stuck to Thai nosh, he's great at that.'

'What are we—?'

The outer door of the restaurant opens. They turn to see an unexpected visitor. A black woman, wearing a maroon and cream baseball jacket with sparkling maroon pants to match. Sarah Gant smiles confidently as she advances towards the startled couple at the bar.

'Hi, guys, what's going on?'

Sarah, Anne and Kline stand together on the sunlit pavement, watching the sign writer perched up on his ladder, adding the final touches to the name 'Nirvana'. Sarah nods approvingly.

'I like the fancy lettering, a touch of the orient but not too much.'

Kline glances sideways at her. In profile Sarah has a disturbing likeness to her younger sister, Dinah. Her dead sister. He shakes the thought from his mind, together with the memory that Sarah had once tried to kill him in order to exact revenge.

'So, Sarah, what brings you here?'

'The police chief who was protecting my interests in New York got busted. My business closed, I needed to lie low for a while. So I decided to let my ladies go freelance while I visit my parents over here. And what do I find, you two moving into the catering business. Why'd you decide to switch?'

'Good question.'

Sarah picks up on a rueful look between Anne and Kline.

'Problems? Hey, tell me, I ran a restaurant in LA way back when. John?'

'The idea was to provide an international menu, European, Asian, Oriental. But we've got a problem: a Thai chef who can't cut the international mustard.'

'Or the local,' Anne adds. 'Some of our customers are connoisseurs of chips.'

Sarah shrugs. 'I can teach him basic cookery. Simple stuff but done right, the customers come back again and again.'

In the pause while Anne and Kline share a similar thought, they fail to notice a beat up Morris Minor turning into their street. Kline sees Anne nod. He looks straight at Sarah.

'Might you be interested in helping us out? We'd cut you in...'

Before Sarah can reply Kline's sixth sense of imminent danger kicks in. He turns to the street, sees a leather clad figure about to hurl a flaming Molotov cocktail towards them. The bottle of petrol spirals through the air. Kline makes a catch, hurls the missile back in the direction of the Morris Minor. The cocktail explodes in front of the car. Seconds before the car explodes into a ball of flame, Dodger hurls himself from the driver's seat and legs it away from the blazing vehicle.

Away from the blazing car, on the other side of the street, Roy Sturt sees Kline pushing Anne to safety inside the Nirvana. Sturt starts to climb up the slatted side of an advertisement hoarding extolling the strong points of Levi jeans. Hauling himself up behind the framework he shuffles along to where a gap allows him to descend a fire escape leading down into a narrow alleyway. Through the gap, he sees Kline appear outside the restaurant and start to look about him. Sturt grins, takes out the last of his firebombs and advances towards the end of the alley. He lights the fuse, takes aim at his target, draws back his arm...

'Stop!'

Roy turns, sees a black woman pointing a Sig Sauer.38 pistol at him.

'Drop it!'

Without thinking of the consequences, Sturt drops the burning bottle. There is just time for him to mouth, '*Oh, SHIT!*' before the Molotov cocktail smashes and envelops him in flames. Silently yelling, the human torch runs away down the street towards the smouldering wreck of his car. Yards away he crashes to the ground.

Running towards the still burning bomber, Sarah and Kline converge. Anne joins them, shudders at the sight of the smoking, blackened body. Kline is the first to speak, his voice bleak and unforgiving.

'How'd you like your petrol bombers, Sarah, well done or medium rare?'

In Roy Sturt's burnt right hand, his voice box emits a faint buzzing sound that splutters briefly before it dies into silence.

46

Lily Li T'ang does not countenance failure. When news reaches her of the botched arson attack on the Nirvana, she looks for scapegoats and finds a convenient one in Mr Yan. With Red Stick at her shoulder, she castigates Yan in vehement Cantonese. Her volley of abuse swirls around the silent machines and hanging chains of the disused factory. Yan stoically takes her recriminations but is distracted as he notices a rattling of the main door. Glad of an excuse to escape the wrath of Lily, Yan hurries to the door, bends to the observation crack and peers through. He straightens, puts his fingers to his lips, motions for Red Stick to join him at the door.

The Triad executioner glides forward, flattens himself against the wall. Yan eases open the catch. After some seconds, the door opens. The Dodger peers in with some apprehension. Red Stick seizes his shoulder and hurls him into the interior of the workshop.

Dodger Dudley lands at the feet of Lily, who looks down at him with cold contempt.

'Ah, Mr Dudley, our failed arsonist. Also, known as "the Dodger", I believe. Well, let's see if you can dodge your just rewards.'

She signals to Red Stick, who, like a kill dog unleashed, leaps forwards. The Dodger runs for his life, weaving between machines, screaming with terror as he goes.

Both men disappear out of sight of Lily and Yan. They hear pleas, cries of pain that reach a crescendo then cease abruptly. Lily lights a cigarette, waits.

There is a rumbling sound of a motor stirring into life. The overhead chain pulley system begins to rattle and shake. Coming towards them, hanging upside down like the dead Mussolini, the lifeless body of Dodger Dudley is delivered to them.

Lily casts a brief look at the contorted features, the crushed skull. She indicates with a wave of her cigarette that she is satisfied with the outcome. Yan presses a release button. The body is conveyed away, the arms of the corpse hanging and swaying as it recedes from them.

47

On the walkway that circles Birmingham city centre, Sarah Gant, wearing a grey pinstripe trouser suit, saunters along towards a meeting point in the shopping mall. She spies the photo booth where the assignation will take place. She notes that the curtains are drawn. Stone-coloured trousers and polished brown shoes can be seen beneath. She looks around at the passing shoppers, hears a voice from behind the curtain.

'Won't you come into my parlour, Mrs Gant?'

There is just enough room for Sarah to squeeze alongside Khan. Their faces are reflected in the glass of the photographic panel. Sarah nudges him.

'This is cosy.'

'Now that you have penetrated Kline's kitchen it's better if we're not seen together.'

'OK. You heard what happened?'

'Yes, it's a pity about Roy Sturt. One more informant who has disappeared in a puff of smoke.'

'Too bad.'

'Yes, I may as well close down that gambling factory.'

'Why not hold off, it might become a staging post for some future drug supply.'

Before Khan can reply, a woman's voice intrudes from outside.

'Ey, yow in there, yow havin' a union meetin' or what?'

Khan pulls coins from his pocket inserts them into the slot before him, calls, 'Won't be long!'

They prepare themselves for the first of three photographs. Khan lowers his voice, speaks out of the side of his mouth.

'I'm interested in who the Triads might choose to replace the leader recalled to Hong Kong. Have you heard anything?'

FLASH!

Sarah blinks, whispers.

'No, I'm waiting to see if there is a move against Kline and Anne. According to that report the Red Disciples always take revenge against those who cross them. Are you going to the opening of the Nirvana?'

'When is that?'

'Tonight.'

FLASH!

'It depends, I have an interesting interview to conduct first.'

'Anyone I know?

'Yes, I think so. A youth has been picked up trying to bribe an embassy official. I'm hoping to link him to Mr Rafiq.'

FLASH!

They leave the booth. An irate elderly woman, wearing a floral headscarf, glares at them.

'About bleedin' time. I need a photo, urgent, like, to renew my bus pass.'

Ever the gentleman, Khan shows his gleaming white teeth in a disarming smile. He invites her to step inside the booth. He takes out a handful of change, encourages the woman to select suitable coins for the machine.

'So sorry to keep you waiting.'

'Well, er, you know, much obliged.'

She draws the curtain. With a slight sigh, a strip of photographs slides into view. Khan extracts the strip, looks down at the images. Sarah strains to see. Khan points.

'That's a good one of you.'

'Not bad.'

Khan tears off a photograph, hands it to her. They go their separate ways.

48

By the bay window of his Edwardian-style living room Rafiq sits at a corner table spitting venom into his telephone.

'Get this into your head, our would be immigrants must be primed fully. Names, local information, what football team they support, everything! If they are turned away either at Elmdon or Heathrow airports they cannot earn money to pay me back my fees. I warn you, Jakir, do not become too smug. I may be thousands of miles away but, if necessary, I will swoop down upon you from a very great height…'

He becomes aware that his butler, Bashir, has entered the room.

'Yes, what is it?'

His servant bows.

'Sir, Mr Khan come.'

Rafiq bangs the phone down into its cradle, sighs mightily.

'Khan, Khan, Khan. That man is an albatross around my neck, an albatross! Where is Miss Lily?'

'Not yet return.'

'When she does, ask her to remain in her room until I've got rid this tiresome Mr Khan.'

'OK, sir.'

In the few seconds of grace granted to him, Aslam Rafiq feels a surge of aching lust sweep through him. He knows it is distorting his judgement in so many ways, but he doesn't care. He has promised himself that only when he lies between the thighs of the divine Lily will relief come. He stretches, gives a shuddering sigh that turns into an effusive greeting to the smiling Asian who has just been shown into the room.

'Ah, my dear Khan, what a pleasant surprise. Can I interest you in a drink, a cigar, a woman?'

'No, nothing.'

The thought of imbibing alcohol propels Rafiq towards the drinks table.

'My dear, I must confess that I have much need of all three.'

Pouring himself a triple scotch to fortify himself against the boredom to come, he looks across at his visitor. Khan's composure becomes a source of irritation.

'Tell me, Khan, do you not find living within the confines of a clear conscience boring in the extreme?'

'No, not at all.'

'That says a great deal about the difference between you and I.'

Carrying his drink like a comforter before him, Rafiq settles himself before the agent of the law. He takes a slug of scotch and opens the batting.

'So, what is it? To what do I owe the joy of your company?'

'I need to enquire about something,'

'Something specific?'

'Perhaps. But what interests me most is why you have lost your ability to stay clear of trouble.'

'Trouble?'

'I have come across your name as part of a report on Triad activity. A Triad whose leader has ambition to import large quantities of heroin into this country.'

'Really?'

'Yes. There is also another matter. Only today I caught an employee of yours attempting to purchase visas and blank passports from an embassy official.'

'This is all very fanciful. Triads, passports, visas, bribery, corruption? I am a boring businessman, not a master criminal.'

'An amount of currency was recovered from the young man. It was intended as a bribe. He hasn't confessed as to who organised the crime, but when he does… '

Rafiq spreads his hands.

'What has this to do with me?'

'I wish you to join me at Police HQ to record your fingerprints.'

'Are you arresting me?'

'Not yet. But if I discover one print of yours on one banknote, that will change.'

Rafiq's thoughts dart around before settling on damage limitation.

'But any such involvement will be difficult to prove. A fine, no more than that.'

'But still a fall from grace. Your position as a leader of the Asian community would be at risk. Some constituents might even be willing to come forward with the details of how you smuggled them in and what fees you charge.'

Bemused rather than alarmed, Rafiq becomes pensive.

'You know, only today I was thinking of that scoundrel Kuldip. An omen of sorts, don't you think?'

'I'm sure you would not wish to join him inside those grey prison walls.'

'Not if a less boring alternative could be found.'

Khan settles back, a chess player who knows he has obtained a winning position. He smiles.

'Orange juice.'

'What?'

'I'll accept one now.'

'Oh, yes, yes, of course.'

As he reaches for the bell that will summon his servant, Rafiq feels a constriction, as if a serpent were wrapping its scaly coils around him.

49

Early evening in the Nirvana restaurant. The newspaper and TV reports of the failed attempt to fire-bomb the restaurant have generated publicity and resulted in healthy bookings for the opening night. The subtle scent of jasmine drifts from joss sticks planted in the mouths of two ornamental Asian tigers that stand guard on either side of the entrance door.

In the steam-filled kitchen, Sarah Gant is very much in charge, supervising, tasting, instructing, chivvying the catering staff into a state of readiness for the action to come.

Inside the restaurant, Rajesh, a young Indian sitar player, sits cross-legged on an array of cushions. Waiters in burgundy-coloured jackets check the tables and side booths one last time. Kline, wearing black evening dress, emerges from the male washroom. He surveys his domain. All is in place. Annie, near the entrance, wears a high necked burgundy-coloured dress that matches the wall panels. From a shelf, looking down on the shaded lights of the oriental palace décor, sits a gleaming brass statue of Buddha, who beams benignly upon all below.

Kline glances at his watch. It is time. He raises an eyebrow to Anne. She turns to the staff member who attends the door.

'OK, Clive baby, let's open for business.'

50

At the time the Nirvana is opening its doors, Rafiq, wearing a green velvet dinner jacket is sighing like a fretful child. From her chair beside the parlour fern, Lily Li T'ang watches him mooch from one side of the room to the other. He pauses by the drinks table, reaches for a glass. Lily frowns.

'Not another drink, you'll be inebriated before the evening even begins.'

'Why won't you come to this opening with me?'

Lily picks a speck from her yellow trouser suit. 'I told you, I doubt if the owner or his lady would make me welcome.'

'But the invitation says Rafiq and guest. You would be with me, no one would dare object.'

'Look, go on your own. Try and enjoy yourself.'

'I would sooner stay here with you. We could enjoy a feast of a different kind.'

He allows his eyes to travel the length of her body. Lily deflects his suggestion.

'You know that is not practical at this particular time.'

'Yes, yes, I know all about such things, but even so.'

'Patience, Aslam, patience.'

'Yes, yes, all right. Have you heard from your father?'

'No.'

Khan's instructions chime inside the mind of Rafiq. They do little to lighten his mood, but he lays down a future marker anyway.

'Lily, we must talk about plans for our future.'

'Soon things will become so much clearer.'

'I do hope so. You must not become involved in Triad wars. Now, will you reconsider your decision? Come with me to the Nirvana, please.'

Lily yawns expansively.

'I need an early night. This has been an exhausting day, not made better by your constant badgering me to do things I have no wish to do.'

'All right, my darling, don't be cross with me. I will see you tomorrow. Sleep well and think of me adrift in the lonely night.'

'Oh, do shut up, will you.'

51

When Rafiq arrives at the restaurant the evening is in full flow. The sitar plays music that Rafiq recognises, sounds that convey longing and heartfelt emotion.

Sarah, with the kitchen operating to her satisfaction, has changed into a glittering white evening dress. She sits at the bar chatting with a pair of customers who are waiting for a table. Anne meets and greets later bookings, providing them with menus and a complementary glass of champagne. The door opens once more. The smile of greeting assumed by Anne fades momentarily when she sees the identity of her latest guest.

'Mr Khan, how good of you to come. May I offer you a drink?'

Khan, smartly dressed in a black bowtie and dinner jacket, looks past Anne to where Kline stands at the bar, a full glass of orange juice held out towards him.

'Thank you, Anne, but it seems my welcome drink is already waiting.'

Anne escorts him across to Kline. Khan takes the drink from him and sips it appreciatively as he takes in the busy scene, with waiters coming to and fro from the kitchen carrying plates of food. Archie, the barman, is expertly plying his trade.

'Congratulations, Mr Kline, I hope your venture succeeds and that the liquor license is a great source of profit for you both.'

'I'm sure it will be.'

Anne mutters, 'Bastard,' to herself as she turns to resume her hostess role.

In a secluded corner of the Nirvana a Chinese man detaches himself from his blonde companion. He leaves the booth and makes his way towards the male toilets at the rear of the restaurant.

The sitar player finishes a long sequence of sonorous notes with a flourish. There is scattered applause. Rafiq, from the bar, claps and calls, 'Bravo!' He wipes a tear, turns to Kline.

'John, where did you find that boy, he plays like a dream.'

'Annie hired him. He's trying to earn enough money to study the sitar in India.'

'I will sponsor him. He has real talent.'

'That's good of you but wait until we're more established.'

'I shall hold my fire. I seem to be doing rather a lot of that lately.'

Inside the area of the washroom, Red Stick stands inside a cubicle, listening intently for any other occupants. Hearing none, he takes out a thin screwdriver, goes to the frosted window that looks out onto a side alley. He begins to loosen the hinges of the window frame.

*

The peak of the evening is past. Anne, near to the main entrance, asks a middle-aged couple if they have enjoyed their meal. Their answer is positive, almost effusive. Clive opens the door and bids them goodnight.

The next couple about to leave are a fit-looking Chinese man escorting a white woman with a riot of blonde hair. The woman smiles at Anne as they pass but the man pays her no attention. A shiver passes through Anne. She fails to understand why.

Lily Li T'ang has changed into a trouser suit of midnight blue. At her throat is a scarf of scarlet silk. She goes into the Edwardian lounge, takes her car keys from a side table. On the mantelpiece, an ormolu clock begins to strike the hour of eleven.

Having thanked the staff for their efforts, Kline, after locking up, pours a brandy for himself and a soda and lime for his partner. He carries them upstairs to their living quarters.

He finds Anne stretched out on the settee. She turns her head to him.

'That was work.'

'Yeah, but good, eh?'

'The money will be good.'

Kline sinks down into a chair. Anne kicks off her shoes.

'Heels, how long is it since I wore high heels? Has Sarah gone?'

'With our old pal Kublai Khan, no less.'

'No?'

'Yes. I saw them walking off into the night as I was locking up.'

Anne laughs.

'She'll put some starch into his undies.'

'Maybe that's what he needs. Talking of which, I'm going to take my drink to bed. You too, if you get a move on.'

He stands, heads for the bedroom. Anne swings off the settee.

'I'm coming, I'm coming...'

She catches up with him, he gives a low tiger growl of welcome. She puts her arm about him. They enter their bedroom.

On the floor below, in the shadowy darkness of the washroom, the frame of the window is being dislodged. Red Stick, now wearing scarlet Shaolin fighting garb, stealthily eases himself through the narrow opening and drops down to the floor. The door that leads out into the darkened restaurant is half open. The Triad enforcer slips through and begins to silently climb the stairs that will take him up to the apartment above.

Kline lies naked in bed, reading a comic book, waiting for Anne to return from the bathroom. He is content with the night's work and looks forward to enjoying a pleasurable end to an exacting day.

Anne leaves the bathroom. She wears a pale grey robe decorated with a green woodland motif. She, too, is in a mood that she finds unusual, one of being about to share sex as an expression of easy, accepting love.

Just a few strides away from the bedroom door, Anne hears a sound from downstairs. She frowns then hears it again. A definite meow. A cat must have somehow got in from outside. She leans over the landing rail, peers down. At that moment, a hand touches the side of her forehead. She feels a wave of disorientation. The hand touches her other temple, two waves meet inside her head, making her confusion complete. She turns to her attacker. Red Stick concentrates his power, he touches a nerve centre on her neck. Anne is washed into unconsciousness by the onset of a crimson sea. She begins to fall backwards. Red Stick catches her, lowers her onto the floor of the landing. He then moves towards the bedroom where John Kline expects to encounter the joys of love, not the murderous attentions of the red executioner.

To be continued…

BOOK THREE
WHILE BEAUTY SLEEPS

52

John Kline lies on his king size bed. He turns over the page of a comic book illustrating the dastardly doings of 'Villains United'. He lays the shiny pages aside and looks up with a smile as someone enters the room. His smile vanishes. He throws the cover aside, leaps out of bed to confront the intruder.

Red Stick goes into his fighting stance. John Kline, in his birthday suit, throws a right cross that misses its target. 'BLAM!' A punch hits him in the mid-riff. 'GAAH!' Kline doubles over with pain. 'WHOOMP!' Straightening, he manages to grapple with his opponent. 'KRAAK!' He brings up his knee into the other's groin. 'OOOFH!' Red Stick staggers back, his foot slips on the fallen comic book. Kline sends in a left jab. 'SWOOSH!' It slides past its mark. Kline feels a steely grip fasten under his armpit. 'BAAA-DOOOM!' There is an explosion of searing pain from his shoulder that shoots up into his brain. 'OWOOCH!' The naked man falls back against the window.

The Red Assassin steps back to give himself space to launch a deadly drop kick. Kline can see what's coming but his limbs are frozen, unable to respond to the wild panic in his mind.

'AAARGH!' Red Stick becomes airborne, flies feet first at his target. At the last second, the paralysis of his victim fades. Kline slumps to his knees. Red Stick's 'AAARGH!' turns into 'AIEEEEEE!' as his body smashes through the window. He falls towards the street below; shards of broken glass and splintered frame accompany him. As the pavement looms, he regains some control, landing on his feet, although the impact sends a 'CRUNCH!' of pain 'KRAKATOOMING!' up his left leg, up into his groin.

With a 'THOOM-THOOM!' a yellow Spitfire open topped sports car hurtles around the corner and brakes to a screaming halt nearby to the limping assassin. With a last attempt to impress the driver, Red Stick flips forward, yells, 'YAAAH!' turns a somersault in the warm night air and lands in the passenger seat beside his employer. Lily Li T'ang, peeved at the result of yet another failed mission, screams, 'IDIOT!' as she guns the engine and speeds away with an angry, roaring, 'BWOOOOM!'

Looking out from the hole in the wall where the window used to be, Kline sees the sports car speed away but cannot see the driver clearly. He hurries from the room, searches for Anne. It doesn't take him long to discover her. He picks her up from the landing floor and carries her unconscious body back into the bedroom.

Gently he eases Anne down and lays her out on the bed. Her breathing is shallow and laboured. He lifts the phone, dials 999, says it's an emergency. He gazes down at the sleeping beauty. He has an absurd thought that if he kisses her on the lips she will awaken. What is there to lose? He bends down, presses his lips to hers. There is no response. In the distance, Kline hears the 'Wah-Wha-WHA!' of an approaching ambulance.

53

After spending an uncomfortable night on a hard hospital chair, nursing an aching shoulder, Kline visits the room where Anne lies oblivious to the world. She has been hooked up to a device to assist her breathing. An ugly black nozzle protrudes from her mouth, a tube running down to an inverted concertina that rises and falls with each halting breath.

A young nurse, all in white, checks readings on the monitoring equipment, notes down details on a chart. Kline, wearing a fawn mackintosh, leans against a wall and stares across at Anne, willing her to wake. He hates everything about hospitals. The smells, the underlying superiority of the staff that says, 'You're sick, I'm not.' A white middle-aged doctor, weary from too many patients over too many years, sits at a table, takes Anne's chart from a pile, glances at it. The latest entry reads 'No change'.

'Thank you, Sally.'

As the nurse leaves, Kline detaches himself from his post and approaches the doctor. The name badge above the top pocket of his white coat reads 'N. A. Middleton'. Kline looks down at the combed-over hair, the sallow dried skin, his unruly eyebrows. The doctor is leafing through a thick file marked 'Anne Darracott'. Kline speaks bluntly, his voice scratchy from lack of sleep.

'Hey, doc, you going to tell me what's happening?'

'There is no change. I see from the file that the patient has a history of drug abuse. Several overdoses of heroin from which she barely survived. Do you know if this state of coma is because of her addiction?'

'No, I don't think so. She's on a methadone recovery programme. I gave her pills to the sister. There were no fresh track marks on her, I checked.'

'Well, we must maintain the methadone dosage. She seems to be suffering stress, which may be due to symptoms of withdrawal.'

'She's stronger than she looks.'

'Let us hope so.'

'So, what are you going to do to revive her?'

The doctor closes the file. He looks wearily up at the man towering over him.

'Specialist area. In the case of a coma, all we can do is wait.'

His tone is as starchy as his coat. He sits and pulls a file towards him, opens it. For him the interview is at an end. Kline reaches over and slams the file shut.

'Don't sit there playing God almighty while she, Anne, oh sorry, *the patient* takes what might be her final breath!'

'It might be of some help if you indicate how loss of consciousness occurred.'

'I don't know, I don't know. There's nothing, no mark, not even a bruise.'

'Well, as I say, we must take our time. Await events, try not to worry too much. I'm sure, she, the patient, will come back to consciousness in due time...'

The realisation that the doctor has nothing to offer, that no miracles of medicine are to occur, hits Kline like a blow to the stomach. He's taken one or two of those in the past twenty-four hours. He has a vision of the raider who attacked him. Suddenly, quick as a karate chop, he sees a way to save Anne. He turns to the doctor.

'You got any Chinese on the staff?'

'Chinese?'

'Yeah, there's a few of them about.'

'None in here.'

'Do you employ a, what you call them, acu... Acupuncturist?'

Doctor N.A. Middleton sucks on the word as if it were a denial of the Hippocratic oath.

'This is a National Health hospital.'

'No place for pin stickers.'

'Certainly not.'

'Well, thanks, doc, thanks a bunch for, you know, nothing.'

54

Holding a breakfast tray, Rafiq taps gently on the door to the White Bedroom, calls Lily's name softly. He waits for a welcoming call but no such sound floats on the morning air. He eases open the door and enters. Dressed in a black silk dressing with an old gold pattern of diamonds that matches his pyjamas, Rafiq tiptoes towards the bed, where an outline of a sleeping figure lies unseen beneath the bedclothes.

'Lily, darling Lileee?' he croons.

Rafiq places the breakfast tray with its glass of freshly squeezed orange juice, its carefully wrapped toasted bread and an assortment of jams and honey on the white lace coverlet. He regards the shape beneath the covers, so near, so very near. He contemplates the sweep of a thigh, the curve of a haunch. It is too much too bear, to be so close to such loveliness. Trembling a little he stretches out his hand, touches where buttock meets hip. The figure stirs, throws back the sheets, looks up blinking in the morning light. Rafiq takes a startled step backwards.

'I… I… You…? Who?'

Red Stick helps himself to a gulp of orange juice. Rafiq scuttles from the room.

Left alone in the White Bedroom, Red Stick stares down at his swollen, bruised left leg. He applies all his power of will to the affected area. The swelling begins to diminish, the mottled purple of the bruising begins to fade.

55

The treatment room of the Chinese Herbal Medical Centre is austere. John Kline lies on the treatment table staring at a painting of the Chinese god of healing, Shennong, a tough looking dude with a bunch of herbs stuck in his mouth.

The shoulder of John Kline resembles a pin cushion, with all the meridian and collateral channels open to drain away the soreness from mangled nerves savaged by the Chinese assassin.

Zheng Meng, a neat man in his late thirties, wears a short white medical jacket. He has an inner stillness that gives his patient some belief in the treatment he is undergoing.

'Just a few more needles then I am done.'

Kline turns to the acupuncturist and nods his thanks.

'It's beginning to ease, I'm glad I found you.'

'How did you come across my name, Mr Kline?'

'With a pin. Yellow pages.'

'Where else.' Zheng acknowledges the pun with a slight bow.

'Yeah, sorry. What I said about my girlfriend, you any idea how she was turned into sleeping beauty? Any suggestion how I can find the magic to awaken her? I tried a kiss, didn't work.'

Zheng starts to insert another needle just above the kidneys.

'There are high masters of the martial arts who can do such things, who can paralyse with a touch to a vital nerve centre. Would your assailant enter into that category?'

'Could be.'

'You didn't see the lady receive the pressure?'

'Uh uh.'

'That's a pity. For what seems dead can be brought alive by those who know.'

'That include you?'

'Unfortunately, no. I think the treatment is now complete.'

Zhen begins to remove the needles, slowly. Kline tries for one last piece of information.

'The guy who laid it on Annie, would he be able to undo the damage?'

'Perhaps. There, we are all done.'

Kline reaches for his purple shirt, manages to find the sleeve without wincing.

'Much improved. Thanks for everything. What do I owe you?'

56

Early the following morning, the Nirvana is deserted except for two men facing each other across a side booth table. A half full bottle of Johnny Walker whisky lies between them. Zahir Khan sees John Kline knock back a tumbler of scotch. Not for the first time, Khan wonders about alcohol and why people would seek to cloud their minds. He decides to break the sullen silence.

'How is your lady?'

'Still in a coma. Every time the telephone rings I expect to hear she's taken her last breath.'

Kline pours himself another shot. He has a menacing air to him that Khan has seen before, a steely determination to take on all comers no matter the cost.

'What is it, John? Why have you called me here?'

'I want the guy who downed Annie. You have any info on who he might be?'

'Did your attacker limp at all?'

'Not when he arrived, no.'

Khan considers the request. Information is his currency, he is reluctant to give any away. But Kline on the rampage against the Triads might reveal many hidden aspects of their drug trade. He decides to divulge a little of his store of knowledge.

'The Triads have two main enforcers, Red Stick and Double Petal. Each are equally dangerous but in different ways. One is a master of the martial arts. The other uses drugs and weaponry.'

'The only weapons he used were these.'

Kline extends his hands across the table.

'Then Red Stick is your man.'

'Red Prick more like. I want the bastard and I want you to tell me where I can find him.' Seeing a flicker of calculation in Khan's expression, Kline smiles a tight little smile. 'What's in it for you, babes? Don't worry, you'll think of something.'

The agent of the law pauses to consider the situation, running through possibilities, playing the odds. Who to sacrifice? Who to save? He smiles as he reaches a decision.

'I have a contact who might have access to the Hong Ming Triad. You must be patient until I can apply a little pressure to this informant.'

'Mr Khan, get off your arse, go find me Red Stick.'

57

In the Edwardian drawing room, all is not well. Rafiq is trying to question Lily Li T'ang, who marches up and down blowing loudly on a bird whistle. As the piercing trills fill the room Rafiq cries out in anger.

'I mean, who is that man upstairs? And what is he doing here, uninvited and in my house? Above this very room and no doubt active within your bed!'

The birdsong ceases. Lily, imperious in a swirling floor length pink robe, decorated with darker pink chrysanthemums, turns to her host.

'Oh, cool it, will you, you're like a mummy hen. Cluck-cluck-cluck-tut-tut-tut!'

'But, darling Lily, Shen T'ang left you in my care.'

Rafiq receives a withering glance and a vehement reply.

'My daddy would know better than to accuse me of indulging in carnal intercourse with a person who is nothing but an employee.'

'Darling—'

'The man upstairs is known as Red Stick. I believe I did mention the matter. Well, I regret to say that last night he fell down on the job rather, and at this moment is recuperating from his injuries.'

'Lily, Lily—'

'I slept down here, if you must know, and jolly uncomfortable it was too!'

She turns away, strides towards the door. A remorseful Rafiq hurries to restrain her. He falls to her knees before her, pleading.

'Oh, Lily, please forgive me…'

He gazes adoringly up at her, sees her hair gathered up in swirls that liken her to an Edwardian beauty. He is determined to pay any price necessary to make her the mistress of his house. Lily looks down without pity. Rafiq tries to explain his emotions.

'I'm sorry, I couldn't think, I just felt the pain of jealousy, like a twisting knife in my heart. Oh, my dear, I cannot bear to think of the dangers that surround you.'

He is favoured by a condescending smile.

'But I am safe here with you, surely?'

She kneels beside him, puts an arm around his shoulder. He grasps her hand, presses his lips to it repeatedly, punctuating his words.

'You might be safe for the moment, but that is all. I have homes in Europe, the subcontinent. We could be safe and happy there, just you and me. No Red Sticks, no John Kline, no Khan.'

Lily, far from persuaded, rises to her feet. She assumes an outraged tone, paces around the room in a state of shocked surprise.

'Are you suggesting that I become, I believe the phrase is, a permanent house guest? A mere paramour? Someone of the demi-monde?'

Rafiq rushes to placate her.

'No, no, no, no, no! No, of course not. I mean, if you want

respectability, then, then, for, yes, for you, I would…'

Once more Rafiq finds himself on his knees, a suitor about to propose to his lady love. Lily leads him ever onward.

'Yes, you would, for me, you would…?'

They are never to know what Rafiq would do for the love of Lily, for, at that moment, there is a rap on the door. Rafiq's butler, Bashir, looks in, only to be instantly met by a tsunami of abuse in Urdu.

'But, sir—'

'Out, out!'

'Mr Khan, he here.'

The atmosphere of love and romance vanishes from the drawing room. Rafiq runs his fingers through his hair, worriedly.

'Khan, Khan, like an albatross still. No, no, a Kraken hanging about my neck! Pursuing me like a monstrous hound from hell!'

He takes Lily by the hand and leads her towards the door.

'My darling, I must ask you to withdraw. We will resume this matter later. In the meantime, I hope that I may hope?'

'I hope you may. What is the problem, exactly?'

'Oh, nothing. Merely an irritation. A glorified policeman called Khan.'

With a shrug that makes her breasts jiggle, Lily dismisses the problem.

'Those who uphold the law have their price, surely?'

'I believe they do. But let us discuss all this later.'

As he ushers Lily through the doorway and into the hallway, his hand touches her waist. Through the flimsy material, he can feel her smooth, warm skin. The touch, slight as it is, deepens his desire. He beckons Bashir to him. Both watch Lily ascend the stairs. Both sigh as Lily gathers her robe around her, the shape of her swaying hips outlined as each stair is climbed. Without taking his eyes from the ascending derriere, Rafiq speaks, softly.

'Bashir…'

'Uh, yes, master?'

'Bashir!'

'Yes, What…What?'

'Prepare a room for Lily memsahib, the one that is next to mine.'

58

Lily Li T'ang enters the bedroom with its virginal white décor. Red Stick, wearing only a scarlet loin cloth, sits cross legged, eyes closed, self-healing on the bed. Lily watches him, smiles to herself. Teasing the lovestruck man downstairs has whetted her appetite for carnal action. She releases her lustrous black hair, arranges it to fall around her shoulders, steps out of her slippers, kicks them aside. Next, she loosens her robe. It cascades down, revealing a body nude apart from a silver necklace of coiled snakes around her throat.

On the bed, Red Stick opens his eyes. They widen as he sees Lily standing naked before him. He takes in the rounded shape of firm medium-size breasts, small dark red nipples, strong, wide hips, long legs. She parts her thighs invitingly. No pubic hair is visible against her tawny skin, which disappoints him. The hired assassin knows what is expected. Women who employ his services often yearn for the delights of airborne sex.

Red Stick stands, notes the damage to his left leg has not yet fully healed. He eases down his loincloth, displays the full extent of his manhood. Lily raises both her hands, adopts a Shaolin fighting pose.

'Right, then, Redders, let us test your capacity for continuing combat.'

With a fevered 'WHOOMP!' their naked bodies meet and mesh together. The frenzy begins.

In the room directly below, Rafiq walks about searching for tobacco for his pipe. He still wears his ornate dressing gown, gold-coloured pyjamas and Moroccan slippers. Khan, dressed in a dark blue safari style suit, sits in an easy chair. There are muffled 'THUMPS!' of activity in the room above. Rafiq finds his tobacco jar, fills his pipe, returns to his discourse after darting a puzzled glance at the ceiling above.

'Why… Why should I know how drugs are brought into the country? And as for this… ('THUD!') what, what was his name, Thick Stick?'

'Red Stick.'

'Ah. I have no idea who he is or what he is up to.' ('THUMP! THUMP!')

Rafiq glances up at the ceiling, which has become a sounding board for some inexplicable activity. Khan notices his unease.

'But you could, no doubt, discover what Red Stick and his partners are up to?'

'How can I when the false words of my assistant, Suraj, threaten me? False accusations of all kinds of infamy, from procuring passports to organising illegal immigration, and God knows what other fantasies.'

'What if that particular worry could be removed?'

With a pull on his pipe, Rafiq senses a deal in the offing.

'Then, my dear Khan, we could see what arrangements might be made...'

('THUD! THUD! THUD!')

They both look up to where the ceiling is rhythmically vibrating. Khan points a finger towards a piece of plaster dislodged from above.

'Repairs?'

'Oh, a little contracting work. Joinery. That sort of thing.'

At the top of the stairs Bashir is carrying a tray of crystal glass tumblers. As he passes the White Bedroom, he hears a sound: a woman's cry, a cry of, of what? Fear? Pain? Something else?' The butler lowers his tray, picks up a glass, presses it to the wall, the better to hear the amplified sounds from within. The woman seems hysterical, what is she saying? Bashir strains to pick out the words being screamed in a manner that is beyond his experience.

'FUCKMEFUCKINGFUCKERFUCKMEHARDHARDERHARD AAAH!'

Bashir drops the glass, shocked by what he has heard. He can only imagine what depravity must be going on inside.

Inside the bedroom, Lily is thoroughly impaled, her arms twined around the neck of Red Stick, her legs locked around his waist. The couple swirl around the room, ending up against a painted panel depicting dancing nymphs. Red Stick gathers the last of his strength, sends in one final surging thrust of power. Lily sobs with a final shuddering cry of release. The couple slowly slide down the wall. They sit slumped, breathing heavily, all passion spent.

Left alone in the room below, Rafiq is having trouble lighting his pipe. Khan's visit has eased some worries but promises only to bring more dangerous involvement in the future. At last the lighter fires. He sucks in the honey dew smoke, settles down in his chair to ponder how best to free himself from the coils of Khan. His cogitations have hardly begun before the door is thrown open and a babbling butler bursts into the room. Red in the face, gulping for air, Bashir claps his hands together like a performing seal. Alarmed, Rafiq rises, goes to his servant.

'Bashir. Whatever is the matter?'

A torrent of explanation in Urdu, ending with the words, 'Miss Lily, jig-a-jig, jig-a-jig!'

Rafiq drops his pipe. Glowing embers of pipe tobacco spill onto the carpet. He does not notice. He stares at the wretch before him, takes him by the lapels of his waistcoat and screams, 'LIAR!' He begins to pummel the unfortunate messenger. Bashir falls to his knees. His master kicks him furiously, losing one of his slippers. The bare sole of Rafiq's foot lands on a patch of carpet that is about to be incinerated. He yells with pain, hops on one leg, stumbles and falls across the back of the cowering butler. There is the sound of birdsong as Lily enters, joyfully blowing on her bird warbler. She takes in the sight of Rafiq athwart his servant in a most compromising position.

'Really, Aslam, can you not find a more private spot to satisfy your lust?'

Rising to his feet, retrieving his slipper, stamping out the spread of fire on his carpet, Rafiq points an accusing finger at Lily Li T'ang.

'How dare you speak of lust. You, who have been, have been…'

'Have been what?'

'Playing the whore with that Red Stick person.'

'Have you gone mad? Are you off your chump?'

'My butler heard you. Bashir, did you not overhear the sounds of jig-a-jig?'

The butler cowers, afraid to rise from the floor.

'Indubitably, sir.'

'WHAT?!'

Screaming with anger, Lily starts to aim savage kicks at the ribs of Bashir. Rafiq pulls her away.

Breathing fire like the dragon she is, Lily directs her scorn from one to the other.

'May I be allowed to speak?'

'Please do.'

'Yes, I was with Red Stick, yes, we were in the bedroom, but what this fool overheard was merely a rather energetic session of Tai Chi. Red Stick has been kind enough to put me through my paces in that particular discipline. What your spy must have overheard was merely the release of tension caused by my participating in a most innocent fitness exercise!'

Trying to take this in, Rafiq slowly looks from one to the other. The tall young Chinese woman aglow with beauty. The cowering, snivelling middle aged minion who understands nothing. His decision is easy.

'Apologise to Miss Lily at once for besmirching her with the filthy outpourings of your depraved mind.'

Bashir climbs to his feet, approaches Lily.

'Mistress, I, I humbly apol—'

'Oh, save it.' She swats him away.

Rafiq pushes his servant towards the door.

'Bashir, to your pantry. Remain there until I decide what is to be done with you.'

When the door closes on the unfortunate Bashir, Rafiq turns to Lily.

'What can I say?'

'Say nothing.'

Lily blows birdsong into his face and leaves the drawing room in high good humour. For her it has been a most satisfying morning.

59

The mind of Anne Darracott has entered a region of nightmare. She follows a livid blue ball of light through a darkened wood. Misshapen night creatures follow on behind. Hanging above her, touched by glistening moonlight, are the bodies of tortured men. Their agonised mutterings convey no sense to her. The blue light blinks and beckons. She follows, not knowing where it is taking her or why she is lost in this desolate place.

Inside the hospital room Kline and Sarah Gant look down at the comatose Anne. Sarah points at the fluttering eyelids. Anne is experiencing the process of dreaming. The eyeballs beneath the lids rotate, move from side to side as if straining to escape from some inner turmoil. Not knowing what to say, Kline looks at Sarah, his expression hopeless and sad.

'That's what she gets for being mixed up with me.'

'Quit that...'

A nurse bustles in.

'Visiting hour ended five minutes ago.'

They ignore her. The nurse speeds away on her mission to return the hospital to the staff and the sick as soon as possible.

'Heard anything from Khan?' Kline asks.

'No, he's out on some caper.'

'What gives with you and him?

'How'd you mean?' Sarah asks.

'I saw you going off into the night together after the Nirvana opening.'

'Nothing like that, though he's a good looking guy. But then, so are you.'

All she gets is non-committal grunt in reply. Sarah realises that Kline has no ego about his looks, something that makes him even more attractive to the opposite sex.

Kline takes a last lingering look at the pale face of Anne unmoving on her pillows. Sarah feels very close to him. She turns him to her.

'We'll get Anne out of this.'

Kline sees Sarah morph into her sister, Dinah, something that drives him further into the depths of guilt and depression.

'How?'

'We'll put our heads together, hearts and minds.'

Sarah hugs him to her. Kline finds the contact comforting in a way he doesn't quite understand. They take their leave of the woman trapped within the grey limbo that lies between life and death.

The machines do their work. They help Anne to stay alive as, outside the hospital, night begins to fall.

60

In the pressing and ironing room of the Noh Wei laundry, a group is gathered to observe a very strange cleaning process.

On one side of a long trestle table covered by a white sheet held down by smoothing irons are Aslam Rafiq and Lily Li T'ang. Facing them are Mr Yan and Lily's father, Shen T'ang, dressed in grey business suits. The only splash of colour in the room comes from the cherry red hue of Lily's stylish short coat. Everyone present watches a laundry worker carefully spread a black skirt. This done he picks up a hair dryer and begins to blow hot air onto a section of the garment. Shen T'ang begins to explain the process in his halting but precise way.

'What you see is a garment I have brought back from Hong Kong, where it was dipped in liquid cocaine. That is what the white patches now becoming visible contain. All we need do is to scrape off the cocaine and we have merchandise to sell.'

Adjusting his camel coat around his shoulders, Rafiq tries to overcome the fumes of bleach, starch and unwashed clothing that permeates the long room.

'That is quite novel but, Mister T'ang, is that the only reason you have returned?'

'I am extremely fortunate. My superiors have decided to exploit a rivalry between the drug squads of London and the Midlands. They are to bring the merchandise through Birmingham airport in future.'

All Rafiq can think of is how this might thwart his pursuit of Lily. Will she return to live with her father? He tells himself to concentrate. He is here to gather information on behalf of the manipulative Khan. He speaks with as much sincerity as he can muster.

'We are all delighted by your return, Mr T'ang.'

'Thank you for taking such good care of my daughter.'

'An honour and a pleasure.'

They all watch the scrapings of cocaine being transferred into a steel bowl. The heated air from the dryer plays on another section of the cloth. Soon another patch of snowy white powder is revealed. Mr Yan and his leader exchange smiles in anticipation of the profits similarly materialising before them. Shen T'ang beams across the table.

'Mr Rafiq, do you remember that we once discussed how best to link our immigrant communities?'

'I remember it very well. That was the first time I had the pleasure of welcoming your charming daughter to my home.'

He glances sideways at Lily, but all her attention is centred on her father, who signals to Yan to expound on their plans to restore the fortunes of the Hong Ming.

'For reasons of security, and due to the setbacks suffered through the intervention of this man Kline, we do not know which of our

Chinese couriers are known to the drug squads. Would you be willing to provide an Asian courier to convey a consignment from Birmingham to London?'

'Well, I…'

Rafiq becomes aware of Lily's hand touching his arm, he tries to concentrate. Mr Yan slides into negotiating mode, his voice lowers, a predatory smile plays on his lips.

'It is a most valuable item of merchandise. You will be well rewarded for merely providing a person to carry a parcel.'

'To what tune?'

'Shall we say five hundred per trip?'

Lily gives Rafiq's arm a squeeze of encouragement. Rafiq turns to her. He gazes into the dark brown eyes that promise so much but deliver so little. He decides not to give up on his quest to possess this exotic creature.

'Yes, well, as your daughter can well affirm, I have a servant whose talents would be best employed elsewhere.'

Lily acknowledges his capitulation with a slight forward movement of her lips. Rafiq interprets this as being a secret vote of thanks. She turns towards her father.

'Very well, Daddy, we may proceed.'

'Good, good…'

Shen T'ang takes out a pen, pulls a pad of blank laundry receipts to him. He scrawls the number 47 in large script across both portions of the ticket. This done he separates the halves by means of the perforation. He hands the receipt section to Rafiq.

'Your man must present this to the shop counter of this laundry. He will then be given a parcel containing four shirts and a weight of cocaine. He will take the 3.48 train from New Street to Euston station. From there he must proceed to Gerrard Street. Somewhere along the route he will be approached by a man who will make this sign…'

Shen T'ang bends the forefinger of his left hand back towards the base of his thumb.

'Your courier must reply with the sign of Kai Ching…'

'Kai Ching, yes, yes… What sign is that?'

Shen T'ang tucks his little finger under his ring finger. Rafiq, all fingers and thumbs, tries to replicate the sign without success. Lily rearranges his fingers into the correct position. The instruction continues.

'Our man will respond with the sign of Xiao Tu...'

His ring finger folds back onto his thumb, his middle and forefingers extend to form a horizontal V sign. Lily watches Rafiq fumbling fingers. She grasps his hands, tugs his fingers into place.

'Your palms are perspiring. Why is that?'

'Excitement at the touch of a virgin, no doubt.'

'No doubt about that, Mr Rafiq.'

61

Lunchtime at the Nirvana, businessmen at tables, lovers in the side booths, waiters serving their culinary needs.

Khan and Sarah sit at a secluded table beneath the statue of Buddha, where they cannot be overheard. Khan wears a dark suit, white shirt, carefully knotted grey and black striped tie. He is rather pleased with himself, believing he knows the position of all his pieces on the board: where his contacts are, what power he holds over them. Sarah regards him thoughtfully. She has been celibate since she arrived in the UK, a condition she does not regard as normal. She squeezes her thighs together, releases them, tells herself to concentrate on what her fellow agent is saying. What the hell *is* he saying?

'...Rafiq had absolutely no choice but to accede to my request for co-operation. I pinned him to the corner of the board.'

'So, what, you pick off a few pawns? That's all they are, these cocaine couriers.'

'And close down the Chinese laundry operation.'

'Why not really clean up? Find out where the routes are in and out of the UK. Who provides the finance, who manufactures the stuff?'

Khan leans back, strokes his moustache as Sarah continues, 'Let me purchase the goods. Where I go, who I meet, what I discover, we can share, straight split. Good for us both.'

'I have pressure upon me to produce results. If what Rafiq tells me is true, the Triads intend to switch their operation to the Midlands. I need immediate success to prove the worth of my ongoing investigations. A few pawns will help me achieve that.'

Sarah looks Khan over, the way she would a john when he enters one of her houses. She sees a handsome guy whose dark good looks should ensure he never need pay for sexual services. So how to play this? Direct approach? Why not? She lowers her voice, leans across the table.

'You're a good looking guy. You and me, we'd make a great couple from any angle, any position.'

'I have only one position, Mrs Gant.'

A pause. Sarah places him as preferring up and down sex of the vanilla variety.

'Yeah, I bet, baby.'

Khan reacts to the scornful look she shoots at him. He rises, annoyed, strides away.

Sarah watches him go, rises from the table, saunters across the restaurant, hips swaying in her close-fitting leopard skin dress. She gives practised smiles at admiring male customers as she progresses towards the bar area, where she knows the owner will be sitting.

Kline sits at a small table, a phone and a whisky bottle placed before him. Sarah joins him, indicates the telephone. Kline shakes his head, pours himself another shot, lifts the bottle in invitation.

'Too early for me.'

She sits at the table. Their knees touch, briefly. She stares at him, wondering if it's cards on the table time. She decides it is.

'I've just left your friend, Khan, or to be exact, he just left me.'

'Nothing lasts forever.'

'It's a professional arrangement, nothing more.'

'He pays you?'

'Not that way. No, we're colleagues.'

'How's that?'

Sarah takes his hand, looks straight at him.

'I'm working for the United States Drug Enforcement Agency.

She watches the play of emotion on the face of John Kline. Bemusement followed by a cynical smile. He detaches her hand from his.

'Who are you spying on, me?'

'No, we wanted to get a lead on the Triads when they attacked you. I saved your ass from that petrol bomber, if you recall.'

'So you did. Thanks.'

'I saw no need to involve you further, John.'

'Until now.'

'There's a scam involving a Chinese laundry operation. The Hong Ming want help to shift a hefty packet of cocaine down to London. I wanted in on the action. Khan refused.'

'Is that the outfit that employs Red Dick?'

'Red Stick, yes.'

'He's the guy that sent Annie into the land of nod.'

Leaning across the table, Kline's manner becomes urgent.

'Tell me what you know. What their scam is and if that red bastard might be involved.'

'We don't know who exactly the courier will be. But there are signs in code to facilitate the exchange of the drugs.'

'What are they?'

'I don't know. Khan wouldn't pass on everything Rafiq told him.'

'Rafiq?'

Kline gets to his feet, looks down at Sarah, who wonders at his sudden switch into action mode.

'John, what is it?'

'I think it's time Mr Khan learned a new Chinese proverb. He who does not pay laundry bills gets taken to the cleaners.'

62

The white bedroom has a cold and empty look. Aslam Rafiq gazes around. With Lily gone from his care it is an Arctic wasteland. He wanders around the room, goes to the side of the bed, looks down at the pillow that has been closer to her than he would ever be. Into his mind a vision surfaces: that of the hated Red Stick instead of the lovely Lily.

Rafiq turns away, growls with anger, glares around the bedroom. Decides complete fumigation and a redecoration is required whilst he is away. His eyes rest on the panel with the dancing nymphs. Their leaping dance seems to mock him. He scowls at the freedom and joy they display. He feels neither. He catches sight of himself in his white suit and tie in the dressing table mirror. Tries to shake himself free of all thoughts of Lily Li T'ang, whose last words to him had been those of every empty promise ever made: 'See you soon.'

Rafiq sighs, is about to turn away when he notices a small bottle of perfume lying beside the mirror. It has a stopper with a pink circlet. He looks at the blue label that reads *apres l'ondee*. He unscrews the cap, inhales the scent. Bergamot, vanilla with undertones of musk. It is Lily's daytime perfume. Sunshine after rain. It brings every poignant memory of the failed romance back to him. Her looks, the promise, the allure of the unobtainable. A discreet knock sounds on the door. For one mad second Rafiq believes Lily has come back to him.

'Come…'

Nazema, his young housekeeper, looks in. There is nothing subservient about her. Rafiq tolerates her general rudeness because of her efficiency in all things domestic.

'A man downstairs.'

'My taxi?'

'No, a big white bloke.'

'Name, name?'

'Kline.'

'Show him into the dining room. I will be down presently.'

Left alone, there is time for one last indulgence. Rafiq allows himself one further inhalation of the essence of Lily Li T'ang before he pockets the elegant bottle of frosted glass.

Kline paces around the drawing room restlessly. He pauses when Rafiq finally appears.

'John, what an unexpected pleasure.'

'Glad I came when I did. I saw the suitcases in the hall. Yours?'

'Yes, I've decided to go on a business trip.'

'Taking Khan with you?'

'Certainly not.'

'You heard what happened to Anne?'

'Yes. Is there any improvement in her condition?'

'That depends on you.'

'I don't quite…'

'Red Stick?'

'That dreadful fellow. What of him?'

'He put Annie out of action, I need something on him to get him to break the spell.'

'What can I do?'

'Give me information. This drug transfer, tell me who the courier is, where to find him and what the secret signs are that will trigger the exchange.'

The mind of Rafiq rapidly assesses the factors involved, the timeline, the departure of his flight, the foiling of Khan, and above all the confounding of the hateful Red Stick.

'The courier is a chap who was once my butler. Bashir is booked on the 3.48 to London Euston. He wears a homburg hat and will collect the goods from the Noh Wei laundry in Balsall Heath within the hour.'

'And the code signs?'

'Give me your hand, John.'

63

John Kline walks through the train soon to depart from platform 4 on New Street Station. He is looking for an Asian man wearing a homburg hat. With ten minutes' leeway before the train starts its journey to London there is some urgency in Kline's search. Near the front of the train, sitting in a first class carriage he spots his man, slides into the seat opposite.

'Mind if I join you?'

Bashir shifts nervously, puts a protective hand onto the brown paper parcel beside him.

'Lots of empty seats, why choose this one?'

'Thought you could use some company.'

'I don't need any.'

'No? Mind if I ask you a question.'

'What?'

'What sign are you?'

'What?'

'Scorpio? Libra? This?'

Kline shows him the sign of Kai Ching. Bashir starts like a rabbit who has just seen a fox. He stammers out a reply.

'Who… Who… Who are you?'

'Someone waiting for the answering sign. The sign of Xiao Tu.'

Bashir twists his fingers to make the sign. Kline nods.

'Now give me the goods.'

'It was supposed to take place in London.'

'There's been a change of plan. Give.'

Bashir hands across the parcel. Kline gets to his feet. Bashir looks out onto the platform.

'I'd arranged to meet my fiancée in Southall.'

'Tell you what, you take the train and I'll look the other way.'

'What?'

'Go to London, see your lady love.'

'Oh...'

'I haven't seen you. You haven't seen me.'

'I don't want trouble, sir.'

'All we've done is play pass the parcel. No harm in that.'

64

Sarah Gant is busy in the kitchen of the Nirvana, filleting fish for the evening ahead. Khan is with her, venting his rage and frustration.

'Rafiq's servant was sighted at every station down the line to Euston. He was observed being met by Triad members. No parcel. No cocaine. Insufficient reason for a drug squad arrest.'

'Hmm. Raid on the Chinese laundry?'

'No, not yet. I wish to confer with Rafiq about that and other matters. I must be certain that there are Class A drugs to be found on the premises.'

'You haven't contacted him?'

'By telephone, but he wasn't at home.'

'Terrific. No drugs, no Rafiq, no arrest, and there I was I wanting in on your information.'

Khan starts to reply, changes his mind, grits his teeth and strides out of the kitchen. Sarah brings down her cleaver with some force, separating a head from the body of a Pollack fish. She looks up as Kline comes out of the cellar carrying a crate of wine.

'Your mate gone?' he asks.

'Yes, he's decided to pursue a few wild geese. You stash the parcel?'

'Yeah...'

'Let's hope they try to recover it soon.'

'I'll be waiting when they do.'

Kline starts to unload the bottles of wine. Sarah goes to the sink to rinse her hands. Watching her Kline realises she has the same figure as her dead sister.

'Sarah...'

'Yes?'

'Just so you know, you're into me for a favour.'

She looks back to him at the table, her skin tingles.

'Mutual advantage.'

'You're a resourceful lady. You could have heisted that parcel as easily as me.'

'Probably.'

She saunters across to him, drying her lean brown arms.

'Well then?' Kline says.

'Maybe I wanted to create a situation where I could ask a favour and not be refused.' Sarah's voice is warm, intimate.

'Ask.'

Sarah Gant gently takes the bottles of Burgundy, places them to one side. Her arms reach up around his neck. She pulls his head down to her, finds his mouth with hers.

In the restaurant, Rajesh is tuning his sitar. He watches as Kline and Sarah start up the stairs. They stop halfway, embrace hungrily before continuing towards the apartment above.

They make it only so far as the upstairs room but no further. There, first on the settee and then the floor, Sarah Gant encounters enough angles to make Archimedes shout 'Eureka!' Now she lies, naked, alongside John Kline on the carpeted floor, satiated. After a while she props herself up on an elbow and looks down on a less than satisfied sexual partner.

'Hey, John, what is it?'

He shakes his head, looks away. She turns his face back to her, speaks softly.

'Look, baby, this is just a one off. No shoes, no rice. We know that, right?'

'Yes.'

'So what is it? Tell me. Your Aunt Sarah knows all about this stuff. Is it about Anne?'

'That's part of it. Not all.'

'Which means what, exactly?'

'I can't come with her. I can't come with you.'

'I noticed. Any idea why?'

After a long moment of silence, he tells her about his belief that he is the angel of death. He brings destruction to all who care about or come close to him. Anne in a coma, Sarah's sister, Dinah, dead for her kindness and shelter. At times of pleasure, he sees her in her coffin and his enjoyment turns to ashes.

'That's bullshit. That Malleson guy did for Dinah. He paid for it. You and I both had a hand in his execution. There's no blame, not from me. You take your guilt, wrap it in a ball, let it go.'

'Not so easy.'

'Give yourself a break, that's an order.'

'Yes, ma'am.'

'I can't sort out your mind, but I can do something about your body. I know various ways to take a gentleman past the point of no return.'

'Is that a fact?'

'Want me to try?

Kline looks up at her, slowly nods his acquiescence.

She reaches for him, begins a slow massage that soon brings a strong uprising. Sarah grins up at Kline.

'Now we're getting somewhere.'

She grasps Kline's erect member in both her hands, commences a spiral movement, one hand climbing above the other in a constant flowing motion. After a short while her hands go their separate ways. One stays above, the other strays below and enters him. The two movements merge into one sensation, Kline emits a whimper of pleasure, Sarah looks up at him, sees his torso tense, his back arch. She goes down on him. Kline feels her mouth suck on the nut of his penis. Now there are three sensations, a convergence of pleasure he cannot resist. The moment arrives, he lets it all go: guilt, blame, pain, all burst from him in spasm after spasm, accompanied by a last cry of shuddering release.

Sarah sits back on her heels, wipes her mouth, gazes down at the naked sprawl of him.

'Well?'

Kline struggles to speak.

'That bad, huh?'

Finally, he gets the words out.

'Thank you, Sarah.'

65

It is as if a hurricane has hit the house of Rafiq.

Zahir Khan storms from room to room searching for the missing

Asian leader. Nazema soon gives up trying to reason with him. She waits for the storm to abate.

Finally, the agent returns to the drawing room to question her.

'Where is your employer?'

'How should I know?'

'You work for him.'

'I'm his housekeeper not his travel agent.'

'He must have left a forwarding address.'

'If he did, I haven't seen it.'

'What other homes does Mr Rafiq possess?'

'I'm not his estate agent.'

'When you hear from him you must inform me, immediately.'

Nazema looks him up and down, her manner just shy of insolence.

'Must I? And who are you to say so?'

Khan frowns with annoyance.

'Ask your boss.'

With a snort of disgust, he marches away.

66

HMP Birmingham has a programme of education and rehabilitation. As a change from staring at blank walls, classes are well attended by prisoners

Today, the English language class is a little baffled to find themselves being addressed by one of their own, with an eccentric way of interpreting English grammar.

Armed with a copy of *Fowler's English Usage* and a pointer stick, Kuldip is trying to explain the meaning of the word 'expletive'.

'We use bloody expletives every day. You lot might call it swearing but educated people like me refer to such dirty words as expletive.'

He thumps the book he is holding with his stick. There is a wild look in his eyes. Faint froth can be seen by the front row.

'Now Fowler bloke knows what he is talking about. He uses a word like "bloody" and cites it as a term in popular use used by persons such as you who find themselves sitting here thinking what the bloody hell is he talking about? Well, if that's the case I suggest you lend me your ears, listen to what Mr Fowler bloke and me have to say about expletives. Any questions?'

The group of a dozen prison inmates stare dully back at him. Some have the stunned look of someone hit across the head with a sock full of wet sand. No questions are forthcoming. The officer at the back of the room checks his watch and wonders if he is witnessing a new form of judicial punishment. Kuldip brings the lesson to a close.

'All right. As for the use of adjectival usage and the pronouncing of expletives in modern societal situations, that can wait until next time, when it is hoped your tutor bloke will have finished being in bed with Asian flu. All right, class over, dismiss!'

Slowly the dazed class rise to their feet and troop towards the door. The guard ushers them back in the direction of their cells. Kuldip lays down his teaching aids and is about to follow them when he sees someone he remembers all too well. He begins to laugh with a high shrill manic sound.

When the laughter fades, Khan says, calmly. 'Hello, Kuldip.'

Hope leaps like a salmon in the prisoner's breast.

'You been sent to prison, too?'

'No.'

'Why you in here?'

'I'm seeking help.'

Kuldip takes a step away.

'Me? From me? Why me?'

'You are acquainted with Mr Rafiq.'

'Expletive bastard him!'

'Maybe.'

'What you want? Why not just say, huh?'

Khan wanders around the classroom. Kuldip watches him, suspiciously. The agent picks up the pointer and jabs it towards the stocky Asian.

'Before Mr Rafiq betrayed you to save his face and skin, you were his personal assistant.'

A shadow of bitter recollection passes across the face of Kuldip.

'Know everything, me. Could have said a lot, me, but who would believe the word of bloody nonentity against mister smoothie Asian leader?'

'I am less than pleased with your former master. Mr Rafiq has sold me a Chinese pup.'

'Pekinese?'

'Let us say he has told me less than the truth, then disappeared before his deception could be discovered.'

'Mr Rafiq has not changed his leopard spots.'

'I have traced him to a number of Asian flights. Might he have gone to India, perhaps?'

Kuldip shakes his head, his mind seeking an opportunity to profit. Khan offers another suggestion.

'Kashmir?'

'Maybe neither.'

'Pakistan?'

'Why should I help you, mate? You incarcerated me inside here.'

'Your sentence was not excessive. You will be eligible for parole soon.' Khan points towards the red armband on Kuldip's left arm. 'You're a trusted member of prison society. Help me bring a criminal to his just desserts, you could be free in no time at all.'

'Why believe word of a bloody copper, eh?'

'I can put in a good word to the Parole Board or I can do the reverse. Kuldip, what better offer are you likely to receive?'

A long, suspicious pause ensues. Finally, Khan shrugs, walks towards the door. Kuldip reaches a decision, calls.

'He sold his Indian operation. He had a boat on lake in Kashmir but that sank. That leaves most likely his travel agency in 'Pindi.'

'Rawalpindi?'

'That's what I just said.'

67

The PIA flight from Birmingham to Islamabad has been a long one. Khan feels that he needs at least one night to gain his bearings before searching for Rafiq in nearby Rawalpindi.

If Khan had expected a peaceful visit to his father, he is disappointed. As his dad serves tea to him in the courtyard, perched around the walls sit more than a dozen village boys. Leaning against the opposite wall are five elders, all interested in this visitor from another world. As the old man pours the tea into white china cups, he looks across at his son.

'I could hardly believe the boy when he told me you had returned. Why are you here, part of your investigation?'

'Yes, I must persuade a valuable contact to return where he will be most useful.'

Khan stirs sugar into his tea, glances around at the audience, who gaze at his father with respect and a touch of awe. The old man strokes his moustache, smooths his tie.

'Would that place be England?'

'Yes.'

'The fellow's here in 'Pindi, you say?'

'I believe so.'

'Still on the trail of the fiends who deal in opium?'

'Heroin...'

The elders nudge each other. They sense that soon there will be a story to entertain them. The boys on the wall lean forward to hear every word. One almost topples to the ground but is grabbed by several hands and returned to his perch. Khan feels he is taking part in a play, with the audience seated on either side of the stage. There is an expectant pause. Khan delivers his lines.

'Yes, heroin. We have had some success but not enough to stop the supply of Class A drugs into Britain.'

The old man looks around at his fellow villagers. They all enjoy his police stories. They smile, willing him to begin. Khan gives his father an opening.

'It is an international problem. One that is hardly new.'

His father accepts the invitation. He adjusts the cuffs of his white shirt, clears his throat.

'In my time, I have brought more than a few drug pedlars to book. I remember, as a young constable, I was involved in the apprehension of a chap called Mumtaz, a dacoit who had brought a reign of terror to our district. The head constable dressed me up in a burqa, sent me out posing as a woman, dashed good I was at it, too. I located the gangster buying fruit in a street market. Pretending to examine a row of mangoes, I sidled up alongside my quarry. Before the fellow could realise he was in the toils, I'd thrust my service revolver up into his beard and told him he was under arrest. Yes, that was my first capture of significance. You know, of all the others that I brought to book after that, even after I was promoted to Chief of Detectives, none gave me greater pleasure than that first good pinch. This, ah, what is it you call him?'

'Rafiq.'

The old man squares his shoulders, looks his son in the eye,

'Do you want any assistance? Surveillance, disguise? Don't mind coming out of retirement, not at all. Methods a bit antiquated, but they work, believe me.'

Khan smiles, gently.

'If there is a difficulty in Rawalpindi, I'll call on your services, Papa.'

'Splendid. Chance of action. Hey, look forward to that.'

The elders nod and smile. The boys clap their hands.

68

The humidity of the monsoon season sucks the energy out of the tubby Asian, crumples his white suit. Rafiq trudges down Iqbal Road towards the site of the AR travel agency. The street steams as the hot sun bears down on men carrying rolls of rugs on their heads. Auto taxis buzz about like demented bees.

Rafiq plucks the damp cloth of his shirt away from his paunch. His eyes flicker around him warily, sensing an attack may arrive at any moment. He stumbles and slides on the muddied street, almost placing his foot into a pile of sickly-smelling offal. A cloud of flies rises in protest. Rafiq reaches into his man bag for a handkerchief. He sprinkles the cloth with a few precious drops of the perfume that once belonged to Lily Li T'ang. He inhales her scent.

A man without legs is wheeled towards him in a low wooden cart. With an inward shudder, Rafiq thrusts a 500 rupee note at the beggar. He hastily weaves his way around droppings of horse manure, past a row of shops selling pots and pans, another with heaps of used tires piled outside. Confused, he looks around in every direction trying to regain his bearings.

At last he reaches Saidor Road. Motley crowds spill out from the nearby Raja Bazaar. He looks up, spies a familiar balcony. He turns gratefully away from the hubbub of motor horns and the teeming hordes of humanity. Sighing with relief he reaches the shop of Mohammed Ali and Sons, Silversmiths. Inside the doorway is a sign that reads 'AR Travel. 1st Floor'.

On reaching the top of the stone stairs, Rafiq pauses, wipes the sweat from his brow. He prepares himself to berate his employees for their failure to bring enough illegal immigrants into the UK.

Seated alongside the white bearded typist on the Sador Road, the Writer wonders where to take the story next. *A chase would be good, not just any old chase but one with a novel aspect to it.* The typist sits, long brown fingers poised. The Writer removes his sunglasses, watches the passing show for a moment before he begins to dictate…

'Exterior. Saidor Road. Day.'

He notices the balcony above the silversmiths.

'Pan up and along a balcony that houses various offices. Rafiq appears from his travel agency. He is tired from a training session with his less than competent staff. He shoots a sour glance towards the noisy hen coops that line the corridor. He ambles towards the archways that give a view to the busy street below. Peering across to a shaded area, he waves for an auto taxi to meet him downstairs. The green and blue taxi, which is little more than a glorified motor bike, filters into the traffic. The Writer pauses. Time to set up the chase… How's this?

'As Rafiq withdraws from our view, his image is replaced by that of Zahir Khan, who appears out of another archway nearby. He beckons to the next taxi, which is a chestnut horse pulling a cart with an awning above.

'Cut to Rafiq climbing into his taxi, driving away without noticing that Khan is behind him. Hopping aboard the horse and trap, Khan urges the driver to follow the blue and green taxi.'

And with that, we cut to the chase.

Leaning back in the taxi, Rafiq sighs, wearily. He feels far from his true home in England. There is too much activity here, too many people. He tries to wave away the diesel fumes that assail his nostrils.

He takes out his handkerchief, tips a little more of the scent of the woman he has deserted, left without a word of explanation as to his sudden absence. Might Lily Li T'ang miss him? Was there any love in her heart for him? He breathes in the precious fragrance of her. A wave of sadness makes him choke with a realisation. At first all he wanted was to appease his lust for her. Now… Now, what was this delicious inner pain? Something that might be called *l'amour*? Ah, he needs to walk, to ponder on this revelation. He calls to his driver, a shifty fellow with a wall eye.

'Stop here!'

Rafiq has just paid his fare when a horse and trap clatters to a stop nearby. A man, wearing a fawn linen jacket and dark trousers, steps down onto the road. Rafiq gulps for air. His hands begin to shake at the sight of his nemesis, Zahir Khan. Behind him he hears the splutter of his taxi.

'Stop!' Rafiq yells at the taxi driver.

'Stop!' Khan yells at Rafiq.

The taxi brakes, skids to a halt. Rafiq scrambles into the rear, orders the driver to escape with all the speed he can muster

The auto taxi turns into Ganj Mahdi Road, encounters a melee of traffic. The horse and trap gallop up alongside. Rafiq and Khan, for a moment, are within touching distance. The auto driver sees a gap, accelerates towards it, forces his way through. A cacophony of blaring horns sound behind him.

Heading towards the entrance of the Raja Bazaar, Rafiq sees a way to escape his pursuer. He will mingle and lose himself in the crowded market. Leaning towards the driver, he points towards the gate and the milling crowds. The taxi slows down, halts. Hurriedly, Rafiq digs into his pocket for notes and change. In a panic to be gone he thrusts all he can find into the driver's hands and hurries towards the bazaar.

Dodging through the tide of humanity that surges towards him, Rafiq has only travelled a dozen steps before he feels the loss of something most precious. He halts, checks the side pockets of his white jacket. Both are empty. He has lost the small bottle of perfume. Aghast, he turns back to where he left the taxi. It has departed. In its place stands the smiling figure of Mr Khan. The pressure of the crowd behind slowly delivers Aslam Rafiq towards the hunter who has tracked him down.

Khan smiles a sardonic welcome. In one hand, he holds the bottle of perfume. From the other dangles a pair of handcuffs.

69

Taking hold of Anne's cold clammy hand makes Kline's throat go dry. The monitor beside her bed beeps. Interchanging horizontal lines of light crawl across the screen, indicating that life remains within the unconscious woman. Kline strokes her hand, searches to say something other than meaningless words.

The hospital room door opens. A nurse looks in, young, pretty, overworked. She doesn't speak, gives Kline a half smile of sympathy before she bustles away.

A few seconds later, Anne stirs. Her lips compress into a narrow white line. Her eyes flutter beneath her closed eyelids. Kline moves closer, willing her eyes to open.

He watches as the feverish signs of her inner distress slowly subside. Kline lifts Anne's dank blonde hair away from her forehead. He finds a napkin in the side locker, moistens the cloth with water from a plastic jug. He places the cold compress across her brow, looks down upon her, fumbles for the right words.

'Annie, come back, please. On my own I do stupid things. Things I'm not proud of. I'm looking for a way to break this spell but, so far, nothing. I'll find a way to bring you back. Depend on it.'

He glances at his watch, frowns.

'Afraid I've got to go, be back tomorrow.'

He takes away the compress. Dries her forehead with a tissue, kisses her unresponsive lips.

70

Inside a gymnasium in Digbeth, a bout between a pair of kung fu fighters is in violent progress. Both contestants wear gloves and protective headgear. One man is dressed all in blue, the other completely in red. After a flurry of jabs and kicks, the blue warrior gives ground. With a banshee wail of pure aggression, the fighter in red launches a throat-crushing drop kick. The blue fighter staggers, chokes, raises a hand in surrender. Red Stick bows to his vanquished adversary.

Huddled together on a bench nearby are Mr Yan and Shen T'ang. Yan is the first to comment on what they have just witnessed.

'He is recovered enough to use against Kline again, should your daughter fail by other means.'

Shen T'ang shifts uneasily. As the fighters withdraw, he stands. Yan joins him.

'To destroy the man Kline is not a problem. As a precaution, I have requested the services of a colleague of Red Stick's.'

'The madman known as Double Petal?'

'Yes. But the recovery of the drug consignment lost to Kline is more important.'

The Triad leader rubs the back of his neck, runs a finger around the inside of his collar. He turns to face his second in command.

'One failure might be acceptable to Hong Kong. Another, following so soon after the first...'

He spreads his hands before him. Yan shows his concern.

'Must that be so?'

'We must accept the truth of things. Lily is our last chance to revive our fortunes. Should she recover our goods, I may yet save face. Should she fail...'

Yan touches the shoulder of his superior.

'Shen T'ang, for all our sakes, let us pray your daughter will succeed in her mission.'

71

Having taken an order from a table of four customers, Sarah Gant is making her way to the kitchen when a flurry of activity at the main door attracts her attention. She passes the order to a waiter, watches as a tall, slim Chinese woman, flanked by two athletic-looking guys wearing black suits, advances into the restaurant. They pause, peering around in the subdued lighting. The young sitar player finishes playing, his last note resonating in the air.

Sensing danger, Sarah moves towards the bar where Kline, wearing evening dress, is pouring himself a Jack Daniels.

'Think you might have company, John.'

He glances past her to where the young Chinese woman, dressed in a black lace wrap and a matching evening dress, is about to approach. He nods to himself.

'About time she showed up.'

'You know her?'

'Yeah, we've been thrown together before.'

'A high class whore if ever I saw one.'

'You could be right.'

'Takes one to know one. Looks like she's dressed to kill.'

Kline makes no comment but watches the party advance. He eases himself away from the bar, feels a tingle of anticipation as the glamorous leader of the delegation halts before him.

'Permit me to introduce myself. Miss Lily Li T'ang.'

She extends her hand. A tiger's eye ring shines on her middle finger.

'What can I do for you, baby?'

'You may escort me to a less public place.'

She picks up a menu, turns, leaves the bar, proceeds towards the staircase. Her escorts follow and plant themselves on either side of the stairs. Sarah grins, watches Lily ascend towards Kline's living quarters.

'Good luck with that one.'

'Maybe she just wants to study the menu in private.'

'Maybe you're on the menu.'

'Yeah, sure, I'm a standing dish.'

'You don't have to tell me.'

Upstairs in the main living room, Lily Li T'ang discards her wrap. She wears a strapless evening gown that accentuates the beauty of her bare shoulders. At her throat is a black pendant. On her left arm are bangles of onyx and a bracelet of black-beaded skulls.

Kline seats himself at the end of the settee and watches his exotic visitor as she studies the menu. She moves around the apartment, allowing herself to be admired from every angle. Lily muses aloud over each dish as if she were trying to reach a decision about what best to order.

'Hmm. Yam Tala? Satay Gai? Pad Thai noodles? I don't think so. Prosciutto e Melonie? Creole Jambalaya? Chateaubriand? Zabaglione? Flammkuchen? Apple pie? How cosmopolitan. Is there an a la carte option?

'No, just what you see.'

With a glint of a smile, she tosses the menu away from her, joins him on the settee, tilts her head, provocatively.

'What have you in the way of tall, strong, attractive men?'

'I'll ask the chef. There might be a couple left in the freezer.'

As he starts to rise, Lily puts her hand onto his.

'Stay. I'm not really hungry for food...'

Kline feels the warmth of her touch. He looks down at her slim hand with its painted black fingernails. He is very aware that she has moved closer to him. He watches a small seductive smile play about her lips as her hand strays up his arm.

'You're not just a pair of flashing fists, strong muscles. There is a brain there and that is unusual. To take over that drug consignment in such an efficient way does you great credit and is worthy of much respect.'

She is now very close to him. Despite himself, Kline can feel her sexual power. He has strayed once already this week. As casually as he can, although the words thicken in his throat, he simply says, 'You reckon?'

Lily places a long black-stockinged leg across his thigh. Her voice is a low, sultry purr.

'I do indeed. May I call you John?'

'You might.'

Kline puts his hand on her knee, feels the touch of nylon that always excites him. He lets his hand wander to where the bare flesh of her inner thigh begins. He feels the slight ripple of welcome to his touch. Their faces are close together. Lily speaks softly but clearly.

'For various reasons, my daddy cannot afford the loss of that particular shipment. He has authorised me to offer you a fair price for the parcel you filched from the train.'

'Money?'

'Together with whatever else is required.'

They are now so close their noses almost touch, He looks down at the curve of her mouth. Lily smiles slightly, presses her tongue to her top lip as if tasting honey. Kline moves his hand inside the elastic of her stocking suspender. Lily's eyes widen, her pupils dilate. She breathes a question into his ear.

'What else might you require, John?'

He lifts the suspender lets it snap back hard against her thigh.

'Red Stick.'

Surprised, Lily pulls away. For a micro-second, there is a flash of the predator within. She regains her composure.

'For what purpose, pray?'

'Resurrection.'

72

Inside Anne's hospital room the green dots on the monitor screen race each other endlessly. The accompanying beeps signal that the heart of the unconscious woman continues to beat.

Her visitors are crowded into the small hospital room. Lily stands besides Red Stick on one side of the bed. Shen T'ang and Kline wait on the other. The Triad leader examines the brown paper parcel. He peers at a red wax seal and decides that it has not been tampered with. He tightens his grip on the package. Kline extracts it from him, places it alongside Anne. Says, firmly, 'No cure. No fee…'

They are interrupted by a middle-aged nurse who surveys the room with stern disapproval.

'This number of visitors contravenes hospital rules.'

Nobody moves.

'Do I have to call Sister?'

No reply.

'There just isn't enough room for you all. I really must insist—'

Lily Li T'ang turns on the nurse.

'Oh, for God's sake woman, shut up!'

The voice of the nurse rises in response.

'Out. Out! Two may stay, two must go. Or would you prefer I call security?'

Before Lily can retort in kind, her father intervenes.

'So sorry, nurse, we will withdraw. Lily, please do as I ask.'

Lily gives the nurse a look of contempt as she sweeps from the room.

Shen T'ang goes to the end of the bed, glances from Kline to Red Stick then back towards Anne. He bows in her direction before withdrawing from the room.

Left alone Kline and Red Stick regard each other, warily. Finally, Kline breaks the silence.

'Shall we push on?'

Moving towards the patient, Red Stick rolls back the sheet, begins to unfasten Anne's hospital gown. His action brings a warning growl from Kline.

'Hey…'

Red Stick reaches inside the gown, detaches the two monitoring pads. The machine squawks in protest. Red Stick hurls them away. The screen goes dead.

With the bed a barrier between himself and the Triad enforcer, Kline feels his mouth go dry. This guy could kill Anne, try to heist the pack of cocaine. He tenses. Any outcome is possible.

Red Stick raises his arms. His fingers resemble talons. He hovers over the length of Anne's body, gathers his inner power. For a few seconds, Red Stick remains unmoving before going in for the kill. One hand delves deep into his victim's solar plexus, the other presses against the nerve centre of her neck.

Every part of John Kline wishes to halt the contact, but he knows, dangerous as the process is, it is the only chance for Anne to return to him.

After a minute of intense fusion, Red Stick steps away. Another thirty seconds pass without response before Anne sighs, shudders, arches her back, locks into a spasm of violent inner upheaval before she falls back. Still unconscious, she begins to pant, heaving, sucking, sobbing with the effort of filling her lungs.

Just as it seems she cannot possibly breathe any faster, the frantic rhythm begins to slow down markedly, until she hardly seems to be breathing at all. Kline is just about to call for help when Anne releases a long shuddering moan. Her eyelids flutter and finally open. She blinks, looks around at a scene from a black and white movie. A room in a hospital, with a sinister Fu Manchu guy, and someone else. Who? She peers at the stranger as colour floods back into her inner world. She holds out her hand. Kline takes it. She struggles to speak.

'Oh... I waited so long. I looked everywhere for you, but the wood was too dark.'

As Kline hugs her to him, Red Stick lifts the parcel of drugs and glides from the room.

At the same time as Anne Darracott is experiencing her resurrection, incoming passengers are leaving the arrival section of Elmdon airport. Amongst them are two men, walking side by side. Khan tugs his prisoner in the direction of two uniformed police officers who are waiting to greet them on the airport terrace. The man in the creased white suit rubs his wrists, trying to ease where the handcuffs chafe his skin. Aslam Rafiq gazes into the distance, watches a large black bird fly slowly across the grey sky.

73

Two days later Anne and Kline emerge from the hospital like two naughty children released from school. They hug and kiss, then kiss some more before hurrying, arm in arm, into the car park. They skip past a parked ambulance. Kline unlocks his black Avenger, they both pile in.

'Where'd you like to go?' he asks.

'Anywhere, everywhere, bit of green countryside. But stay away from dark woods.'

Behind the steering wheel of the stolen ambulance, wearing a driver's uniform, Red Stick watches the black saloon pull out of its parking space. He lifts a walkie-talkie to his lips, speaks in Cantonese.

'Stand by.'

Kline is just about to pull out of the car park when a DAF lorry, heavily loaded with the trunks of trees, crosses ahead of him. He slots in behind, glances into his rear mirror. An ambulance is now driving close behind them.

Soon the suburbs of Birmingham are behind them. They are driving along green lanes, between open fields. Kline frowns, impatient at being held up by the lorry ahead. He tries to overtake but the lorry swerves to prevent his manoeuvre.

The ambulance starts to tailgate him. With growing alarm, Kline tries to assess the danger. Ahead of him, protruding from the rear of the lorry, are heavy tree trunks capable of decapitating them both. The ambulance thuds into the Avenger, reducing the space, eliminating the option to swerve away.

Boxed in, Kline frantically tries to escape, to reduce his speed. There is no option but to keep driving forward.

From behind the driving wheel of the ambulance Red Stick gives the order to execute his plan via intercom.

Inside the cab of the lumber lorry, the Chinese driver replies, 'OK. Fall back. Doing it now!'

He stamps on the brakes. The wheels of the heavy truck lock and squeal in protest.

Close behind, Kline tries to swerve but it is all too late. The heavy logs clear the bonnet of his car and hurtle, like so many battering rams, towards the windscreen. Petrified, Anne sees death rushing towards them…

To be continued…

BOOK FOUR
DOUBLE PERIL

74

Through the ambulance intercom, Red Stick gives the order to execute his plan for Kline's destruction.

Inside the cab of the lumber lorry, the Chinese driver replies, 'OK. Fall back. Doing it now!'

He stamps on the brakes. The lorry skids to a halt.

Close behind, Kline tries to brake but it is all too late. The heavy logs clear the bonnet of the car and hurtle, like so many battering rams, towards the windscreen. Petrified, Anne sees death rushing towards them...

Kline reaches for the auto switch that releases the seat position. A split second before the tree trunks smash into the windscreen and shear through the upper structure of the car, the couple are lowered into a horizontal position. Anne yells with pain as a coil of twisted steel scrapes across her upper arm. Kline, entangled in roofing and showered with glass, is pressed against her.

'Anne, Anne, you OK?'

'I'm alive, if that's what you mean.'

Her voice is trembling with shock. Kline feels the stickiness of the warm blood running down her arm.

'How bad is the cut?'

'I'll live.'

'Close your eyes. Time to play dead.'

'What?'

'Do it. Do it now.'

Outside the wrecked car, Red Stick and the driver approach and peer into the interior of the mangled Avenger. They see two inert bodies lying side by side, covered in fragments of glass. The woman has a bloodied arm thrown across the chest of her companion. Neither moves. Or breathes. Red Stick nods his satisfaction at a job well done. The driver points towards the inert bodies.

'Fucking round-eyed bastards.'

They both return to the truck. The engine of the DAF starts up. As the Chinese prepare to leave the wrecked car and the stolen ambulance behind, John Kline hauls himself from the wreckage of his car, scrambles up onto a lower log and clambers up towards the top tier of tree trunks on the loaded lorry.

The vibration of the powerful engine reverberates through the wooden trunks, shaking Kline as the truck drives away from what could have been the scene of his death.

Left behind in the Avenger, Anne sits up and looks out from where the windscreen used to be. She groans in disbelief as she sees her man climb aboard the truck, his figure briefly silhouetted against the summer sky. She moans, 'John…' Looks down at the blood oozing from her arm, feels a wave of pain from the torn expanse of skin. She lies back along the length of the seat, cradles her injured arm, begins to cry.

Lying amongst the trunks, the wind tugging at his hair, Kline can smell the scent of pine resin. The truck rumbles along, going deeper into the countryside.

After a little while they round a bend, bump onto a deserted side road that leads to a distant farm. From his vantage point Kline can see, in the distance, a farmer operating a muck spreading machine.

John Kline feels the truck begin to slow down. Ahead of them lies a parked red Ford Granada saloon. The DAF rumbles to a halt. He hears the cab door open below. He ducks out of sight as Red Stick and a burly Chinese man, wearing green overalls, leave the truck.

Kline lifts his head just in time to see the driver chuck the keys to the stolen lorry away to the side of the road. Red Stick, neat in his black ambulance uniform and shiny shoes, settles himself in the passenger seat of the Granada, waits for his henchman to join him. When he does so, the red saloon car drives away, leaving the truck and its cargo of lumber behind.

Seconds later, John Kline retrieves the keys to the DAF truck from the side of the road.

As they drive along Red Stick wonders what his next assignment will be. This last one has not been one to enhance his reputation, but it's over, the troublesome Mister Kline has been eliminated. At that moment of satisfaction, Red Stick glances into the side mirror and sees a truck loom into view. Behind the wheel sits a familiar figure back from the dead. A ghost, a demon spirit? Red Stick punches the driver's arm.

'Faster, go faster.'

The red Ford accelerates away down the quiet country road.

Seeing his quarry speed away, Kline curses the slow response of the heavily laden lorry. The car ahead takes a bend and disappears from his sight.

Slowing to take the bend safely leads to the sight of a herd of cows lumbering towards him. Marooned in the middle of the bovine bunch is a static Ford Granada. The driver abandons the vehicle when he sees Kline heading towards him. He vaults a wooden fence and disappears into a leafy wood. Red Stick follows, quickly overtaking the lumbering man in the heavy green overalls.

The driver is not someone who takes a great deal of exercise away from the wheel. He can hear his pursuer crashing through the bushes behind him. He pants towards the crest of a rise, dares not pause to look behind or study ahead. He loses his footing, slithers down a bank and ends up face down in a fast-moving stream. He attempts to rise but is shoved back underwater by a foot using his body as a stepping stone. When he shakes the water from his eyes, he sees the back of John Kline chasing after bigger game.

Coming out of the wood there is only a short run to reach a farmyard surrounded by sheds for cattle, storage and, by the sound of clucking and squawking, a shed full of caged poultry. Parked around are various items of farm machinery, tractors, a mini JCB, a bulldozer with a bale-lifting fork attachment.

Standing next to a slurry pit, Kline can smell the results of a season of livestock excrement. He looks around for any clue as to the whereabouts of the assassin Red Stick.

He is just about to search elsewhere when a sickening blow to the base of his skull sends him down on his knees. Trying to recover he feels a kick to his kidneys that thrusts him face down with a 'SPLAT!' into the pit of slurry. Spitting out liquid excrement, Kline feels the shit seep into his clothes. He rises, claws away the crud from his eyes, peers around, sees a door closing in the nearby poultry shed. Dripping crap as he goes, Kline limps across the yard, determined that this will be the last encounter between Red Stick and himself. Only one of them will survive this final round.

After sidling past the hens trapped in their cages, Red Stick prepares for battle. He sheds his clothes as he goes, stripping himself to the waist. Placing his shoes on a wooden crate full of eggs waiting to be shipped to market, Red Stick listens, hears the door open and close, causing an increase of noisy expectation from the poultry population.

The trail of abandoned clothes takes John Kline to a pair of shiny black shoes placed neatly on a long wooden box. Before he realises this is a trap he is leapt on from above. He crashes onto the wooden crate, which gives way under his weight, mixing egg yolk with the blood and shit already staining his suit. He fends off his attacker with a quickly raised knee but gains only a limited respite. Under a rain of blows and kicks Kline is forced back into a wall of hay bales stacked together ready for storage.

Red Stick launches a final attack. Kline counters, grabs his opponent's arm and throws him onto the wall behind. Red Stick counters with a kick to the solar plexus, follows it up with a backhand chop to the throat. Kline reels back, sinks down into the bales of hay. Red Stick backs a few steps away, makes ready to launch his speciality, a death kick to Kline's throat.

Exhausted, struggling to regain his feet, Kline grasps at the straw and feels his hand fasten onto a roll of netting used to hold together the bales.

Red Stick launches himself, Kline hurls the loosened roll of netting. Rolling aside, Kline sees the net entangle the assassin. Red Stick struggles to free himself, stumbles out into the farmyard, leans against the metal railings of a fence, frantically plucking away the netting. He has almost succeeded in freeing himself when he hears a motor rev into life across the farmyard. A bulldozer, its lifting spikes extended, rumbles towards him. Red Stick realises he is trapped, and from the expression on the man driving the spikes towards him, knows there will be no mercy. Red Stick's final thought is that death is fitting when you lose to the better man. Then all thought ceases as the prongs of steel stab into his chest.

75

Deep inside the HQ of the Midlands police force, Khan releases the handcuffs that have linked him to his prisoner. Rafiq rubs the inflamed skin on his wrist and stares in puzzlement at his captor, who is grinning at him.

'Does my predicament amuse you so much?' Rafiq asks.

Khan jingles the handcuffs together. His smile broadens.

'Did you really believe you were under arrest? A common criminal under extradition from Pakistan?'

'Then why the need for handcuffs?'

'I wanted to be sure of your companionship.'

The handcuffs are placed in a drawer. Khan seats himself behind his desk. Rafiq stands before him trying to assess the developing situation, to search for answers. Khan waits. Finally, Rafiq can wait no longer.

'Why bring me to this place of law enforcement?'

'To give you a choice. Information on a Triad gang might make me pause about proceeding with your passport offences.'

'Courts may fine or imprison but Triad gangsters inflict capital punishment on those who betray their secrets.'

'Oh, you'll be protected, even arrested if it is necessary to maintain your cover. Afterwards you will be released.'

Inspector Khan watches Rafiq wander around the office. The man in the white suit does not take long to make up his mind. He seats himself, leans forward, his usual assurance beginning to return.

'I could inform my Chinese friends that I've concluded my business abroad and am available for consultation.'

Khan pushes the telephone across his desk in reply. Rafiq wants to pick it up and hurl it at the head of his tormentor. He hides the impulse, although his words are tinged with resentment at Khan's manipulation.

'Very well, my dear Khan. I do not wish you to be a dagger at my jugular vein for evermore. I will re-establish contact with the Chinese gangsters, given the assurance that you will not besmirch my good name in future.'

'You have my word.'

Khan extends a hand of invitation towards the telephone. After a moment's reluctant pause, Rafiq picks up the receiver.

76

After several showers, John Kline decides the stink of slurry no longer hangs about him. Wearing a dressing gown, with a yellow bath towel slung around his neck, he is seated at a table in the deserted Nirvana restaurant, devouring a chicken curry and rice with some gusto. Watching him, seated around the small round table are Sarah Gant, flashily dressed in a red and white satin baseball top and sparkling red-rhinestone-encrusted trousers, and Anne, more soberly attired in a cream kaftan with brown braiding around the neckline. Her right arm is bandaged from wrist to elbow. Kline pauses to drink from a glass of Chablis. In the pause, Sarah brings up the obvious question.

'Did anyone see Red Stick suffer his "accident"?'

'No. It'll remain an unexplained tragedy.'

'The Triad guys will guess who is responsible.'

'Maybe, or perhaps they'll back off.'

'Don't count on it, John.'

'I won't.'

Anne listens to the casual exchange with growing anger. She leans forward, stares with disbelief across the table.

'They attacked us. We escaped decapitation by a microsecond. Why did you leave me to face the police on my own?'

'What did the law say?' Kline asks.

'They'll look into it.'

'Oh yeah?'

Kline pushes his plate away. Anne stares at him.

'Why did you run after the Chinese? Why?'

Her voice trembles with hurt and anger. Kline is in no mood to explain or apologise.

'Because your way doesn't work, Annie. You want me to keep my head down. Well, baby, I need to tell you something, I'm tired of being a target for those Triad bastards.'

'Why not remove the target?'

Their eyes focus on each other. Anne's voice softens.

'Let's cut our losses, John. Up and off. Let's do it... Please.'

'We can't. Not yet. We have obligations.'

He glances at Sarah. She nods in acknowledgement of the debt. Anne picks up on the unspoken acknowledgement.

'Obligations. What obligations? Sarah?'

Sarah Gant looks steadily across the table, a gambler about to show her cards.

'I gave John the information and the means to hijack the consignment of snow. It was something for him to barter so Red Stick could return you to the land of the living. In order for him to hijack the parcel of cocaine, I had to put my job on the line.'

'Job? You mean, here?'

'I have another job.'

Kline takes over the narrative.

'Sarah works for the US Drug Enforcement Agency.'

It takes Anne a few seconds to register this information.

'Oh, that's nice...'

'I've even got a badge to prove it,' Sarah adds.

Inside Anne, a searing anger takes over.

'What a pity you didn't show it to me before now!'

Before an argument can ensue, Kline jumps in, trying to head off trouble.

'We have to help Sarah. Least we can do after what she did for us. There's a meeting with Yan tonight. I've agreed to go with her as back up.'

Looking from one to the other, Anne senses a bond between them that wasn't there before. The DEA agent becomes all business.

'Khan will be back in operation soon. If I'm to get the goods on Yan before he does, I need to get my agency to release enough of the green stuff to instigate a sale.'

She stands, places a hand on Kline's shoulder.

'See you tonight.'

Watching Sarah Gant stride away, full of confidence and purpose, sends Anne deeper into a growing depression. Kline takes out his cigarettes, offers her one. She shakes her head. He lights up, inhales, looks across at her.

'Everything OK?'

In reply, all he gets is a long bitter sigh.

'Talk to me, Annie.'

'Everything's great. I've been asleep for a hundred years. Just been lacerated during a car wreck. Just discovered I'm still lost in a dark wood, a long way from home.'

Her voice trails away, dark thoughts emerging like wood demons to torment her. After a strained pause, Kline offers her a lifeline.

'Annie, you're home now.'

'I wouldn't say that.'

She stands, leaves him alone at the table. He watches as she walks away from him, her shoulders hunched, head bowed as if expecting further blows to fall.

77

The home of Shen T'ang is an oasis of Chinese tradition placed in the heart of Edgbaston. The décor of the room displays crimson wallpaper embossed with golden dragons, pink tiling, red carpet, cabinets with decorated panels depicting trees in blossom. Lamps hang from the ceiling casting soft light onto a wide low table.

Seated on ample brocade cushions Shen T'ang presides over the crisis meeting. On his right hand, a worried Yan waits for his leader to decide their next move. Both men wear business suits, with neat collars and quiet ties. Opposite to Yan, long legs curled beneath her, sits Lily Li T'ang, impatient with her father's dilatory ways. Finally, she can stand the indecision no longer. She slaps her hand on the tabletop.

'It is against all reason to linger here.'

There is no response. She reacts, anger and fear driving her words.

'We'll be held responsible for the death of Red Stick. Even now, another of the assassin category 426 may be on his way here to inflict punishment on us all.'

The frown lines on the forehead of Mr Yan deepen.

'The mad dog who kills under the name Double Petal.'

Lily has a chilling thought.

'Or his master, White Devil.'

A frost of apprehension descends. Yan struggles to dismiss the prospect.

'Surely the ending of our insignificant lives would not merit his direct employment.'

A thump on the door from outside makes them all believe that the master of assassins is about to pay them a call. They exchange looks of apprehension. Finally, Shen T'ang points a trembling finger at Yan and then in the direction of the door.

Manfully, Yan pulls himself upright and walks unwillingly towards the door. Is it his imagination or can he detect a whiff of sulphur in the air? He springs the catch, steps out of the line of fire. Rafiq steps into the room surrounded by a haze of smoke. He puffs on his pipe. Everything about him oozes confidence: his pink cashmere overcoat slung casually about his shoulders, his freshly cleaned white suit designed to dispel any thoughts that he might be a traitor to their cause. Shen T'ang has no such thoughts. He calls out a warm greeting.

'Ah, Mister Rafiq.'

'Mister T'ang.'

Watching the Asian leader bow to her father Lily tries to recall the last act of the romantic charade she had indulged in with the chubby Asian. She decides she really can't be bothered to maintain the pretence.

Shen T'ang smiles at his visitor.

'How was your trip?'

'Oh, quite hectic, you know, lots of chasing around.'

He takes in where Lily is seated. Her black sleeveless top, blue satin pants and black boots all raise the beat of his heart. He takes the opportunity to seat himself beside her. Lily promptly stands and moves away. She stares down at him, haughty and indifferent.

'To what do we owe the honour of your esteemed presence?'

'I come to pay my sincere respects to you and your father.'

'We don't have time for such niceties anymore.'

Shen T'ang intervenes before his daughter can reveal too much of the danger that threatens them all.

'Lily, let us just say we would welcome an alternative view. Mr Rafiq may help us find a solution to our problems.'

Lily folds her arms, glowers in turn at all three men seated around the table. Shen T'ang addresses their visitor.

'Mr Rafiq, we may have a chance to redress our fortunes through a meeting with a woman buyer.'

'Do you know her name?'

'Mrs Sarah Gant.'

Thoughts racing, Rafiq nods.

'I know her.'

'Is she trustworthy?'

Time to endorse the deal.

'She is no lover of the law.'

This seems to placate some of the fears of Shen T'ang. Some, but not all. He continues to ponder.

'If you can vouch for her that is of some significance. Though why an American should know of our operation is the cause of my concern.'

Yan wears a look of brooding anxiety. Lily waves a puff of pipe smoke away as if it were a plague of locusts. Shen T'ang ruminates. Rafiq waits for an outcome to emerge. Finally, a decision is reached by the leader of the Hong Ming Triad.

'I am tempted to favour a meeting with Mrs Gant. She has agreed to pay a high price for our goods. She also promises to pay well for future shipments, using Britain as a pipeline to America. Such prospects would diminish the scale of disasters that have occurred under my leadership.'

Lily stamps a booted foot.

'We have no time for this! It may well be a trap. We must disappear abroad, Daddy. Malaysia, Singapore, anywhere until the dust of this debacle settles.'

Shen T'ang speaks slowly and sadly.

'Lily, we have no choice but to cast the dice. Our hope must be that they fall favourably, allowing us to avert dishonour, disgrace, death.'

In a low voice, heavy with concern, Yan speaks directly to Shen T'ang.

'To gamble with money is recreation. With freedom, life itself, that is madness. I not only think of my safety but of yours.'

The two men exchange long looks that convey their deep respect for each other. Rafiq reaches a solution to his own dilemma. How to fulfil his promise to Khan and protect his interests for the future safety of Lily Li T'ang. He knocks the dead ashes of his pipe into an ashtray. The sound draws attention to him. In tones of silk and satin he makes his play.

'Might I suggest that I accompany Mr Yan to wherever the meeting is to be held and assist in the exchange of goods and currency. You, Mr T'ang, together with your lovely daughter, could remain in a position of safety with all routes of escape still open to you.'

With a bow, Shen T'ang acknowledges the wisdom of the strategy.

'Truly, a man's fortune lies in the love of his friends. Thank you, Aslam, for your most valuable contribution. My decision is made. Yan, you will attend the meeting tonight. Mr Rafiq will accompany you.'

Yan stares with distrust at the urbane Asian. Rafiq's hands, out of sight beneath the table, sweat, his fingers intertwined with tension. Above the table his look is one of unconcern. Lily assesses the situation. She soon sees where her advantage lies.

'Yan, my father is still head of what remains of the Hong Ming.'

Yan turns his gaze towards Shen T'ang, his expression sombre.

'I have been loyal, Shen T'ang. In this, as in everything, I obey. But should I fail to fulfil my mission, I beg you, do not stay or hope for mercy from those who hold the power.'

Shen T'ang's response is a solemn one.

'We must cast the dice. I will accept how they fall.'

78

Seated on the settee in their apartment Anne watches Sarah Gant carefully pack wads of fifty pound notes into a plastic takeaway meal container. The phone rings out. Anne stretches to pick up the receiver. Sarah takes it from her as Kline comes in from the bedroom. Sarah answers the caller.

'I know it. There'll be two of us, OK?'

The phone goes dead. The DEA agent looks across at Kline.

'The deal's on.'

'I'll get my coat.'

He goes back into the bedroom. Anne hesitates then follows. Inside she watches him start to put on his fawn raincoat.

'Don't go.'

'My acting as back up to Sarah squares the account.'

'Does it? She'll be just like Khan. Using you for one favour then blackmailing you into another.'

Sarah stands in the doorway.

'Ready?'

A wave of unease sweeps through Anne. She feels threatened by the intrusion.

'Why do you need him? Why not get back up from the boys in blue?'

'What I'm about to do is outside the UK law. Time to go, John baby.'

She leaves the couple alone. Kline is impatient to get on with the night's events. Anne tries to hold him back.

'I've a bad feeling about this. Stay with me, now, tonight.'

'I made a deal. We owe Sarah.'

'Do we?'

'Yes. So far, you've said nothing positive, not even thanks. Not to me, not to Sarah.'

'Thanks for what?'

'For your life.'

'Oh, that…'

She gives a small shrug of indifference, sits on the bed, plucks at the bandage on her right arm. Frowning with annoyance, Kline turns and leaves.

Anne lies back on the bed, hugs her kaftan around her, closes her eyes. Now the waiting begins. Waiting for the call to say your man is hospital, paralysed by a bullet in his spine. Or that he's on a charge for murder. Or 'Can you help us identify the body of John Kline?'

'Oh, for fuck's sake, I can't stand this anymore!'

She jumps from the bed begins to tear at her clothes, strips to her underwear. Goes to a drawer in her dressing table, takes out a razor blade, looks down at it for a long time before she puts it away. She takes out a black dress from the wardrobe, slips it on, looks at herself in a long mirror, imitates greeting an imaginary customer with a welcoming smile.

'Hello, how are you? Welcome to Nirvana.'

79

Yan's fist raps on the grey wooden door. Once, twice, once again. Standing behind the second in command of the Hong Ming, Rafiq presses tobacco down into the bowl of his pipe. He is just about to light up when a panel slides open in the upper part of the door. The surly face of a young Chinese looks them over. The panel slides shut, followed by the drawing of bolts, allowing the rickety door to swing open. Yan gestures for Rafiq to follow him into the Noh Wei laundry.

Yan walks between bundles of washing into a dreary rectangular room with a long table scattered with steam irons. Rafiq follows. The young Chinese wastes no time. He immediately unlocks a wall cupboard and presents Yan with the sealed package that contains freshly laundered shirts and a quantity of high-grade cocaine. As Yan inspects the seal, a signal knock is heard on the outside door. Yan points. The young worker hurries to answer the call. Yan and Rafiq move behind a steam press, out of sight of their visitors.

Sarah Gant and John Kline are ushered in. Sarah, brightly dressed in her designer baseball top and sparkly red trousers, stands out vividly against the grey-painted walls. She carries a plain brown carrier bag. Kline looks around for danger, tenses as Yan and Rafiq appear. Kline is surprised to see the Asian community leader. Rafiq gestures with his pipe in friendly acknowledgement.

No words are exchanged between the quartet. None are necessary. Sarah takes out the takeaway container, strips off the foil, shows Yan the currency inside. Yan slides his parcel across the table as the box of money is delivered to him. Sarah starts to rip open the parcel, Yan to count the money.

A splintering crash is heard as the outside door shatters. Shouts are heard, together with pounding footsteps. Kline moves to protect Sarah. Yan tries to hide the money from view as the laundry room fills with half a dozen armed police officers. They surround the table. The last person to enter is Zahir Khan. He enjoys his slow advance to the table. Once there he relieves Sarah of the drug consignment.

'Check mate, Mrs Gant.'

80

Seated behind his desk Khan watches calmly as Sarah Gant rages around his office.

'You son of a bitch, you've screwed my whole operation!'

'You were caught purchasing Class A drugs, Mrs Gant.'

'Oh, come on!'

'Mr Yan says that was the purpose of your meeting.'

'I was about to nail him as a dealer. You weren't around to help.'

'But Mister Kline was.'

Sarah stops pacing. Khan gets to his feet like a lawyer about to lay his case before the jury.

'In the car returning here, Mr Yan was quite talkative. I asked him where the drugs had come from, he gave me quite a surprising answer. John Kline.'

'What is this?'

'When those drugs were originally stolen on their way to London, I was made to look a fool, not only to my superiors in the West Midlands but to the London drug squad.'

He pauses, trying to hold down his anger against the woman who stares back at him defiantly.

'I believe you must have told Kline of my plans for the movement of the cocaine. I believe he was the one who intercepted the courier provided by Rafiq. You employed Kline to thwart me and to claim a success to show your bosses in America.'

'That's your theory.'

'There is enough evidence to raise charges against you.'

'How will you do that? Kline won't talk, Rafiq likewise. Yan's words, if he spoke them, are worthless, he'd say anything to wriggle off the hook.'

'You went behind my back. Co-operation between our agencies meant nothing. I'm ready to charge you with illicit drug dealing, Mrs Gant.'

Sarah laughs derisively.

'Are you crazy? My agency will make such a blast you'll need a fallout shelter to hide in. You've no case. My word against Yan's. I was about to arrest him when you jumped us.'

'Maintain what you like, Mrs Gant. I intend to prove otherwise.'

'You'll need an independent witness to stand any chance of having me indicted.'

'Yes, someone who was part of the planning but not directly involved. I wonder who that could be?'

Khan turns away from her. He has just seen another move he can make. His ill-temper ebbs away into cold calculation. Sarah finds his calm demeanour more worrying than his anger. She attempts to shore up her position.

'Kline won't help you. Rafiq knows next to nothing about me.'

'Yes, probably.'

'So, who else can support your case?'

A smile appears on the face of Zaheer Khan.

81

Anne is just about to go to bed when she hears a crash against the door downstairs. She pulls on her white kaftan and heads for the stairs, only to be overwhelmed my three uniformed policemen and a woman in plain clothes brandishing a warrant card at her.

'What's going on?'

The woman cop pushes Anne back into the bedroom, shoves her against the bed, forces Anne face down against the coverlet. Feeling the woman's hands run over her body sends Anne into a frantic struggle to break free. She sits up and sees, all around her, bedroom drawers being pulled open, their contents searched and scattered. A burly cop grips the mattress and turns it over, depositing Anne onto the floor. The woman detective grabs her by the arm and marches her towards the door. Anne jerks free.

'Where are you taking me?'

'Someone wants to see you.'

'I can walk downstairs on my own, OK?'

When Anne reaches the bottom of the stairs, she sees a light at a solitary table in the darkened restaurant. Seated there is Inspector Khan. Anne curls her lip as the raid begins to make some sense.

'Why it's Mister Nice Guy, the bloke everyone hates.'

The woman cop pushes Anne towards the table. Khan looks at her enquiringly.

'Anything?' he asks the woman officer.

'Nothing, except for this.'

She tosses a small pill bottle to her boss, who catches it and studies the label. Watching Khan holding her lifeline seems the ultimate intrusion. Anne tries to hold her panic in. She assumes a cool manner she is far from feeling.

'That's mine. Prescription Methadone. Check if you like. This bitch here, she on the suppository squad?'

Khan stands. Anne is bundled towards him. He catches her, pushes back the sleeves of her kaftan, searches for tell-tale track marks. Failing to find any he jerks his chin for his assistant to act. Anne feels her hair pulled painfully from behind, forcing her head back. She closes her eyes, but they are soon forced open and the light from a pencil torch shone into each in turn. When there is no reaction to the light she is released. Trying to regain some dignity, Anne tosses a few bitter words towards the main intruder.

'Life's full of little surprises, isn't it?'

'The weaning process is not a cure.'

'But it's within the law.'

'As you say.'

'Look, Khan, what is all this?'

'Drugs. Cocaine. We are holding a group for questioning. Mr John Kline, Mr Aslam Rafiq, Mr Robert Yan, Mrs Sarah Gant.'

'But not old Annie, right? You've nothing on me, pal.'

Khan makes no response. Anne turns away from him. Khan's manner becomes more demanding. His voice takes on a sharper edge.

'Mrs Gant works here. You know who and what she is.'

'What if I do?'

'I need an independent witness to support me against Mrs Gant and to prove she planned to make an illegal purchase of Class A drugs.'

Anne laughs, incredulously.

'You can't mean me?'

'Why not, don't you wish to vent a little spite, Miss Darracott?'

'You been at the orange juice or what? The only spite I'd want to vent is at you.'

In the pause that ensues Khan and Anne regard each other. The agent of the law and his victim. Khan decides to go in for the kill.

'Your man and Mrs Gant, during your stay in hospital, their relationship was far from platonic.'

'What?'

'Not all of your staff are on your side. A sexual relationship between the pair has been reported to me.'

'Who would say such a thing?'

'Someone no longer in your employ.'

Rapidly recalling the staff register leaves only one possibility.

'Do you mean the kid who played the sitar? He's the only one who has left.'

'To study in India, I believe.'

'With your blessing?'

'Musicians see a great deal of what goes on before them. The boy was quite disgusted to see Mrs Gant make a play for your man. A play that succeeded.'

Anne absorbs the toxic information. She concentrates all her hurt and anger on the smooth talking cop before her. She saunters up to him, gazes up into his unsmiling face.

'Fuck off.'

'You can reach me anytime.'

'Just your throat would be enough.'

82

It is well past midnight when Rafiq returns to the haven of his home. Weary of heart and uneasy at allowing himself to be coerced by Khan, he needs a nightcap and some restorative slumber. Rafiq enters the dimly lit Edwardian-styled living room.

To his surprise, when visiting the drinks trolley, he finds his best bottle of Hennessy five-star brandy completely empty. He gazes around at the disarray of the normally elegant room. Empty glasses, a plate with the remains of a half-eaten fruit cake. What has been going on? Then he hears a snuffle and a snore and looks down at a figure stretched in sleep on the Bergere settee. Rafiq slams down the empty bottle angrily. The impact causes the sleeping intruder to struggle back to consciousness. Rafiq blinks unbelievingly at the person he sees.

'Kuldip?'

The stocky Asian sighs, sits up, brushes crumbs from his charcoal grey suit. Adjusting his turquoise shirt with its matching tie, he reaches for a brandy glass three quarters full of Benedictine. He helps himself to a corona-corona cigar, puts his feet on the low glass-topped table and contemplates his former master with unfeigned arrogance.

'Good morning. Welcome to your home and mine, Mr Rafiq. How nice it is to have my freedom and to see you here.'

Kuldip picks up the table lighter, tries to get it to light several times. When no flame appears, he hurls it and the cigar away from him. He grabs a handful of ice from a bucket and furiously crams it into his drink. He leers up at Rafiq, who, dazed, requires a further moment to come to terms with the fractured syntax of his unwelcome visitor.

'How was 'Pindi? Does the excremental smell linger like the last bad breath of spring still?'

'Why are you no longer rotting within the confines of your prison cell, Kuldip?'

His question is met by a snigger merging rapidly into a chortle.

'Got friends in high places, me. They say, "Dear Kuldip, mate, let's unlay the injustice done unto you." So me, I say if you do, I return favour gladly. So I'm out of my cell. I'm given freedom and the role of watchdog. Grrrrr!'

'What?'

'I watch your every move, Mr Rafiq! Every time you visit the little boy's room will be noted on my report...'

Rafiq glares at him.

'Report? To whom do you report?'

Almost immediately the answer comes to him.

'Ah, of course, Khan. It was you who brought about my swift return from Pakistan. Many, many thanks, Kuldip.'

He bows with a brief ironic flourish before the heat of his anger takes him over.

'There are words for people like you. Turncoat! Traitor! Nark! Rat! Scum!'

Kuldip giggles as each word is hurled towards him. When his glee subsides, he points at his former boss.

'You much better back here in Brum so I can keep a big beady eye on you.'

Rafiq gropes his way towards a chair, sits, holds his head in his hands.

'I used to enjoy my life. Oh, go get me a cup of tea, Kuldip, please, like a good chap.'

'Get it your bloody self, Mr Rafiq, sir cock!'

83

Her thoughts in turmoil, Anne Darracott busies herself trying to restore her bedroom to something like normality. After order is restored, although it is the middle of the night, she decides to get dressed in a mauve two-piece suit. After that, she pulls out a suitcase and begins to pack a selection of her clothes. She is halfway through packing when the door opens behind her. John Kline enters. He takes in Anne as she kneels at the foot of the bed, folding clothes, placing them in an open suitcase before her.

'What's up?'

'Amongst other things, a visit from the drug squad. They turned a few things over.'

He comes to her, places a hand on her back, caresses her.

'Leave it. Let's get some kip.'

Anne tries to ignore the touch of his hand, steels herself.

'I think if I fill this suitcase and make the catches go click, that means I should go. Leave.'

She steals a quick glance up at him. He frowns, takes his hand away. Sits on the bed.

'That time, is it?'

After a painful pause, he continues.

'Who took charge of the raid?'

'Mister face-and-charm.'

'Khan? They find anything?'

Anne resumes her packing, folding a blouse and thrusting it into the suitcase.

'There's no need to ask. You know there's nothing to find.'

She packs several more items before she reveals her main source of hurt.

'Mr Khan wanted me to implicate you. He thought he had a big lever. He said that you and Sarah G have been making two-backed black and white beasties. Here in this very room.'

Kline's look away tells her all she needs to know. She transfers a pile of underwear into her case.

'I told him to vacate the premises. I said… I said he couldn't touch me with his lies.'

She stands, faces him full on. Kline looks up at her.

'I'll deny it if you want.'

'Tell me nothing. Is that what you and Sarah decided?'

Her anger brings Kline to his feet, he steps in close to her, his tone more forceful than pleading.

'There was nothing to decide. I mean nothing, not from me. Sex, that's all. Two bodies in need. Hers more than mine. She's a pretty determined lady.'

'Oh, rape, was it?'

'I needed her information, something to bargain with. Something to save you. She gave me the information. I hijacked a drug parcel, arranged to return it if that assassin bloke brought you back to life. I chose the obvious way to reach Sarah Gant, but that's just me.'

'Yes, it seems so, yes.'

She starts to close her suitcase. Kline reaches across to stop her. She resists, stands, breaks away from his touch.

'Why, why do it, you bastard?'

'Annie…'

'Stay away, don't touch me. I thought I could take everything you could serve up. Assault, crashes, drug squad, next door to death… All of that but you screwing Sarah. Screwing her right here, I can't take that.'

'It didn't happen in here.'

Anne laughs, bitterly.

'Oh, that's all right then.'

'One thing it did was lay the ghost of her sister.'

It takes a moment for Anne to understand.

'You came into her?'

'It finally happened. I'm no longer haunted by what happened to Dinah. I'll think about it, sure, but now I can move on.'

'You fucked her in a way you couldn't do with me. Bastard, bastard, *bastard!*'

She slams the lid of the case closed. Kline goes to her, pulls her into him.

'You know better than all this emotional one-man-one-woman crap.'

'No, John, I'm afraid I don't. I've started to see things differently. I've been wondering lately what Mr and Mrs Smith might get out of life.'

'The hope of what you're running out on?'

She holds his gaze for a long time then shakes her head.

'No.'

Anne reaches across and clicks the catches down on her suitcase. Kline makes a last appeal.

'Annie…'

'I want to find out what an ordinary life feels like. I need to find out, I really do.'

He is very close to her. He puts his arms around her. She does not respond to his embrace.

'Let me go. Please!'

Kline steps away. After a long moment, he lifts his hand towards the direction of the door. Anne picks up her suitcases, brushes his hand aside, hurries out of his life.

Left alone, Kline eases himself onto the bed. He lies back and stares up at the ceiling, trying to come to terms with what has just happened. His closing thought, before sleep overtakes him, is that something needs to be done about Mister fucking Khan.

84

The journey through the deserted streets of night-time Birmingham is an uncomfortable one. Anne, weary, empty of emotion, constantly needs to point out directions to the Asian taxi driver, who is so disoriented he must be one of Rafiq's illegal immigrants.

She brings the journey to an end at the bridge that leads down to the tow path, where she hopes to find her house barge, *Anne Carol*, untouched by vandals. As she walks alongside the dark waters of the canal, lit only by the light of a waning moon, her suitcase becomes a dead weight.

With some relief, she finds the craft unharmed, despite it having been a while since she last lived within its narrow confines. She turns the key in the padlock, detaches the chain, lowers herself down the steps into the kitchen area. Something cold and clammy brushes across her face. A tentacle wraps itself around her legs. About to give a squeal of terror, Anne gropes for the light switch. In the light, the alien space monster reveals its identity. She had forgotten a bag of potatoes and, left to their own devices, they have grown into a bunch of Triffids, spreading their pale tendrils in every direction.

'Give me a fucking break!' she yells, hacking the alien growths aside.

She pushes through a bead curtain into the main section of her living space. The air is musty, damp, cold. She shuffles to where her bed is waiting, an old friend. With only enough energy to shed her clothes, she curls up under the chill sheets and covers. Shivering and shaking, Anne waits for some warmth to steal over her.

She begins to remember her life when this barge was her means of distributing drugs via the inland waterways. Dropping packets of heroin, picking up stashes of money. Enjoying unlimited supply of the stuff that made life bearable. Other less pleasant fragments of memory flit across her mind. Her former boss, Rawlinson, forcing himself on her in this very bed. John Kline making her go cold turkey in his quest for information as to how the drugs were brought into the country.

'Bastards,' she mutters as, at last, she succumbs to sleep.

85

Watching the dawn light creep through Birmingham streets reminds Khan how tired he is. The night that started with all his cards in play has been a disappointing one. Without an independent witness, he has been forced to release not only Mrs Gant but also Rafiq and Kline. All that remains to him now is to continue to question the enigmatic Mr Yan.

He turns from the window, takes a swallow of lukewarm coffee, sits at his desk. Across from him, Yan sits impassively. Khan eases the police issue pistol from his shoulder holster, places it on the desk before him, resumes the interrogation.

'Your superiors within the Triad known as the Hong Ming—'

'Triad is the name you keep using, Mr Khan, what does it imply?'

'It implies that Shen T'ang, your leader, is in danger of elimination now that yet another venture ends in failure.'

Yan twists in his seat, half turning away from his questioner.

'Perhaps.'

'You have respect for him?'

'As a man, yes.'

'Not so much as your Triad leader?'

'What can I say?'

'You can tell me where I may find him. Bringing Shen T'ang in for questioning might allow him to enjoy a peaceful old age.'

'In a UK prison. Shen T'ang would rather die.'

Turning around to face Khan, Yan places his last card on the table.

'Mister Khan, you have kept me here long enough to alert all my friends. I am sure that by now they have made alternative arrangements to ensure their safety. Any information I can give will now be totally redundant.'

86

Kline wakes up mid-morning. There is someone in the room. For half a second he believes Anne might have quit her pursuit of 'normality'. He peers up at Sarah Gant, dressed in a smart fawn trouser suit with waistcoat, brown trilby hat, tinted glasses. Her manner is brisk, all business.

'I want to tell Anne those changes to the menu will have to wait. Where is she?'

'Departed. Your mate Khan marked her card about you and me.'

Sarah takes in the news, shrugs.

'Not much to fill in.'

'Yeah, as you say.'

Kline sits up, rubs his forehead, feels a dull throb of pain interfering with his thoughts. He focuses on the black woman standing before him. He remembers her naked, the warmth and wetness of her.

As if reading his mind, Sarah shifts her hip, tips her hat a little.

'So, where does that leave us?' she asks.

'Anywhere. Nowhere?'

'I have to fly to Paris, no doubt to receive a final warning from the head of the agency. "Produce the goods on the Triads or you know what will happen." '

'Back to whoredom and boredom?'

'Worse than that.'

'Jail time?'

'A lot of it.'

A pause. Kline tries to make light of the threat hanging over her.

'Well, Sarah, case we have to wait for a conjugal visit, how about coming to bed now.'

He pats the mattress invitingly. Sarah adjusts her glasses.

'Your timing's somewhat off, baby.'

'Story of my days.'

'Yeah.'

He watches her turn and go without even a fare thee well.

Kline lies back on the bed, the trace of a bitter smile on his lips. This has been the second woman in the last twelve hours to dish out the arse treatment. He doesn't like it. He does not like it at all.

87

Later that same morning, a few minutes before noon, Lily Li T'ang and her father sit at a table in a coffee shop that overlooks Victoria Square. Shen T'ang checks his watch, looks across at Lily. His eyes are sad, almost tearful.

'Lily, I am so sorry to leave you like this.'

'It is best to separate, safer that way.'

'I must believe it is.'

'It is time for you to go, Daddy. The car will be here soon.'

'Yes.'

Lily takes the lead, stands and moves ahead of him. Shen T'ang sighs, picks up his briefcase, follows his daughter out into the sunlit square.

Above them, concealed behind the ornate iron railings of a balcony alcove, a Chinese man, wearing a pinstripe suit, peers down at the couple. The young woman wears a rose-coloured shantung silk suit, the man a dark overcoat and a trilby hat. This must be the couple he has been waiting for. The assassin takes out a Glock 9mm pistol and begins to screw a silencer onto its barrel.

Standing on the lower steps of the town hall, Shen T'ang sees the limousine ordered to take him to the airport sweep into view. It purrs to a halt.

The Triad leader leaves Lily before he can change his mind. She reaches for him, but he is already on his way towards the sleek black car. As he hurries towards its safety, the town hall clock begins the first of its twelve strikes. At the first chime, a bullet strikes Shen T'ang between the shoulder blades. He falls on his face. His brief case flies open, wads of bank notes scatter on the concrete beside him.

Lily screams, 'Daddy!' She runs to his aid, turns his body over. Blood runs from his mouth. She sees the light die in her father's eyes as the last chime of the clock above the square fades into silence.

A strong hand grips her arm, pulls her to her feet. Lily stares into the face of the man who has just slain her father. He wears a black fedora with white edging. His eyes are hidden behind shades. Lily knows who the killer must be.

'Double Petal.'

88

Seated in the outer office of the Helen Bowden secretarial agency, Anne stares ahead, ready to begin a new life. She scans the opportunity board, reads the neat rows of cards offering temporary employment within the business community. She feels oddly detached, as if invisible in an alien world. The door of the inner office opens to allow an agency client to exit. This is it. Anne gets to her feet, ready to begin her quest for a fulfilling life amongst law abiding citizens.

Helen Bowden is a businesswoman in her late thirties. A brunette, she is dressed in a white shirt, brown skirt, a paisley cravat at her throat. She lowers her school ma'am glasses, the better to take in the appearance of her would be client. Helen likes what she sees. The woman seated opposite is fair haired, with the contained manner of a young Marlene Dietrich. Helen likes that. The two women regard each other before Helen refers to her notes.

'Anne Darracott?'

Her voice has authority, the result of conducting many interviews such as this. She reminds Anne of her Careers teacher back in school.

'Yes.'

'Typing speed?'

'What's good?'

'Well, that's for you to say.'

'Seventy-five?'

'Yes...'

Helen writes down the number on a file card.

'Shorthand?'

'Yes.'

'Salary required?'

'What's good?'

'The going rate?'

'Let's start with that.'

There is something unusual about Anne Darracott, Helen decides, difficult to place. Perhaps not, time will tell.

'Right, Miss Darracott, you have references and qualifications that can be produced if required?'

'If required.'

'Fine. No problem. We'll have you placed in no time. Plenty of work for temporary positions now. Welcome to my agency. Yes?'

'Yes.'

'I'm sure it will be a profitable arrangement for us both.'

'When do I start?'

'Wait outside, I'll make a few phone calls.'

89

The Nirvana is gratifyingly busy. The annual motor show is in town and the tables are full of salesmen and good-looking babes hired to bring allure to the product; buy a car like this and you can have a woman like me.

Even with Anne and Sarah missing, their staff training holds up. Dinners are being served to the customers within a reasonable time, drinks are flowing, refined piano music underscores the chatter. The owner of the restaurant couldn't care less. Seated at the end of the bar, he wears dress pants and a frilly white shirt. The rest of his evening attire lies untouched on the bed upstairs. Seated alongside him, Aslam Rafiq is more formally dressed in a black velvet jacket, white shirt, dark grey tie.

While Archie, the barman, attends to customers, they share a bottle of spirits. Both are determined not to become maudlin, but as the bottle of Johnnie Walker slowly empties their resolve ebbs away. Kline throws back his shot of whisky, western style, mutters to himself. Rafiq leans towards him, enquiringly.

'What was that, John?'

'I said, I didn't reckon on it, being run out on.'

'Ah, women. Only when they are lost to us does their true worth emerge.'

'Mine walked after I was ratted out by Mister bleedin' Khan.'

'Please don't mention that fellow to me. Do you know, he has installed that felon, Kuldip, in my home as a watchdog? To visit you tonight, I had to sneak out of my own house!'

Kline re-fills their glasses. Rafiq produces his gold cigarette case, offers cigarettes. They light up, inhale deeply. The Asian notices a bitter smile appear on Kline's craggy face.

'What is it, John?'

'Just a thought. If your watchdog caught rabies and sank his teeth into Khan, both our problems would be solved.'

'Ha... No, one mustn't laugh. Rabies is no laughing matter... Ha!'

They both burst into laughter. Rafiq tries to regain his composure.

'To be serious, just for a moment. One wouldn't wish rabies on one's worst enemy. No, no, no, I think a more humane method has to be devised if we are to be rid of the odious Mr Khan.'

'Let's drink to that.'

They clink glasses solemnly.

90

Inside the red room of Shen T'ang's home, Double Petal, dressed in his gangster garb, pinstripe suit, black shirt, white tie, sits reading a Hollywood fan magazine that has a bullet hole torn through the middle.

Lily Li T'ang stands across the room, leaning against a large slatted cabinet, weeping.

Double Petal's assistant, Lo, stands guard by the door.

Lowering his magazine, the Triad enforcer tosses a cigarette into his mouth. Lo hurries to light it for him.

'I bring you coffee now?' Lo asks.

Receiving the curtest of nods, Lo scurries from the room.

Lily's tears continue to flow. Her sobs increase in volume until Double Petal has heard enough. He jumps to his feet.

'Save the sob stuff, sister. Cry tomorrow. Right now, I need to figure how best to ice John Kline.'

Having learned English while working as a film projectionist in Hong Kong, his speech is influenced by the idiom of American gangster movies.

Lily turns away from the cabinet, her face wet with tears.

'He was my father!'

'Count yourself lucky to have known one. Me, all I had was a mom. Know what that makes me?'

'I'd have guessed, given time.'

Double Petal advances towards her.

'Time we don't have. You're in for the big squeeze, sister. The Wo Shing Wo will move in quicker than you can say Edward G. Robinson.'

'Not while breath remains in my body!'

Inadvertently, Lily has fed him a line from a movie. He takes off his shades, glares into her face.

'How long do you want to keep it in?'

He giggles with delight.

'Vince Edwards, *Murder by Contract*, 1959.'

'Stop this nonsense! When my father suffered disgrace, I asked to lead the Triad of the Hong Ming. Now he is dead I must restore the reputation of our name.'

'I love it when you snarl.'

'The organisation I build will have round-eyes in its ranks. I will mould them into a lethal force.'

'You're a good-looking dame. Why not settle for a cottage in the country and a nursery full of kids?'

'I'd sooner take the veil.'

'Wise up, what you're facing would make Al Capone pay his taxes.'

With a look of contempt, Lily tries to assert her position.

'Listen, you cretin, this is a matter of honour.'

She kicks a cushion out of her path. Lo brings in a tray with a pot of hot coffee, cups and saucers. He places them on the table and withdraws to stand guard at the door.

Double Petal sits, reaches for the coffee pot. His hand trembles, he looks up at Lily standing close by to him. He aches to become Lee Marvin in *The Big Heat*. To hurl the boiling coffee into Lily Li T'ang's arrogant face. Like Gloria Grahame she would remember him for the rest of her days. But there are other fish to fry, and he needs this bitch to turn on the gas. He pours the coffee into a cup, calms himself by spitting a few home truths in Lily's direction.

'Let me put you straight, doll. The Hong Kong syndicate have a deal going with a rogue cop here in Birmingham. Your buddy, Mr Yan, is about to sing like a canary to Mr Khan. When he does, you'll lead the sewing circle in the big house for the next seven to fourteen years. Savvy?'

Lily glares at the hit man. 'Yan will be silenced. Khan will be nullified. You will not kill Kline until I say so. Is that clear?'

Double Petal grins but makes no reply.

'Now I have things to do.'

Lily strides towards the door. Lo hesitates, then stands aside to let her through. Double Petal makes a sign that he should shadow Lily.

Left to himself, the mobster from Hong Kong tips back his fedora, eases back the jacket of his black pinstripe suit, reaches into his pocket, extracts a thin chain with a key attached. He swaggers over to the cabinet and inserts the key into the lock. The doors open onto a small shadowy room containing a chair on which sits a woman. Sarah Gant pops a marshmallow into her mouth and ducks out into the main room.

'I heard. Let's wish Lily baby lots of luck, shall we?'

'Yeah? Oh, yeah!'

Double Petal's grin grows into a wild burst of laughter.

91

Returning to his home, Rafiq feels in better spirits for sharing his troubles with John Kline. He enters the hallway and finds Khan's creature, Kuldip, waiting to greet him with his newly assumed arrogance.

'Where've you been, cock?'

'That is no business of yours.'

'Been keeping a lady waiting, haven't you?'

'What nonsense you talk, Kuldip.'

Rafiq gathers his camel hair coat around him and sweeps into the lounge. Standing with her back to him, a black coat draped over her drooping shoulders, is a familiar figure.

'Lily…?'

Lily Li T'ang turns, a picture of misery.

'Lost her father, her.' Kuldip points.

'Have you?'

'She says murder most foul done unto her dad.'

Rafiq, in a fury, attempts to bring Kuldip to heel.

'I dislike mistreating servants, but I will unless you leave us, right now!'

Kuldip tuts and mutters but does as he is ordered. Rafiq shrugs off his overcoat, trying to come to terms with the unexpected reappearance of a woman he believed lost to him. He approaches her cautiously.

'And why have you come back, my little gazelle?'

Lily shakes her head, wipes a tear, makes a dart for the door.

'Wait!'

Sniffling, Lily pauses, allows Rafiq to approach her, to turn her around.

'Tell me, tell me everything, please.'

Like a chastened child, Lily tries to hold back her tears.

'M-Mister Yan has been arrested. H-he is about to inform Khan of everything he knows about me. I will be a-arrested and imprisoned for t-trafficking in d-drugs… With my father now gone, they will b-blame me.'

Rafiq wipes a tear from her cheek.

'There must be something we can do.'

He turns away, trying to evaluate the situation. Behind him Lily cries out in despair.

'If only I had someone, a friend to depend on for shelter and friendship!'

Gates of opportunity fly open, sunlit uplands beckon. Rafiq turns to his lady love.

'Oh, Lily, Lily we could never just be friends. Lovers, yes; a fiancée, yes.'

He takes her hands, raises them.

'A wife, yes?'

'This is so sudden. What can I say?'

'Say yes.'

Lily considers, sniffs, shrugs.

'All right.'

'Really?'

'Why not, as long as the proprieties are observed as befits a fiancée.'

'Ah, proprieties...'

He pauses to kiss the tip of each of her fingers in turn.

'Lily Li T'ang, you have made me the happiest of all men. Except...'

He drops her hands, wrings his hands together in anguish. Lily is baffled.

'What is it?'

'Jealousy! Jealousy! I cannot bear to think of other men gazing on your beauty.'

'But I have to go out. I have business to attend to. Police enquires into my daddy's death, his funeral arrangements, my freedom to protect.'

'Ah, then, there is something you will need.'

Bemused, Lily watches her fiancée skip across the room. He opens a drawer of a bureau and takes out a bundle of black silk. He bears it back to her, beaming with anticipation. He shakes the sheer material free.

'Wear this as a symbol of your commitment to me. It is a burqa. A veil to hide your beauty from the eyes of lustful men.'

'But I may display myself to you?'

Lascivious joy envelops Aslam Rafiq. He shakes open the burqa, places it over Lily's head.

'May I?'

Taking her silence as a sign of agreement, Rafiq loosens the thin black veil, allows it to fall. He clasps his hands together in ecstasy as her beauty is obscured.

92

The Anemos is a Greek restaurant on Queensway that Anne knows of but has never frequented. Now, after her first full day of her temporary employment with Soper, Travers and Edmund, Solicitors, she is sitting across the table from a junior partner of the firm, James Partridge.

The work had been routine: typing up reports on cases of divorce, managing of trusts, invoices for payment. Towards the end of the long day she had been called on to take dictation from the man now seated opposite to her.

His suggestion that they go out to dinner was a surprise, but Anne told herself that's what office girls do. Most husbands are found in the workplace, so she heard herself saying, 'Yes, that might be nice.'

James had asked if she liked 'Chinese?' She passed on that one. The next suggestion was to try a new place on Broad Street that had received good reviews. He couldn't remember the name, but Anne could.

'The Nirvana?'

'That's it.'

'No, thanks.'

So Anemos it was. Now at the end of the meal all their chit chat has been exchanged.

Her escort is tall and thin. Early thirties. Not as tall as Kline but tall enough. His hair is thinning; it is only a couple of years before his scalp will begin to show through.

Watching James settle the bill, Anne notices his wallet will hardly close over the thickness of the banknotes stuffed inside.

Now, with the meal paid for, the wine consumed, Anne wonders what might happen next. The solicitor seems flushed, animated. What is coming? They go to a hotel room, or out to the empty house of his mother in Edgbaston? The question is academic. He might not know that but she does.

But when the suggestion is made, it is neither of these alternatives. The proposal is that they should 'try their luck at the tables'. He is a member of a Casino that is 'only a short walk away'.

93

Kline surveys the customers seated at the Nirvana tables. His attention settles on a woman in black, wearing a veil, a plain glass of water placed before her.

On his arrival at the table he makes what he hopes is a gentle enquiry.

'Evening, madam. Everything to your satisfaction?'

In reply the woman lowers her head and begins to sob. Kline sits down at the table across from her.

'Oh, come on, the food isn't that bad.'

Lily raises her head. Through the veil, Kline recognises who she is. He calls to a passing waiter.

'Pete, bring me a bottle of the stuff that bubbles.'

Further sobs emanate from behind the veil. Kline reaches across and lifts it away from her face. He gently wipes away her tears with a caress of his hand.

'There, there. Tell me what's happened.'

'My father is dead.'

'No. How did that happen?'

'At the hands of an assassin.'

'That's why you're all in black?'

Lily nods and sniffs at the same time.

'Forgive me, I should not have come. Only, only…'

'Yes?'

'Mr Yan has been arrested. He's about to inform Khan of everything he knows about me.'

'That's quite a lot.'

'I know, I know. I will be arrested and imprisoned for trafficking in drugs. With my father gone, the blame will fall on me.'

'That's true.'

'You were the only person I could think of who might save me.'

'Well, let's hope so. It would be such a waste of your talents.'

He covers her hand with his. Lily darts a look up at him.

'Where is that blonde person?'

'Gone to pastures new. Now, tell me what I can do.'

Before Lily can reply, a bottle of Bollinger champagne is presented at the table. She gives a brusque instruction to the waiter.

'We'll have it upstairs.'

94

Uniformed doormen open the doors to the Fairplay casino. Inside lies a world of lush carpets, male staff in evening dress, pretty girls wearing costumes that belong in the fantasy world of girly magazines. James is known here. He receives warm greetings from the management as he makes his entrance. Obviously a valued member.

Anne, quietly chic in a vintage Jean Muir black dress, should feel at ease, but the ambience reminds her of nights, too many nights, when her former boss, Rawlinson, had taken her along to his clubs as window dressing.

After signing her in, James disappears, only to return with his hands full of blue gambling chips. A half dozen of these are presented to her with a small flourish.

'Just in case you feel the urge to play.'

He takes her arm and guides her swiftly past the rows of slot machines towards the inner sanctum, where tables are at play. A small group of punters stand around the roulette table, clicking chips, impatient for the next spin of the wheel.

Anne watches as her date hurries to join them.

He is soon absorbed in the play. The ebb and flow of fortune, the stifled groans as the ball nestles in the zero slot, meaning all stakes are cleared from the table for the profit of the house.

Anne can't stop thinking about her old boss, his contempt for the gambling fraternity. He had once explained why he had so many one-armed bandits installed at his clubs. 'For every hundred quid put in, I only pay out eighty. Yet still the stupid bastards go on playing.'

All at once Anne tires of the whole scene. James is lost to her. He fails to notice as she goes to the cage to redeem the chips given to her.

To her surprise, she receives three hundred pounds in return. He's been playing with fifty-pound counters. Anne shakes her head, heads for the door. She'll return the money in the morning.

In the taxi the overweight white Brummy driver keeps glancing back at her. Finally, he makes his usual enquiry.

'How was your luck tonight, love?'

'Not good.'

Her words slip out without thought. The driver nods. That is what he wanted to hear. He often picks up fares from this casino. It gives him an opportunity to prey on the newly impoverished.

When the taxi draws to a halt on the bridge over the canal, he switches off the engine.

Anne reaches into her purse.

'What's the damage?'

'Depends.'

'On what?'

'Whether you fancy a bunk up.'

'Go fuck yourself.'

Anne thrusts a tenner at him and pulls open the door. As she hurries down to the tow path, she fears he will come after her.

She hears the taxi-cab engine start up.

At least her first day of normality will not end in rape and murder.

95

Lily Li T'ang sits in a high-backed wicker chair, a paisley-patterned wrap draped around her. She pushes a cigarette into her ivory holder, lights up and glances across to where the naked body of John Kline lies curled up in sleep. A depleted bottle of champagne stands on his bedside table.

She had not needed to utilise too many of the sexual techniques her mother had insisted she learn from Hong Kong's most notorious courtesan, Madame Chi. Just basic man-woman interaction had been enough to bring about a satisfactory conclusion. Now he is linked to her emotionally, she can concentrate on finding a survival strategy.

Lily draws on her cigarette. The outstanding problem is Khan. Not that difficult to kill, but wouldn't that bring the forces of law down on her rather hard? Yan would still be able to trade information concerning her involvement in one or two unsolved murders. Both enemies must be neutralised. All right, how?

There had to be a way. Kline, Rafiq, Double Petal, that little angry guy, what was his name? Kul..? Ah, yes, Kuldip. Khan's creature, how loyal was he? Could he be turned? Through what? Sex, no. Money, possibly. Flattery, perhaps. Whatever secret information Kuldip reported to Khan would be believed. There it was, the solution. A way to bring Khan and Yan out into the open. A subterfuge to eliminate both dangers at once.

She stands, shrugs away the wrap, reaches for her clothes. There is much to do.

After dressing, Lily looks down at the sleeping Kline. He is unlikely to survive the outcome of her plan. A pity, but in war there are always casualties.

96

Outside the white bedroom, Rafiq and his housekeeper, Nazema, who carries a breakfast tray, pause. Rafiq gives a discreet tap on the panel. He is just about to try again when he hears the familiar haughty tones of his fiancée from inside.

'Yes, what is it?'

Rafiq enters carrying the breakfast tray.

'Good morning, darling Lily.'

He places the tray on the bedside cabinet.

Lily sits up in bed, gathers the white sheets about her. Allows a peck to her cheek, reaches for the orange juice, sips. Rafiq frets a little.

'What is it?'

'Your absence last night; I was worried, that's all.'

'I was visiting John Kline.'

'Whatever for?'

'Things to discuss.'

'Things? What things, pray?'

'About how best to rid ourselves of a common problem. Mr Khan.'

'Khan? How?'

'Come and join me.'

With some alacrity, Rafiq starts to climb into bed with her. With a sweet smile, Lily halts his progress.

'Please stay outside the covers, Aslam, there's a good chap.'

'Must I, with heaven so very near?'

'Yes, you must listen to me, this is more important than carnal satisfaction.'

'I somehow doubt that, but what is it you wish to say?'

'We must be awfully nice to Kuldip.'

'What? Kuldip? How can you sully your lips with the name of that fellow? John Kline? Kuldip? Lily, what is going on?'

'A way for us all to escape from the shackles imposed by Inspector Khan. Now, if you can desist from peering down the front of my nightgown, I will endeavour to explain.'

97

A little later that morning Anne receives a summons to the partner's room.

Inside, James Partridge is waiting for her. After closing the door to the oak panelled room, he turns to her, his watery blue eyes red rimmed through lack of sleep.

'Why did you run out on me last night?'

'I'd forgotten how boring those places are.'

It was as if she had informed a four-year-old child that Santa didn't exist. Anne reaches into her handbag, pulls out the banknotes she exchanged for the gambling chips.

'Here, this is yours. Two ninety, I used a tenner for a taxi.'

'How kind, how noble of you. Thank you, much obliged seeing as it's the very least you can do, considering.'

'Considering what?'

Running his fingers through his thinning hair, he starts to pace up and down before her.

'You took my luck away with you.'

'What?'

'Yes, I'd decided to play the colours. Rouge or noir. I glanced across to where you were standing, saw you in your little black dress. I began to double up on black, very successfully, until I looked for you and you had gone. A succession of seven reds followed, which did considerable damage to the contents of my wallet.'

'That's bullshit.'

'My luck—'

'Fuck your luck.'

The solicitor takes a backward step, ducks away as if expecting a blow.

'Who are you, what are you?'

'Someone who wanted to work here.'

'Yes, well, obviously you are far from being suitable. Not suitable at all. It's best you and your foul mouth leave immediately.'

'Just like that?'

'Your agency will be paid for a full week's work if you agree to say nothing of the events of last night.'

Anne looks him over with contempt.

'A confidentiality agreement?'

'You could put it that way.'

'Let me put it this way, James. I'm not interested or bothered enough to talk about your pathetic addiction. Do yourself a favour, get some help.'

Before he can close his slackened jaw, she turns and walks away from Soper, Travers and Edmund, Solicitors.

98

Inspector Zahir Khan sits behind his office desk and drains the last of his morning coffee. Seated opposite is his prime informant.

In a gloating, self-congratulatory voice Kuldip explains the reason for his visit.

'I play Mr Rafiq like a tickley-trout. He thinks once bent I'm always twisted.'

'What news do you have, Kuldip?'

'Rafiq wants me to stand lookout while he and his gangster mates bring out antiques from Edmonson's storage warehouse place, tonight, six o'clock, through gate number four.'

Khan moves his coffee mug towards the side of his desk space.

'Antique shipments are not illegal.'

Kuldip grins.

'Filled with bloody heroin, they are.'

Khan leans forward, scans the grinning face of Kuldip intently.

'You're sure of this?'

'Overheard Lily person and Rafiq discuss it, didn't I.'

'And the destination?'

'United States of America.'

'This is happening at six o' clock tonight?'

'That's what I said, didn't I?'

'This storage warehouse, how might one gain entry?'

'I'm not a bloody oracle, am I? Except…' Kuldip draws closer to Khan's desk, drops his voice. 'You need two qualifications. One is to be Chinese…'

He puts a forefinger on each side of each eye and pulls the skin taut. Khan sighs, disapprovingly. Kuldip adds, hurriedly, 'The other is to be a recognised member of Lily Li's Triad. Is good info I bring you? Good dog, me, yes?'

'It might be useful.'

'Should I go gung-ho with the crime tonight?'

'Play along but do not become directly involved.'

Kuldip jumps up, throws an extravagant salute.

'Got it, Mister Khan, sir, boss!'

After watching his informant exit the office, Khan flicks the switch on his intercom. A throaty female voice answers his call.

'Sir?'

'Have Mister Yan brought up right away.'

99

The derelict storage warehouse is a casualty of the times. Formerly a factory manufacturing farm equipment, it is now a forlorn relic filled with industrial detritus. Above the yard stretch empty offices with many broken windows.

Khan, accompanied by a team of three detectives, arrives outside gate number 4. It is a little after six o'clock. All the lawmen are armed. They leave the sand-coloured car. With them is Mr Yan.

Across the street, concealed behind a clump of weeds, Kuldip grins as he watches the team of detectives gather outside the dingy yellow-painted gate.

Around the corner Kline sits, in his restored Avenger, smoking, waiting.

Khan raps on the wooden door. There is no reply. He checks that the number above is correct. He pushes the door. It creaks open, revealing a long empty yard filled with rusting machinery, abandoned containers, coils of wire.

Cautiously, Khan leads his team into the yard. He halts by a door that opens onto the lower floor of the disused factory.

Above them, on the roof of the building, Rafiq appears. He signals across to the adjoining roof, where Lily Li T'ang, dressed in black leather, her burqa fluttering in the evening breeze, passes on the signal to Double Petal below. The assassin grins, begins to screw a silencer into the barrel of his Glock pistol.

Inside the building below, the air is stale. There seems only a jumble of broken furniture, no sign of antique items anywhere. Khan indicates that the team check out all the adjoining corridors and workshops. He and Yan will explore further ahead.

Halfway along the short corridor a door is ajar. Khan opens it fully, looks inside. The floor is stained with oil spillage. Racks and shelves fill the walls of what once was a motor pool leading out into the street. He sees a statue of a Chinese god of death glaring hate at him. A metal trolley, placed in the centre of the room, attracts his attention. On it is a lacquered black box, adorned with motifs of golden dragons. Behind him, Yan slips away, unnoticed.

Seeking to make good his escape, Yan turns a corner and comes face to face with a grinning Chinese guy, wearing a black fedora and holding a gun.

Yan tries to turn away. A bullet smacks into his chest. Blood stains his white shirt. He crumples to the floor.

Double Petal steps over the body and ducks into the room where Khan was last seen. He finds the cop examining packets of heroin taken from the black box. He creeps up behind him, a pad soaked in chloroform ready in his hand.

The smell alerts Khan a second too late. The pad is clamped to his mouth and nose. There is an intense struggle. Khan's head begins to fill with fumes, his grip slackens, his knees give way. Double Petal lowers him to the ground. Lily steps forward from the darkness.

'Good work.'

'It isn't over yet, sister.'

'What?'

'I've other fish to fry.'

He goes to lift the box containing the heroin. Lily tries to stop him.

'That's mine!'

'Not anymore, doll!'

He pushes her away. She stumbles over Khan's body.

Double Petal grabs the burqa from Lily's head, and before she can protest, he runs away, leaving Lily and the unconscious Khan alone together.

The remainder of Khan's team meets up in the factory yard. There is a general shaking of heads. They have just decided this raid is a non-starter when a figure wearing a burqa, carrying a cardboard box, is seen running towards the gate. They yell and give chase.

Outside, Kline starts the engine as he sees the hooded figure running towards him. His passenger piles into the rear seat of the car. Kline drives away at speed, turns a corner seconds before his pursuers appear.

Kline looks in the mirror at his hooded companion.

'How'd it go, baby?'

'Pretty good, baby, pretty good.'

The obviously male voice alerts Kline, but before he can react further, he finds a knife at his throat. A burst of manic laughter fills the speeding car.

100

Lying on the greasy floor of the garage, Khan comes awake. His head aches, his mouth feels full of sand. He realises that his gun is within reach. The wooden door is rattling, shouts reach him from beyond it. He makes to reach for the weapon and attempt to rise to his feet.

Something prevents him. A sharp tug on his wrist. He realises he is handcuffed by his left hand to the dead body of Mr Yan. On the chest of the corpse are scattered three polythene packets of heroin.

Before he has time to realise the implications fully, the outer doors crash open.

Sarah Gant, flanked by four uniformed officers of the law, strides purposefully towards Khan and his murdered victim…

To be continued…

BOOK FIVE
ENTER THE WHITE DEVIL

101

Handcuffed to the corpse of Mr Yan, Khan allows Inspector Peterson to take the Glock 9mm from his hand. The handcuffs are removed.

'You've some explaining to do, Khan.'

'I—'

'At headquarters.'

Sarah Gant watches Khan being hustled away. She pops a sugared almond into her mouth.

With a knife held to his throat by the man in the burqa, John Kline drives in the early evening traffic.

'Where we headed?' Kline asks.

'Roxy cinema, know it?'

'We on a date?'

Double Petal hisses into Kline's ear.

'Yeah, there's a movie I've been dying to see.'

102

The movie on screen is *the Dark Eyes of London*, the first British film to receive an 'H' certificate.

The flickering black and white images light up John Kline as he sits alone, bound and gagged, in a mid-row seat in the empty circle of the Roxy cinema.

On screen, the actress Greta Gynt is being forced into a straitjacket by Jake, the monster. He throws her over his shoulder.

'No, no, Jake! Please, Jake, don't!'

He carries her away.

Kline struggles, tries to free himself.

On screen there is a cut to an upper floor of the warehouse, where the murders take place. Greta has a fearful realisation.

'Jake, where's Lou, Jake? He found him, Orloff got rid of him. Like he got rid of all the others before he dumped them into the river.'

Jake, the monster, lurches away. In a rage, he proceeds to destroy the laboratory equipment of Bela Lugosi.

Downstairs, from their seats in the stalls, Lily Li T'ang, dressed from head to toe in black leather, sits next to Double Petal, who is absorbed by the destruction on screen. Lily glances at her companion, who grunts along with Jake, the monster.

A slim Chinese youth slips into a seat behind them. He touches Double Petal on the shoulder. With a sigh, the mobster nudges Lily, stands, pulls down his black and white fedora, steps out into the aisle. As Lily follows, she feels the weight of her Luger pistol. She eases the gun away from her hip and conceals it beneath her leather coat.

As they cross the foyer, they pass an usherette eating an apple. She sees them ignore the 'Circle Closed' sign and start to climb the stairs. She thinks about calling after them but decides to go into the stalls and watch the climax of the film instead.

The executioner and his assistant enter the Circle. The Chinese youth joins them. He points down toward the helpless Kline as on screen they hear, 'Hangman, hangman, hold that rope...'

'Make no mistake this time, Kay.'

Double Petal intends that there will be no mistake. He stands behind Kline, takes out a thin cord, loops it around his victim's throat. As he tightens the garrotte he begins to cackle with glee. Kline's head jerks back under the choking pressure. Standing a little way behind, Lily takes out her Luger pistol. The laughter of the Triad hitman escalates into hysteria.

On screen a posse of police arrive. The monster is shot in the gut by Bela Lugosi.

As he fires, so does Lily Li T'ang.

The cord slackens. Double Petal slumps back into his seat. His white hat band stains with blood. The young guy, frightened for his life, runs down towards the exit. Lily fires after him as, up on screen, an exchange of gun fire covers the sound of her shots.

On screen, Bela Lugosi takes a bullet in the shoulder. Jake, the monster, fatally wounded, grabs hold of Lugosi, hurls him out of a loading bay into the river below.

Lily frees Kline. They hurry to escape from the cinema.

Double Petal stares at the screen, hears the closing dialogue.

'Has he gone?'

'Yes, when a dog goes mad, he has to be destroyed.'

As his life ebbs away, Double Petal mumbles, '*The Dark Eyes of London*, starring Bela Lugosi, directed by Walter Summers, circa 1939. When Double Petal goes mad, he has to be destroyed...'

As the music builds to a crescendo, the last image he sees is of Bela

Lugosi being sucked into the mud of the River Thames.

Lily and Kline reach the street. Behind them, a dozen or so members of the Wo Shing Wo Triad, waving machetes, knives and swords, charge after them. Lily turns and fires. The gang scatter, Lily fires again, sees a Chinese mobster crumple to the ground. She gives a whoop of joy.

Kline realises that against such odds they have little chance of survival. Across the street, he sees a car slow and halt. He runs towards it, Lily follows. Kline opens the driver's door, pulls a somewhat surprised elderly gentleman out of the driving seat and takes his place behind the wheel. Lily runs around the other side, scrambles in beside him.

As the blue Escort begins to pull away, a gun toting Chinese reaches the car and levels his pistol at Lily's head. She beats him to the draw. The car window shatters, spraying her with his blood. Their attacker falls away. Kline accelerates away from danger. Lily is ecstatic.

'Wonderful, wonderful, I feel so alive!'

'Danger does have that effect.'

'I wanted to avenge my father, but I realised there was another emotion involved.'

'What was that?'

'I love you.'

The driver responds with a touch of irony.

'This is so sudden. I hardly know you.'

Lily puts her arm around Kline's neck. He can feel the heat of the gun against his cheek.

'Lay that pistol down, babes.'

Unable to contain herself, Lily hugs and kisses him. The car swerves towards the pavement, mangles a bicycle before crashing into the rear of a parked white van. Lily's cries become ever more joyful as Kline reverses, joins the flow of traffic.

'Wonderful, ah, wonderful! Oh, that was absolutely amazing!'

As the blue Escort speeds away, a ten-year-old paper boy emerges from an apartment building. He stares down at the wreckage of his bicycle.

'Bleedin' vandals!'

He begins to cry.

103

In the outer office of Petfix Ltd, Anne awaits the arrival of Sub-Divisional Manager Anthony Buckram.

Helen had been very understanding of the sudden curtailment of her previous employment. 'Damaged creatures are everywhere,' she had said. 'Most of them possess a penis.'

Her latest boss finally makes an appearance. Anne is determined to be cool, professional, proficient.

Buckram says nothing, prowls around the office, checking files, peering into desk drawers. Finally, he finds what he is looking for in a wastepaper basket. He extracts four sheets of crumpled A4 paper, smooths out their surface, begins to read their contents.

Anne decides he must be aged about forty. A little extra weight puts strain on the seams of his business attire. His steel blue eyes look up from the document he is reading. They rest on her. There is a moment of cold appraisal.

At last he speaks in the sharp tones of the privately educated.

'My former secretary…' He taps the retrieved papers. 'Not the most efficient.'

'Oh.'

'Yes, exactly. Well, ah, Miss Darracott, welcome.'

'Thank you.'

'I must warn you things can be pretty exciting here. Though your time with us might be only temporary, it coincides with the need to clarify my presentation to the full board. My suggestions for new products in the pet food market that, should they become commercially successful, might lead to my promotion to that self-same board.'

Anne gives a non-committal smile. Buckram frowns.

'Ah, you're thinking how foolish to profess such vaunting ambition.'

'I didn't think anything, Mister Buckram.'

'No? I'm an expert in the interpretation of the silences of the fair sex. Plenty of practice, I'm afraid. You see, I'm fortunate enough to be blessed with an entirely female household. Mother-in-law, wife, teenage daughter. You remind me a little of her, in appearance. Blonde hair. Yes, well, like all families, all marriages, all filial relationships, they fluctuate, and never more so than now, when I'm trying to survive within this company.'

'What do you want me to do?'

'The basic things.'

'Typing, dictation?'

'As a beginning, look this over, provide me with a clean copy, incorporating all my textual alterations.'

He hands her four sheets of closely typed paper. Anne glances at the scribbled notes and changes; it is as if a colony of ants have dipped themselves in red ink and marched hither and thither across the paper.

About to make his way to the adjoining office, Buckram pauses and looks back at his new secretary as she attempts to assimilate his proposal. She could be his daughter, bent over her homework.

104

A little after dawn, by the side of a quiet lake, Sarah Gant watches as two members of the Wo Shing Wo Triad wedge the body of Double Petal into the stern of a rowing boat. His fedora hat is placed on his head, ready for his final journey.

Sarah nods her approval.

'Good job, guys, you can leave the last rites to me.'

Left alone, Sarah pulls on a pair of light rubber gloves. She extracts a plastic evidence protector that contains a small packet of heroin from her bag. After carefully removing the packet, she tucks it into the breast pocket of the deceased enforcer. This done, Sarah Gant straightens, places her foot on the bow, gives the boat a shove towards a bridge that leads into the main section of the parkland lake.

As the craft moves slowly towards the tunnel beneath the bridge, Sarah gathers her fur coat around her, watches Double Petal float out of her life. She tips her hat, strikes a tough pose.

'When a gal's partner's killed, she's expected to do something about it. *The Maltese Falcon*, Warner Brothers, circa 1941.'

105

Waking up in his own bed, Kline winces against the morning light. His throat feels raw from the garrotting; a livid half-moon weal remains as a memento. He shifts his naked body, tries to remember the wild night that followed their escape from the Roxy. Lily riding him like a bull rider whooping and hollering in a frenzy of climatic energy. Where is she? He can see her clothes scattered around the floor. He is just about to get out of bed when the door opens and Lily Li T'ang, draped in towels, fresh as morning rain, sweeps into the room.

'You have a rather boring selection of shampoos, John.'

'I'll get in touch with Liberty's right away.'

'No time for that, we have things to do, a war to win.'

'Against who, exactly?'

'The Triad of the Wo Shing Wo.'

'Ah, who else?'

'That cinema is their headquarters. Double Petal must have been in alliance with them, hence his double crossing of me and your abduction.'

'Who framed Khan with the death of Yan?'

'Who do you think?'

Kline realises.

'I'm looking at her?'

'I had to eliminate two threats at the same time. I needed to discredit a police source and ensure Yan could not implicate me.'

Lily shows little emotion; her words could have been about the time of day rather than the death of one man and the disgrace of another. Kline gives a shake of his head.

'Khan behind bars, that I've got to see.'

'There will be no time for prison visits. Wo Shing Wo will target you, that is a certain fact. I will contact Hong Kong. I will seek their permission to recruit disaffected members of another Triad, 17K. I will also make a request to lead. I must lead. I simply must.'

'Must?'

'It is my destiny. Now kiss me, then rouse yourself.'

'Again?'

'There is a time for sex, this isn't it. Go take a shower.'

'Yes, ma'am.'

Kline throws her a salute.

106

The lone fisherman casts his line into the dark water beneath the bridge. It has been a while since a bite on his line, so when the rod is almost pulled from his hands, he thinks for a second that he has got his hook into Big Barney, the legendary pike that rules these waters. His excitement wanes rapidly as he sees the prow of a rowing boat cut through his line.

'Hey, you, you're across my…!'

The full length of the boat emerges, the fisherman sees a slumped figure wearing a pinstripe suit and a black hat with a white trim. The boat turns and drifts into the bank. The impact makes the occupant sag and fall forward.

'Hey, mate, you drunk or what?'

Double Petal makes no reply.

107

A hearty breakfast of two eggs, four rashers of bacon and a mess of mushrooms and tomatoes goes some way to filling the void within John Kline. Lily contents herself with a toasted slice of wholemeal bread and a cup of organic green tea. Kline wonders where her energy springs from. He feels languid after the excesses of the past night. His coffee provides no more than a minor hit. He raises his hand to attract the attention of Archie, who is re-stocking the bar.

'Hey, Archie, bring me a Buck's fizz.'

Waiting for the drink to arrive, he gazes across at his breakfast buddy. Absorbed in plans of conquest, she makes notes on a napkin, her eyes made bright by thoughts of the battles yet to come. Then she falters, frowns, strikes a line through her latest jottings.

A piano is being wheeled across the floor. The pianist, a replacement for the sitar player, who is on his way to India, is the last guy Anne hired before her departure. Kline tries to recall the name of the sad, dumpy, middle-aged man who seems to know every popular piano piece ever written.

The orange juice, laced with champagne, is delivered to their table. Kline notices that the barman averts his eyes from Lily, his way of disapproving of Anne's replacement, no doubt.

'Thanks, Oh, Archie, what's the name of the new pianist?'

'Stan. Stan Guthrie.'

'Thanks.'

Lily fits a cigarette into her holder. Kline lights it for her. She nods, crumples her napkin, squeezes it into a tight ball. Kline, not used to her displaying any sign of uncertainty, extracts it from her tense grip.

'Relax, baby.'

'Yes, yes, I must.'

'What is it?'

'I've just realised that the ultimate assassin might be sent against us.'

'What's he called, Green Custard?'

'He uses many names, appears in strange disguises. We know him as the White Devil. Some say he is a monster, a demon who hides behind a mask of levity; others say he can kill by applying the merest touch.'

'Sounds an interesting bloke.'

'Compared to him, Red Stick and Double Petal are amateurs.'

'I look forward to meeting him.'

'Don't say that, don't ever say that. If our paths converge with his, our lives will be in utmost peril. Oh…'

She shivers as a cold blast of air sweeps through the restaurant. Kline looks around expecting to see a wide open door or a window, but all seem closed. He takes a pull on his drink.

'This White Devil bloke, why should he bother with us?'

'We have caused the death of two Triad enforcers designated 426. That is a category that automatically triggers swift revenge. We are wasting time. We must be about our business.'

'Let's linger a while. Let me finish my drink.'

'Don't be difficult. If survival doesn't interest you, perhaps money will. I intend to export a cargo of antiques that will contain, within each item, a substance that will enhance their value a thousand fold.'

Her words have little effect. Kline yawns. Lily changes tack. Her manner softens towards him. Whereas she can play Rafiq like a fish on a line, this one needs different tactics.

'John…'

'That's me.'

'I need an enforcer to help wage war against the Wo Shing Wo. What is stopping you joining me? The blonde woman? She's no longer around.'

'That's true.'

Lily takes his hand, places it against her breast.

'Oh, darling, how thrilling it is to have a lover I can look up to physically. Someone as tall and as strong as you.'

With a slow smile, his hand cupping her breast, Kline leans his head towards hers.

'I know what you're doin' but go on doin' it.'

'Not "in", darling, "ing". Doing. Doing it. Do. Doing. "Ing" it.'

'Got it.'

'Then what are we waiting for, for God's sake.'

Their lips meet and melt into a deep, binding, kiss.

108

Pacing around his living room, Aslam Rafiq is wracked with worry.

'What are they doing? Where are they? What are they up to? *What?*'

Sprawled in an armchair, Kuldip offers little comfort.

'Don't ask me, cock. I look outside, the missing Lily is still amiss along with Kline bloke bastard.'

Glaring at the man who was once his dogsbody but is now his watchdog, Rafiq strides across to confront Kuldip.

'Listen, listen, you… You will refer to my fiancée as Miss… Miss Lily.'

'Bloody did already, didn't I?'

The snarl of aggression gives Rafiq some pause.

'Er, Kuldip?'

'What, Rafiq?'

'You say you saw Miss Lily get into Kline's car?'

'Wearing a burka, couldn't miss that.'

'Then where the bloody hell are they?!'

He takes a turn around the room, agitated and full of foreboding. He pauses by the drinks table, grasps the brandy bottle, pours himself a heart starter.

'What happened to Khan and Yan inside that warehouse? Perhaps we should have lingered, but direct confrontation with the law is always best avoided.'

He waves his brandy glass in the direction of the sullen Asian.

'Now, that is an axiom, my dear, Kuldip, that you would do well to remember, for he who sups with Mr Khan needs a very long spoon.'

'Only if he lands in the soup, eh, Mr Rafiq?'

While Kuldip cackles madly, Rafiq downs his brandy, wanders towards the statue of the goddess Kali, makes a silent plea for the safe return of Lily Li T'ang.

109

On a visit to Rawalpindi police headquarters Khan's father is the recipient of disturbing news. He turns over the paper informing him of his son's arrest on the charges of corruption and murder. A former colleague, Jamal, offers his sympathy. This is brushed aside.

'These lies against my son must be disproved.'

'How can that be done at this distance?'

'It can't. I must make my way to England to ensure the innocence of my son is established conclusively. Do you have an airline schedule to hand?'

110

Less than half an hour after the plea to the goddess the doors to the salon are thrown open and Lily sweeps in with John Kline in her wake. Rafiq is overjoyed. He hurries to greet her, pauses at the sight of her naked features.

'Where is your burka?'

For answer, Lily fires an accusatory broadside.

'Listen you, when one has been in a horrific car smash, one is less than concerned at the revealing of one's facial features!'

'Car… Smash?'

Rafiq clasps his hands together, stares at his betrothed with concern.

'But you're not hurt? You are still my pretty darling?'

Kline sees the oasis of the drinks table, skirts around Rafiq, replies, in passing.

'Nice of you to ask, but I'm OK.'

'Lily? Are you concealing any damage to your person?'

'A few bruises, most of them spiritual at your abandonment of my person when I was inside that filthy warehouse.'

'Darling Lily, I thought you had escaped. Kuldip, as usual, was less than dependable with his information. What is this?'

He gazes down upon her left hand thrust beneath his nose.

'It is bad enough, Aslam, that you have not yet decorated this hand with a galaxy of diamonds to proclaim your troth. Well, so be it. I may as well inform you that I am less than enamoured by your performance on the field of battle.'

A further cackle of derision issues from Kuldip.

'Not one of nature's doughty warriors is he, Miss Lily?'

'He is not.'

Bewildered by this attack from two fronts, Rafiq spreads his hands helplessly.

'But what else could I do, what can I do now?'

Perched on the arm of the settee, Kline observes how Lily has taken centre stage. Rafiq stands humbly before her. Kuldip shifts a little uneasily in his chair. Lily looks around at each man in turn.

'We are faced with a problem…'

Rafiq gives a warning cough, nods towards Kuldip, the spy in the room.

'Let him stay,' Lily orders.

'Are you sure?'

'I just said so. Sit down and stop interrupting.'

'Yes.'

Kline makes room on the settee for Rafiq.

'Thank you, John.'

'Be my guest.'

Lily brings the room to order.

'When you've both finished, it is time to assess the situation in which we find ourselves. I am faced with a chronic shortage of personnel. Kuldip has a choice. To stand as accomplice to the murder of Yan by the not so clever Mr Khan…'

'What?'

Squirming in his chair, Kulip can't decide whether to bare his teeth or wag his tail.

Lily continues, 'Or, Kuldip, you can agree to accept the strict discipline required by a disciple of the Lily Li T'ang Triad.'

Shaking his head in admiration, Rafiq leans into Kline and whispers.

'Isn't she wonderful?'

'A little too quiet for my taste' is the dry rejoinder.

They both watch Kuldip wrestle with the choice Lily has placed before him. He seeks further clarification.

'Hey, what, Lily… Miss Lily, what you come here and say about Mr Khan, eh?'

In a calm voice, Kline addresses the confused Kuldip.

'Her ladyship reckons that your mate Khan is in the frame for killing Yan. I can't see it myself but that's the way the picture's being painted, kid.'

As the truth finally sinks in, the stocky Asian barks with rage.

'That bloody tealeaf crook. Khan, murder man, is he? Well, well, bloody hell. Trust not in the majesty of the law. That's when the scales depart from my eyes.'

Realising his servant is now back on the leash brings Rafiq great joy. He stretches, enjoying the realisation that he is, once more, the master of his fate.

'I say, Kuldip, would you care to purvey a little brandy from over there to over here?'

'Boot on other bloody shoe, isn't it?'

In silky tones of condescension, the master asserts control over his servant.

'No, no, Kuldip, no. Not when I believe you have just pledged your loyalty to me, to us, to the cause of Miss Lily. What a fortunate choice, for now that Mr Khan finds himself in dungeon deep, you are, once again, the servant of one master…'

His tone changes to one of brutal command.

'So, brandy, Kuldip, brandy!'

Feeling deep satisfaction, Rafiq watches his servant scurry towards the drinks table. He stands, raises his hands to the heavens.

'Ah! Oh, freedom, freedom, freedom! Comfort thyself with the thought, Kuldip, that only in perfect service is there perfect freedom.'

He smiles at Lily.

'Book of Common prayer, actually.'

'I know' comes her curt reply.

At the drinks table Kuldip growls and mutters as he measures brandy into the bowl of a glass. From across the room, his owner calls.

'Did you say something, Kuldip?'

'Oh, no, Mr Rafiq, nothing, Mr Rafiq…'

He trots across the room, holding the glass of brandy in his hands. He bows his head.

'Your brandy, Mr Rafiq, sir.'

With a chuckle of pure delight, Rafiq accepts the offering, pats his servant on the head.

'Good boy.'

111

As her first day in the employ of Petfix ends Anne wonders if she will ever become used to sitting in one place, facing the same desk, for hours and hours on end. But that's what people do. And she is an office worker now, she tells herself, her choice, so get used to it.

The door of her office opens. Mr Buckram sidles in. In his hands, he holds the typescript of the proposal Anne has been deciphering for much of the day. He stands before her, his lips form a slight smile.

'End of our first day together.'

'Yes. That proposal document, was it OK?'

'Oh, yes, as far as it goes.'

Anne blinks.

'Oh, yes, this is just the first of what, no doubt, will be many drafts. But be assured that each draft will bring the ultimate draft ever nearer.'

'Oh, I see. Will it? I mean, I'm sure it will.'

'As am I. We will achieve a proposal that will revolutionise not only the firm's fortunes but also mine.'

Anne nods. Buckram looks down at her intently.

'May I ask you a question?'

'All right.'

'Which of my three ideas intrigue you the most?'

'Oh, I think they are all OK.'

'They have to be more than "OK", Miss Darracott.'

'I favour the dog collar that shows how many walkies have been taken.'

'Rather than the "Doggie Chox" option?

'Marginally. What option do you favour, Mr Buckram?'

'I do rather like the customised feeding bowl. Big doggie, big bowl, small chap, smaller receptacle. Yes, well, I've redrafted a few ideas, made a few notes, ready for our next attempt at reaching ultimate clarity.'

He hands the sheets of paper to her. The first page is full of crossings out and scribblings across the margins. She glances at other pages; they, too, are covered in hieroglyphics. Buckram hovers.

'I suggest you leave the work for tomorrow. Fresh start, I think.'

'Thank you, Mr Buckram.'

'Not at all.'

He turns away, then, after a brief tussle within, turns back to her.

'Would you care for a snifter? Celebration, sort of thing, one full day in my employ?' Anne gives him a less than delighted look. His assurance falters a little. 'Er, no, not a good idea?'

'Thanks, anyway.'

'Oh, it's just as well. I go home smelling of the cup that cheers and all sorts of accusations get flung forth. Everything from alcoholism to my reeling from riotous orgy.'

Anne smiles, mischievously. 'Well, perhaps we should have one.'

Buckland takes a step towards the door.

'No, not tonight. Better not. Yes. Second thoughts. Well, maybe tomorrow… Yes, tomorrow. Madam and my daughter make their annual pilgrimage to the horse of the year show. Tomorrow is another day.'

'Which is followed by another night?'

'Yes…'

She pauses as an idea surfaces, a naughty idea, a *wicked* idea. Buckland watches her expression change from disinterest to something else… A look of anticipation in her hazel eyes?

'Yes, perhaps a quiet dinner somewhere?' he suggests.

'Perhaps.'

Anne smiles at the prospect of what tomorrow night could bring.

112

The black taxi rattles down a street of boarded up shops, past rows of houses built when Queen Victoria was on the throne. Behind the houses loom concrete towers, smoke blackened mill chimneys.

The taxi pulls up outside a small hotel. The Albany. A dapper man in a pale linen suit, hat, collar and Rawalpindi cricket club tie alights, pays the driver. The taxi drives away, leaving Khan's father alone on the empty street. He looks about him. The day is dull, overcast. As his eyes scan the bleak industrial landscape, a poem of Rudyard Kipling enters his mind. '*I am sick of endless sunshine, sick of blossom-burdened bough. Give me back the leafless woodlands where the winds of springtime range. Give me back one day in England, for its Spring in England now!*' The old man gives a sigh, picks up his suitcase and rings the bell of the Albany hotel.

113

Waiting inside the salon of Rafiq's mansion, the group who are the nucleus of the Lily Li T'ang Triad are awaiting the appearance of the lady herself. They can hear her voice rising and falling as she engages in discussion with the crime bosses of Hong Kong. As the conversation takes place in Cantonese, they are none the wiser as to how her request is being received.

Before making the call, she ordered her members to cease drinking. They obeyed, but Rafiq remembers where another stimulant is to be found. The rear of the Goddess Kali yields her secret hoard of grade one marijuana, complete with skins for the rolling of joints.

Hearing Mistress Lily complete her phone call, he drops the grass and cigarette papers into Kline's pocket with a naughty wink.

'An allowed fillip to the proceedings, I feel.'

'Gotcha.'

Kline grins as Lily, flushed with pleasure, bounds into the room, 'Gentlemen, I have permission to become your dragon head!'

Rafiq claps his hands. Kline nods. Kuldip seems baffled by it all. The two silent Asians youths recruited by Rafiq remain silent. They all move to a long table and take their seats with Lily at the head. She calls the meeting to order.

'My father, God rest his soul, made more than one mistake, which I do not intend to replicate. Wo Shing Wo have property of mine, stolen by the traitor Double Petal. Property that is hidden, no doubt, within the citadel of the Wo Shing Wo.'

'A flea pit called the Roxy cinema,' Kline adds.

'Quite.'

Rafiq frowns.

'Property, darling, what property?'

'A substance that was entrusted to Double Petal by my daddy. A trust that was betrayed. The strategy was for us to purchase a range of small Victorian sculptures, mostly fakes, of course, and to conceal, within those items, the means of achieving our ultimate fortune. It is imperative, therefore, that we form an army to regain that drug consignment.'

'An army? Comprising, what, me, him and him?' Kline points across the table at the two uncomfortable Asians. 'Some army.'

'I will bring another nine members of the 17K to augment our ranks. That should be sufficient for a frontal attack on the Wo Shing Wo.'

Kline reaches into his pocket, takes out the bag of weed, begins to construct a joint.

'I'm all for frontal attacks,' he says to Lily.

'I'm aware of that.' Their eyes meet for a brief second before Lily turns to the rest of her troops.

'You, Aslam, seeing as you do not qualify as an exponent of the martial arts, will organise my HQ here. You will also purchase enough antique items to fill a container for export to the United States. Kuldip will ensure that the sculptures are primed and concealed in such a way as make their unpacking by customs a rather daunting task. They will not delve beyond the first few layers, I feel.'

A dissenting hand is raised by Rafiq.

'Darling, if I may interrupt, wasn't this your father's plan?'

'It was, but despite that I believe this method of illegal importation to be a sound one.'

'Seems a lot of trouble for the exporting pots of junk ornaments,' Kuldip says.

With a deep sigh, Rafiq turns to his servant.

'Kuldip, we are discussing matters of some importance.'

'I'm sorry, Mr Rafiq, but what are these discussions about?'

Drawing in a first drag on his newly rolled joint, Kline holds it in then slowly exhales. He looks at the puzzled Kuldip with some amusement.

'We're talking of the smuggling of heroin, kid. You're in the big time, now.'

He passes the joint to Lily, who, surprisingly, takes a puff, passes it on to Rafiq without comment. Kuldip tries to absorb what is happening. Rafiq seeks to enlighten him further.

'Lily, as our leader, would you say that we are about to set up a trail for the white elephant to follow?'

'We are indeed.'

Still struggling with the detail, Kuldip thumps the table.

'And what is the size of this elephantine's droppings?'

Lily calculates.

'Somewhere in the region of a quarter of a million profit per each cargo.'

'Dollars?'

'Pounds,' Rafiq says, pleased by the impact of his words. 'And that, Kuldip, is merely the beginning.'

The Asian is transfixed. His master snaps his fingers, attempting to bring him out of his trance.

'Kuldip, Kuldip, where are you, Kuldip?'

Kline, beginning to feel mellow, leans across the table.

'He's recovering from the thought of a quarter of a million smackers, isn't that right, kid?'

Fervent nods confirm Kline's diagnosis. Lily gives Kuldip a nod of approval.

'Overcoming the Wo Shing Wo means we will control the market for distributing drugs throughout the UK.'

The roach is passed from a benign Aslam Rafiq to John Kline. Kuldip finds his enthusiasm increasing by the second.

'Mr Rafiq…'

'Yes?'

'Sir.'

'Yes?'

'Why have we been wasting our precious time on illegal persons when we could have been raised to rich rewards by the trunk of the white elephant? I like the thud of Jumbo's feet, Miss Lily. I want very much to travel his trail up and down and all along it.'

'You will be given an opportunity to follow.'

Kline can't help but add, 'Yeah, with a brush and shovel.'

A chortle of delight issues from Rafiq. Kline joins in. Their leader is not amused.

'When you've both settled down, I would like to continue…'

Her latest recruit attempts to restore order, fixes the giggling pair with a stern eye.

'You heard what Madam Lily said, didn't you? Let us concentrate on giving her some attention, shall we?'

Wiping his eyes, Rafiq turns to Lily.

'Obviously, you have found a new disciple.' He glances across to Kline. 'How quickly his loyalties turn. Compared to Kuldip, Judas Iscariot would seem as constant as the morning star.'

More laughter ensues. Kuldip begins to serenade his leader.

'Twinkle, twinkle, little star, eh, Miss Lily?'

Lily claps her hands together, decisively.

'The meeting will come to order. Before we set out on our quest, I want us to take a moment of contemplation, to go within ourselves and ask the spirits for courage and guidance. Let us pray to Kwan Yu, the god of gangsters, to crown our enterprise with great good fortune.'

She clasps her hands, closes her eyes. Kuldip follows suit. Rafiq, after a brief shrug, shuts his eyes, assumes a pose of meditation.

Kline's eyes remain open, watching his fellow soldiers at prayer. He wonders what they are asking for: strength, power, luck, love? And what about him? What would he ask for? To know what happened to Anne, to know where she is right now? Can she really be happy in the vanilla life? He slumps back, the pleasures of the cannabis fading fast.

Had he but known what disasters lay ahead, John Kline would have called on Kwan Yu to protect him from the gathering forces of darkness.

114

Khan's father sits in the bare, white-painted visitor's room in the psychiatric wing of Birmingham prison. With a lifetime of policework behind him he has been in this position many times, waiting for a criminal to be brought to him for interrogation. Now the prisoner is his only son.

The glass-panelled door is opened by a uniformed guard. Zahir Khan is escorted to the table and seated on a grey canvassed-back tubular chair. Father and son are left alone in an ever lengthening silence. Eventually it is the younger Khan who speaks.

'I cannot believe this is happening. That you have come to England or that you find me in such a place.'

'You have to answer the charge of murder to me. I've seen your solicitor. I know the details of the murder, together with the evidence against you.'

The senior Khan studies his son.

'Look at me. Speak to me from your heart. Did you kill Yan? Accidentally or otherwise?'

'I did not.'

A few tense seconds elapse before the old man says, 'Fair enough.'

He removes his hat, sits down opposite Khan. Takes out a well-worn notebook and an indelible pencil.

'I believe you. But we must find out who did. That's why I'm here in England.'

'Unfortunately, other pieces of evidence have been brought against me. The body of another Chinese has been discovered floating on a lake. On him was found a portion of heroin that contained traces of elements used in police tests. My fingerprints were found on the packet containing the drug sample.'

'How could that be?'

'I've handled such items, drugs taken in recent police raids.'

'Yes, well… Anything else?'

'Money found within my desk. Planted, obviously.'

After jotting details into his notebook, Khan senior raises another question.

'I say, I've tried to see the officer in charge of the investigation. He thinks he's rather too busy to see me. Why is he being so hoity-toity, hmm?'

'Simple. I'm a police officer corrupted by Triad money. Someone who sells confiscated drugs back onto the market. They believe there was a quarrel over payment, that's why I killed Mr Yan.'

'You were handcuffed to him.'

'Yes.'

'Why, how?'

'I don't know, I was rendered unconscious. Yan was dead, chained to me when I woke up.'

'I must think about this. We must work back through the events and decide who is the most likely source of engineering this trumped-up case against you.'

Zahir Khan looks out through the glass panels of the door to where two prison officers are sharing a joke. He turns back to his father, says with concern, 'How are you coping with England?'

'Oh, I've hardly encountered the true England, much too busy with your case. Looking forward to it, though.'

'Be careful, it is not all you might imagine it to be.'

'No? Obviously, though Birmingham fits Blake's description of dark satanic mills, never fear, we'll visit the real England after you are declared innocent.'

The old man gets to his feet. Not easily, Khan can't help but notice. He, too, stands, watches his father glance around the bare white walls.

The prison smell of sweat and disinfectant has never seemed more apparent. He watches as the dream is resurrected, a gleam returning to those rheumy eyes.

'Yes, heart of the nation, I saw this great city called. Surely that heart beats with a sense of fair play. People will talk to me, have no fear. I've solved cases equally daunting as yours and against odds just as long. Know what was once said about me?'

Khan says, gently, 'No, tell me.'

'Inspector Khan can gaze into men's souls, see hidden truths. So, my boy, let us begin. Whom do you suspect? Who's on top of the list?'

115

Sarah Gant picks her way between the moss-covered gravestones that lie within the grounds of St Stephen's church. The day is damp and chill. She snuggles into the fur collar of her coat.

On the wall beside the weathered wood of the church door, there is a ring that releases a latch inside. The door creaks open. Beyond the porch lies an inner door that takes her into the main church. Sarah looks around her, sees nothing but rows of empty wooden pews, choir stalls, the pulpit. The light filtering through the stained-glass windows gives a diffuse, eerie light. She is just about check her watch when a deep voice, redolent of the Southern States, sounds behind her.

'Might you be the arch sinner known as Sarah Gant?'

Sarah turns. A large black man wearing the classic lawman garb of dark suit, white shirt, striped tie looks down upon her.

'Are you she?'

'Yeah, that's me, who the hell are you?'

'My name is Marcus Mason. *Agent* Marcus Mason. They call me the Preacher Man. I'm here to save not only your soul but your job.'

116

Lily Li T'ang is inspecting her troops in the hallway of the mansion belonging to her fiancée. They muster a dozen strong. Nine are Chinese with the hardened careless look that marks men of violence. Kuldip waits at the end of the line. Kline stands alongside Lily while Rafiq hovers in the background, relieved that he will not be required to take part in the forthcoming battle.

Satisfied at what she sees, Lily addresses the ranks in ringing tones.

'Members of the 17K, welcome. With me you will find action that will lead to wealth and status. The LLT Triad to which you now belong will become famed and feared. Today, under the leadership of John Kline, you will do battle against the scum that operate behind the honoured name of Wo Shing Wo. They are not warriors, they are dregs, hopeless gamblers, unemployed waiters, men who would rather suck on the pipe than battle for the glory of success. So, gentlemen, go forth and make me, your head dragon, satisfied and proud. John, you may inform us of your plan of attack.'

Stepping forward, Kline is reminded of his army days, the tension in his gut before violent, bloody action. But then he was amongst trained, hardened soldiers, not a multi-racial rabble. But he has given his word to help Lily Li T'ang, so help he will. He begins the briefing.

'OK, guys, the strategy is simple. We arrive at the Roxy in time for their matinee. Kuldip and I will go to the box office to purchase tickets. We will cause enough delay there to hold up the queue. You will be in the queue. When we are inside the foyer, me and Kuldip will head for the manager's office. We believe the stuff we are after will be found in the office safe. Your job is to hold back the Wo Shing Wo forces long enough to allow us to complete our business with the manager. Any questions?'

A query comes from Lily.

'John, am I right in believing that you have had some dealings with the Wo Shing Wo on a previous occasion? Won't that mean you might be recognised instantly?'

'Maybe not, these might help…'

He produces a pork pie hat and a pair of sunglasses, puts them on for her inspection. Lily claps her hands, delightedly.

'Not sure the hat works as a fashion statement, but for our purposes it should suffice.'

'Let's go then.'

The group pick up their weapons, knives, clubs and chains and move towards the cars waiting outside on the driveway. Kline goes to follow. Lily catches his arm.

'Just a private word.'

She pulls him in the direction of the salon. Rafiq goes to join them.

Lily points a manicured finger of denial.

'Aslam, make a start on those phone calls, I'll be with you presently.'

Before Rafiq can respond she has taken Kline into the salon and closed the door.

As soon as they are inside Lily grabs hold of her chief of staff and kisses him fiercely. Putting his arms around her, pulling her into him, he can feel the pulse of excitement running through her, the rush of the gambler as the wheel begins to spin. They break apart. Lily, eyes bright with desire, voice vibrant with excitement, punches him in the chest.

'I'd give anything to be going with you!'

'They might overlook me, but the last thing you are is anonymous.'

'I know, for once I wish that wasn't so. All right, my love. If you come back on your shield, so be it, but if you succeed, I'll give you a night that you will remember until your dying day...'

A diffident knock sounds against the door. A plaintive voice is heard.

'Lily, is everything all right?'

'Yes, come in.'

Rafiq's anxious face appears. Lily takes the initiative.

'We were engaged in a strategy meeting.'

'Oh.'

Gazing at Kline, Rafiq says, simply, 'Goodbye, John, I pray we will meet again, once the battle is won.'

117

Sarah Gant watches Marcus Mason bow his head in reverence before the altar. Her mind is abuzz, trying to calculate the angles as to why he should want to visit her in England. Lack of success on her part? Surely she has done enough? And through her clandestine liaison with the Wo Shing Wo, the reports she has delivered promise more. So why in God's name had he demanded this meeting?

Marcus, finished with praying to the almighty, joins Sarah in the front row of the pews. Sarah glances at him. She's known clients with a religious bent. Stern men, fond of flagellation, full of anger because not everyone shared their interpretation of God's rules. What is the story on this 'preacher' guy? What would grant him grace? At last he breaks the silence, his voice echoing through the silent church.

'Your last report mentioned a Triad named the Wo Shing Wo.'

'What about it?'

'They are of interest to me.'

'And me. I hope to discover their lines of distribution. Indications are they run drugs through Amsterdam into Britain then on to the States.'

'Yes. That is a discovery that would help ease your position with the agency.'

Sarah ventures a little wry humour.

'Much rejoicing when a sinner is saved, huh?'

'In the agency as in heaven. Sarah, have you heard, in your dealings with Wo Shing Wo, any mention of a super assassin?'

'One guy called Red Stick, and another Double Petal.'

'Neither are with us anymore, is that correct?'

'It is.'

'The man responsible for their demise?'

'John Kline.'

'A criminal?'

'Not really. They keep sending their enforcers against him, he keeps sending them back dead.'

'Good for him. Will the Triad bosses seek revenge?'

'Who knows. They'd be best to call it quits.'

'We don't wish for that.'

Sarah gets to her feet, turns to face the agent.

'What's going on here, Marcus? Why are you here? What do you want from me?'

'Have you heard, in your dealings with Wo Shing Wo, mention of the White Devil?'

About to shake her head, she suddenly recalls Double Petal saying that he had once assisted someone with that name. She gives the information to Marcus Mason.

'That's more than likely,' Mason says. 'I've been following the trail of this man, if he is a man, for the past year and a half.'

'If he's not a man, what is he?'

'A demon, perhaps.'

'Oh, come on, you might believe that stuff…'

'I believe this devil kills for money, he flaunts danger, some say he can kill with a look, a touch. When the Triads wish an enemy to be removed, they pay top dollar for his services. He has victims on each of the five continents, presidents, a Saudi prince, a mafia boss, and we suspect many more. Wherever there is an unexplained death, he is rumoured to have been seen in the vicinity.'

'That's quite a build-up, Marcus.'

'He was last seen in Macau. It is no coincidence that the leader of the Shun Wing X Triad was found with a six-inch nail hammered through his head.'

'Ouch.'

'Yes. I must also warn you that he has a habit of impregnating women.'

'Sounds a busy boy.'

'Oh, he is. Some of the women say his genitals are somewhat, ah, unusual should we say.'

'Bent, serrated, corkscrewed, what?'

The agent shuffles his feet, looks away, mumbles something that sounds to Sarah like 'Passage to Venus'.

'Say again?'

'Some say he has a prehensile penis.'

'*What?* You mean this dude can swing from the trees using his johnson?'

She laughs in disbelief.

'It's probably only a legend, but the children he has sired are real. Some of the older ones are showing disturbing tendencies. We monitor those we know about, but I wake in the night fearing the antichrist may be growing up among us.'

'The antichrist?'

'Yes.'

'I must keep taking my pill, just in case this White Devil guy rocks up in Birmingham.'

'If he does, a mere contraceptive pill may not provide sufficient protection.'

Sarah blinks, asks unbelievingly, 'That potent?'

'Perhaps. The main question at issue here is that we wish the Wo Shing Wo to send him on a mission to Birmingham so he can be apprehended.'

'By me?'

'When and if that time comes, I will be there with back up.'

'You want me to consort with him. What if I end up with a nail through my head, or even worse, pregnant?'

'Survive your encounter with the White Devil and I promise you total immunity from prosecution for your past sins. A place within the Company, if you want it. I give you my word.'

Sarah looks him over thoughtfully, then asks pointedly, 'What's your word worth?'

'Everything. I will place my hand upon the holy book should you so wish.'

'Just remember you made that promise here in God's house.'

'I will.'

118

The film showing at the Roxy has the title *Jumping Ash*, a product of the Hong Kong film industry.

Kline reaches the head of the queue, gives the surly middle-aged cashier a winning smile. Kuldip is at his side. Other members of the raiding party filter in and join the growing line of cinema-goers anxious to purchase a ticket. Kline assumes the role of an anxious parent.

'Hi, nice place you've got here. It's our first visit. Tell me about the movie.'

'It's directed by Po-Chi Leong.''

'Is he good?'

'He's a she.'

'What's the film about?'

His question is greeted with a deep sigh of impatience.

'It's about warfare between rival Triads, very sexy, very violent. Good entertainment.'

With a worried frown, Kline indicates Kuldip.

'Sex and violence? That worries me. I wouldn't want my lad to see such things, he's led a very sheltered life.'

Kulip gives her an innocent grin to confirm this.

'You want a ticket or what?'

'That's a difficult decision.'

The cashier looks more closely at the customer before her as the line shuffles impatiently behind. Take away the dark glasses and the silly hat and he could spell danger. She presses an alarm button beneath her desk, asks suspiciously, 'Don't I know you?'

'I used to be big before the talkies came in.'

He feels a touch on his shoulder, a signal that his troops are in position.

'Give me two tickets, Anna May.'

Out of the corner of his eye he sees members of the Wo Shing Wo appear from the offices that lie beyond the foyer. He notices that the projectionist, carrying film canisters, is about to enter the overcrowded foyer.

Kline removes his sunglasses, hurls his hat away, points at the enemy, shouts, 'Now!'

Battle is joined. Kline leads the charge. He is met by two Chinese warriors, drops the first with a roundhouse swing. He sends a fierce jab at his second opponent, who ducks. Kline feels his knuckles crunch against a very hard head. All around him are grunts and groans, curses and the cries of men battling in hand to hand combat. Knives appear, clubs break heads. Had the battle been depicted in a comic book, there would have been a plethora of 'SPLATS', 'BAMS', 'KERPOWS', 'AAHS' and 'OUCHES!'

Caught up in the melee, the projectionist has the canisters dashed from his hand. Reels of film spill out to curl around the ankles of the grappling fighters.

Having served the customers inside with ice cream and popcorn, Doreen, the usherette, appears. She leans back against the wall, holding her tray, as she watches the violence without interest or emotion. It's just another movie.

Dodging a kung fu kick, Kline picks up a film canister and smashes it down on his assailant's skull. The Chinese groans, staggers back as, from a side door, an overweight man in a blue suit peers out at the ongoing mayhem. He quickly withdraws. Kline leaps over a fallen body, reaches the door, opens it just in time to see the man in the blue suit hurry into an office.

The usherette decides on a change of scene. She pushes open the doors and returns to the auditorium. Half a second later a flying meat axe thuds into the woodwork behind her as on screen a police informer who pretended to be blind is blinded for real.

The door to the office has been locked. Kline kicks at the lock, once, twice. The wood splinters and crashes open.

Kline finds himself inside a small office that holds a metal safe. Blue suit cowers behind his desk, Kline advances, is just about to grab the manager by the lapels when a blow thuds into the nape of his neck. He falls to his knees. A Chinese gangster he dimly remembers from his previous visit pulls back his head. A knife appears and moves for his throat. Kline tries to thrust himself upright but his legs refuse to do his bidding. As he feels the edge of the knife blade on his windpipe, he hears a shot that reverberates around the confines of the office. The grip on his head loosens, the knife disappears. His attacker falls back, a bullet hole perforating his forehead. Kline looks up into the smiling face of Lily Li T'ang and at the pistol she holds.

'Hello, John. I couldn't bear to miss the fun. Sorry if I shot your fox.'

'I forgive you.'

He rubs his throat. Lily toys with her gun. She addresses the manager, who sits transfixed behind his desk.

'I do hope you will grant us access to your safe.'

A shake of the head in reply. Lily fires. His right ear lobe disappears. Blood stains the collar of his shirt. Lily examines the pistol.

'This gunsight must be faulty. I never miss what I aim for.'

'Aim for his other ear, you might miss and part his eyebrows.'

The Triad leader gulps for air. Lily smiles and takes aim. No words come, but a shaking hand points at a filing cabinet. Lily lowers her weapon. Kline goes to the cabinet, pulls open a steel drawer, lifts out a bunch of keys.

'Try them,' Lily orders.

The third key Kline tries turns the lock. The door of the safe swings open. Neatly stacked inside are rows of polythene bags containing the stuff that nightmares are made of. Lily smiles with delight at what she sees. She leans down, addresses them lovingly.

'Hello, boys, Mummy's here.'

119

The afternoon seems interminable. Anne has typed the word 'pets' over a million times, or so it seems to her.

Now, at last, the proposal papers are done. Her boss hovers over her. She hands him the neatly typed sheets, gives him a polite smile.

'One set of proposals, version number forty-three.'

'Oh, not that, surely. Not quite.'

His eyes scan down each page. A pause. Buckram taps his fingers against the pages.

'Yes, Miss Darracott, very good. Yes, I think we may put this aside and move onto the next phase.'

'Next phase?'

'Yes, I've had a rather exciting idea. One that might even outshine all the rest. We will develop it in the same way as we did the others. I scribble out my ideas, you give me a copy, I clarify my thoughts until the new proposal reaches a level fit to be presented to the board.'

In a small voice his secretary asks, 'What's your idea?'

Buckram begins to pace around, stops, decides to share.

'I'm going to suggest a range of soups for doggies. Petfix can market a whole range, liver, beef, chicken, rabbit, even vegetarian. My daughter would insist on that option. Yes, just think of it, a whole variety of ingredients for doggie taste buds to savour. I've even come up with a generic name. "Poochy Soup..." Something like that.'

Only one idea occurs to Anne: bullshit.

'Sorry?' Buckram frowns.

'Erm, I'll do anything you think fit, Mr Buckram.'

'Really? Oh, good, good. Maybe we can make a start. You said you wouldn't be averse to staying late. Perhaps a little more typing?'

Anne slumps back into her office chair. Buckram changes tack.

'Followed by a little eaties, perhaps?'

'Oh, I don't know,' Anne replies, wearily.

'No. Forget the typing. Go home and change. I'll meet you. We'll go somewhere swish on expenses. Anywhere, you name it and we're already at table.'

A wicked thought surfaces. Anne gazes up at him, her expression brightening as the idea fully forms.

'Have you heard of a restaurant called the Nirvana?'

'Erm...'

'All the best people go there.'

'Oh, the *Nirvana?*'

'Yes.'

'I never quite... I've always meant to go, of course, is it as good as they say?'

Anne smiles bewitchingly at him.

'Well, I can promise you an evening you won't easily forget.'

'Excellent, excellent. Tonight, hopefully, we shall experience Nirvana together.'

'Perhaps we will.'

120

Sarah Gant enters the field of battle. Slumped around the wrecked foyer lie the defeated warriors of the Wo Shing Wo. Some are nursing broken heads, others tending battered bodies. She pauses by a display of goodies that have miraculously escaped the mayhem. She selects a packet of chocolate Smarties and makes her way towards the inner offices.

In the main office, she finds the blood-stained Triad leader Michael Lam, bound to his chair by means of a complete reel of celluloid (a John Woo film starring Jackie Chan) wound tight around him. A flyer for next week's movie, *The NEW Fists of Fury*, is stuffed into his mouth.

After cutting him free, Sarah pops a blue chocolate into her mouth, requests a report on the attack.

'Tall round-eye, young Chinese woman with a gun, mad bitch, she do this!'

He points at his bloodied ear. Sarah is more interested in the empty safe.

'Hijacked?'

'Shipment stolen.'

'Not good. Especially for you.'

Michael Lam groans in agreement. Sarah reaches a decision. One that will imperil many lives, including her own.

'OK, Michael baby, here's what I suggest. Get that ear seen to. Before you do, put the phone to your good ear, make a call to your bosses in HK, tell them to send in the big guy before John Kline brings more woe to the Wo Shing Wo.'

121

Kuldip unwraps a white plaster bust. Along the dining table lie a collection of pottery and porcelain items taken from the cardboard boxes that litter the floor of the salon. Rafiq sits across in an armchair, pen poised over a notebook.

'Yes, Kuldip, what is the next item?'

'Don't know, head of some bloke trying to look clever-clever.'

Rafiq looks at the bust under review, shakes his head, returns to his inventory.

'Item twenty-seven. One bust of Beethoven...'

He is interrupted by his stand-in butler. A large lumbering fellow wearing a short white jacket, he closes the door behind him as in muffled tones he announces the arrival of a visitor.

'Jamal, please speak up a little, please.'

'Mr Khan!'

'What? I thought he was in prison.'

Almost dropping a Crown Derby ginger jar, Kuldip panics.

'I don't like the turning up of this Khan!'

'Neither do I. Cover the shipment, quickly, there is a tablecloth somewhere.'

While Kuldip scurries around opening drawers, prising open cupboards, Rafiq composes himself for the meeting with Khan.

'Found it, Mr Rafiq...'

'Good lad. Cover the items, place the boxes under the table.'

Once all the antique wares are out of sight, Rafiq calmly says to his servant, 'Very well, Jamal, you may show in our visitor.'

Jamal opens the door. Iqbal Khan steps into the room. He addresses Kuldip.

'Mr Rafiq?'

'No, Grandad, I'm far from being Mr Rafiq.'

Khan's father turns his attention to the other Asian in the room.

'To whom do we have honour?' Rafiq asks.

'I am Iqbal Khan. Inspector, 'Pindi Cantonment Police. Retired. I wish to question both of you as to the events that occurred on the 25th last, staged events which led to the false imprisonment of an officer of the law.'

Rafiq and Kuldip exchange wary glances. Both have the same thought: *Who is this relic?*

122

Dressing for her 'date' with Buckram, Anne searches through her wardrobe in the cramped quarters of her houseboat.

There is a jumble of styles and colours to choose from, most of them bought when she had a big score to celebrate. Not all though; a few had been bought on the instructions of her former boss, the gang leader Rawlinson.

She reaches along the rack, pauses at a black chiffon dress she can't remember wearing, certainly not at the Nirvana. She takes the dress out, examines it critically. There is a glittering spray of sequins spread from bust to shoulder, bringing glamour to the otherwise sombre black outfit. Yes, it could be described as 'piss elegant'. Just the thing for paying a visit to an old flame.

123

Seated opposite to each other while Kuldip busies himself at the drinks table, the ex-police inspector conducts his interrogation of Rafiq as if he was once more the head of detectives.

'You deny any responsibility in the spinning of the web of falsehood within which my son finds himself entangled?'

'Of course. And I find it difficult to raise much sympathy for an officer of the law who, if what I hear is true, was involved in, what's the expression, Kuldip?'

Pausing in his polishing of a brandy glass, Kuldip searches for just the right expression.

'On the double take, Mr Rafiq.'

The voice of the old man rises with disdain.

'I do not know criminal jargon, I recognise truth and innocence. I also recognise dacoits no matter how great their veneer of culture, wealth or sophistication.'

'Dacoits? Dacoits? Do you recognise that word, Kuldip?'

'He mean gangster folk, Mr Rafiq.'

'How insulting.'

In a flurry of anger Iqbal Khan jumps to his feet, takes a step towards his adversary.

'You forget, or perhaps do not know, that my son visited me in my village when you had gone to ground in Rawalpindi.'

With a casual wave of his hand Rafiq dismisses the implication.

'Yes, Mr Khan requested my return to help him with information that could lead to preventing the rise of the Triads.' Rafiq's voice rises in indignation. 'I would never have agreed to return had I known it was merely a pretence to protect his investment in corruption.'

'Oh, balderdash!'

'Balderdash?'

Kuldip interjects. 'What is this balderdash?'

The old man glares at each in turn, his lip trembling beneath his greying moustache.

'I know of your involvement in the trade of illegal immigration, the trafficking of human cargo. Why you're still at liberty, sir, completely escapes my comprehension.'

Stretching lazily, Rafiq ignores the outburst. He turns to his assistant.

'Where is the orange juice for our guest, Kuldip?'

'Oh, yes, yes, very sorry, I will convey it right away, sir.'

While Kuldip fetches the drink, Rafiq gazes at his visitor.

Kuldip hands the glass of orange juice to their accuser with a humble bow.

'What you will experience, my dear Mr Khan,' Rafiq begins, sagely, 'is that life in this great city will add little towards enlightenment. You will find, for instance, that English justice is most discerning between the innocent and the guilty, which is why, if you will pardon the comparison, your son now resides within a prison cell and I am entertaining you in my humble home.'

Kuldip sniggers at his master's words. Iqbal shakes his head.

'Hypocrisy is the most dispiriting path a man can take, Mr Rafiq.'

'Which is why I advise you to make an early return to the simplicities of village life. Leave the board to players who know the rules of the game.'

Kuldip giggles, points at the old man, sticks his fingers into his mouth, emits a loud whistle like a referee calling full-time.

'Go to jail, do not pass go, do not collect two hundred pound, no double sixes either. Do what Mr Rafiq say, go sling your hook!'

Overcome with loathing the ex-inspector of police advances a step towards Kuldip.

'I would sooner not be than listen to the likes of you, a liar, mean as a collier's whelp. You who are free only through the influence of my son, you who gave information as false as the smile on your master's mouth.'

Snarling, Kulip snaps back.

'Your bloody son, he say, "Tell me what you hear or else your back in nick, mate." I tell him what I overhear from Kline. Not bloody well my fault if your boy add up two and three and make a four.'

He cackles with laughter. Iqbal Khan recoils.

Rafiq asks, silkily, 'Mr Khan, by whose authority have you…?'

He breaks off as Lily Li T'ang sweeps into the room, cradling a terracotta nymph in her arms.

'Keys to the strong room, please…'

She sees the old man, frowns, then becomes the social hostess.

'I don't think we have been introduced. Aslam?'

With some pride, Rafiq makes the introduction.

'My fiancée, Lily. Lily, this is Mr Khan,' adding, 'Pere.'

'Son Pere?'

'Oui.'

('Yes.')

'Que veut-il?'

('What does he want?')

'Pour sauver son fils de prison.'

('To rescue his son from prison.')

'Il en a le pouvoir, l'autorité?'

('Has he any power, authority?')

'J'en doute.'

('I doubt it.')

'Alors pourquoi sommes-nous en train de perdre du temps avec lui, stupide? Débarrassez-vous de cette relique de l'Empire britannique, passer à faire cet inventaire.'

('Then why are we wasting time with him, stupid? Get rid of this relic of the British Empire, get on with making that inventory.')

Lily shifts the sculpture from one hand to the other.

'I need to prime this, so keys, keys…'

While Rafiq searches for the safe keys, Lily offers her hand to Khan *pere*.

'Awfully nice to have met you.'

The old man smiles, takes a step forward, replies in fluent French.

'Et je vous. Avec Kipling, je crois que la plus sotte femme peut gérer un homme intelligent mais il a besoin d'une femme très intelligente pour gérer un fou.'

('And I you. With Kipling, I believe the silliest woman may manage a clever

man, but it needs a very clever woman to manage a fool.')

Lily covers her *faux pas.*

'Oh, well, quite.'

Glancing around at the surprised faces around him, Khan asks, in English, 'Where may I find this man Kline?'

'Anywhere there is trouble, Grandad...'

Kuldip pauses as the phone rings, hurries to take the call. Rafiq turns impatiently to his unwelcome visitor.

'Look, Khan sahib, we are busy. If there are no further questions or insulting quotations from Kipling, I trust you will excuse us.'

'Excuse the likes of you? Never!'

124

Fastening buttons on a dress shirt with a swollen fist is not easy but, finally, Kline snaps on his bow tie, ready for the evening. He tries to ease the muscles in his neck, stiff and aching from the blow suffered at the Roxy. He wonders if pleading a headache might postpone the 'night to remember' promised by the warrior queen. *Aspirin,* he decides, *I need aspirin.* Where to find it? None in the bathroom, he knows that for sure. His eyes rest on the table beside Annie's side of the bed.

Crossing to the bedside cabinet he opens the drawer, looks down on the bits and pieces she has left behind. Amongst them are a tab of paracetamol together with a silver strip of birth control pills, half-used. Kline removes the paracetamol, closes the drawer, shakes his head, winces at a stab of sudden pain.

125

On their entering the Nirvana, Anne holds her head high, unsure of her welcome. For all she knows she might have been barred. Archie, the barman, is the first to notice her. He indicates her arrival to Max, the head waiter, then hurries smiling to greet her.

'Ah, good evening, Miss Anne, lovely to see you here again.'

'Thank you, Max.'

He shows Anne and Buckram to a table with a view into the bar area. Stan, the pianist, catches her eye, winks, starts to play 'As Time Goes By'. Anne grins across at him. Archie brings her a tonic with ice and lemon.

'Thanks, Archie.'

The barman ignores Buckram. Anne calls him back. Archie asks Buckram, curtly.

'What would you like?'

'A large gin, rather pink, I think.'

Gavin, a young black waiter, passes the table.

'Hello, Miss Anne, nice to see you here again.'

Anne smiles, looks across the table at her escort, who seems a little disconcerted at the warmth of the welcome she has received.

'You have been here before, I see.'

'Oh, once or twice.'

She looks past his shoulder, sees the stairs that lead up to what she once called home. Her expression follows her thoughts. Buckram notices her sadness.

'Something wrong?'

'No, no, it's just this tune…'

'Bad memories?'

'Something like that.'

The piano music becomes louder as Kline descends the stairs. He reaches floor level, points at the pianist, begins to make a joke.

'I thought I told you never to play it…'

Stan inclines his head towards the corner table. Kline turns and sees Anne sitting with a business bloke in a grey pinstripe suit. He recovers what he hopes is some poise as he approaches their table. Anne avoids eye contact with Kline, smiles at Buckram.

'You asked about the proprietor, here he is.'

Buckram stands, extends a hand.

'Ah. How do you do.'

'How do you do,' Kline responds, touching the offered hand.

Buckram glances around at the décor, the subdued lighting, other couples at other tables.

'This is a most interesting café, I congratulate you.'

'I congratulate you,' Kline says.

'What for?'

'On your choice of partner.'

'Why, thank you. Would you care to join us for a drink?'

'I never drink with customers. Enjoy your meal.'

Anne lifts her eyes to watch John Kline move towards the bar. He has lost a little weight; his black dinner jacket now fits him perfectly. Buckram tries to hail a passing waiter without success. Anne realises she is being spoken to.

'Sorry, what?'

'Well, I was going to share some of my ideas for new doggie products.'

'You've already told me about them more than once.'

'Oh, sorry, sorry.'

During the pause that follows, Buckram stares at Anne. He realises how attractive she is, so alluring yet so familiar. Those grey-green eyes, the honey-coloured hair he so longs to touch.

'Tell me about your wife and teenage daughter,' Anne says.

Buckram welcomes the topic. He leans towards her, takes a pull on his pink gin.

'Now that is a story and a half...'

From his perch at the bar Kline sees Buckram and Anne put their heads together. Talking about what? He tries to divorce his thoughts from the upsurge of emotion. It isn't easy. He feels something touch his elbow. He looks down and sees a bottle of bourbon. He looks up as Archie slides a glass towards him.

'Thanks, Archie, you're a pal.'

The last notes of 'As Time Goes By' fade away.

Kline pours himself a double, sighs, drinks.

126

Feeling like a schoolboy presenting his homework for stern appraisal, Aslam Rafiq watches as Lily scans down the list of items for export to America. She looks up, purses her lips, shakes her head.

'This simply isn't good enough. Detail, detail, it totally lacks convincing detail. This wouldn't fool a blind child of three, let alone a sharp-eyed US customs officer.'

'Darling, I have many talents but describing antique pottery is not one of them.'

'Then find someone who can. Three out of ten, try harder.'

She thrusts the list back at him.

'And don't take too long about it. I'd like to see this shipment on its way before we draw our old age pension. I have to go out, advance me a hundred pounds.'

'Where are you going at this late hour?'

'A dragon head cannot afford to rest. I have a clandestine meeting with a defector from the Wo Shing Wo. He says he has vital news regarding our continued wellbeing.'

Opening his wallet and extracting banknotes, Rafiq watches Lily Li T'ang put on her fighting garb, a long leather coat and jaunty hat. She pulls out a gun from her pocket, checks it is fully loaded. Rafiq begins to understand the allure of leather-clad lovelies. He shudders pleasurably at the prospect of licking the boots of such a cruel creature. Lily notices his agitation.

'I know what I'm doing. I can look after myself.'

'I'm sure you can, but why not take Kuldip along as, what's the term? Backup?'

'Not necessary. But I do need that money, I may have to buy the information.'

'Yes, of course, here you are, my darling. Please be careful, that's all I ask.'

'I will.'

'Can I make one further request?'

Halfway to the door, Lily turns in a swirl of leather.

'What is it?'

'Wear your burka.'

'Don't be ridiculous.'

127

Toying with her portion of chicken and coconut sauce, Anne wonders why she expected this visit to achieve anything. All the three principals seem to be doing is seeking solace in drink. Kline at the bar with his bourbon, Buckram with his champagne, she with her empty glass of tonic. She raises a finger towards the bar, sees the proprietor nod. Archie begins to pour her a fresh one.

Stan, the pianist, starts to play 'Moon Glow', so softly it becomes almost subliminal.

Laying down her knife and fork, Anne looks at the side dishes scattered on the table. Once delicious they are now congealing into a sad memory. Anne stares up at the man who believes he is still her boss.

'Tell me something,' Anne says.

'Yes?'

'What is the best outcome for you from tonight's little tête-à-tête? Tonight's little rendezvous at, what did you call it? "This most interesting caff"?'

'Caff? I'm sure I would have said "café".'

'I'm sure you would, baby…'

The diminutive barman approaches the table, places her drink before her.

'Thanks, Archie. I've missed you. Be a pal, don't relay that message.'

'Got it. Are you OK?'

'I can cope.'

She watches him return to the bar. Takes a sip of tonic, gives Buckram a quizzical look.

'You've told me about your position on doggie products, how much you despise your wife, your family, how you fear for your position. But you say nothing about your daughter, or why you're so attracted to little ol'… well, little *young* me. Why? Is it because I remind you of your offspring, because I act like her?'

There is no reply to her question. Anne stares across the table, waiting for his answer.

'Speak.'

Buckram drains his champagne glass. He has the fevered look of a man who is about to reveal a hidden longing.

'Oh, so many questions. What did I hope to get from tonight, from being with you? Well, Anne, the answer to your question is something beyond what you might imagine.'

'Like what, exactly?'

Anne watches his eyes mirror his inner desire.

'I still possess her school uniform.'

'My size?'

'Oh, yes. Yes.'

'You want me to wear it?'

'Would you mind?'

He stares at her. His eyes cloud, a sheen of perspiration glistens on his high forehead. Anne has a moment of clarity.

'If I did it would be nothing. Not even a therapy, just a pathway into further sickness. Like me, tonight, realise the truth about something. Try and live with that. It's a demanding bedfellow but worth satisfying.'

He reaches across the table, grips her hands, holds her fast in a crushing grip.

'I'll give you truth, truth about your kind. You don't know whether to be whipped by men or treat them like animals. Want to put a saddle on me, dig your spurs into me until I bleed?'

'Not particularly.'

'No? Ah, you wish to be told what to do, to experience my total dominance.'

'Just try.'

Anne gives him a hard, defiant stare, picks up a fork, goes to stab the back of his hand. He releases his grip. His face contorts with anger. She lowers her voice, tries to avert the growing conflict.

'Look, let's bear no rancour for tonight's termination of our personal and business relationship. Let's just quit.'

'Quit? Shit! I'm the boss. You, you're only the bloody secretary. I tell you what to do. I dictate, I control. "Oh, it feels wonderful, Mr Buckram, whatever you say Mr Buckram." What I say, what I say, what I *say!*'

As Buckram pours out his bile and drunken anger, Anne ladles sauces from their side dishes onto her plate until it swims with an admixture of spicy Thai gravy, coconut sauce and a wodge of sticky rice. She picks up the plate, balances it, smiles sweetly, says, 'I'll tell you what, Mr Buckram, you have your meal on the firm, I'll have my meal on you.'

'What…?'

Anne empties the plate of congealed food and condiments onto his head. Buckram stands, claws the gunge away from his eyes. He kicks the table over, strikes out at her.

'Bitch, fucking cow!'

Backing away, Anne sees him bearing down on her, his fists raised. Before he can strike a blow, Kline intervenes, hustles him away. Waiters converge. Kline points at Anne, gives curt instructions.

'Take her upstairs, I need to get this bum out of here.'

The waiters hustle Anne away. Buckram squares up to Kline.

'I used to box, you know?'

'What, kippers? Manx kippers?'

Buckram's reply is a feeble right cross. Kline evades, turns the impetus of his attacker, grabs the businessman in a half nelson, frog marches him towards the exit that leads to the street.

Kline and Buckram are almost at the door when a well-dressed elderly Asian man enters. He stands aside as Buckram is ejected from the premises without ceremony.

Khan senior follows the tall man in evening dress as he apologises to diners for the disturbance. As they reach the bar area the old man manages to speak out.

'Oh, excuse me, could you tell me where I might find Mr Kline, please.'

'That's me. What can I do for you?'

'I would welcome a little of your time. My name is Iqbal Khan, I believe you know my son, Zaheer Khan.'

With his mind on other things it takes a moment before Kline realises who his visitor is.

'Oh, Khan. The old man, you?'

'Yes.'

'Look, right now there are matters I have to deal with. Have an orange juice, I'll see you later, all right?'

'Yes, yes, of course.'

On his way towards the stairs, Kline pauses to give instructions to the head waiter that Khan's father is to be looked after as a welcome guest. This done, he begins to climb the stairs.

In the apartment above the restaurant, Anne has perched herself on a corner of the bed. Archie stands across from her, wanting to speak but unable to find the right words to say.

John Kline comes into the bedroom. His assumed expression is one of contained indignation. Anne stands, ready for anything. Archie looks from one fighting cock to the other and decides his bar downstairs requires his services urgently. He hurries away, leaving the couple facing each other. Kline is the first to speak, his tone one of pained reproof.

'Nice, very nice. I'm trying to run a business here. I can't have drunken executives and their frustrated secretaries creating scenes in my caff, can I?'

'What are you going to do about it?'

'I can either bar you, or…'

'Or…?'

There is no reply, only a burst of action. Kline takes two steps towards Anne, sweeps her into his arms, carries her towards the bed.

128

At this late hour, the dingy multilevel car park that overlooks the garish lights of the Bull Ring is almost empty of vehicles. Lily Li T'ang drives her yellow sports car up the ramp leading onto level three. She sees a white saloon car waiting in the middle of an empty row. She drives alongside, waits for the man inside the Datsun to make a move. She eases her Beretta out of her handbag and holds it out of sight.

The window of the adjoining window is lowered. The red glare of the neon advertising hoarding in the street below shines onto the face of a Chinese thirty-something with a white plaster across his nose. Lily opens her window in turn.

'Well?'

'You want information, I got good information.'

'Give me an inkling about that information.'

'What you mean?'

'A hint.'

'No money, no info.'

Lily sighs, takes out a ten pound note, offers it across from her window to his. Her offer is met with a snort of derision.

'You think I sell my life so cheap?'

'Fifty. That's my final offer.'

The banknotes are whisked from her hand. Lily shows the informant what she holds in her other hand. There is an instant response.

'Not necessary to shoot, I speak. Wo Shing Wo want you and John Kline dead.'

'Of course they do. Give me back my money.'

'They have negotiated big fee with someone they call the White Devil. He is on his way to Birmingham.'

Lily lowers her Beretta.

'You're certain of this?'

'Dead certain. I was in the office of the Roxy manager when he got the news.'

Lily feels a shiver run through her. She looks around the bleak concrete walls, the oil-stained floor, as if the ogre might be about to materialise. She recovers from the chilling moment.

'All right. Stay in touch.'

The white Datsun reverses, speeds away down the ramp, disappears. Lily sits back in her seat, her mind filled with apprehension at the news. She decides it is imperative that she warn her chief enforcer right away.

129

The evening at the Nirvana is almost at a close when Lily Li T'ang makes her entrance.

Kevin is the first member of staff to try and head her off.

'Good evening, madam, may I help you?'

'No, thank you.'

'We've stopped serving food, but may I order you a drink?'

'Just get out of my way.'

The next line of defence is Max, the head waiter.

'May I be of assistance, madam?'

'No.'

'Are you quite sure?'

'Yes, quite sure.'

Lily sweeps towards the stairs that lead up to the apartment. Archie makes a final desperate attempt to divert her.

'Mr Kline's out at a meeting!'

'Rather late for that, isn't it?'

All the staff watch as she ascends the stairs. Archie shakes his head, despairingly.

Lily enters the bedroom to an unwelcome sight. Her enforcer is lying naked with the blonde trollop sitting up beside him. Both are bathed in a glow of post-coital satisfaction. For once Lily is lost for words. Kline smiles lazily across at her.

'Sorry to disappoint you, baby, but I've already had a night to remember.'

Anne chimes in, pointedly.

'Not keeping you, are we? Am I?'

For one savage second Lily thinks to put a bullet into each of them.

Then she remembers all the staff downstairs. Looking from one to the other, her expression hardens into a cold fury.

'I'll piss on your graves.'

Kline is unmoved.

'Be my guest.'

Lily flounces out of the room. Anne gives him a look.

'You and her?'

'Yeah. But there was nothing to it, just sex.'

'Oh…'

Anne lies back. Kline leans on his elbow, looks down at her.

'Know what I think?'

'No, tell me.'

'There's got to be more to sex than just sex.'

'A four-letter word beginning with "L"?'

'Lust?'

'Ah, you… I'll teach you…'

She pushes him away, begins to tickle him fiercely, armpits, ribs, the inside of his thighs.

'No, not there, ow, stop…ha, Annie, stop!'

She eventually stops the good-natured assault.

Kline lies back, grinning, stretching. Anne rests her head on his chest, inhales the smell of him. Feels the fall of his seed. Knows she is home.

130

The scenic valley where the Writer lives is full of early afternoon sunshine. All is quiet. Cattle and sheep graze in fields that lie beyond drystone walls. The country road lies straight before him, which is more than can be said for the thoughts whirling convoluted inside his head. He pushes his one-year-old daughter ahead of him in her pram. This walk is a daily occurrence, a way to lull her into a mid-day sleep and for him to wrestle with his story problems.

The toddler yawns, a promising sign. A dozen more steps and her eyes flutter and close. The Writer returns to thoughts of a character he is about to introduce for the first time. He's done the foreshadowing, built the bugger up, now the time has arrived for him to take centre stage.

A white car with a loudspeaker on its roof turns the corner ahead and speeds towards them. The car slows. As it comes by the man with the pram, a metallic voice booms out, 'ROUND BRITAIN CYCLE RACE COMING PAST IN THREE MINUTES!'

His daughter sits up as if an electric shock has been administered. Her father yells, 'Stupid fuckers!' He hurries the pram to where a seat is located at the point where two roads converge. He takes the child up into his arms as a phalanx of bike riders sweep around the corner. In the centre of the pumping thighs, whirring wheels, is a rider in a yellow jersey. The race wheels away down the country road followed by motor bikes, support vehicles, a pair of police cars.

Quiet returns once more. The Writer decides to return homewards. The kid will not settle for sleep now, so they may as well trot back to the cottage. But surprisingly she decides to lie down and look up at the scudding white clouds against the blue of the Quernmore sky. Seconds later she is asleep once more.

Where was I? The writer asks himself. *White Devil. Who is he? What is he?*

With the cottage now in sight he wonders what there will be for lunch. Then a thought floods into his mind, an inner voice that says, 'Death comes to Birmingham disguised as W.C. Fields.'

What? What the fuck does that mean? But the blockage has been dislodged, ideas are breaking the fourth wall, taking the writer on a surreal journey of supernatural elements, florid language, all the stuff that scares you when you're writing a thriller that is supposed to stay within the safe confines of its genre.

All right, so Death comes to Birmingham disguised as W.C. Fields, does it? Well, let us at least consider the matter, decide to what strange shores it might take us to...

131

It is a morning when the sun has refused to show its face. A grey mist lingers over Birmingham, turning the high-rise apartment blocks of the city into ghostly monoliths.

A trio of urchins stare into the foyer of the Imperial hotel. A one-legged blind man, propped up by a crutch, waits for guests to buy matches from the wooden tray that hangs from around his neck. With the fog chilling his bones he stands beneath the overhang of the hotel entrance.

His acute hearing warns him that a smooth-sounding motor car is approaching. He begins to fumble with the items on his tray, hoping that his first sale of the day might be imminent.

A white Rolls Royce bearing the number plate 'W.D.1' emerges from the gloom and draws to a halt on the driveway. A rear door swings open to allow a figure that might have stepped out the pages of a Dickens novel to emerge. A portly man, in his middle years, he wears a grey top hat with a black band, a cravat of the same hue, a white shirt, a purple waistcoat, a dark tailcoat, close fitting trousers, shiny black shoes, matching white socks and gloves. In his right hand, he holds a silver topped cane.

The three urchins run towards him, hoping to beg a coin. They are met by a savage growl and a raised cane. The children start to scatter. The youngest sobs as he tries to evade the hefty kicks being aimed in his direction.

Inside the Rolls, his chauffeur, Jenkins, looks on impassively. W.D.s assistant Lemmy, a puny Chinese youth dressed in similar fashion to his master begins to fill a cocktail shaker with gin and vermouth.

Once the children have been cleared from his view, the White Devil, for it is he, spies the sign worn by the beggar. 'Blind,' it reads. The W.C. Fields lookalike approaches, casually hooks his foot around the end of the crutch and slowly, very slowly, shifts it away from the perpendicular until the blind beggar crashes to the floor. His goods are scattered all around him. As he gropes helplessly on the ground, his tormentor considers the view of the city now emerging from the mist. He shakes his head, speaks in a wheezy drawl, 'Birmingham, eh? On the whole, I'd sooner be in Philadelphia.'

He grins to himself, sweeps into the hotel foyer, approaches the reception desk where a clerk waits doing his best to keep a straight face. His visitor speaks in pompous tones.

'I have a suite reserved under the name of W.*D*. Fields, Not W.C. Fields, don't make that mistake. One is synonymous with comedy, the other with tragedy. What has this to do with you, sir? Nothing. I will therefore proceed to the bridal suite without further ado.'

Twirling his walking cane, he strolls towards the elevators. Lemmy, a violin case in one hand, a silver cocktail shaker in the other, follows at a respectful distance.

132

Ensconced once more in the white bedroom of Rafiq's mansion, Lily Li T'ang lies in bed still smouldering at being bested by a blonde trollop. The traitor Kline is not aware of the danger he will be in once the White Devil hits town, and she, Lily, certainly isn't going to tell him. So, what to do? What move to make, what vengeance to wreak? The aim must be obliteration. Only then will the wound of rejection start to heal. She begins to consider how best to bring about the downfall of the reunited couple. A plan begins to form. A discreet tap on the bedroom door interrupts her vengeful thoughts.

'Yes, what is it?' she calls.

Venturing into the white bedroom, Rafiq holds glasses of orange juice. He looks towards the bed and is greeted by a radiant smile.

'Good morning, Aslam, how lovely to see you. And orange juice, how thoughtful you are.'

'Well, I try, darling, I do try.'

'Won't you join me?'

Lily folds back the sheet, invitingly. Rafiq takes a quick step towards the bed, places the glasses of orange on the bedside table.

'Are you sure?'

'We are engaged.'

'We certainly are.'

He removes his dressing gown, slides in beside her. The warmth of her thigh through the thin cotton of her white nightdress makes coherent speech difficult. He clears his throat.

'Last night...'

'What about it?'

'You seemed to be out rather a long time.'

'I popped into that awful Kline person's restaurant. Once there I then asked myself, what am I doing here? Why am I not with my Aslam?'

'Why not indeed?'

She snuggles up to him. Feeling her against him, her breasts a mere touch away, makes Rafiq tremble.

'Are you cold?' Lily asks.

'Quite the reverse.'

'Yes, sorry about that.'

'No, don't move away, please don't.'

'There are things I must do. Did you manage to assemble a container of antiques?'

'Yes, they are at the warehouse.'

'And the inventory, has it been changed?'

'No.'

'It won't do as it is. We need authentic titles to describe the fakes. I don't have that expertise, neither do you. Perhaps you might know someone?'

'No, I don't. Well, yes, I might. John Kline's woman knows about such things, but they are no longer together.'

'She has wormed her way back into his affections. Some women are quite shameless. I happened to come across them last night, quite the loving couple.'

'Well, why don't we ask her to help us out?'

'Better coming from you. I don't think she likes me very much.'

'No, why ever not?'

'Aslam, women know these things.'

'All right, I shall ask her to visit the warehouse, put proper names to the items as a personal favour to me. Talking of favours…'

He reaches for her. She eases herself out of reach, steps out of the bed, looks down at him. He holds out a beseeching hand.

'All in good time. Let's get this shipment off to America first.'

'After that?'

'There will be time for recreation.'

'For consummation? May I dare to hope?'

'You may indeed.'

'Ah, Lily, how I long for that consummation, like a parched man longs for water, as a hungry lover craves the flesh of his beloved…'

'All right, enough, you've made your point.'

133

The bridal suite has many garish features, the most notable a large lowered window shade painted with naked cherubs preparing a bride for her nuptials. The king-sized bed is raised on a platform with sunken coloured lamps inset around its base at regular intervals. On the bed is a pink satin coverlet. Laid out on this lies a languorous Sarah Gant polishing her nails.

Hearing voices, she sits up, lowers the neckline of her red slip dress, prepares for her assignation with the deadly assassin.

The twin doors are thrown open, a Victorian-looking gent in a top hat strides in. Sarah gapes at him.

'What...?'

'You must be Sarah Gant, undercover agent for the Wo Shing Wo?'

'Yes.'

'Ah, my dusky moor, my sweet Azande!'

He opens his arms in an expansive greeting. Sarah stands, her expression one of utter disbelief.

'*You're* White Devil?'

The vaudevillian bows, begins to glide about the room, making flowery gestures to illustrate a discourse that is delivered from the side of his mouth in a barking accent from the east coast of America.

'You seem a trifle discombobulated.'

'You could say.'

'Once I showed my true visage, my features, in Alexandria, and five hundred people died at a glance...'

He sends a brief glance in Sarah's direction. She feels a cold hand clutch her heart. For a second she glimpses the reality behind his mask of deception. He nods, returns to his adopted persona, continues his progress around the room. His servant, Lemmy, stands by the door, holding onto the cocktail shaker, watching the performance.

'So, my divine Sarah, I adopt the guise of a buffoon, so all are lulled, dulled into a sense of false security, cosy within the confines of their contempt, little realising that I have brought about the deaths of presidents, kings, emperors and struck down the wise and the worldly. I accept tasks such as this as a means of keeping my deadly skills well honed. Yes...'

He pauses. Lifts his cane, gestures towards the window behind the bed. Slowly the painted frieze lifts, revealing an expansive view of the city of Birmingham. He takes it in, lifts his cane, looks along it as if it were a samurai sword.

'I have, within my luggage, a scythe, and on that scythe is writ the name "John Kline". Whatever the variables in this uncertain life, know his death to be a certainty!'

He turns to his servant, lowers his voice. The Fieldsian tones disappear, his pattern of speech is without accent. He could be from anywhere.

'Pour me a Martini, Lemmy, you know how much that bloody speech takes out of me.'

134

Anne and Kline walk together towards the factory that once housed the gambling operation of Shen T'ang. As they near the battered blue wooden door, Anne hesitates, catches his arm.

'Do we have to do this?'

'Rafiq asked for a favour, something about antiques. Let's see what it involves. You don't fancy helping them out, we walk. OK?'

'Isn't he engaged to that Lily Li T'ang bitch?'

'He says it's just a favour to him.'

'OK. Let's see what's what.'

The door still creaks and shudders on its hinges. It bangs shut behind them. What was once an engineering workshop is now a warehouse. Wooden crates and containers are stacked around the walls. A forklift truck is stacking a series of smaller crates ready for transportation.

They enter further into the warehouse. There is no sign of Aslam Rafiq. Chinese workers wearing blue overalls are sealing crates, using black paint to stencil 'New York' on the white wooden sides. From the far end of the building a whirring, rumbling sound begins to be heard. Kline and Anne stare upwards as a loading mechanism activates. Trundling along, high in the air, a heavy wooden crate is being ferried towards them.

Unseen by the couple, Lily Li T'ang emerges from a side office. As the heavy wooden container looms above Kline and Anne, she signals to the driver of the hoist. He operates a lever. The harness holding the cargo opens, releases the wooden crate. It hurtles down towards the couple standing directly below...

To be continued...

BOOK SIX
EAST OF THE EQUATOR

135

Unseen by the couple, Lily Li T'ang emerges from a side office. As the heavy wooden container looms above Kline and Anne, she signals to the driver of the hoist. He operates a lever. The harness holding the cargo opens, releases the wooden crate. It hurtles down towards the couple standing directly below as Rafiq enters from the side office. Seeing the crate plunging down, he yells a warning.

'John, Anne, look out!'

Kline sees the crate about to crush them. He pushes Anne clear, rolls over. The crate smashes to bits on the concrete floor, splinters fly. Kline protects himself, feels his hands peppered with flying debris, shards of broken pottery and splinters of wood.

Anne scrambles to her feet in time to see Lily make her exit through the main door. Rafiq reaches them, looks from one to the other, anxiously

'My God, are you all right?'

Kline regains his feet.

'Where's that bleedin' driver?'

'An accident, surely,' Rafiq suggests.

Anne cuts in.

'So how come there's nobody around to apologise?'

They stare down at the planks of shredded wood, the litter of broken pots. All three reach the same conclusion. This was no accident.

136

Seated at the bar Anne watches Kline pour himself a scotch. He pushes a club soda in her direction. She nods her thanks, marvels, not for the first time, at the way this man can shrug off a near death experience. As if reading her thoughts, he gives her a wry smile.

'What?' she asks.

'That crate could've shortened our stature.'

'With me, that's no joke. I saw her, you know, that slant-eyed, sallow-faced bitch sneaking away from the scene of the crime.'

'Hell hath no fury, that it?'

'She's no woman, she's a brat. One who needs educating with the toe of my boot.'

Kline leans across the bar, brings his face close to hers, speaks softly.

'I'm getting worried about you, Annie. First you go attacking my customers, second you invade my bed, and now you're threatening my ex-lovers with all sorts of mayhem.'

'She tried to flatten us. We're going to let that go?'

'Forget about it. Only damage suffered was this…'

He holds up his forefinger, shows a festering splinter of wood under the surface of his skin.

'Get it seen to.'

'I am.'

As he begins to nibble around the offending sliver of wood, the door opens from the street and an elderly well-dressed Asian enters. He approaches the couple at the bar, doffs his hat.

'Good morning, Mister Kline. Are you Miss Darracott?'

Anne looks askance at Kline, who makes the introduction.

'Mister Khan, senior.'

'I waited as long as possible last night, Mister Kline, right up to the time you closed, in fact.'

Kline remembers.

'Sorry, I got distracted. Things kept coming up.'

'I can vouch for that.' Anne smiles a satisfied smile at Iqbal Khan. 'What can we do for you?'

'My son is in jail, falsely accused of corrupt practice and murder.'

With a shrug, Kline replies, 'Life's a bastard when you weaken.'

'My son has a great respect for your integrity. I appeal to you, tell me what you know of the mysterious happenings on the night of the 25th. I'll respect your confidence, man to man. Now, this is hardly easy, but please, I beg you.'

Looking from one to the other, a puzzled Anne asks, 'What's Khan supposed to have done?'

'Shot Mr Yan over a drug deal.'

'What? No…' Her disbelief lessens as a thought occurs. 'Tell me, might the opium queen be mixed up in all this?'

Kline ponders.

'She might.'

'John, tell Mr Khan what you know. You owe that bitch nothing.'

Still Kline hesitates. His reluctance to snitch irritates Anne.

'Why should you do her any favours? Do you want to protect her or what?'

'All right. She was out to get Khan at the beginning, not so sure about her involvement at the end.'

Iqbal Khan produces a notebook and a pencil.

'Please continue, Mr Kline.'

137

Sarah Gant approaches the portals of St Anne's Catholic church. While seeking directions, she has been told that once upon a time the writer J.R.R. Tolkien worshipped here. The tall redbrick tower has the look of a fairy tale castle incongruously set in the grey wasteland of downtown Digbeth.

Inside the church, she gazes at the white arches that support a yellow stained-glass roof that casts a pale primrose light down upon the altar, with its centrepiece of Christ crucified.

Beside the altar is a statue of St Anne. A cluster of mourning women light candles before her. Other candles flicker in supplication and remembrance in the offertory stand, below the feet of the saint.

There is a faint trace of incense in the air. Sarah looks around for the man she has been summoned to meet. There is no sign of the preacher. She is about to leave the church when a muffled voice nearby calls out to her.

'Sister Gant, come to confession.'

Looking behind her, in the direction of the voice, Sarah sees a confessional booth.

Pulling aside the curtain reveals a wooden step and alongside this a grille with the outline of a shadowy seated figure waiting behind.

'Come in, Mrs Gant.'

Inside, the curtain is drawn across. Sarah, forced to kneel in a position of penitence, decides to regain some initiative.

'Been a while since I confessed to anything, Marcus.'

'I can believe that.'

'OK, I get it. This is your chance to play Holy Joe, but why in hell's name am I here?'

'To confess.'

'To what?'

'Consorting with the Devil.'

'You mean the White Devil?'

'They are one and the same.'

With a short laugh of derision, Sarah peers through the lattice.

'Have you seen the guy? You'd die laughing if you did.'

'Don't believe all you see. He is everything I've told you and more. I need your report.'

'OK, I was told by you to make myself available to him. I was informed of his arrival by the Wo Shing Wo. He's booked into the bridal suite of the Imperial hotel. You can arrest him there any time you like.'

A deep sigh of frustration comes from the other side of the divide.

'There is a change of plan. The Agency wish to weaken Triad activity by pitting the Wo Shing Wo against another Triad known as the 17K. The White Devil is in the UK to assist the Wo Shing Wo. You will render all assistance to him in achieving this end. You will also keep me informed of White Devil's aims and intentions.'

'Is that all? Would you like me to whistle Dixie while I'm about it?'

'I am merely the messenger, Mrs Gant. Your position remains as before. You can only obtain your freedom by delivering the success the company requires.'

'I'm to buddy up with the Devil. Thanks a lot.'

'Sister…'

'What now, you going to give me a penance, a dozen Hail Marys?'

'I will ask the heavenly host to protect you, I will pray for the safety of your soul.'

'Gee, thanks a lot.'

Leaving the confessional, Sarah steps into a shaft of sunlight that, for a moment, blinds her. Blinking, she gazes around the church, thinks about lighting a candle or two as protection from the forces of darkness. She dismisses it as mere superstition.

On exiting the church, she muses about the White Devil, recalls that evil glance of his that sent an icicle of fear into her heart.

Maybe lighting a few candles wasn't such a bad idea after all.

She turns, retraces her steps and re-enters Saint Anne's church.

138

Lily Li T'ang, still seething at her failure to exact vengeance on John Kline's strumpet, can't directly blame Rafiq for thwarting her plans.

But now a suitable opportunity to vent her spleen has presented itself.

Like a pair of sheepish schoolboys admitting a transgression before their headmistress, Rafiq, aided by Kuldip, informs her of the disaster at the warehouse.

Hands on hips, eyes glinting, lips compressed, she glowers at the two bearers of bad tidings.

'Let me understand this, in my absence, you allowed an oaf to destroy a crate of our antiques?'

Rafiq owns up to the fact. Kuldip is quick to deny any involvement.

'I wasn't there, Miss Lily.'

'So, this disaster is all down to you, Aslam.'

'No, I wasn't driving the apparatus. If I hadn't acted, Kline and Anne would have become flattened.'

'Oh, that would never do.'

Lily advances across the room.

'This means I must find a replacement for the lost crate. You must call Hong Kong and explain what has happened. Ask them to send another shipment of false antiques and an extra supply of heroin.'

Rafiq winces.

'Heroin, my darling, should that be mentioned on an open line?'

'No, call it... Yes, excreta of the white elephant.'

Kuldip giggles, turns the phrase over on his tongue.

'You have a fine way with words, Miss Lily.'

'Thank you, Kuldip, coming from you that is praise indeed.'

She gives Kuldip a winning smile. Rafiq feels isolated from her affections.

'Why not let Kuldip talk to the boys in Hong Kong. The Chinese will understand his mangled mode of expression rather that the purity of mine.'

Bridling at the insult, Kuldip becomes vehement in his own defence.

'Insults is it now? You think I sound like Chinese chaps having a sing song?'

'I rest my case.'

Seeing Kuldip about to descend into a glowering sulk, Lily tries to placate him. She puts her arm around his shoulders, gives him a gentle squeeze.

'He's a good boy, aren't you, Kuldip?'

She kisses the top of his head, turns to her fiancée.

'I only wish you were half as useful.'

Watching the two together, Lily and her pet poodle, makes Rafiq spring into jovial action to cover his pangs of jealousy. Whisking her away from Kuldip like a gallant cutting in at a ball, he twirls her into the middle of the room, speaks with style and panache.

'Given the opportunity to make myself useful, I would compose an exquisite symphony of love to play on the strings of your heart, zing! Zing! ZING!'

Lily is not impressed.

'We've no time for mush. Anyway, where is my engagement ring? That most precious precursor to a band of gold?'

Taking her hand, Rafiq presses it against his heart.

'Oh, Lily, darling Lily, even now, in the deepest depths of Kimberley, black miners search for stones of the palest blue to bedeck your third finger with the very root of adamantine fire.'

'Oh, that's all right then.'

'Lily…'

'Must dash, things to do.'

She departs, leaving a crestfallen Rafiq with only his assistant for company.

'Oh, is it worth it, Kuldip?'

'You want to get back into her better books?'

'Yes, but how?'

'Make that call to Hong Kong.'

Kuldip hands his master the telephone.

139

The White Devil, in his W.D. Fields persona, tips his straw hat, surveys the dozen Chinese youths sent to him for martial arts training by the Wo Shing Wo. Lemmy, his assistant, holding a cocktail shaker, watches impassively. His master jerks an aside in his direction.

'By the great balls of Beelzebub, it looks like an outbreak of yellow jaundice in here. Still, to business to business…'

Playing the schoolmaster, he introduces his training programme to the would-be warriors.

'Gentlemen, you will learn from me the hidden mysteries of the Mexican Malice, together with the delights of the Ganges Groin

Grapple. Mastery of these will be sufficient to destroy anything the K17 can send against you.'

The group are less than impressed by the portly, red-nosed figure before them. The White Devil smiles a sardonic smile then continues.

'Now you are all thinking, what's the bum got? Is he just a bag of bombast? Well, boys, one of you is about to find out the hard way. I always exert myself once for demonstration purposes, although I usually adhere to the principle that he who has truly mastered the art of the warrior has no need to fight at all. So, whomsoever is your best fighter, let him sally forth.'

The group grin slyly at each other. A youth, taller than the rest, is encouraged to step forward.

'Ah, the sacrificial lamb. What is your name?'

'Toi.'

'Ah, Toi, strange heathen name, but what can you expect when you scrape the gutters of Hong Kong and employ a yellow cur such as you?'

'You insult me and all the Chinese people!'

'Yes, so I do. How will you avenge such a coarse and gratuitous insult?'

Hoping to gain a quick advantage, Toi aims for his opponent's throat with a kung fu chop. There is a blur of movement, a shift of the hips that sends Toi hurtling towards the panelled wall of the bridal suite. With a sickening thud, he crashes against the woodwork and slithers, unconscious, to the floor. W.D. surveys his handiwork.

'Ah, the Balkan Buttock, never fails.'

Chastened, the group turn as the door to the suite opens. Sarah Gant, wearing a skin-tight leopard skin suit, saunters into the room. The White Devil takes in her voluptuous figure, opens his hands in a gesture of welcome.

'Welcome, my ebony princess, my queen of the night.'

Sarah steps over the fallen warrior.

'Not interrupting anything, am I?'

'No no, a little demonstration of who's who and what's what.'

Toi regains consciousness. With a scream of anger he charges at the White Devil, who catches the blow, glares into his attacker's eyes with a basilisk stare that freezes Toi into instant immobility. The Chinese youth stands, one arm raised, a frozen statue in the centre of the room.

His companions stare at W.D. with a growing sense of awe.

'Now, boys, anyone else want to push his luck, try to win a kewpie doll?'

He advances towards them. They back away fearfully.

'OK. Now, form pairs, let me see a little sparring here, show me what I must do to turn you into a fighting force that would make Caesar's legions shake in their sandals.'

The Chinese legion stare back blankly. Their troubled looks centre on the frozen state of their champion. W.D. waves a dismissive hand.

'Oh, him, he'll survive. Lemmy...'

He waves his servant forward. Dutifully, Lemmy comes across, uncaps his cocktail shaker and passes it under Toi's nose. At the same time W.D. snaps his fingers. The bewildered warrior comes back to life.

Lounging on the bed, Sarah watches the White Devil move amongst the Triad members, who have begun a frantic, noisy sparring session with much yelling and thudding of feet. He adjusts a jab here, points to a nerve centre there. He is a still presence amongst the whirling throng. She begins to speculate about him. Who is he behind his comedy mask? She realises he is looking across, that the smile on his face is for her alone. A glow of anticipation envelopes her. A soft whisper settles into her mind, a seductive voice that says, '*Tonight, my love.*'

The telephone shrills out. W.D. strides across to answer it.

'W.D. Fields, yes? Ah, the manager... What's going on up here? This is the bridal suite, what the hell do you think is going on up here?'

He grins at Sarah, replaces the receiver, summons Lemmy.

'Lemmy, you may pour the lady a Martini.'

A glass with rounded ice cubes is produced, an olive placed, the liquor poured. Sarah sips, W.D. waits for her appreciation. She glances up at the White Devil.

'You call that a Martini?'

'What would you call it?'

'Sewage.'

'*What?* Lemmy's been trained by the best shakers of a cocktail from Cipriani's in Venice to the Plaza in New York.'

'Waste of time.'

'I sense a challenge here. You produce a better Martini and he will grovel at your feet. Lose and you must perform whatever perversion he desires.'

'Done.'

Sarah hands the glass to W.D. He sips, then drinks the remainder.

'Seems OK to me.'

'Wait till you try the real thing, baby.'

140

The spluttering bulb in the ceiling over the inner entrance to the Nirvana bothered Anne throughout the previous evening. Now, the following afternoon, she stares up, trying, by strength of will, to reach a steady illumination.

'Try this...'

Anne turns, sees Kline holding out a bulb. She takes it from him.

'We still need a ladder.'

'No need...'

He flicks the light switch off, lifts her towards the ceiling. Anne reaches for the offending bulb. It is warm but not enough to prevent her twisting it free. She inserts the new bulb, calls down to the man who is holding her aloft.

'Try the switch.'

Kline does so. A clear, steady light shines down upon the couple. Kline lowers her a little, whirls her around in his arms, hums the tune of 'As Time Goes By'. After a second Anne joins in.

'*Da-da-da-dah-dum...*'

Halfway through Kline halts abruptly, manages to lower her to the floor before he staggers and almost falls.

'John, what is it?'

'Dizzy, whoa, just for a moment...'

He steadies himself, stares at his swollen forefinger. Anne loses patience with him.

'Why don't you see a doctor?'

'It's just a bit of fester. I'll pour some Scotch over it.'

'Why don't you just see a doctor?'

'Why don't you stop nagging me, OK?'

Anne shakes her head, goes behind the bar, presses a glass against an optic, hands the scotch to him across the counter. He places the glass before him, sits on a stool, dips his finger into the alcohol. Looks across at her, gives a slight smile of acquiescence.

'Ah, you're right, I'll go and see the quack tomorrow. I don't feel too good. I feel as if someone's put a hex on me.'

'Like who?'

'Take your choice. Mysterious assassins, the vengeance of Lily Li T'ang. I even hear the surviving Rawlinson brother is getting out of nick soon. He's making dire threats against my person.'

Anne gives a long sigh, hunches over the top of the bar.

'Life at the Nirvana. An everyday story of gangster folk.'

'I've a good mind to take your advice.'

'And what's that?'

'Something about a clean pair of heels being better than a clenched pair of fists.'

He looks down at his swollen right hand, sucks the scotch from his finger. Anne watches him, warily.

'I don't offer advice. If there's one thing I've learned, it's not to chuck my two penneth at you, matey.'

There is a pause. Anne straightens a bar towel, checks her watch. The kitchen staff will be arriving soon. Kline seems lost in a train of thought. She waits. She knows that look, knows something is percolating. He begins to share what he has been turning over in his mind.

'Suppose we put the "For Sale" notices up. Reckon we'd show a good profit?'

'Probably, it's doing well enough. But this is your place.'

'But in your name.'

'A front for a license.'

'Maybe I should be taking steps to secure my investment.'

A little unsure as to where the conversation is leading, Anne sidles along the bar until she is standing before him.

'Oh yes?'

'Oh yeah. In case you decide to run off again. A wedding might be good insurance against that possibility.'

Anne blinks, laughs. Kline elaborates.

'Full showstopper. Cathedral, Bishop of Brum to tie the knot. Morning dress, you in virgin white. Reports in the press: "The happy couple left for an undisclosed destination." Happy because, amongst other things, they'd decided not to come back.'

He gazes at her. Anne shrugs.

'What do you say? Annie?'

'As a proposal, it's a bit business-like. As a deal, it's too much bother. And anyway, white lace does nothing for my complexion.'

Reaching across the bar, he pulls her close to him. His voice is low, his eyes intent on hers.

'You know what I feel about you. Well, sometimes I cover things up. But you know what my missing words would want to say.'

'Do I?'

'Even the barman knows about you and me.'

Close to him, Anne wonders how she can respond in kind. She wants to say the right words, sculpt her thoughts so they express what has gone unacknowledged between them for so long. Haltingly at first, the words form, taking on a clarity of understanding she has long sought. When she speaks, it as much to herself as for John Kline.

'In the past, I've said and used the word "love", and I always needed to hear that word returned to me. Yes, that little word. A word I never once said to you. You're right, we hide our emotions, cover up what everybody knows. Commitment, that's what I choose. Commitment to you. Oh, I love you. We can marry or not marry. I can choose, you can choose. We can choose. We can sell this place or stay. We can do whatever we want.'

She presses her face to his, recoils in surprise.

'Oh, you're burning.'

Kline makes no reply. He leans into her.

'I love you very much. I only wish I had the energy and strength to show you just how much.'

Anne takes in his words. Although they are everything she ever wanted to hear, they obscure other concerns that need to be dealt with. She comes around to his side of the bar, puts her arm about him.

'Why don't you rest? I'll make sure we're ready to open. Come on, bed.'

Hauling himself upright, Kline says, wearily.

'Just for an hour.'

'I'll call you.'

She leads him to the foot of the stairs, watches as he starts to trudge up one slow step at a time. Halfway up he turns and looks down at her.

'Thank you.'

In reply, Anne lifts a hand, points a forefinger towards him. A gesture that conveys the unspoken words, 'Here's looking at you, kid.'

141

The Writer comes awake with turbulent sound beating all around him, a sensation that something is nibbling at his feet.

Coming fully awake he realises that the intense power of the monsoon rains are penetrating the straw roof of his hotel chalet and pouring water onto his bed.

'Oh fuck!' He throws the sodden sheets aside, hurries into the adjoining bathroom, shucks off his shorts and t-shirt, wraps himself in a bath towel, sits on the edge of the bath, trying to remember where he is and what he should be doing. It's the middle of the night, should he trudge through the downpour, ask for an immediate change of accommodation, or leave it until tomorrow? He is now fully awake. His thoughts turn to the script of episode six. The last episode there will ever be of *Gangsters*. The filming in Pakistan is OK now; they've found a typist to alter and develop the pages, including the still to be decided ending. Ending? Endings? The script structure gurus advise against multiple endings. Well, bollocks to them. There are eight story strands that demand resolution, the seeds have been laid, so why not allow them to sprout and grow?

142

Within the bridal suite of the Imperial hotel, the battle of the Martinis is about to commence. Standing behind a glass-topped table are Sarah Gant and Lemmy Sip. Before them are two art deco-style chilled glasses containing their offerings for the delectation of the grave looking W.D. Fields.

He gazes from one to the other, holds up a white gloved hand. Reaches for a tumbler of mineral water, takes a mouthful, swirls it around his palate, expels it accurately towards an ice bucket on the floor behind him. Addressing the two contestants he drawls, 'Now, my chickadees. The rules are these, I will take one sip of each dry Martini in turn. I will be the sole arbiter of their quality. There will be no appeal, my decision is final. The loser will pay a tribute as agreed. Should it be

Lemmy who fails to deliver he will be required to grovel at the feet of the victor. If you, Sarah, fail to match or better his marvellous Martini, then you will be at the mercy of his perverse desires. Agreed?'

They nod in unison.

'Very well, let us begin.'

W.D. lifts an elegant glass by its stem, swirls the liquor prepared by his servant. He sniffs, checks the ice and olive, nods his appreciation. He drinks slowly, holds the spirit on his tongue, swallows. Closes his eyes, gives a slight shudder of pleasure.

'Excellent, but then I would expect nothing less. Now, for your opponent. Let us see if she can compete with your most delectable offering.'

He lifts the glass of mineral water, rinses his mouth, ejects the water over his shoulder. Once again it finds its way unerringly into the ice bucket. Taking up the glass offered by Sarah, he sniffs at the contents of the bowl, wrinkles his nose as if unsure of the bouquet. Finally, he takes a sip, then another. He shoots a startled glance towards the statuesque Sarah, shakes his head from side to side as all his taste buds dance in ecstasy. He slowly lowers the glass, places it back onto the table reverentially. He tips his straw boater in Sarah's direction.

'By the whiskers of Wotan, we are in the presence of a woman of true talent. On your knees Lemmy, you have been bested by the best. Sarah, seat yourself and prepare to receive your due reward.'

Sarah sits on the end of the bed. Lemmy falls to his knees, slowly removes her shoes, begins to kiss her feet, licking them slowly, sucking each toe in turn. Sarah reacts with some pleasure, watches the White Devil take further sips of the winning drink. He gazes at her, his expression full of wonder.

'What is your secret, my dear Sarah?'

'It's just that, a secret. It includes an ingredient known only to the initiates of a select cult of Yucatan Indians. Mm, that's enough, Lemmy, you may move your ministrations to the digits of my other foot.'

W.D. pauses in mid prowl before the black woman being pleasured by the ministrations of his ecstatic servant.

'I shall not rest until I wrest from breast, brain or womb the secret of your genius for commingling the spirits that, all alone in this frigging world, warm and comfort my heart. What is your secret, what?'

He advances towards her. Sarah lies back, languorous as a jungle cat, smiles up at him as he makes his plea.

'What do you want? Money? Love? Sex? Power? Advancement within the Wo Shing Wo? Speak! Speak!'

Sarah withdraws her big toe from Lemmy's mouth. The servant whimpers in protest like a child removed prematurely from its mother's breast. She sits up as Lemmy begins to dry her feet with a paper napkin.

'Send this sucker out for some swizzle sticks. We need some talking space.'

Lifting Lemmy to his feet, W.D. guides him towards the door.

'My boy, I want you to visit the hotel safe. Once there, you must withdraw our store of olives and examine each one for contamination. I believe their staleness explains your failed bid to win the Martini crown. So go.'

Lemmy bows, glances at Sarah, smiles with a little twitch of secret satisfaction. As he leaves Sarah saunters towards W.D., who stares longingly into his empty glass. She nods after his departing assistant.

'Say, as a matter of interest, had I lost, what would Lemmy baby have laid on me?'

'He's a foot fetishist.'

Sarah throws her head back, laughs.

'I was in for a saliva foot bath whatever happened?'

'It's a win-win situation, Sarah.'

'I'm all for that kind of outcome.'

'Then, my dear, my sable Sarah, let us work towards that end. But first, I beg of you, pour for me, your aching acolyte in the brotherhood of booze, another dispensation of your perfect ambrosial nectar.'

He watches her sway towards the refrigerator, take out a small glass jug, return to him and slowly refill his glass as if it were indeed a libation stolen from Mount Olympus. He can wait no longer. He slowly takes in the cocktail, lets it linger in his mouth, swallows, reacts, holds up the glass as a tribute to Sarah Gant.

'Ah, even with a slightly stale olive it is as different as a Paris Saturday night to a Birmingham Monday morning! So, speak, my goddess of the night. What is it you want? If it is within my considerable powers, I will grant it.'

Coming in close to him, she smiles seductively, a dusky Mae West.

'Well, I saw your expertise in the martial arts of mankind. I simply wondered about your proficiency in kindling the flame that resides in womankind.'

His answer is preceded by a knowing grin.

'I am the master of the eighty-seven positions of coital pleasure.'

'Did you say eighty-seven?'

'I will grant you that the final seventeen require the uses of a well-equipped gymnasium, but I am confident the Olympic committee will grant their validity as being kosher.'

Sarah regards him, shakes her head in disbelief.

'You're the most incredible guy I've ever met.'

'I take that as a compliment, coming from someone who I hear once ran a sporting house of considerable range and repertoire. OK... A deal. The mix of the most magical Martini in exchange for multitudinous multiples of mutual orgasm.'

'Well, let's get to it.'

He reaches for her breast, stops himself. She frowns.

'What is it?'

'I have a task to perform. To give the touch of death to one John Kline. For this I need all my senses unalloyed. I may only have the barest moment to touch the very centre of his being. Once my task is done, once his destruction is activated, we will meet, you and I, to celebrate the fusion of the Caucasian with the flower of Africa. The old world and the new, from which will spring who knows what, who knows who?'

He places his hands on either side of her face. For a second she feels a whirligig of pleasure and anticipation. Mason's warning of the powers of the White Devil to seduce and impregnate surface but only in a minor key. W.D. removes his touch.

'Tonight, tonight, when my task is done, we will meet for a fusion of complete consummation.'

'The time?'

'A little before the witching hour. After my touching encounter with Mr Kline.'

143

A distant ringing sound wakes John Kline from a death-like sleep. For a moment, he cannot focus his mind or define where or who he is. Then, like a boxer being led back to his corner, his head clears. He can hear

Annie talking to someone downstairs. He forces himself up, moves towards the door of the apartment.

Talking on the telephone, Anne sees Kline descending the stairs. She ends the call with 'OK, I'll tell him' and replaces the receiver.

Joining her, Kline notices her worried expression.

'Who was that?'

'Sarah.'

'Oh?'

'She wanted to warn you. She's heard there's a guy in town seeking to separate your soul from your body.'

Kline grins, unconcerned.

'Well, he'll need to join the queue.'

He looks at Anne, who takes no comfort from his words.

'You OK?' she asks.

'Yeah.'

'Those things you said to me…'

'I meant every word.'

'That's all I need to know. Let's go to work.'

Kline throws her a salute.

'Yes, ma'am.'

144

In the small square interview room of the psychiatric unit, Zaheer Khan sits hunched over a small table. His father sits opposite to him. Outside the glass-panelled door, warders and orderlies argue over the merits of their rival football teams.

Since they last met, the old man notices a change in his son, a growing depression as he broods on the magnitude of the charges to be brought against him. Iqbal Khan leans forward across the table, tries to lift Khan's spirits.

'You must not despair. I can see a pattern forming in the plot against you. I've talked with John Kline.'

'John Kline? What does he say?' Khan leans forward eagerly. He knows Kline, although not involved in the setup, could be instrumental in proving his innocence. 'Will he agree to help?'

'He has been a help already. I intend to pay him a further visit. He has promised to provide me with further information on the export company run by Aslam Rafiq. But for the moment we must concentrate on who could have conspired to perpetrate this crime against you. As you know, I've always suspected a woman to be involved. Who would have most to gain from your fall from grace?'

145

Seated before a vanity mirror in the bridal suite, Sarah Gant surveys the perfumes and potions laid out before her. She is unsure of what the night might bring, but the promise of physical consummation does not faze her. She is ready to test the rumours, explore the legendary status of this buffoon-like character who calls himself the White Devil. Not to mention the supposed prehensile properties of his penis.

Sarah turns her head from side to side, checks the blending of her foundation, dusts it down a little more. Gazes critically at the reflection of her large brown eyes. What image would best suit the midnight assignation? Maybe she should smoulder a little more, see if this guy really can make her burst into flame. She reaches for a white liner pencil, carefully begins to highlight her lower eyelashes.

146

The White Devil, seated at a corner table in the Nirvana restaurant, is indulging in his favourite sport of baiting waiters by making impossible requests and demands.

Tipping back his straw boater with the black hat band, he looks down at the steak tartar on his plate then stares quizzically up at Max, the head waiter.

'You see, my good fellow, it's like this, I usually sprinkle my vittles with powdered seaweed from the wide Sargasso Sea. Do you have such a condiment on hand in this glorified hash joint?'

'I'm afraid not, sir.'

'Why am I less than surprised at this mortifying news. Tell me, who's the proprietor here, case I need to complain later?'

'Mr Kline is that tall gentleman at the bar, sir.'

'Yes, I see him. A handsome cove, indeed. Well, that information might qualify you for a tip, but I doubt it.'

'That is at your discretion, sir.'

'Sure, it is. Well, waiter, I'd like to eat now, if that's OK with you.'

Max withdraws. W.D. Fields stares across the room at his target. He cuts into his slab of medium rare roast beef, begins to eat.

At the bar, Anne and Kline enjoy the luxury of being together, unaware that death is about to threaten their nirvana.

147

Sprawled in an armchair Rafiq is haunted by maudlin thoughts, fuelled by the brandy he has been drinking for the past few hours.

Across the lounge his companions in crime huddle together, waiting for a call from New York that will signal triumph or disaster. Rafiq becomes convinced the outcome will be the latter. Watching Lily pace up and down, elegant in her green satin mandarin top and close-fitting trousers, only torments him further. And as for Kuldip hovering over the telephone, he is like a jackal ready to pounce...

The phone rings, all three tense. Kuldip answers the call.

'Hello, yes, this is me, mahout to the white elephant... OK, you may shoot... Yes, yes, I see. Yes, I bloody understand your colonial accent... Tell me... I see. Yes, I will tell them. So long, buddy-mate.'

He replaces the receiver. Lily takes a step towards him.

'Well?'

'Miss Lily, our shipment has arrived in New York, it is awaiting customs clearance.'

'How long will that take?'

'Not long, the official blokes are approaching our container now.'

From across the room, Rafiq sees prison looming.

'Discovery, disgrace, the omens are everywhere. Oh, Lily, I will see you at our trial but never again for fourteen long years.'

Lily turns on him, furiously.

'Stop wittering, will you.'

'Have a brandy.'

'No, thank you, one of us needs to stay sober.'

'They won't serve Courvoisier in prison, you know.'

'Oh, shut up, will you, you're like a vegan at a barbeque.'

The telephone rings. Kuldip answers, Lily crosses fingers on both her hands, closes her eyes tight. Rafiq stands, sways from side to side.

Kuldip says, flatly, 'I understand.' He lowers the receiver, looks from one to the other with a grave expression.

Lily and Rafiq speak in unison.

'Well?'

Kuldip shakes his head. Rafiq puts his head in his hands.

'All is lost.'

Lily is frozen with horror at the news.

Kuldip looks from one to the other, grins.

'Only joking. US Customs have passed our shipment without a second look.'

Rafiq, incensed, lunges at Kuldip.

'You… You… *Idiot*… Stupid… *Idiot!*'

Lily protects the cowering Kuldip.

'Leave him!'

Panting, Rafiq steps away.

Lily gives Kuldip a searching look.

'Now, Kuldip, no more silly games. Tell me, what did our informant say?'

'American guy, he say route now open for progress of white elephant. With one shipment through, others may follow.'

'Oh, Kuldip, you are a very naughty boy, but I forgive you. Oh, we are on our way at last!'

She gives him a congratulatory hug.

Rafiq watches their embrace. He reaches for the last of his brandy, downs it in one savage swallow.

148

It is late evening in the Nirvana restaurant, a time to settle bills, serve last orders.

Rising from his corner table, the White Devil places a two pence piece on a pile of coins used to pay the bill. He changes his mind, pockets the paltry tip.

Standing nearby, Max, the head waiter, remains impassive, stoically refusing to be drawn into a reaction despite a sly look from the strangely dressed diner.

W.D. takes up his walking cane, holds it like a magician would a wand and sways jauntily towards the bar where Anne and Kline are sorting bills and making note of payments received.

His sashay complete, W.D. addresses John Kline.

'Excuse me, sir…'

Kline turns, stands. Anne, sensing a complaint from their eccentric customer, joins him. She stares at the straw hat, the cravat, the black jacket, the herringbone fawn trousers, the snowy white gloves as Kline asks, 'Yes?'

'You are, I believe, the proprietor of this most excellent palace of gastronomical delight?'

'I own the joint, yeah.'

'I have just enjoyed the most satisfying of repasts. Truly the name of Nirvana is almost apt, for all but one of my desires are now replete.'

'What's missing?'

Knowing the moment is approaching, W.D. smiles winningly. He begins to ease the white glove from his right hand as he speaks.

'I merely seek the opportunity to shake the hand of the man responsible for creating the means of such culinary delight.'

He extends his hand. Kline shows his right hand, which has a bandage encasing his forefinger.

'I have to disappoint you, sorry.'

'Well, perhaps another time…'

He regards the figure of John Kline admiringly.

'Sir, it is a mystery to me how you maintain such a trim epigastrium when assailed by so much temptation towards gluttony and greed.'

The White Devil knows the moment of decision has arrived. He smiles, extends his hand, makes an unseen rapier thrust, touches the nerve centre below the solar plexus of his victim. Kline hardly feels the deadly contact as he replies.

'I take plenty of exercise.'

His task accomplished, the White Devil turns away, regards his right hand as if it were a thing of wonder. He wriggles his fingers in self-congratulation as he moves away.

'Wonderful, wonderful, such control.'

Watching their strange guest trundle away towards the exit, Anne shakes her head in disbelief.

'Who was *that*?'

Kline shrugs.

'Some drunk.'

He closes his jacket, covers his trim epigastrium, unaware that an assassination has just taken place.

149

The mood of Aslam Rafiq becomes darker and darker as the brandy fuels his feelings of jealousy. He scowls across to where Lily and Kuldip are examining a map of America. He mutters to himself. Lily glances across.

'What did you say?'

'I said you show more bloody affection to Kuldip than you do to me.'

'Poor you. Here, will this help?'

She crosses, plants a cursory kiss on his cheek. Rafiq groans theatrically.

'Oh, a drop of water to a man dying of thirst!'

'What else do you expect, what else do you deserve?'

'Respect, affection, love? A little mercy for one who is afflicted by unrequited love?'

He holds his arms out in supplication. Lily curls her lip.

'God, I hate self-pity. I'm going to bed before you start blubbing in your brandy.'

'Take me with you, please.'

'You're too drunk to manage the encounter.'

'Not true, all I lack is the opportunity.'

'You need to take yourself in hand.'

'Is that the only consolation left to me?'

'You really are quite disgusting.'

Lily turns her back on him, glides towards the door, bestows a gentle smile on Kuldip.

'Goodnight, Kuldip.'

Kuldip beams.

'Goodnight, Miss Lily, till morning come.'

When they are alone, Rafiq stands, sways a little.

'Oh, how cruel she is, Kuldip. How sparing of her favours.'

From the skies above the country house a faint rumble of thunder begins to be heard. Rafiq glances around the room, looks up at the ornate ceiling.

'How heavy the air is tonight. Thunder in the air, lightning, a storm.'

Standing by the dining table, Kuldip tries to maintain a brave exterior.

'I'm over the fear of those claps, Mr Rafiq, I don't frighten through the heavens' roar…'

A flash of lightning followed by a thunderclap interrupts his protestation.

'Oh, what was that?'

Rafiq comes to comfort him.

'Merely Indra and the god of rain in argument again.'

'What?'

'All above your head, Kuldip. Go and get yourself a brandy. Pour me one too, let us drown our desires and sensibilities in drink.'

A clap of thunder explodes above the house.

'Oh… oh!'

'There there…'

Rafiq steers the trembling Kuldip towards the solace of the drinks table.

150

Kline stands alone at the bar of the now deserted Nirvana restaurant. He reaches for a bottle of Napoleon brandy as the thunder clouds rumble, bringing the storm ever nearer.

The doors from the kitchen swing open, Anne comes in.

'All hatches are battened down, the storm can do what it likes.'

'Just like us.'

Anne grins.

'I'll go on up.'

'Yeah, sure, be with you in a minute.'

Anne yawns as she begins to climb the stairs. Kline selects a pair of brandy glasses, opens the bottle, begins to pour.

151

Sarah Gant has arranged herself in a seductive pose on the bed. To her annoyance, the attention of her would-be lover seems to lie elsewhere. He stands at the foot of the bed dressed in a multi-coloured robe. He still wears his straw boater, puffs on a corona-corona cigar, all the while contemplating an antique pocket watch. Sarah's patience runs out.

'What the hell are you waiting for?'

'Time, love, birth, life, death,' W.D. replies.

A rattle of thunder sounds above the hotel. W.D. listens as if the elements were whispering their secrets to him. He nods his head, gazes at his pocket watch, observes the second hand approaching two minutes to midnight

'All beings have their time, a time to live, a time to die. A time that is almost now.'

Carrying a pair of brandy glasses, Kline moves towards the foot of the stairs. As he ascends the first step he doubles over as if hit in the guts by a pile-driver. His head fills with meaningless confusion. Searing pain blots out his consciousness. He sprawls back onto the stairs. The glasses of brandy fall to the floor, splinter and their contents spread like blood from a newly opened wound.

The White Devil listens as the storm outside begins to abate. As it moves away, he nods to himself.

'It is done, take a life, begin a life. Yes, the time draws nigh for the conception of princes.'

He surveys the woman pouting on the bed.

'Now, my dusky Desdemona, I think you have awaited fulfilment long enough.'

Sarah believes the time for action has finally arrived. She watches W.D. stub out his cigar, pitch his straw boater towards a hat peg across the room. It catches. The peg wavers a little before it settles into place.

W.D. unfastens his robe of many colours. Sarah Gant is no stranger to the sight of male genitals. This one is above average in length if not in girth. She reaches across to give the erect member a welcoming caress. She is unprepared for what happens next, for the penis takes on a life of its own, curls itself around her wrist. She screams in shocked surprise. The White Devil laughs, releases his prehensile grip.

'What? How? How can you do that?' she stammers.

'Mind over matter, a little party trick to whet your appetite.'

Sarah reacts as would Mae West.

'Not only my appetite.'

W.D. chuckles, reaches, dips his forefinger into the glass on the bedside table that holds his Martini. He circles each dark nipple with the alcohol, smiles as the areolas react and blossom. He places his lips around each nipple in turn and imbibes what, for him, is another form of nectar. For Sarah, the delicacy of his touch is quite surprising.

152

Wondering about the delay, Anne, in her white cotton nightdress, calls from the head of the stairs.

'John…?'

She sees his inert body at the foot of the stairway. She hurries down, nearly losing her balance in her rush to reach him. Kline is still breathing, but his eyes are empty, as if he has been hollowed out from within. Anne tries to lift him, but his weight is too much for her strength.

Tears cloud her vision as she stumbles towards the phone and attempts to dial 999. Finally a voice asks, 'Police, fire or ambulance?'

'Ambulance.'

153

Sarah Gant awakens to the sound of an aria from *I Pagliacci*. It takes her a moment to locate the sound as coming from the bathroom. The voice must belong to the White Devil, singing not in the abrasive drawl of his speaking voice, but in a lyrical, pleading tone, powering the words with heartfelt emotion.

'Vesti la giubba, la facia in farina, la gente daga, rider vuole qua…'

Who is he really? The sad clown singing so plaintively, or a spirit from Hades? She is no wiser for having spent a tumultuous night of lovemaking with him. At times it felt as if she was being possessed by two different beings, one pudgy and tender, the other hard and cruel, a rider driving his mount with demonic intensity towards the gates of hell.

Sarah allows herself to luxuriate in the afterglow of satisfaction. Then a voice enters her thoughts, a nagging voice reminding her not to be fooled by someone who might be a master of the one night stand but was also… What had Marcus Mason called him? 'A monster, a killer of men, with "wives" and children scattered all over the planet.'

She is due to meet the CIA agent later in the day. He will expect her to snare the White Devil or suffer the consequences. Getting laid was fine; sex might be emotion in motion, but a gal must look to her future.

The aria complete, the singer emerges, pink and naked. Seeing her he slips back into Fieldsian mode.

'Ah, the divine Sarah, how are you this effulgent am?'

'Well, between you and me, I'm ready for a little loving.'

'What!?'

'A joke.'

'Godfrey Daniel, have I found a woman with a sense of humour. If so, we must marry forthwith.'

'Marriage is an institution, I've no wish to be in an institution.'

'Who does.'

He picks up his watch, stares down at the time.

'Oh, drat. I'm needed to instruct members of the Wo Shing Wo on how to smash the 17K. Advanced tuition in the art of emasculation through the correct application of the Ganges Groin Grapple. So, my precious chickadee, what might this day hold in store for you?'

'Couple of meetings, nothing special.'

'OK, let us part with sorrow while being aware that it is naught but a temporary hiatus.'

'Will we meet back here?'

'Nothing will keep me from your arms or the pleasures of your Martini.'

Watching him dress, Sarah wonders how long it will be before Marcus Mason locks him inside an institution for the rest of his days.

154

The route to the hospital room seems depressingly familiar. Then Anne realises the nurse is leading her to the same bed where she had once been trapped in a deep coma.

Entering the room, seeing John propped up on a bank of pillows, eyes closed, his skin pale as parchment, makes her turn to the middle-aged nurse.

'Tell me what's happened, what treatment has been prescribed?'

'The doctors are treating it as a case of septicaemia but there's been little response to the treatment so far.'

Anne makes no reply. She looks at the wan features of the man propped up against his pillows. He is unmoving, his breath shallow. Kline's face reminds her of a death mask.

Sensing her upset, the nurse adds, 'I'm sure a solution will be found to help him pull through.'

A chill of realisation runs through Anne.

'He can't die, can he? I mean, not like this, not just like that?'

She receives a smile of compassion.

'I'll be just outside.'

Left alone, Anne draws a chair right up against the side of the bed.

'John… It's Anne…'

Kline stirs, his breath labours. Finally his eyes open and stare upwards at the ceiling. Beside the bed a monitor records his heartbeat, beeps sounding as a line of light dances across the screen.

Anne again tries to reach him.

'Anne, Anne, remember?'

Deep in the recesses of Kline's mind vivid images begin to emerge. Anne, Anne, yes, there she is, in the drug unit, her sweating face, her cowering body, her pleas for him to help her, help her, please. Being with her in the countryside. Laughing, joking. Other images far less pleasing tumble into his mind. Punches thrown at him, their crunching impact on his jaw. Guns pointing, firing, his enemy, Malleson, smiling with contempt then agony as his hand is trapped in a car door. Sarah Gant, jaunty in her fedora hat. Lily Li T'ang stretching a long leg across his thigh. Drinking at the bar of the Nirvana with Aslam Rafiq, laughing together. Mr Khan, smiling, smiling, telling him he is in trouble. 'Better run, Mister Kline.' Yes, yes. Now running, running, panting, struggling for breath, heaving for breath, for… breath… breath… Heaving… gasping, reaching for just one more breath, seeing someone through the mist… Anne, seeing Anne receding, hearing her calling his name, her voice blurring… fading… fading…

The screen of the monitor with its bobbing, repeating line gives a final beep, settles into a whining monotone as life leaves the body of John Kline.

Anne throws herself onto the bed, punches his chest, begs him not to leave her.

The nurse comes running in, her look of panic triggering anger within Anne.

'Do something, get a crash cart... Something!'

'It's too late, I'm very sorry...'

'Sorry? He can't be dead. John, John, don't leave me, please!'

The body of John Kline lies on the bed. His sightless eyes hold no expression, his jaw sags open in death.

Anne stretches out beside him. Places her arms around his body. The bleak truth of his passing strikes into her soul. She begins to sob at the realisation of what has just been stolen from her.

155

It is late afternoon when her contact within the Wo Shing Wo informs Sarah Gant of the death of John Kline. The news saddens her, makes her think of the role the White Devil might have played, but she is told the death certificate states 'complications ensuing from septicaemia'. So, what to believe, who to believe?

She enters a desolate municipal graveyard to find a black-clad Marcus Mason reading the pious inscriptions on gravestones.

Hearing her footsteps, he turns to greet her. No preamble, just a curt request for information regarding the White Devil.

Omitting details of their personal relationship, Sarah confines herself to the facts. Kline's death, W.D.'s training of the warriors of the Wo Shing Wo.

'Let us walk.'

Walking beside the US secret agent Sarah casts a sideways glace at Mason, lost in thought as he strokes his aquiline nose, an eagle planning to swoop down on its prey.

'I think we have followed instructions sufficiently to satisfy our masters. The time has come for you to deliver the demon into my custody.'

'Me? Why don't you just arrest him?'

'Mrs Gant, we are in a foreign country. The devil has committed no crimes here, all my evidence against him lies beyond these shores.'

Pausing by a statue of an angel seems to give him inspiration.

'If I apprehend him, he can be flown out in secret by US military transport. We will join him. He will be in chains, you will be free.'

'Suppose I don't want to go back to the States.'

'You must, for the sake of your future career. There is kudos to be gained for both of us.'

'You can have mine.'

'Once I have him, Mrs Gant, your mission is complete, all past transgression will be erased once you make your report.'

'He's a resourceful guy, he won't be easy to fool.'

'If only we could tempt him into a holy place. Once there his power might be weakened.'

Sarah is just about to retort sarcastically when a possibility occurs to her.

'Say, Marcus, there might be a way to do just that.'

'Well?'

'Kline will have a funeral. I can ask W.D. to escort me...'

'There will be a chapel or a church nearby. Excellent, lure him there and I will do the rest.'

'Let's not get carried away, there are a few imponderables here.'

'Of course, but you are a resourceful woman with some expertise in manipulating the male sex. That is why you were chosen as part of God's plan to overcome the forces of darkness.'

'Wow, I've never been part of God's plan before.'

'Well, now you are. Let us pray for your success.'

He takes her hand, closes his eyes. Sarah stares at him, trying to come to terms with the decisions that now lie ahead.

156

Alastair, a gravedigger, switches off his mechanical digger, climbs stiffly out of the cabin, pockets the ignition key. He surveys his morning's work. This grave won't be required until the next day. There are rocks to remove and sides to shape, but seeing as it's a quiet time for the burial business, why not have a few drinks at lunchtime, finish the work later? Yes. He looks up at the gathering rain clouds, feels the beginning of a fine rain. He adjusts his Stetson-style headgear, begins to trudge up the slope that leads towards the chapel.

The pall bearers of the coffin containing the earthly remains of John Kline are members of the staff of the Nirvana restaurant. Leading the way out of the small chapel towards where the burial will take place is a portly vicar wearing black and white vestments.

As the procession proceeds towards the grave, made ready only yesterday, the gravedigger pauses, removes his hat in a show of respect. Once the mourners have passed solemnly by, he replaces his Stetson and heads off in the direction of the pub that should be called the Gravediggers Arms, but instead rejoices in the name of the Albion.

The funeral party make its way along an avenue of gravestones. The fine rain intensifies, causing black umbrellas to be raised as shelter from the weeping sky.

Anne Darracott, dressed in a black cloak, wearing a headdress with a semi-translucent black veil, follows the coffin, each step an effort of will. Behind her, wearing the same attire, donated by the White Devil, walk Sarah Gant and Lily Li T'ang, who arrived on the arm of Rafiq.

Enjoying the sight of the three elegantly dressed women ahead of him, comes W.D. Fields, together with Jenkins, his uniformed chauffeur. W.D. adjusts his grey top hat and glances back in the direction of the chapel, wondering what has become of his assistant, Lemmy Sip.

Zahir Khan and his father have a prison guard for company as they follow on behind.

Aslam Rafiq and Kuldip are the last to join the circle that now stands before the open grave. The funeral attendants wait patiently for the signal to lower the polished wood coffin into the ground.

A latecomer, Archie, the barman, hurries into view. He carries a violin case that might contain an automatic rifle. Archie opens the case and takes out a bunch of flowers. He joins the group at the graveside as the vicar begins to intone, 'Man that has been born of woman has but a short time to live...'

Inside the chapel, Marcus Mason and two members of the US security services bind the Chinese assistant of the White Devil, securely. They place sticking tape across his mouth. Marcus removes Lemmy's hat and hands it to Fallon, the thin-faced senior operative who immediately leaves the chapel.

Lemmy is forced to take a seat in a front pew by Kovac, a nervy guy who takes much comfort from the weight of the .44 Bulldog weapon he holds. Lemmy's eyes move from side to side in panic above the tape that seals his mouth. He strains against the steel wire restraints that cut into his wrists. He slumps back, an unwilling Judas goat laid out to tempt his master into a deadly trap.

Marcus faces the altar table with its bouquet of plastic flowers placed before a heavy brass crucifix.

He bows his head and silently asks for divine protection during the battle that is soon to come.

Outside, the rain intensifies. It beats down upon the fabric of the black umbrellas clustered around the open grave, its pattering building into a sombre roll of drums.

Beside the grave Anne cannot bear the sight of her man going down into the darkness alone. She steps forward, intent on joining him. Iqbal Khan is the first to act. He catches her arm, pulls her back from the brink. She starts to struggle against his grip but, overwhelmed by the reality of her loss, turns into his arms to steal a moment of comfort and warmth before she manages to recover enough to watch, shaking with emotion, as the coffin disappears below ground.

Anne takes up a red rose, grasps a handful of wet earth, casts them down onto the coffin as her final token of farewell.

It is over. There is nothing more to say. Nothing more to do other than to return to the cars that will take them away, leaving the dead behind.

Not all visitors to the graveyard are sad, however. An old enemy of Kline has heard of his death. He has come to spit on the grave of the man who caused him to fall from the fourth floor of a building site. A swan dive that placed Dermot McAvoy in the wheelchair he now occupies.

Poised at the top of a sloping walkway, the Irishman watches as the funeral party straggles away from the last resting place of John Kline. Dermot begins to cackle with delight. He might not have the use of his lower limbs but he is still alive, while that bastard Kline is food for worms and maggots. This realisation provokes a fresh bout of laughter that spooks a pair of blackbirds, who depart from a nearby bush in a swift rush of disapproval.

But the outpouring of malicious joy proves to be somewhat short-lived, for, in his moment of unrestrained glee, the Irishman loses control of his wheelchair. He tries to grab hold of the wheels to slow his progress, but the momentum is too great. McAvoy's laughter becomes a screech of fear as his wheelchair careers towards an open grave, with its lining of sharp, uncovered stones.

The wheelchair tips at the edge, hurling its occupant skywards. Yelling with fright, Dermot travels through the air. He lands, with a skull-crunching thud, into the gaping grave.

During the silence that ensues, the blackbirds return to a perch on the arm of a yellow-painted mechanical digger.

Had we been able to place a camera inside the coffin of John Kline, we might have observed an upward twitch of his lips.

157

The white Rolls Royce stands out amongst the black Daimlers of the funeral directors. W.D. wonders what has become of his assistant. He asks Sarah, who informs him that Lemmy was last seen inside the chapel searching for his hat.

W.D. asks if she will accompany him in the Rolls? Sarah looks away, says she feels she should travel back with Anne to the Nirvana. W.D. nods. There is something wrong, but he can't fathom what. He says he will see her later. Sarah nods, ducks into the funeral car, closes the door. Watching the cars depart, W.D. muses to himself.

'Mm, Sarah anxious to fly the scene. Why should that be?'

As the cars begin to drive away, he strolls back towards the chapel, a stately Victorian undertaker with his top hat and walking stick.

Inside the porch, lying on the stone step, he sees a grey hat.

The White Devil looks about him, takes in the trees dripping with rain, the grassy spaces, the lines of gravestones, the fading flowers, a mechanical digger. All cars have now departed, leaving only his Rolls Royce and, yes, just visible beneath the overhang of a willow tree, the bonnet of a black sedan. Aha. The White Devil picks up the grey hat and cautiously pushes open the doors of the chapel with the tip of his stick.

Looking about him, he sees the hunched figure of Lemmy Sip sitting in the front line of pews. Before he can ask why, he receives an answer. A hoarse voice with a New Jersey accent rasps into his ear.

'Hold it there.'

W.D. feels the point of a gun barrel dig into his back. From behind the altar Marcus Mason rises above the crucifix. Fallon steps out from behind the organ. He waves his 9mm Glock at the White Devil.

'Come on down, why don't you.'

'Delighted, don't mind if I do.'

Ambling forward down the aisle, W.D. arrives at the forefront of the chapel. One by one he surveys his captors.

'Ah, Marcus Mason, we meet at last, what a fortuitous conjunction of fate.'

'One that will bring you to justice.'

'Ah, justice. Given that we meet on foreign soil, may I point out that you have no jurisdiction in this green and pleasant land.'

Mason is about to reply when Fallon, impatient at the exchange, interjects, bluntly, 'This isn't an arrest, it's an execution.'

He dashes the stick from W.D.'s grasp. It falls to the stone floor with a clatter.

Fallon clicks the safety catch free, levels the Glock at the prisoner's head.

Mason intervenes.

'My orders are he goes back to the States for trial.'

'Homeland intelligence says it's best if this joker is blown away. Any problem with that, Marcus?'

Mason looks upwards towards heaven for guidance. The White Devil clasps his hands in prayer.

From his seat on the front row, Lemmy, mouth sealed by silver duct tape, his wrists wired together, can only watch the imminent execution unfold. He hears W.D. plead for his life, offer gold, names, sees him fall to his knees, begging Mason for mercy. Then Lemmy understands the reason why W.D. is grovelling so abjectly.

He sees the White Devil reach for a fallen object, sees him pull out the sharp-edged steel sword that is concealed within his walking stick.

The White Devil leaps to his feet. With a stroke of demonic force, he slashes downwards, severing the wrist of agent Fallon, whose hand, still gripping the Glock, falls towards the floor. Before it can land, W.D. lunges, piercing Fallon through the throat with the point of the sword. Withdrawing the blade from his gurgling blood-choked victim he aims a fearsome backhand at the neck of Marcus Mason. The head of the decapitated preacher man soars through the air and lands, like a thrown cabbage, onto the lap of a petrified Lemmy.

The spray of blood from the headless body of Marcus Mason clouds the vision of the White Devil momentarily. When his sight clears, he sees Kovac, standing at the centre of the aisle, outside the range of W.D.'s bloodstained blade. He points his standard issue revolver at the heart of the White Devil.

Kovac extends his arms, clasps the firearm in both hands, steadies. His finger closes on the trigger. W.D. waits to feel the impact of the slug that must follow. A shot is fired. The White Devil, to his surprise, feels nothing.

The US agent sags as a bullet rips into his back. A second shot blows the back of his skull away. He crumples, falls at the feet of Sarah Gant, who, holding her Sig Sauer, steps over the corpse, advances to join the blood-soaked party before the altar. W.D. is surprised by the identity of his rescuer.

'I thought you'd set me up, ratted me out.'

'A lady has a right to change her mind, doesn't she?'

'I'm delighted you decided to exercise that prerogative. Forgive me if I pose the question. Why?'

'When I figure it out, I'll let you know.'

'Release Lemmy, would you? I must decide as to what the hell we do next.'

While Sarah cuts Lemmy free, W.D. contemplates creating a gruesome tableau, a display of lifeless bodies before the altar.

The headless corpse of Marcus Mason would be in the centre, a dead US secret service agent on either side completing the unholy trinity. The cherry on the top would be the head of Marcus Mason impaled on the brass crucifix. No, he decides, it would draw a little too much attention. He needs time to complete his plans to bring destruction to the 17K Triad.

Sarah joins him. Lemmy, rubbing his lacerated wrists, kicks the head of the agent known as the Preacher. It rolls, ends up at the feet of Sarah Gant. They pause to contemplate the doleful features of the dead agent. Sarah speaks first.

'Marcus Mason, gone to his due reward.'

W.D. adds his thoughts.

'Yes, happy at last. I have decided that it is fitting that he and his companions should be placed in consecrated ground. You, Sarah, take my Rolls, tell Jenkins to convey you to the funeral feast, then he must return to collect Lemmy and myself.'

'What about the car these guys used?'

'That will be deposited elsewhere.'

'A long-stay car park would buy us some time.'

'That would be most advantageous.'

'What will you do here?'

'Arrange another burial service.'

Searching through the room at the rear of the chapel, Lemmy finds a cupboard containing cleaning equipment and bleaching fluids.

While his assistant washes blood away from the altar and its surrounds, W.D. is equally busy. He utilises a steel catafalque, used to wheel coffins, to transport the bodies of the dead agents into the graveyard.

Selecting a weed-covered grave, he leaves the bodies sprawled on the grass and goes to examine the mechanical digger. The cabin is open, but ignition keys are nowhere to be found. W.D. wrenches out wires that lead from the ignition, strips them with his teeth, presses the bare wires together. The digging machine splutters into life.

Driving the mini tractor, he trundles back to the site he has selected for burial. It lies in a part of the cemetery that time has passed by. After a few abortive tries he manages to use the claw-head at the end of the boom arm to dig down into the soil of the grave. With a grunt of satisfaction, he feels the claw strike a solid object. It has reached a decayed coffin buried deep in the wet earth.

Seeing Lemmy appear from the chapel he beckons him over. His assistant carries a round object.

'You forgot this.'

He places the severed head of Marcus Mason at W.D.'s feet.

'Ah yes, how remiss of me. Right, Lemmy, let us give these cadavers the old heave-ho.'

Pulling together, they heave the three bodies into the excavated grave.

The White Devil picks up the head of the agent known as the Preacher. He looks at it closely, becomes lost in thought. Finally, he speaks.

'Marcus, you have given me the glimmering of an idea as to what my next persona might be. Thank you.'

He plants a kiss on the cold lips of his victim and casts the head down into the grave.

Only one task remains.

W.D. mounts the digger and shovels the displaced earth back into the grave. Jiggling the guide lever, he battens down the earth to form a neat mound.

Their final act is to choose a selection of flowers from nearby tombs to place on the grave, whose stone inscription declares the last resting place of the family Cowgill.

W.D. nods towards the faded names on the weathered tombstone.

'I'm sure the Cowgills will be pleased to accommodate their long lost American cousins.'

When the white Rolls returns, Lemmy and W.D. are relieved to escape from the graveyard only minutes before the next funeral party are due to arrive.

Driving away from the chapel, Jenkins, the chauffeur, glances at his bedraggled passengers. He makes no comment about their blood-soaked, mud-spattered appearance. He has seen stranger sights while in the employ of the White Devil.

158

On returning from the funeral reception at the Nirvana, Rafiq and Lily Li T'ang sit across from each other in the Edwardian-styled drawing room. Rafiq gives a gloomy sigh.

'Pity about John Kline, he was an amusing chap, very droll, I certainly shall miss him.'

Lily flicks a speck of dust from the sleeve of her cloak.

'As will his common-law widow, I should think.'

'Yes, if there was only something one could do to ease the pain of her loss.'

'There is. I have sent Kuldip with a little gift of condolence.'

'How thoughtful you are, my darling. There really is no one like you.'

159

There comes a time when all the caring support has gone away. When only an empty space remains. Anne stares around the empty tables, looks at the silent bar, sees the stairs that lead upward to a space made hollow and desolate. Inside her head, she knows demons lie in wait, stirring, scratching at the crumbling edifice of her self-control.

She has only taken a few steps towards the stairs when there is a rattle at the outer door. Wearily Anne goes across to allow access to a late visitor.

Kuldip, wearing an expression of concern, stands outside.

'What is it, Kuldip, forgotten something?'

'I bring you something Miss Lily sent.'

He weighs a flat rectangular package, gift-wrapped in shiny black paper with a small crimson rosette attached.

'What is it?'

'She didn't take me into her confidences. But she did say it will help ease the grief of your condolence.'

He wanders further into the restaurant, looks about him.

'Seems a bit dead in here.'

'We're closed for the rest of the week.'

'I was sorry to hear about your dead chap, as a live bloke he wasn't all bad.'

Anne rests her hands on a table, struggling to contain the emotions that swell inside. Finally, she manages a flat response.

'Go away, Kuldip.'

After placing the package on the table beside her, Kuldip sidles away without a word.

The outer door closes. Anne reaches for the gift sent by Lily Li T'ang. She slowly tears the paper aside. A polished wooden box appears. She opens the lid, looks down at its contents. What she sees stabs at her heart with its cruel invitation. She begins to cry, deep racking sobs. Her tears fall into the open box that contains a hypodermic needle and a packet of heroin.

160

Wrapped in a white towelling wrap, Sarah Gant emerges from the steamy bathroom to find a pensive White Devil sitting by the bed. He also wears a white towelling bath robe.

The only light is from a shaded bedside lamp. Beside him, on the bedside cabinet sits a glass of Martini, untouched. There is still the faint aroma of a recent cigar permeating the bridal suite. He has exchanged very few words since she returned from the wake held for John Kline at the Nirvana.

His silence, in contrast to his habitual verbosity, is unnerving to Sarah.

W.D. watches as she undoes her robe, lets it fall. Nods his appreciation at what he sees, pulls back the covers of the bed, indicates she should retire between its sheets. Sarah does so, sits up, stares enquiringly, breaks the silence.

'Something you want to say?'

'I thought I knew you, Sarah. Seems there are depths yet to be explored.'

'That a bad thing?'

'Not necessarily.'

'But there's a bug up your ass about something.'

'I ask myself a question or two. Have I been blinded by the allure of your dusky pulchritude? Did you rescue me only so you can claim the bounteous glory of turning me over to the US authorities?'

'I'm not that devious.'

'No? You stitched up your fellow agent Khan, took him out of the picture. Why not set me up for the self-same fall?'

'Yes, well, I didn't. I saved your ass.'

'You did. I want to know why.'

The White Devil concentrates. His green eyes gleam in the lamplight as he watches Sarah hunch up, wrap her arms around her raised knees, stare ahead, her expression troubled. W.D. says nothing, waits. After a long pause, Sarah begins to speak, at first haltingly, the words dredged up from a murky pool of memory.

'You want to know why I came back for you, why I brought down that agent before he blew you away?'

'I like a good bedtime story. Why did Mrs Gant return to the chapel? Was it in hope of rescuing the prince and living happily ever after?'

'Screw you and your fucking wordplay.'

'A thousand pardons, my lady.'

'You want to hear? You want to listen?'

'I long to partake of your life's history.'

'Forget it.'

'No, speak, bright angel. Please enlighten this dumb fuck.'

'Will you stop, for fuck's sake!'

'Ah, for the sake of fuck, I certainly will. Please begin.'

A pause. Sarah considers. W.D. smiles engagingly, sits on the bed.

'The stage belongs to you, my sweet.'

'Not easy to explain, it goes back a long way.'

'How long a time?'

'Seems a lifetime…'

Sarah falters, W.D. takes her hand.

'Look at me.'

'Well? What?'

Sarah looks back at him, feels him drawing out what has been buried within her for too long a time.

'I want to hear what needs to be said. Let it out. Please.'

Sarah nods. There is a long pause before the words start to emerge, not in a tumble but in precise order.

'I was married once, to Darius Gant. We lived in LA. We scraped by but were happy enough, until Darius was left enough money to open our own restaurant.

'We called it 'The Olive Grove'. It did well, Italian food, simple but good. I thought we were on our way until I discovered that the finance had come not from a legacy but from the wise guys. It was mob money. The gangsters wanted not just to skim profits but to have a secure place to meet and transact their family business. Stupid me thought they visited so often because we had a great Italian chef.'

She breaks off. Reaches across for the Martini, takes a sip, replaces the tall art deco glass.

'Your husband, what happened to him, did he sell his soul, did he become indebted to the mob, did he fall foul of the authorities?'

A bitter memory pulls down the corners of Sarah Gant's generous mouth.

'Both. He agreed to play both sides of the street. He allowed the mob's permanently reserved table to be wired for sound. The wire was discovered. Retribution followed. I knew nothing until, one night, Darius failed to come home. When I went to open the restaurant the next morning, I found my husband seated at the main table. A bullet through his eye, his dick hanging from his mouth.'

She shudders, swallows, clears her throat, continues.

'Today I sat in the funeral car, next to Anne. I knew what was about to happen back in that chapel. I had a vision of you, dead in the way my husband was dead. I couldn't take the thought. I said I'd forgotten something, got them to drop me back at the graveyard. That's how I came back.'

'But not why you came back.'

'I just said…'

'No. You need to think why. Why did you come back? Was it for me, how you feel about me? Could you not bear to say goodbye to my johnson and all the little tricks he is delighted to perform?'

Sarah Gant fights with her emotions, shakes her head from side to side. W.D. places a calming hand onto the base of her throat. She slowly regains some composure, places her hand onto his, speaks like a child recovering from a nightmare.

'I want to understand what is happening to me. Who you really are, your true name. I don't feel I'm in control of my thoughts, my mind, my body.'

She lies back, shivering, shaking as if possessed by something inside her body, something struggling to get out. Taking her hands, W.D. lays them across her belly, eases her down onto the pillows. Places both palms of his hands on either side of her temple, closes his eyes. Sarah reacts to his soothing touch; her eyes begin to drift and flutter towards sleep. The White Devil murmurs softly.

'Go to sleep, you need to sleep, you must sleep, you will sleep, sleep deep, so deep, let go now, let go…'

He looks down upon her dark head against the white pillow as she descends into sleep. If Sarah is confused about her feelings for him, he is also in two minds about her.

Feeling the need for a contemplative smoke he leaves the sleeping woman and crosses to a wardrobe, slides it open, takes out a black leather Gucci travelling bag.

After unlocking the bag, he takes out a wooden cigar box, opens it, selects a cigar, bites off an end, lights up the corona-corona. He begins to pace, trying to bring order to his thoughts. He halts by the bed, looks down at the sleeping black woman, thinks about what he has just heard. It explains why she is reluctant to perform fellatio. He pulls on his cigar, makes himself explore the perils of his present situation. He begins to wander around the darkened room, wraith-like in his white robe.

He tells himself that the time left on this assignment is limited. There are other offers being made from the States, tempting offers, one of a million dollars to bring about the demise of the highest person in the land. That was in the future. What about the now, could he trust Sarah Gant? Did he want to trust her? She is a witness to all his recent crimes. She is erratic, might become his enemy once more. Can he risk that? Can he afford to leave loose ends?

Like a judge weighing up the evidence for and against the accused, he mooches around, the cigar tip glowing in the semi-darkness. The red glow becomes a steady point of light. The White Devil has reached his decision. He stubs out the cigar in a brass ashtray, flexes the fingers of his right hand, moves towards the bed, gently eases the covers aside to reveal his victim's naked body.

The hand that conveys the touch of death hovers over her solar plexus. The White Devil, about to deliver his deadly touch, hears a voice, a child's voice coming from the mouth of the sleeping Sarah.

'No, don't...'

Startled, the assassin recoils, recovers, places a soft hand on the womb of Sarah Gant. With a half-smile, he mutters to himself.

'Well, well, fate has taken a hand.'

He crosses once more to his leather bag, peers inside, lifts a bundle of passports, discovers the jewel box he has been seeking. He returns to the bed, gazes down at the sleeping Sarah. He takes hold of her long fingers, smiles to himself, softly drawls a favourite line.

'Ah, what symmetrical digits.'

The first ring is too loose, the second too tight, the third is just right.

W.D. slips the platinum ring, with its large crystal orb, onto the third finger of the left hand of Sarah Gant.

161

Khan's father follows a guard down a corridor with walls painted a metallic grey more appropriate to a battleship than a prison psychiatric unit.

Staring at the back of the guard's neck he notices tufts of hair curling up from beneath the blue uniform cap. Slovenly. A chap in need of a regulation haircut.

As they proceed through a succession of barred metal gates there grows a pervading smell of disinfectant that masks but does not conceal the early morning odours of defecation. Behind locked cells there is the sound of muffled angry shouts and, later, a prisoner screams as they pass, 'I'll pay you cunts back for this, you bastards!'

Waiting for the final barrier to be unlocked, the old man wonders why his son is being held on remand in a section for the mentally unstable. Do the authorities doubt his sanity? Or is it because men held prisoner in the main section of the prison would take revenge against the agent responsible for their captivity?

At last they reach a square box of a room with a glass-panelled door. A space that has never known natural light or felt a whisper of fresh air. A room where generations of prisoners have attempted to prove or deny their sanity under psychiatric examination.

Zaheer Khan sits at a small table. His usually immaculate fawn suit is creased and crumpled. The collar of his maroon-coloured shirt lies limp and in need of laundering.

When the glass-panelled door is unlocked to allow father and son to meet, there is an awkward silence while the surly overweight guard checks the bare interview room before closing the door and settling himself outside.

Khan senior, as is his way, comes straight to the point.

'I have some progress to report. I now know where Sarah Gant resides. After the funeral gathering at the restaurant, I followed her to the Imperial hotel.'

'How can that help us?'

'You say that Mrs Gant acts for the United States government as a narcotics division agent.'

'Yes.'

'Therefore, we must surmise that she is only really interested in tracing an illicit drugs route into that country so that, what's the word, she can make a, a…'

'Connection?'

'Thank you. A connection that can be followed to the top so that one complete international drug ring can be destroyed. That seems to be her aim.'

Khan, not seeing where the old man's logic is taking him, sighs with frustration.

'Just as mine is to stop the Triads' infiltration into this country or, should I say, *was* my intention.'

Hearing the bitterness in his son's voice pains Iqbal Khan.

'Try not to blame your superiors.'

The advice makes Khan grimace.

'Why not?' Do they believe what I say? Am I not undergoing mental assessment and testing here, am I not on remand for murder?'

He stands with an upsurge of violent emotion. All the repressed hurt and anger of the unjustly accused spills out. Hastily, Iqbal tries to avert the storm.

'Calm yourself, come, sit down, sit or you will bring the warder in to terminate our meeting. Come, sit back down, there's a good chap.'

With an effort to regain control of his seething anger, Khan obeys his father, who searches for the words that will engender patience and hope.

'Rather than blame your superiors, let us concentrate instead on bringing down the criminals that have brought you to this sorry pass.'

His words have little effect. It is obvious from his resentful stare that his son does not see any hope of salvation. Khan grinds the words out with bitter resolve.

'When, or if, I prove my innocence, I intend to put this country and its system of justice behind me. I no longer believe the ethics you taught me to expect from the British. They no longer care for justice, only the application of the law, particularly to those whose skin is of a different hue.'

'I do not wish to listen to this defeatist talk.'

'Then find a way to have me released.'

'That is what I intend to do.'

'How?'

'We must examine what facts we know, what conclusions may be drawn from them. The most obvious being that you are on remand for murder because your interests conflicted with those of Mrs Gant. She framed you so she could act independently.'

Khan gives a somewhat condescending nod.

'I had realised that some time ago, actually.'

'You must forgive your father. In my day, agents of the law trusted and respected each other.'

He leaves his chair, begins to pace around, the way he once had in his Rawalpindi office.

'The key to proving your innocence lies with Mrs Gant. She who trapped you in the coils of conspiracy could clear you if given a large enough incentive.'

'Such as what?'

'Ah, there you have it. That is the crux of our problem. One that I will think through, but never fear, Inspector Khan always gets his man.'

'Or woman.'

'Quite.'

162

Kuldip, with Rafiq hovering at his shoulder, is preparing the latest invoice of antique items for a shipment of illicit drugs into the United States of America. They look up as the door to the drawing room is thrown open. An exultant Lily Li T'ang bounds into the room.

'Oh, I am so excited!'

Rafiq hurries across to his fiancée.

'What is it, my darling, what has happened?'

'I have just heard our second shipment has cleared US customs.'

Her excitement spreads to Kuldip.

'Your star rises with each success of white elephant, Miss Lily!'

Aslam Rafiq tries to dampen the excitement that has invaded his drawing room.

'But this is not new, we have enjoyed similar success before, have we not?'

He watches Lily dance around like a child given a longed-for present. Finally, she pauses, takes calming breaths, begins to outline the news that has brought her such joy.

'It's not just that, HK have asked me to contact the 17K in Birmingham and to take high rank within that organisation. At last, oh, at last my father's failure has been erased by my complete and utter success!'

She whirls around the room, her words tumbling out in a stream of constant delight.

'The 17K must be regrouping as rivals to the Wo Shing Wo. Oh, to be given the task of leading their resurrection is honour indeed. Oh, oh, I can't keep still, I can't wait to get to work.'

She slows, begins to calculate, to plan her next move. Her dark almond eyes glitter with the fires of unrestrained ambition.

'Means of distribution will be the key, yes, heroin distribution will be organised from the upper reaches of society right down to school yard level. The link to America can remain, but this United Kingdom is in for a thorough trampling from the white elephant!'

Equally excited, Kuldip stands and raises his arms to heaven.

'I will ride white elephant with you, Miss Lily!'

Miss Lily, in business mode, speaks curtly to Rafiq.

'Tell your servant to shut up.'

'Yes, yes, please vacate the room, Kuldip, my fiancée and I have intimate matters to attend to.'

Unseen by Lily, he indicates his ring finger. Kuldip understands, gives a knowing wink, hurries from the room, leaving the field to his master.

While Lily stays wrapped in clouds of future glory, Rafiq goes to the mantelpiece, feels behind the black statuette of the goddess Kali. His fingers close on a small black jeweller's box. After taking the box from its hiding place, he clears his throat to gain attention. He tries again, more loudly, holding the box enticingly towards her. Finally, she glances in his direction, frowns.

'What?'

'Come see, I promise you won't be disappointed.'

Lily condescends to cross to him. He snaps the box open to reveal a diamond engagement ring nestling on a cushion of blue velvet. A sample of the jeweller's art that would pay a servant's wages for a dozen years.

He extracts the ring from its box, slips it onto the extended third finger of the left hand of Lily Li T'ang.

With the look of a wary pawnbroker, she examines the oval-shaped diamond solitaire set in its mount of platinum and diamonds.

Rafiq beams in expectation of warm loving gratitude. Lily continues her assessment, waving her hand to capture the light and bring sparkle to the stones.

'How many carats?'

'Er, three, I believe.'

Rafiq takes an impatient step towards her.

'Tell me that you like it, tell me it is a fitting token of the love I bear for my darling Lily.'

'It will suffice.'

'Suffice, suffice? Please don't tease me, not at this confluence of our lives.'

'What do you mean?'

'My ring, on your finger, tells the world we are engaged to be married, my angel.'

He puts his arms about her, smiles lovingly.

'Does that not merit at least a kiss?'

'I know what kisses from you might lead to.'

'They will lead you away from dangerous ambition. You will find all the excitement a woman needs when you become my wife in charge of my home.'

'Oh, really?'

She raises an exquisite eyebrow.

'Yes, really.'

Rafiq hugs her to him. The softness of her body has a hardening effect on his nether regions. He breathes in the musk of her perfume. The heady essence mixed with the dry scent of her flesh, the upper tones of bergamot and vanilla remind him of a perfume-soaked handkerchief in a far-off street in Rawalpindi. He looks up into her eyes, longingly.

'Oh, how I wish I could enter the estate of matrimony now, be given a taste of your precious virgin treasure now.'

Stepping away from his embrace, Lily gives him a seductive smile. She looks down demurely.

'Maybe you can.'

Believing he has misunderstood her words, he asks, 'We can? Did you say, we can?'

'Yes.'

'When?'

'Now.'

'Where?'

'Here.'

'Here, you mean, here, right here?'

'Right now.'

Lily stands quite still as she allows herself to be undressed by the fumbling fingers of Aslam Rafiq.

Pulse racing, he savours her beauty like a starving man brought before a feast.

Made awkward by extreme tumescence he finally shakes himself free of his undergarments.

As he nuzzles at her breasts, Lily looks past him towards the black statue of the goddess of chaos and destruction. She takes the lolling red tongue of the deity as her cue, nods and begins to apply the amorous skills once taught to her by the madame of the most exclusive brothel in Hong Kong.

To Rafiq it is as if Kali herself has erupted into life, somehow possessed his lover and unleashed her anarchic powers upon his naked body. It seems to him as if Lily Li T'ang is not only exploring every orifice of his body, but is inside his brain, knowing when he is about to spend himself, then, like an expert torturer who senses that their victim is about to escape into oblivion, pulling back so the agony will be prolonged.

Sensing the next peak, Lily withdraws, waits before resuming her relentless torment, slapping his face, biting his buttocks, nipping at his nipples, raking his back with her talons, riding him into the throes of madness until, finally, she allows release.

Rafiq cries out, writhing in agonal orgasm. His mind detaches from his body, making seconds extend into eternity.

Lily disengages her body from his. The abrupt uncoupling jolts Rafiq back to reality.

There are to be no loving caresses, no sweet aftermath of shared pleasure. Agitated in mind and body, Rafiq can smell her stale perfume mixed with her sweat on his skin. He tries to wipe it away as if it were eating into his flesh.

Panting, sweating, stretched on the floor, he sees Lily wipe away his essence with an expression of distaste.

Hauling himself onto an elbow, he tries to speak words that pool like acid in his throat. Finally he blurts out, 'You… You didn't learn those lewd lessons in the best girl's school in England.'

Lily takes up her suspender belt, fastens it around her narrow waist.

'Oh, didn't I?'

She searches amongst her scattered clothes, selects a flesh-coloured stocking, begins to ease it up her left leg as she adds, 'I've always found ways of breaking through confines.'

She inserts a suspender, smooths the stocking, attaches the rear suspender.

'I do what I want, when I want.'

'Then that time with that Red fellow, Stick, up there, in the bedroom above, that… That was true?'

Easing into her second stocking, Lily shrugs.

'Probably, I really can't remember, there have been so many since.'

She steps into loose satin panties as Rafiq sits upright, his face mottled with anger.

'So, you finally tired of this pretence, this farce, this Edwardian pantomime of virtuous virginity… Oh, God, oh my god! I could weep bitter tears of my heart's blood!'

Buttoning her blouse, she looks down on Rafiq with icy contempt.

'I only granted your desires to prove a point. I just don't fancy you. As business partners, we can continue, but I will be much too busy to maintain this playacting nonsense of being your dutiful fiancé. Now, I expect you want your ring back – you're the type who would.'

Removing the engagement ring, she offers it to him. He makes no move to accept it but instead gathers all the venom he can muster in reply.

'No. I expect to pay for my mistakes. To pay the toll of bitter experience. Keep it!' He spits at her feet, then continues, 'Keep it as your due, Miss Lily Liar's Tongue! As the labourer is worth his hire, so the high-class whore her due reward.'

After the briefest of pauses.

'That's jolly white of you, Rafiq, thank you.'

163

Under the covers of the king-size bed that lies on its raised platform in the centre of the bridal suite, Sarah Gant comes awake. She stretches languorously, delightfully well rested after the deepest sleep she has enjoyed in months.

Standing at the foot of the bed the White Devil watches her with much pleasure. Dressed in his W.D. day garb, his straw boater at a rakish angle, he waits for her discovery of the bauble he has placed on her finger the night before.

It doesn't take long. Sarah stares, frowns, holds the crystal orb up to the light. Prismatic reflections dance across her breasts.

'What's this? Who put this on, you?'

The White Devil gives a courtly bow.

'Why? And why on that particular finger?'

'Symbol of our burgeoning relationship. You may consider yourself to be engaged.'

'To you?'

'Yes, congratulations.'

'Are you crazy?'

'You must understand, there is a need for respectability, for the sake of our little nipper.'

'Nipper? A child, what child?'

W.D. gives a satisfied smile.

'That's impossible.'

'Is it?'

Sarah suddenly remembers the warning Marcus Mason gave her. About children of this devil being scattered throughout the world. She leaps out of bed, rushes at him, scratching and kicking. He throws his arms around her, hugs her to him. His strength is far above hers. She hisses at her captor.

'If I am pregnant, it won't be for long.'

Released from his grip, Sarah sees a transformation take place, hears a voice, icy with intent, issue from the gaunt satanic figure that has just appeared before her.

'You will be the mother of a girl. The first female sired by me. You will do her no harm. You will bring her forth and love her all your life. Do that and you will want for nothing. Love her and I will love you. Hurt her and you will suffer the torments of hell.'

He returns to his human form. Sarah gropes her way to the end of the bed, sinks down, rests her hands on her knees, hunches forward. The White Devil watches as, after a pause, Sarah straightens, stands, cups her breasts, then places both hands on her womb. Holds them against her dark skin as if they were sensors probing the hidden secrets of her body. She looks across at him, the White Devil nods, opens his arms. Sarah hesitates, feels she is being drawn to the edge of an abyss.

She steps into space, swoops towards him. He catches her, enfolds her in a close embrace. Sarah gives a sob of relief.

After a long moment, he releases her. If she expects soft words, she is to be disappointed. W.D.'s mind has turned to other matters.

'We both have work to do.'

He points to the corner of the room where the ornate, garishly-coloured head of a pair of Chinese ornamental lions stare at them with unblinking eyes.

'What the hell are they?'

'The means of destroying a Triad known as the 17K.'

164

Later that same morning, making her way along Broad Street amongst flurries of snow that cling to the black fabric of her coat, Anne strides along, struggling to absorb the news she has just been given by John Kline's solicitor.

Anne had thought she was all cried out, but now she knows there are more tears to come. In her mind's eye she sees the gift box sent by Lily Li T'ang. She had tried to muster the strength to destroy its contents but now she is glad it is still waiting for her inside the Nirvana.

As she feels for her keys, with eyes clouded with tears, a hand touches her shoulder. Turning, she sees an elderly Asian, dressed in traditional native clothes, shivering in the cold.

'What do you want?' Anne says.

'Just a little of your time, Miss Darracott.'

She has heard that cultured voice before. Peering closely at her visitor, she recognises the features of Khan's father.

'You? What's happened, why are you here? Why the change of clothes?'

'I can explain. May we go inside?'

'I suppose.'

The empty restaurant seems forlorn and unwelcoming.

Following Anne towards the bar area, the old man glances around at the empty tables, their white cloths hanging like dust sheets.

'Have you shut up shop?'

'Closed for a week. Respect for the dead.'

'That's very, ah, fitting, a most suitable gesture.'

'Yes. My decision. My name above the door, you see.'

She reaches the bar where a half-empty whisky bottle stands beside an empty glass. She reaches for the bottle, pours a shot. Iqbal Khan watches her swallow the drink in one swift motion.

'Whisky. Does it help at all?'

'I'm giving it a trial.'

'Are you sober?'

'All the time, that's the trouble.'

She pours herself another shot, stares down at the golden liquid.

'John started this bottle. I'm finishing it for him.'

She raises her glass, toasts the silent space, the deserted tables.

'To John Kline. To one sly bastard.'

'I hardly think he deserves such…'

'Oh, he does. I met with his solicitor this morning. The last will and testament of John Kline. He left me this place.'

'Surely that is good news.'

'I suppose, but it's just like him. Was like him.'

She goes to drink. The old man stops her, takes the glass from her hand.

'What are you doing?' Anne asks.

'Trying to help. We all suffer grief in our lives. My wife died eleven years and sixty-one days ago. My mind accepts it, but my heart never will.'

Anne turns away from him.

'I think we'd better get off this grief kick.'

'I was only trying to—'

'Yes, yes, I know. What do you want, why are you dressed like that?'

'I bought this native outfit at an Asian clothes market. I needed to affect a disguise, practice a little subterfuge. I went to that container base where Mr Kline had his accident. I pretended to be in the employ of Aslam Rafiq. I obtained copies of invoices listing details of antiques being exported to America under his name.'

'What's this to do with me?'

'I hope that you will assist my investigation.'

'How?'

'You went with Mr Kline to that storage place, why was that?'

'It was a favour. I was asked to look over some antiques.'

The old man produces several sheets of paper, smooths them on the counter of the bar.

'Could you possibly look at the items listed? See if anything might strike you about their authenticity?'

Anne takes up the sheets, runs her eye down each page in turn.

'No, nothing untoward, just run of the... Wait a second...'

Frowning, she checks one page against another, shows him two identical entries with a stab of her finger.

'There are duplicate items in both shipments, see, same description of Burne-Jones terracotta figures. No way will you find those babies two weeks in a row, not if they're genuine.'

Folding the invoices, Khan's father allows himself a smile of satisfaction.

'Thank you, Miss Darracott, I believe we now have a fulcrum to shift towards an advantage.'

165

Sarah Gant replaces the telephone next to the bridal bed. The conversation with the American drug enforcement overseas controller has been a worrying one. Enquiring about missing agents, reminding her of the need for results if she wishes to remain outside prison walls. She sits on the white bedcover and reviews her prospects. Looking down at the crystal ring on her finger worries her. She decides to remove it but finds it impossible to shift. The ring seems glued to her skin. What sorcery is this? She stares into the crystal orb and in its depths sees herself holding a newborn child against her cheek.

166

The home of Aslam Rafiq holds too many memories of Lily Li T'ang for the comfort of the rotund figure sat puffing on his pipe, the drawing room hazy with blue smoke as if from a bonfire of his illusions.

Impatiently, Rafiq glances at his watch. He has decided to curtail his drinking, promised himself that he would not imbibe before noon. It is now five minutes to twelve. He makes himself wait for the chime of the clock in the hallway outside. Good discipline, a way to return to ordered ways now that the curse of blind lust has been removed, a cruel lesson instigated by Kali, the goddess of destruction but also, he reminds himself, the instigator of new beginnings.

A bell chimes. *Ah, at last,* Rafiq thinks, then realises it is the sound of the doorbell. He hears an exchange of words at the front door followed by footsteps. The door opens. His butler steps inside.

'Mr Khan, sir.'

'What?'

The announcement lifts Rafiq to his feet as Iqbal Khan, dapper in his western clothes, advances inside. Recovering some poise, Rafiq waves his unexpected visitor towards a chair as the clock outside begins its midday chimes.

'Drink?' Rafiq asks, hopefully.

'I would sooner come to the point of my visit.'

'Which is?'

'My son is held in captivity, as you know...'

'Yes, I do know.'

Rafiq settles himself into a chair opposite to the older man, steals a longing look towards the decanter of Napoleon brandy, then addresses the matter in hand. He feels tired of intrigue, of dealing with lies and subterfuge. He decides to cut the interview short.

'I say, Khan, sahib, what exactly is the purpose of your visit?'

'I wish to release my son from jail.'

'I'm sure you do. But I have no connection to him. So, if you wouldn't mind...'

He waves a dismissive hand in the direction of the door. Khan senior makes no move. His expression becomes magisterial. He makes no attempt to disguise his feelings of dislike for the man before him.

'I came here to offer you a chance to save your neck. I suspect you of owning a business which is but a cover for illicit drug activity. If I do nothing else, I will alert the authorities that you are a smuggler of opium.'

'How ridiculous, I am a bona fide businessman.'

There is a pause. The old man finesses his next ploy.

'Who may not know his business is being used for illicit activity.'

Rafiq has the sensation that he is about to be manipulated. He regards Iqbal Khan and considers the threat of disclosure that had just been made. In a quieter tone, he says, 'You really are Khan's father, yes, I believe that, I do indeed.'

The old man knows the time has come to bring about the outcome he is seeking. He sits back in his chair. His manner changes to one of reconciliation, his words softer and more amenable.

'Of course, perhaps I do you a complete injustice. Perhaps you have been but a dupe. Perhaps what I say to you is a complete surprise causing you to burn with a sense of outrage.'

'That is always possible. I do have a particular aversion to being duped by any man.'

Iqbal Khan pauses, then ventures, 'Or woman?'

'Perhaps.'

In the longer pause that follows much waits to be decided: revenge, escape, release.

The old man takes the initiative, his manner jovial, as if he were addressing a fellow member of a gentleman's club.

'I say, my dear fellow, look here, earlier today, quite by chance, I discovered something I feel you should know about.'

'Oh, and what is that, my dear Khan?'

'My dear fellow, I discovered drug smuggling is being perpetrated under the cover of your good name.'

'My God! Tell me more.'

'You sound outraged.'

Rafiq quivers with false indignation.

'What innocent man wouldn't be?'

167

Circling the bridal chamber, Sarah's mind is ablaze with unanswered questions. What is the White Devil up to? He is supposedly fulfilling his contract to train the Wo Shing Wo for their forthcoming battle against the 17K; this, through her connections with the Wo Shing Wo, she knows to be true, but he has not divulged just how he plans to destroy their rival Triad, now led by Lily Li T'ang.

Who is the White Devil? Is he just that, a devil incarnate? What is his real name? Was she crazy to listen to his ramblings? Is she really going to bear his child? Isn't it time to put her own interests first?

Sarah realises her wanderings have brought her alongside the built-in wardrobe. Might there be some clues as to the identity of the White Devil inside?

Sliding open the door reveals, on the clothes rail, another W.C. Fields costume, the formal one worn at the funeral of John Kline.

Perched on a black leather hold-all lies his grey top hat with the broad black band. Shifting the hat aside she examines the Gucci bag, double locked with combination cylinders for protection. Lifting the bag reveals a certain heaviness. Exploring along its length she feels the shape of at least three weapons. Maybe guns taken from the slain agents? The rest of the contents seem to be documents... Passports?

Deciding she is simply indulging in guesswork, Sarah returns the bag to its position, reaches for the top hat, ready to return it to its former place atop of the soft leather hold-all. The hat is difficult to balance, tips over on its brim. Attempting to re-position it, Sarah notices something that looks like padding inside the hat. She eases it out. It is a wad of paper, carefully folded, tucked into the lining.

Opening the papers shows her part of a map of the southside of Birmingham. Drawn with a black marker pen, a strong line traces what seems to be a route snaking from Ladywell Street into Hurst Street and ending with an arrow halfway along Thorpe Street, pointing to the letters 'KKKK'. Written alongside this, in exuberant capitals, are the words 'HAPPY NEW YEAR, SUCKERS!'

Staring at the map, tracing the route with her forefinger, she feels baffled. The New Year? That was weeks past. Ah, she remembers the heads of the ornamental Chinese lions that W.D. took great pains to have delivered. Light dawns. She begins to understand how the White Devil intends to close in on the 17K.

Mulling over how best to turn this information to her advantage, her thoughts are interrupted by the ring of the telephone.

'Yes? Sarah Gant... Who's...? Ah, Anne, sorry, didn't recognise your voice...'

168

An hour after putting in the call requested by Khan senior, Anne is in the room above the restaurant toying with the deadly gift sent to her by Lily Li T'ang. She can hear voices below, the formal tones of Iqbal Khan and the confident replies of Sarah Gant. Anne puts the flat black gift box aside, unscrews the top of her methadone bottle, dry swallows a tablet and leaves the room on her way to join the pow-wow downstairs.

When Anne descends the stairs, she sees Sarah Gant in her flash baseball jacket leaning across a table, listening intently to Iqbal Khan. The Asian is once more dressed like an English gentleman, rather than the scruffy underling who last visited the Nirvana.

The voices become audible as Anne approaches the only table in use inside the restaurant. Sarah Gant is questioning the old man.

'You say this drug route to the states can be left open. How can you guarantee that?'

'Because I have discovered the smuggling method involved. The owner of the transportation business, when I tackled him, was so outraged that there is no reason for his innocence not to be believed.'

Anne pulls a chair up to the table and sits down.

'Might this owner of the transport firm be Aslam Rafiq?' she asks.

'I believe that is his name, yes.'

'Isn't he engaged to be married to that Chinese bitch?'

The old man winces at the language used, shakes his head in reply.

'I believe that is no longer the case, Miss Darracott. They may still be business partners, but I believe she is no longer his permanent house guest.'

'How do you know this?'

'Servants like to gossip about their masters and their mistresses.'

'OK...'

Sarah brings the discussion back to the matter in hand.

'What's the deal here, Poppa, why so anxious to involve me?'

'Aslam Rafiq, to help the authorities, has agreed to allow the next consignment to America to go through to completion.'

'Allowing my guys to follow it through and close down the operation.'

'Many arrests would be made. Your stock would rise, Mrs Gant.'

'I guess it might.'

'There is, however, a stipulation. I will only provide evidence if you, I believe the expression is, "play ball with me". I wish to bargain with you for the freedom of my son.'

Sarah shifts in her seat, the light glittering on the glossy sleeve of her red baseball jacket. Anne watches the players approach the ninth innings. Sarah is the first to speak.

'I have no official connections with the British police.'

Anne intervenes.

'Just who do you have connections with, Sarah?'

'I get around. That's my job.'

'You mean that strange bloke in the top hat, the Chinese Triad mobsters?'

'OK, I'm undercover, supposedly assisting the Wo Shing Wo while trying to discover a way to stop their infiltration here and in the States.'

A pause descends on the table. Iqbal Khan plays his best card.

'The price for my information is that you assist in the release of my son.'

Watching Sarah calculating all the angles irritates Anne. All she can think of is that here may be a way to strike back at Lily Li T'ang.

'Sarah, give him what he wants,' Anne says, abruptly.

'I suppose I could use my contacts to inform the law that a hitman carried out a contract on Mr Yan.'

'That, I venture to say, is exactly what happened,' the old man says.

Drumming her fingers on the table, Sarah begins to construct a scenario.

'A corrupt colleague of your son planted false evidence, drugs, cash, gave an anonymous tip off, knowing the hit on Yan had already taken place and your son had been handcuffed to the body. That would hang together, yes?'

'Who's to be the corrupt colleague, anyone we know?' Anne says.

Sarah grins.

'No, but there's no shortage of fall guys.'

'It would be a service to the community to expose police corruption.'

'That's right, Poppa.'

'You must share the success of thwarting these triad gangsters. Kudos for you in America, plaudits for my son in Britain.'

'All right, it's a deal. What we need to come up with next is a suitable event, something to bring about mutual rejoicing.'

A slow smile appears as Sarah realises just how she can hit the ball right out of the park.

169

The day of the Chinese New Year begins quietly. Musicians with their gongs, drums and cymbals begin to gather in Ladywell Street. All are dressed in traditional red costumes.

Chinese dancers watch as members of their group begin to don the lion costumes, each couple to form the legs that will propel the long tubular body behind the massive grinning heads of the ornamental beasts. Anticipating that the dance and celebrations will soon begin, a crowd begins to gather.

A local television crew checks their camera, a soundman muffling his microphone against the distortion of a rising breeze.

As the troupe comprising Triad members of the Wo Shing Wo assemble, their festive costumes belie their sombre pre-battle mood.

Standing on the second tier of a multi-storey car park, the White Devil, Sarah Gant at his side, observes the preparations taking place below. Behind them Lemmy and Jenkins wait inside the warmth of the parked white Rolls Royce.

In the doorway of an empty shop on Hurst Street, Iqbal Khan waits for his son to join him. He hopes that by now his release from custody will have taken place.

Across the street, in an alleyway grandly named Harpers Close, there is a smell of last night's urine and a litter of yesterday's discarded food cartons. Anne stays out of sight, the collar of her black woollen coat turned up against the chill wind. Behind her a painter begins his solitary task of whitewashing the rear wall of the Love at First Bite Burger Bar.

Anne is the first to see the woman in red stride down the street.

Lily Li T'ang, bristling with ambition, is eager to usher in a year of great good fortune. To ensure this, she has purchased a new red outfit, a bright red beret, and underneath her clothes she feels the luxury of scarlet silk underwear. *If that doesn't bring luck my way, nothing will,* she decides, as she pushes open the door of the Kan Kan Kash and Karry.

Seeing Lily Li T'ang disappear inside the oriental food suppliers, Anne steps further out onto the pavement and signals across the street to Iqbal Khan, who in turn raises a hand towards the upper reaches of the car park.

'Here we go,' Sarah murmurs to her companion.

'Yes, indeed. It's time for the lions to perform their deadly dance.'

The White Devil removes his top hat and waves it in the direction of his troops below. Almost at once there is a clash of cymbals in reply, the sound carrying towards them on the freshening wind.

Inside the food emporium, the Chinese youths recruited by the Triad of the 17K stand as Lily, their new commander-in-chief, walks down the line inspecting her troops.

Chiang, the owner of the food store, is an old man with a face lined by more wrinkles than a year-old apple. His wispy grey beard straggles in fronds down to his sunken chest. His eyes are bright and alert as he observes Lily complete her inspection of the young men drawn up before her. There is a surly look to some of them. They either resent her as their leader or dislike being called to muster on this, the first day of the Chinese New Year.

'Splendid,' Lily begins. 'I see before me a fine fighting force to further the interests of the 17K.' She produces her most enticing smile. 'I look forward to knowing each of you on a close, one-to-one basis.'

This veiled promise has the desired effect. The men stand straighter before the tall beauty who stands enticingly before them.

Turning her attention to Chiang, Lily orders, 'You may show me the imported merchandise from Hong Kong.'

Lily is led to the rear of the store. Boxes containing packets of noodles and rice are piled on shelves all around, the air filled with the scent of spices: anise, fennel, cinnamon, all blending to create for Lily a memory of her mother's kitchen in far off Canton.

Chiang shifts a cardboard box containing tins of fried catfish, places it to one side. He lifts another box labelled 'White Elephant Lychees'.

Opening the sealed box reveals a consignment of grey labelled tins. The manager selects one, passes it for Lily to examine. She frowns, not knowing what response is expected. Taking the tin back from her, Chiang deftly turns a false top to show plastic squares of pure heroin stuffed inside. For Lily, this is rainbow's end, a crock of gold that will fund her future glory. She nods calmly. It is not meet for a leader to show too much excitement.

'Very good. We will export them once the New Year celebrations are over.'

The old man bows in obedience to her wishes. He does not approve of women in business, but his loyalty is to the Snakeheads in Hong Kong who have appointed Lily Li T'ang.

On re-joining her men, Lily Li T'ang senses their resentment at being summoned to work on this, the first day of the Spring Festival. Considering whether she should allow them to disperse, she becomes aware of music playing in the street outside, the clash of cymbals, the deep sound of a gong, accompanied by a crackle of firecrackers, merging with the frantic beating of a drum.

All members of the 17K cluster at the window in time to see a pair of ornamental lions come dancing into view. Behind the massive ornamental lion heads are half a dozen dancers in red satin trousers and loose yellow tops. Their progress forms a bright whirl of colour against the dull background of Hurst Street.

All the while the accompanying musicians keep up the beat, interspersed with the throb of the gong and the clashing of the cymbals, sounds that draw the 17K, led by Lily, into the street to join in the celebrations.

Delighted to express her joy at having attained control of the 17K, Lily begins to dance with a man who seems somehow familiar. With a jolt she recognises him as her informant from within the Wo Shing Wo. Out of the corner of her eye something else is amiss. The Lion dancers are casting aside their costumes. They advance towards her and the 17K, wielding baseball bats and machetes.

Caught in the middle of the clash, Lily kicks and punches alongside her troops, while 'THUDS! SPLATS! OOOPHS! THWACKS!' echo all around her. The musicians, caught up in the affray, abandon their instruments and run for their lives.

An attacker launches himself at Lily with an 'AIEEEEE!', trying to bring her down with the Ganges groin grapple. He forgets W.D.'s warning only to use the manoeuvre on an opponent who owns a pair of testicles. When the man reaches for her groin all he gets is a handful of red cloth and, instead of her throat, the soft rise of her breasts.

Bringing her knee up sharply makes the grappler-after-groins regret that he is a member of the male sex. He doubles over, emitting an instant 'OO-OO-HHH!'

A brass cymbal whirls past Lily's head with a 'WHOOSH!'; at the same time a brass gong rolls up and settles at her feet. She seizes the gong and brings it down with a 'BOOOOM!' on the skull of the groin grappler. As the reverberations fade, another sound starts to be heard: the 'WAH-WAH-WAH!' of police sirens.

At either end of the street police cars block off all means of escape. Climbing out of the leading car Zaheer Khan leads the police charge towards the warring Triad mobsters.

From his vantage point the White Devil sees the police cars seal off the street. Turning to Sarah Gant, he snarls, 'I detect the odoriferous whiff of law enforcement. Who could have tipped off the constabulary,

I wonder?'

'No, idea,' Sarah says, innocently.

Two things become apparent to Lily Li T'ang: her men are being bested, and she needs to escape before she is arrested by the police.

She runs back towards the KKKK store, then decides there is not enough time to rescue the goods. Better save herself. Looking desperately around, she notices the entrance to a side street.

Running around the corner she sees a clear way ahead. A street free of police and Wo Shing Wo gangsters.

Lily hurries away, heading for freedom, relieved by her narrow escape.

As she passes a side alley, a woman's arm thrusts itself across Lily's midriff, halting her progress.

'Who…?' Lily pulls the restraining arm away.

Anne Darracott stares at Lily Li T'ang, Lily Li T'ang stares at Anne Darracott.

'Come here, you!' Lily cries as her hands claw into Anne's hair.

Anne yells with pain, catches hold of Lily's wrist, kicks out at her shins. This time it is Lily's turn to yowl with pain. The women grab hold of each other, a pair of wrestlers each seeking to overthrow the other.

Turning and twisting, trying to break the grip of her attacker, Anne retreats into the alley where, at the end of the cul-de-sac, a painter is covering a wall with whitewash.

Using her superior height and strength, Lily breaks Anne's grip and slams her back against the wall.

Anne sees Lily smile as she comes in for the kill, her right hand raised kung fu style.

The guy in the white overalls decides to ignore the cat fight. He goes on with his painting.

At the last moment, Anne ducks the savage chop aimed at her throat, shoves Lily Li T'ang away from her. In the moment of respite Anne notices a bucket, half-filled with whitewash…

Once the forces of law and order have subdued the warring Triad gangs, Zaheer Khan is anxious to search the storeroom of the KKKK.

Together with a pair of detectives from the Drug Squad, Burt and Conway, he enters the premises. At first glance the cash and carry outlet seems deserted until, from the rear, comes the sound of a flushing toilet.

Pulling back a tobacco-coloured plastic curtain reveals a wizened Chinese gentleman sitting on the lavatory, his trousers around his ankles, an empty lychee tin clutched in his hand.

'This private business,' Chiang bleats.

'Stand up, Grandad, let's see what private business you've been up to,' Khan says.

Protesting, kicking, Chiang is lifted from the toilet. Looking down into the bowl the cops see packets of heroin choking up the foul-smelling bowl.

'Expensive shit, that,' Conway observes. He glances at his colleague, who produces a coin and tosses it into the air. He catches its fall, slaps the 50p down on his wrist.

'Heads,' Conway calls. Burt shows him the result of the toss.

'Oh, shite,' Conway says, rolling up a sleeve before plunging his arm deep down into the contents of the toilet bowl.

Back on the street once more, Khan surveys the battlefield, the discarded Lion heads, a broken drum, a constable collecting abandoned weapons, another carrying a brass gong.

From the corner of Smith Street, Khan's father waves for his son to join him.

On reaching him, Khan senior wastes no time.

'I say, that woman in red, she seems to have slipped from your grasp. I saw her escaping down this street.'

'Let's see if there's any sign of her.'

'I doubt it, but one never knows.'

They begin to walk down the street with little expectation, but on reaching Harper's Close, to their surprise a bedraggled figure crawls out onto the pavement. Her once red suit is now covered with white paint, her face a ghostly mask, her hair matted and caked.

Anne Darracott follows, places her foot on the rump of her victim, and with a shove delivers the woman to the feet of the Khans.

'Here's the lovely Lily Li T'ang, she's all yours.'

170

Sarah Gant sits beside the man she knows only as the White Devil. He has removed his incongruous top hat and stares out at the passing motorway traffic as the Rolls Royce carries them north from Birmingham towards the Hilton Park Service station, where W.D. has a meeting with a Chinese paymaster.

Finding the silence of the usually verbose W.D. disturbing, Sarah begins to worry as to what he has in mind for her. She knows he suspects her of betraying his plans to the law. Would he punish her, gun to her head, body buried in a wood? He was capable of anything, but what if she was really carrying his child? Would he kill the mother of his child?

Sarah moves her handbag onto her lap, feels the weight of the gun inside. If there is to be gunplay she will try to draw first.

Up ahead Lemmy sits next to the driver, Jenkins. Sarah senses a brooding tension inside the vehicle. Now that she has delivered a successful mission, destroying a drug route, she is free of the DEA. Free to do what? Return to her former life… Was that possible, even desirable?

The Rolls leaves the M6 motorway and enters the parking area laid out before a low building with towers that reminds Sarah of an airport.

When the car comes to a halt, W.D. tells her to stay put. She watches him and his assistant walk across the concourse. Both are wheeling suitcases. What is inside she has no idea. Jenkins removes his peaked chauffeur's cap, turns to her.

'Get you a coffee?'

'No.'

The driver turns back to face out front. Without his peaked cap she notices his close-cropped hair has flecks of grey. She puts her hand into her handbag, feels for the gun. She could place its muzzle against his neck, order him to drive. Where? Anywhere.

Before she can decide, Jenkins yawns.

'Think I'll stretch my legs.'

'OK', Sarah says, watching as the chauffeur leaves the car and wanders away.

Left alone, Sarah becomes uneasy. Was this some sort of test, see if she would try to escape?

Across the car park she notices a guy leaning against the cab of a lorry, smoking. Easy to cross to him, ask for a ride. The guy is young enough, horny enough to believe a sassy black American woman to be heaven sent. Still she hesitates, part of her wanting to move but something, some presence inside holding her back.

Her gaze shifts to the sight of a well-dressed Chinese man unlocking a black sedan car. He bears a resemblance to Shen T'ang. The dead Triad leader's brother? Is he the paymaster W.D. was to meet?

The lorry driver finishes his cigarette, grinds it underfoot. Now or never… She reaches for the handle of the door as a black shadow falls across the window. The door opens. A soft voice from beyond the grave asks her to step outside.

Standing before her is a preacher dressed in a black suit, a white shirt with a twin-tailed black cravat. On his head sits a round-brimmed black hat. Behind him, Lemmy stands, dressed in identical attire. Sarah shakes her head in bafflement at the transformation of the White Devil.

'Who the hell are you now?' she asks.

'Harry Powell. I'm the Reverend Harry Powell.'

'What church?'

'That's between me and my maker.'

His voice is different, the rasping throaty tones of W.C. Fields replaced by the soft drawling speech of the southern states of America. A voice uncannily like that of Marcus Mason, deceased.

'May I invite you to accompany me on a pilgrimage, Sister Sarah?'

The preacher opens the door and, with a courtly gesture, indicates she should step back inside. Behind her the lorry pulls away; the red letters on the side of the lorry read 'Gateway Pipes'. Sarah Gant enters the Rolls.

When they are settled in, Jenkins asks, 'Where to next, Reverend?'

'Elmdon Airport. Our mission here is now complete. We must carry the word of the Lord to those in need of enlightenment.'

Jenkins starts the engine, the Rolls reverses. The white car whispers away towards the motorway.

Sarah sees the Reverend Harry Powell settle into his new role. She is sure there is a film reference in play, but she can't place the title. All she knows is that the man seated beside her seems happily content, an actor with a rich and satisfying new role to play.

Reaching into his side pocket the Reverend pulls out a small blue cloth bag with drawstrings. He passes it over to Sarah.

'A small token of appreciation, Sister Sarah.'

'Oh…'

Sarah separates the strings, peers inside. At the bottom of the bag she sees a cluster of grey stones. She frowns, not understanding how to react.

'What…?'

'Industrial diamonds, my favourite form of fee. Keep them. They will be a nest egg for the fruit of our union.'

'I can't take these.'

'Think of them as manna sent from Hong Kong. Let us give thanks for such munificence.'

With an unholy grin, Harry Powell places his hands together in prayer. With a start of recognition, Sarah sees inscribed across the back of the fingers of his left hand the word 'H-A-T-E'. She reaches across, separates his hands, turns them over, sees 'L-O-V-E' inscribed on the fingers of his right hand.

'Ah,' she says.

'Yes,' he replies.

With a smile, the Reverend Powell begins to sing, in his strong tenor voice, snatches of a bluegrass revival hymn.

'Waiting for the harvest and the time of reaping,
we shall come rejoicing, bringing in the sheaves.
Bringing in the sheaves, bringing in the sheaves,
we shall come rejoicing, bringing in the sheaves.'

Waiting to re-join the motorway southbound traffic, Jenkins adds his bass voice to the refrain. Lemmy joins in. Sarah shakes her head in wonderment then begins to sing in harmony with her companions.

'Bringing in the sheaves, bringing in the sheaves,
we shall come rejoicing, bringing in the sheaves.'

171

In the days following the round-up of the rival Triad gangs, Zahir Khan has been instrumental in the closing of the drug smuggling operations created by Lily Li T'ang. Facing a seven year stretch inside prison, Lily quickly agreed to co-operate in exchange for a lesser sentence, implicating not only her American connections but also the Snakeheads in Hong Kong.

While making her information available to his American counterparts, Khan pays due credit to the part played by Sarah Gant. When asked as to her whereabouts he replies, truthfully, that he has no idea.

Khan's father has used the time while his son re-established his reputation to diligently search for the England of his imagination. He has visited Kipling's house at Burwash, looked out on the downs described by the author as 'blunt, bow-headed, whale-backed'. Now back in Birmingham after a trip to Stratford-upon-Avon, with a little time to kill before meeting his son, Iqbal carries the presents he has bought to take back to his home village, a taste of the culture he loves so much.

Dressed in a navy-blue overcoat, a grey homburg hat, he carries a cloth carrier bag that contains his favourite book by Rudyard Kipling, mugs with the image of the Bard, tea towels listing all the works of the playwright, and a collection of tourist doo-dads that he knows the village children will value as treasures from a distant land. His most precious purchase, a small bust of Shakespeare, he cradles in the crook of his arm.

Passing by a football ground he hears the chanting of the crowd, a sound filled with hate and fury.

Outside the ground, police are ejecting a group of young men draped in red and white scarves, carrying a Union Jack. Hurling abuse at the policemen, spitting, shouting in unison about some football team the old man has never heard of. A line of Kipling surfaces in his mind as he hurries away from the feral youths. '*It was not taught by the State, no man spoke it aloud when the English began to hate.*' It is time to go home.

Wandering through Victoria Square, he pauses before a statue of Queen Victoria, regal, holding the orb and sceptre that symbolised her power over the British Empire.

Iqbal checks the time, decides to take a stroll along a walkway on his way to keep the rendezvous with his son.

The towers and buildings are shrouded in a fine grey mist, still something of a novelty to someone used to endless sunshine.

He climbs the steps that lead up to an overpass that takes pedestrians above the traffic. On reaching the wide walkway he notices, coming towards him, the four football followers he saw abusing the police a short time ago. They are still shouting slogans, pausing only to take long swigs of beer from cans.

Deciding to give the youths a wide berth, the old man veers towards the railings that skirt the concrete overpass.

The fans shout at him.

'Hey, you, wog-face, where y'going?'

'Trying to avoid us, are you?'

'That's not very social.'

They surround Iqbal Khan, jostle him, shoulder charge him from one to the other.

'I say, steady on,' the old man protests.

'Ooo, get him, talkin' posh.'

'I really must insist you let me past, I'm late for an appointment.'

Carl, the leader, who sports a swastika tattoo on his cheek, glares at the elderly Asian with contempt.

'The only appointment you've got, pal, is with us. What the fuck's this?'

He grabs the bust of Shakespeare. The old man begins to protest.

'Stop this tomfoolery at once!'

'Easy, mate, we're just curious as to why a bleedin' wog thinks he's better than us.'

'I think nothing of the sort. But I insist you give me back my property.'

'Sure, no problem. Oops, butterfingers.'

The plaster cast shatters on the floor at Iqbal's feet.

Oddo, not to be outdone, seizes the carrier bag and upends it. The souvenirs scatter and are trampled under the boots of the gang. Crezza, who can hardly read his own name, picks up a book, shows it to Jacko, who translates the title for him.

'Puck of Pooks Hill.'

'Fuck of what fucking what?' Crezza reaches for the offending object, rips the binding apart, throws the torn pages at Iqbal, who, angry and distraught, glares at each one of his tormentors in turn,

'Animals! Animals! I cannot believe that the blood of England now reposes in the veins of such as you.'

'Cheeky twat.'

'Bastard!'

'Cunt!' Oddo adds. He grabs the grey homburg hat and plants it on his own head.

'Britain for the British!' Crezza shouts. He grasps the elderly Asian by the lapels of his overcoat and throws him to the ground.

Iqbal sees the boots coming, tries to turn his back. The kicks are random, but one finds his kidney; the pain makes him retch, his vomit falls on the boots of his attackers. The attack would have continued but for a shout from an angry Asian guy who runs towards them.

'Leave him!' Khan yells. 'Police!'

The kicking ends, the four thugs prance away, taking turns to try and grab Iqbal's grey hat from each other as they cavort and dance their way back into the shelter of their city.

Khan kneels beside his father, sees the blood on his face, the stained overcoat.

'Let me call the hospital.'

Iqbal Khan feels something has died deep inside him. He tries to cover its loss with a stoical response.

'That might be a good idea. Several of my ribs seem to be dented a little.'

172

Anne Darracott, wearing a new black dress bought for the re-opening of the Nirvana, sits on the settee facing the stairs that lead down into the restaurant.

She can hear the murmur of conversations, the tinkling of a piano, some laughter. Laughter no longer figures in her life. Listless, she tries to rouse herself, tries to make ready to face the staff, to give a 'life goes on' smile to the customers. All the while carefully avoiding the sight of the empty place at the bar.

On a table within her sight sits a shiny flat box that contains a hypodermic needle, a sachet of smack, a spoon. A present from Miss Lily Li T'ang.

Anne has tried to fight the temptation to sample the goods within. She has succeeded so far, but now she feels overwhelmed by loss, by grief, by the pointless exercise of living through each day. What does it matter if she falls back into the arms of Mister H? If her surrender leads to destruction, degradation, death? At least there will be highs along the way. Highs? Yeah, highs rather than this endless parade of fucking lows.

She stands, her decision made. She takes a step towards the black box, falters as a wave of nausea envelops her. As she sways and fights against throwing up, she tells herself it is only her mind anticipating the first fix, her body knowing that what is coming next is the real thing, not the daily dose of methadone.

The nausea grows into an urgent need to vomit. She runs to the bathroom, just makes it to the wash basin before heaving up the contents of her stomach.

When it is all done, the bile washed away, she cups her hands beneath the cold water tap and rinses out her mouth, wonders what the hell is going on with her body. This isn't the first time this has occurred; the last time was only this morning. This morning? Sickness in the morning... No, her periods were erratic at the best of times, and yet...

She sits down on the closed lid of the toilet, thinks back to the night of her reconciliation with John Kline. Frantic lovemaking, no thought of contraception, each trying to outdo the other in the giving of pleasure.

Yes, she tells herself, it might be, it could be and, if it was, no child of theirs was going to enter the world addicted to any shit whatsoever.

She stands, regards herself in the mirror above the sink. She feels the fight flow back into her. The way ahead is very clear.

Anne strides back into the living room, picks up the black gift box from the table. The contents rattle, call to her. She marches towards the stairs that lead down into the restaurant.

Watching her descend the stairs the staff wonder how she will cope with the evening ahead. They are soon to find out.

Anne beckons Dev, an Indian waiter. When he reaches her, she thrusts the black gift box at him.

'Incinerator.'

Her eye falls on the tablecloth of an empty table. She notices the faint outline of a wine stain that cleaning has failed to remove.

'Max...'

The head waiter hurries to her.

'This tablecloth, change it, and check for stains more carefully in future.'

'Yes, Miss Anne.'

Anne turns away as the tablecloth is replaced. She is about to enter the busy bar area when a couple of visitors rivet her attention. She turns to face the pair with a growing sense of disbelief. The two city gents pause, lean on their rolled umbrellas, remove their bowler hats in deference to her.

'I say, Anne,' Rafiq begins, 'I do hope we are still welcome here.'

Kuldip looks around the crowded restaurant.

'Yes, it is a fine place for eating people.'

'Sure is. What are you two up to?' Anne asks.

'That and this,' Kuldip replies.

'We are sort of combating the drug menace.' Rafiq pauses, then adds, 'One might say that we are associate agents of the United States Narcotics Bureau.'

Anne looks at the pair of pinstriped scallywags before her. She throws back her head and laughs.

'That's got to be the end.'

She gestures for Archie, the barman to come to her.

'Get these bums a drink.'

Anne gazes around the restaurant that now belongs to her. She senses a presence at her side, hears his whisper in her ear. She raises her voice, makes a gesture that includes everyone present at the re-opening.

'Fix everyone a drink. It's what John Kline would have wanted.'

Rafiq starts the applause that pays tribute to Anne. Neither he nor anyone present can know that within her womb is an embryo that will eventually become another John Kline.

173

It is the end of the journey. The train that has brought Iqbal Khan from Islamabad to his home village of Jullander chugs past him, sending smoke into an azure sky.

There is no one to meet him on his return from England.

The village is almost a mile away. He transfers his suitcase from one hand to the other and begins to trudge away on the path that leads from the train halt. He feels low in spirits, his ribs still ache, but there is no longer blood in his urine.

After a while, with the sun forming a haze ahead, he sees a figure running towards him. He recognises his nephew, Ahmed, full of life and of joy. When the two are reunited, a question forms on the boy's lips.

The old man straightens, Ahmed takes his suitcase and gazes up expectantly at the world traveller.

'How was England?' The boy asks.

Iqbal considers his reply.

'How was England? Wonderful.'

He puts his arm around the boy's shoulder.

They begin to walk towards their home village.

174

The Writer sits next to his typist, side by side in an alcove off Saidor Road, Rawalpindi. The Writer takes in the crowd of onlookers clustered six-deep behind the cameraman and the director. He feels a buzz of adrenaline. This will be the final shot of the series. The end of the endings.

'ACTION!'

Turning to Mohammed, the Asian typist with the neatly trimmed white beard, the Writer gives his final instructions.

'E,' he says, pointing at the ancient keyboard. Mohammed hits the 'E' key.

'N.' Ditto.

'D.' The word 'END' appears on the last page of the final episode script.

It is done.

The Writer stands, nods his thanks to his helper and picks up the pages of the script. He expects to hear the director call 'CUT' but the scene is not yet over.

Behind the camera, Alastair, the director, indicates that the loose pages of the bulky script should be thrown up into the air.

The Writer nods. Pauses to build the tension then hurls the completed script high into the air.

The pages swirl and float above the rapt brown faces.

Later, when the showing of *Gangsters* reaches its end, there will be a freeze-frame of the falling pages. The screen will be inscribed with *Looney Tunes* lettering accompanied by appropriately zany music. A final caption will be written across the screen.

'That's all folks!'

And so it was.

END

Available from Candy Jar Books

100 OBJECTS OF DR WHO BY PHILIP BATES

"So, all of time and space, everything that ever happened or ever will: where do you want to start…?"

100 Objects of Dr Who is a celebration of everyone's favourite sci-fi show. Perfect for fans, no matter your mileage – whether you've just started your journey through all of time and space, or have lived through the highs, the lows, the Wildernesses, the Androzanis, and the Twin Dilemmas.

Inside, you'll find: A terrifying army of three Daleks! Death's Head's head! A really quite astonishingly heavy door! Dinosaur fossils! A framed piece of wall!

And much, much more!

This is a book about *Doctor Who*. But probably not the one you're expecting.